THE FINAL HOUR

THE FINAL HOUR

TOM WOOD

sphere

SPHERE

First published in Great Britain in 2017 by Sphere

3 5 7 9 10 8 6 4 2

A CIP catalogue record for this book
is available from the British Library.

Hardback ISBN 978-0-7515-7014-4
ISBN 978-0-7515-6569-0

Typeset in Sabon by M Rules
Printed and bound in Great Britain by
Clays Ltd, St Ives plc

Papers used by Sphere are from well-managed forests
and other responsible sources.

MIX
Paper from
responsible sources
FSC® C104740

Sphere
An imprint of
Little, Brown Book Group
Carmelite House
50 Victoria Embankment
London EC4Y 0DZ

An Hachette UK Company
www.hachette.co.uk

www.littlebrown.co.uk

THE FINAL HOUR

ONE

The priest was a short man who was stooped in posture, making him shorter still, but he carried himself with gravitas, especially when he spoke. His voice was deep and boomed without effort. He was often told he could not whisper. A useful trait when addressing his congregation, but not so useful when hearing confession. He compensated by cupping his left hand over his mouth. It helped keep the sins of his flock a little more private.

The confessor was already in the box, waiting with patience, so quiet and still that the priest almost didn't notice him. He decided not to comment on the confessor's own impatience. It was only right to wait outside until the priest was ready to hear the confession. No matter, but he would try to mention it at the end. Manners were a close third after godliness and cleanliness.

He knew he should not, but he couldn't help but speculate who might be so eager to confess. The priest knew

1

almost everyone in the area by name and by voice. They were decent people, but ones who sinned in thought and deed like any others. As a young man he had served in towns and cities and heard confessions that had reddened his face in embarrassment or caught his breath with shock. Here though, the sins were what he called 'baby sins'. People lusted, but didn't commit adultery; they envied, but didn't steal; they could succumb to wrath, but only with their fists. They were simple people and now he was old he enjoyed the simple life he had built with them. The priest was well liked because he relished his whiskey as much as the villagers and didn't give them more Hail Marys than they could handle.

The church was set atop a low hill overlooking a village. The village was located on the southwestern tip of Ireland, in County Cork. It was a small, isolated place, with a single bus service that made the trip to Cork and back once per day. A handsome village in the priest's humble opinion, populated by those who loved the Lord and whiskey in equal measure. There were but four shops in the entire village, but also four pubs. The church was built in the middle of the nineteenth century and was still standing tall and strong. Larger than the village needed, but a fine building nonetheless. The floor of the nave was composed of tiles, aquamarine, white and pale green. The interior walls were white and the beams that supported the roof overhead were stained dark. The pews were simple and in need of some sanding and polishing, but where was the money for such frivolity? It was dedicated to Our Lady, Star of the Sea and Saint Patrick.

The confessor said, 'Forgive me, Father, for I have sinned. It's been exactly one year since my last confession.'

The priest was intrigued by this exactitude. Most confessors spoke in general terms to ease their own guilt. A few days meant a week. A week meant ten days. A couple of weeks was a month. A year meant eighteen months. A long time meant several years. I don't remember meant a lifetime ago. The priest was a precise man and respected others who were also precise.

The voice that spoke to him belonged to no Irishman, which was rare. The confessor had almost no accent, if such a thing could be true. The words were well enunciated, perfect in pronunciation, but flat and monotone. An Englishman, he presumed, but a traveller who spoke several languages, and had lost any quintessential Englishness from his speaking voice. The priest liked to hypothesise when dealing with new people. Uncommon now, but it was a habit that had served him well in his past life. The Englishman was no doubt here to explore rural Ireland – the Ireland of postcards and folk songs.

The screen that separated them offered privacy, but no secrecy. Through the lattice the priest could see the confessor, who was a dark-haired man in a grey suit.

The priest said, 'Tell me about your sins, my child.'

'I have killed many people.'

The priest was unfazed. 'Is this some kind of joke, because it's neither funny nor original. It's one thing to waste my time, but it's another to waste the time of this church and squander that of those who are in need.'

'I assure you, it is no joke.'

'I see,' the priest said, and settled himself for what would follow.

It hadn't happened to him since he had moved out here to the wilds, but when he had worked in areas with larger populations he had dealt with the occasional oddball. Some confessors were borderline insane or outright mad. They confessed outlandish crimes, looking for attention or even believing themselves responsible. He had listened to many a Hitler who had survived the war and had been in hiding ever since. He had heard the confessions of many a Satan.

'Okay,' the priest said. 'We'll start from the beginning. Why have you killed people?'

'I'm a professional assassin.'

'Yes, of course. And how many people have you killed?'

'I'm not sure.'

Despite the ridiculousness of what he was hearing the priest couldn't help but think about the fact he had taken the confession of real killers before. Those who had fought in the Troubles. He was still disturbed by the things he had been told.

'How can you not know how many people you killed?'

'I poisoned a woman recently,' the confessor answered. 'I'm not sure if she died.'

'Why did you poison her? Were you paid to?'

'No,' he said. 'We were enemies, then allies of convenience. After that alliance was no longer necessary, I considered her my enemy again.'

'I see.' He didn't. 'Why are you not sure whether she died?'

'I told her how to beat the poison. I gave her a chance at

4

life if she was strong enough to take it. It's not yet safe to check whether she was or not.'

'Why did you give her this ... *chance*, as you put it?'

'She convinced me I might need her help one day. She had already proven herself capable of fulfilling such a role.'

It was a fantasy. It was a delusion. The confessor really believed what he was saying. Which was frightening in a different way. The priest hoped there was help out there for him. For now, the best the priest could do was humour the fantasist to keep him calm. The priest didn't want to cause a scene that would upset those who were genuine in their need.

'Do you care if she lives or dies?'

The English confessor was quiet for a moment, then said, 'If she dies, then I have eliminated a dangerous threat. If she lives, then I have gained a useful associate.'

'In which case, if she does indeed survive, maybe you should send her flowers. But that's not the answer I wanted.'

'It's the only one I'm able to provide.'

The priest rolled his eyes and said, 'Are you sorry for what you have done? Is your conscience heavy with guilt?'

'No,' the confessor said.

'Then why are you even here?'

The confessor was quiet for a time. The priest didn't hurry the answer. Instead, he waited, curious.

'This is something I have to do. Habit, or perhaps addiction would be a more appropriate word.'

'Explain.'

'This, here and now, is a remnant of the person I once was.'

There was a neutrality in the confessor's voice that belied the sadness of the words. The priest was intrigued as to who might create such a broken delusion, and what life they sought to escape in doing so.

The priest said, 'What do you hope to achieve with this confession?'

'What do you mean?' the confessor asked.

'You don't seek absolution. If you don't feel remorse for your sins then this process is pointless. You have to accept your sins if you want forgiveness.'

'And God will forgive me, no matter what I've done, if I only ask for it?'

'Yes, that's how it works,' the priest said to bring the conversation to a close. 'Say nine Hail Marys and ten Our Fathers and you will be absolved of your sins.'

'Thank you, Father.'

He said, 'Go to confession more than once a year.'

'I'll try.'

The priest smiled to himself. Never a dull moment. 'And don't kill any more people.'

The confessor said, 'I can't promise that.'

TWO

Dying didn't hurt, but coming back to life sure did. Rehabilitation was agony. The central nervous system cannot be shut down and restarted without consequence, she would be told. It was a needless observation. She had begun her second life paralysed. She could breathe. She could groan. But that was about it. Movement was slow to return. Feeling was slower. She could scratch herself before she could sense the nails on her skin. The pain was always there, though, but without focus, without a cause. Her limbs had a constant ache. Muscles in her back would go into spasm without warning. The faintest light could ignite her retina into spectral flames, yet darkness could do the same. A pneumatic drill hammered against the inside of her skull at all times, wielded by a sadist.

You'll have to get used to it, one physician would explain, adding 'I'm afraid', in some token sympathy. She had lots of doctors and specialists and consultants asking her questions and examining her notes. At first, this had reassured her, but it wasn't long before she understood that she was but an interesting anomaly to them. None of them cared about her.

It took a day or so before she could talk, which meant no one knew what had happened to cause her heart to stop. She had been dead on arrival, then unconscious in intensive care once they had brought her back, then mute and immobile when she had awoken. Because she hadn't been able to talk she couldn't tell them what had happened, and even if her lips and tongue worked again she didn't know the name of the poison she had ingested. It was a neurotoxin, her murderer had told her.

The doctors therefore had to hypothesise, they had to guess, they had to investigate. They loved that part. She could tell they were having fun with it, with her. She didn't mind that, if it meant they brought her back to full strength faster. She hadn't spent this long in bed since college, and then it hadn't been to rest.

'Did you see that?' a disembodied voice said. 'She smiled.'

'I didn't see anything. You probably just imagined it.'

'Don't tell me what I saw or didn't.'

'Is this about last night?'

When she could talk she told them nothing of substance. Nothing useful. She said she didn't remember. She said maybe someone had given her something to drink. That part was true, at least, and she figured they might have pumped her stomach and found traces of whatever it was that had poisoned her in her blood, or the remnants of it.

'You're very lucky to be alive,' a young doctor told her.

'I don't feel lucky.'

'Your heart stopped for over two minutes.'

If you're strong enough, they'll bring you back, her murderer had told her.

'Thank you for not giving up on me.'

'You're very welcome, but in truth the credit goes entirely to you.'

I'm strong enough, she had told him.

The doctors were happy to have her conscious and compos mentis, but she wanted to know more, she wanted to know when she would be well again, when she could leave. No one wanted to tell her, else they didn't know themselves. Lying in bed, it was hard to comprehend the full extent of her condition, but she knew it was beyond bad. She knew she couldn't be any weaker. Her hands told her that. It was a struggle to make a fist. There was a ball of iron in her grip that she had to flatten just to make her fingertips meet her palm. Her arm shook under the strain. She started to perspire. She gasped for air upon giving up, as infuriated as she was disheartened.

There was some police involvement, which was expected. Two local cops asked her some questions but grew bored of her telling them she didn't remember, she couldn't be sure, it was hard to recall.

'We'll come back in a couple of weeks when you're feeling better.'

She wasn't trying to protect her murderer. She wanted to protect herself. There were a lot of people out there south of the border who would be keen to finish the job he had started. As a living Jane Doe in a Canadian hospital she was pretty anonymous, but she had already been here too long. It was easier to stay alive when on the move, and if anyone came for her in her current state, she wouldn't be able to run, let alone put up much of a fight.

After a few days she could sit up by herself, and once she could bend her knees it wasn't long before she could push back the bedclothes and attempt to stand. She acquired a lot of bruises. Hospital floors were hard.

'You're not ready to walk yet,' a different doctor told her.

'I need to get to the gym.'

The doctor laughed, figuring she had made a joke.

'Look at me. I'm atrophying all over the place.'

'You must let yourself recover properly. This is a slow process. Physiotherapy will come eventually, when you are ready.'

'I'm ready.'

'Let's not push you into anything you can't handle.'

'I can handle it. I came back from the dead, didn't I?'

She was doing push-ups the next day – only three, using her knees to assist her – but by the end of the week she was doing five unassisted. She exercised at night when the lights were off and she wasn't checked on for hours, which gave her time to lie on the floor in an exhausted sprawl before she regained the energy to climb – and she had to climb – back into bed, tears wetting her face because the pain of exertion was so bad. She used the pillow to muffle her cries.

She did grip-strength exercises in bed, every hour, squeezing the metal support bars until they were left with handprints of sweat. She made herself eat, always asking for another portion, another meal, snacks, leftovers, ignoring the constricted feeling of airlessness in her weakened throat as she forced food down, ignoring the bloated nausea of fullness to make sure she consumed enough calories to stop herself wasting away, using both hands to clamp shut her mouth and pinch her nostrils tight to trap the inevitable vomit and swallow it back down so no nutrients were wasted.

The clock on the wall showed her the day in that little plastic window next to the three. *We'll come back in a couple of weeks* ... She had to be gone by then. She couldn't risk another conversation with the police. Each day she was better than the last and looked it. They wouldn't relent so easily next time. There would be proper questions. A proper statement required. That would put her on their system.

That was her fear. That's what she needed to avoid.

Those who wanted to find her would see that entry on their own systems, because their electronic tentacles reached everywhere. Their search algorithms would flag the telling details. Someone would notice. Messages would be sent. A decision would be made fast and acted upon without delay because the mysterious woman without a name or memory bore an uncanny resemblance to one Constance Stone, aka Raven, former government operative, rogue agent, assassin ...

Kill on sight.

THREE

Her client stood by the window. He kept the curtains closed, but peered out into the night through the thin gap between curtain and wall. He was dressed in his grey suit – he was always dressed so fast – but had not showered. He never showered, and she had stopped offering him its use. It was strange as he always seemed so clean, but he didn't want to be undressed around her any longer than required. Ashamed of his nakedness, she had guessed, although he had no reason to be. She had never been with a man in better shape. His skin seemed shrink-wrapped over muscles so dense they hurt if he pressed himself against her with too much force. It was the scars he was ashamed of, she reasoned. He had so many scars – far more than she'd seen on a single person – and some were horrible to look at, but she didn't find them ugly. Quite the opposite, in fact. She saw them as a multitude of unknown stories – each scar the page of a book she longed to read.

He was a Russian, tall and dark. He never said where he was from, but she recognised the accent. She had known many of his countrymen. She observed him at the window whilst she found a robe and collected up her own clothes from the foot of the bed. It took her longer to recover and get herself together again.

'She's not out there,' she said.

The dark-haired Russian didn't look at her. 'Who isn't?'

'Your wife.'

He had given her a name that she didn't believe was his own – she was well used to being lied to by clients – but she didn't let on. She always played the part she was paid to play.

'I'm not married,' he said.

'Sure,' she replied, 'which is why you always have to check who's outside, before and after. You think I don't notice, but I do. You think your wife is going to catch you. That's why you never really enjoy yourself.'

'I assure you I enjoy my time with you.'

'That's not what I meant and you know it. If you didn't have to worry about her catching you in the act then you could truly relax more and make the most of our time together.'

'I don't worry,' he felt the need to state.

It was a strange thing to say, or at least it would be, coming from another person. From him, who was more than a little strange, it was almost normal. She had spent enough time with men to understand how they worked; to know what made them tick; to interpret their actions and decipher their subtext. This one remained an enigma. She had worked out the window thing. That was easy enough. Men cheated on their wives and their wives weren't dumb. It didn't take paranoia for a man to be concerned his wife might follow him to his hired mistress. On the other end of the scale was the bed. It had taken her a couple of his visits before she noticed he had dragged it a little way from the wall. She noticed the absence of the headboard thumping. Her home was a two-storey house and the bed was positioned against an exterior wall, so she had never had to fear angry neighbours banging at her door. That's why it was set there, after all. And men, she had learned, liked to hear that thump. They liked to feel powerful. Not this one, though.

She yawned. It was getting late and she was sore. 'Same time tomorrow?'

She dropped the clothes into a laundry basket and checked her hair in the vanity table mirror. She kept the room simple, but tasteful. It was her second bedroom. She didn't entertain clients where she slept. She was okay with how she made her living, but she was not *that* okay. She wanted her own space. She wanted separation between work and her personal life, and she wasn't comfortable being personal by choice with anyone in the same room where she was personal for money.

She was well educated, with two degrees and a master's, had travelled and volunteered, but she made more money doing this than she could ever hope to in the real world. Her father was a drunk and her mother had died in childbirth. She'd had no advantages in life except her looks and the charm to go with it. The degrees were achieved through hard work and the desire to better herself, but the world judged her on how she looked over what she thought, so it was only logical to play along. If she couldn't be who she wanted, then she would do whatever she could to exploit who she was expected to be.

The dark-haired man hadn't answered her, but he didn't talk a lot. He spoke only when spoken to. She wondered if there would be only silence otherwise, if he would be happy with no communication beyond the physical.

'What should I wear? The white dress again? You liked that one, didn't you?'

She smiled to herself, remembering his reaction when she had first worn it.

He said, 'I'm leaving Sofia first thing in the morning.'

'Then you really should have had more sleep, shouldn't you?' She winked at him. 'When are you coming back to me then?'

'I won't be.'

Her smile faltered. 'What do you mean, you won't be?'

He faced her. 'I'm moving on. I'm not coming back.'

'You know you are. You've seen me every night this week.'

'It was a mistake to keep returning,' he said without a hint of emotion. 'I don't usually do that kind of thing. I know better. I should know better.'

'But I'm a special case, aren't I?' she asked, knowing the answer. 'I'm the one who makes you break the rules. I know you like me. You can't help yourself. I have that effect on men. They can't resist me. They always come back.'

'Not me. Not again.'

'Why?' she demanded rather than asked.

'I don't stay in the same place for long. A few days, a week at the very most. This is the seventh night in the same town. I've been pushing it as it is.'

She couldn't keep the confusion from her face, nor the rejection.

He said, 'If I've somehow misled you then I'll pay you now for tomorrow night, but I won't be back.'

She turned away. 'No, I don't want any more money from you. I could take a month off with what you've paid already.'

'Then what is the problem?'

'Who said it's a problem that you can just end things without warning?'

'I didn't know I needed to provide any forewarning. I thought we had established the terms of this transaction.'

'I know, we did. But you said yourself you don't usually do this.'

'Which is exactly why I can't do it again.'

'You didn't deny it when I said you like me.'

'I don't understand,' he said, and it was infuriating that he didn't. He was so naïve, so simple. No, he was stupid. His stupidity was ridiculous.

'Of course you don't get it, why would you?'

'I never said this would be a long-term arrangement. Maybe I was unclear about that. I can only apologise if I've inconvenienced you or if you were relying on my continued custom.'

She laughed; a hollow, ironic sound. 'Are you trying to be an asshole? Look at me. Do you think I'm struggling for

16

clients? I pick and choose. I thought I made that quite clear. Ten years from now I'll still be able to pick and choose. And you dare to say "relying ...."? You couldn't be any more insulting if you tried. *Jesus.*'

He frowned. 'I really don't like blasphemy.'

'Oh, do forgive me. I thought that, given you've been screwing the *holy hell* out of a call girl every night for a week, blasphemy would be pretty low on your list of moral concerns.'

He waited a moment – it seemed out of politeness only – and said, 'I'm going to go now.'

He walked across the room and she let him, furious at him for going and more so at herself for letting him. She didn't turn around until she heard the door click shut and she listened to his footsteps on the landing, then on the stairs, then gone for good. Then she noticed he had left another night's payment on the dresser by the door. She grabbed the pile of crisp notes and tore them to shreds before her back slid down the bedroom door and she sat on the carpet with her knees to her chest and her hair over her face.

FOUR

'The messages from your brain to your muscles are delayed,' yet another doctor told Raven. 'The synapses are firing. The messages are sent on time, but they're not getting where they need to be. Your nervous system has so many routes, so many pathways, it's like a maze. The messages your brain is sending have forgotten which way they're supposed to go. They're getting there eventually, but they're getting lost on the journey. They're taking the scenic route, if you like. It's going to take time and patience to help them relearn the maze.'

'Time and patience are two things I don't have.'

'It would really help if we knew what you had been poisoned with.'

'No traces at all?'

He shook his head. 'Bizarre, isn't it?'

Not really, she didn't say. She was no stranger to toxins herself. Raven had killed many people with poisons that couldn't be detected. Potassium chloride – one of her favourites – a classic poison that induced heart failure, because it was so hard to detect due to the fact it broke down into its component elements after death, both of which were present in the body already. The neurotoxin that had paralysed her and stopped her heart could be long gone from her system or still present, but they didn't know what to look for.

'Are you okay?'

She smiled through the agony. 'Never better.'

The pain kept Raven awake at night. It kept her awake in the daytime. There was no escape from it. She hid the full extent of it whenever she could.

A consultant from the UK tried to explain it to Raven in her weird, posh accent: 'You're in constant pain because your nervous system has been overstimulated and now it's responding to a stimulus that isn't real. The nerves are sending messages to your brain informing it of injuries that don't exist.'

'You're saying it's all in my mind?'

'In a way, I suppose I am. The pain you're experiencing is very real, I assure you of that. But your central nervous system is confused. It's had a factory reset, only the firmware isn't up to date.'

'Now I'm as confused as my nervous system.'

'Sorry,' she said. 'I'm trying to explain it in the simplest way and I'm not doing a very good job. Basically, your CNS has gone arse over tit.'

'*What?*'

'Never mind,' she said. 'Just be patient.'

'I'm getting really tired of people telling me that.'

Raven was always tired, so tired. But she couldn't sleep for long when the pain seemed to subside. Her muscles would cramp and she would wake up fighting back the screams, else she would dream of spreading paralysis and the madness of being trapped inside a body she could no longer control.

The specialists came and went. There was a revolving door of doctors and consultants, nurses and therapists. They had their own ideas. Contradictions were common.

'Hold on, are you saying my central nervous system needs to rebuild itself?'

'No, that's not really what I'm saying. Relearn would be a better way of describing the process.'

Process. She heard that a lot. Such a clinical, soulless term for what she was going through. Like she was a project or experiment for them – and in a way, she was.

Every day there was improvement, the pain easing as her mobility increased. After a week she could hide the cramps and spasms from the doctors, pretending to be better than she felt so they would speed up the process of rehabilitation. They weren't taking any risks with her recovery, they kept telling her. They wanted their money's worth, more like. They still didn't know what had caused her complete neurological shutdown.

'You want to write a paper on me,' she couldn't help but retort to some smug consultant who flew in every few days to check her progress and ask stupid questions. 'You want to solve the mystery and then brag to your peers.'

'I assure you that's not the case.'

'Then leave me the hell alone.'

When they believed her to have been painless for forty-eight hours she was allowed outside, supervised, of course. The afternoon sun felt so good on her face she almost felt free of pain for the first time she could remember.

The nurse who accompanied her said, 'Let's take a nice slow stroll around the garden.'

He was cute, with dimples and blond hair tucked behind his ears. He was pretty young too, but strong. There was an innocence in his smile. She couldn't help but like him. Typical that she was holed up in a hospital, in an awful gown, pretty much the worst she'd ever looked. Not that it mattered. She didn't remember the last time she had asked a guy for his number. There wasn't much time for dating in her chosen career – ex-career – path.

'I want to go this way,' she said, trying to steer him.

'There's nothing to see over there.'

There was. Windows and exits and cameras and vehicles. She analysed the perimeter while the cute, well-meaning nurse offered his arm for support.

'That's probably enough for today,' he said.

'One more lap.'

He started to shake his head.

'Please,' she said.

She didn't know the hospital, and it was too big and she too immobile to learn, even if they would let her explore on her own. So she did what she could. She made do. Raven could hobble from her room and around the ward without too much interference. She could ignore the shaking heads and dismiss the offers to help her back to her room with a smile. She had a nice smile and she made it work for her. Not on the women, though. They knew those tricks. To the women she acted brave, so she had their respect. To the men she acted vulnerable, so she had their veneration.

She received flowers. A beautiful bouquet of lilies arrived one afternoon. The cute nurse brought them into her room. She was drowsy, having just awoken.

'Oh, Lionel, you shouldn't have,' she said to the cute nurse.

He set them down on the bedside table. 'Aren't lilies what you give at funerals?'

'It's a joke,' Raven said. 'What does the card say?'

'*We'll always have Coney Island*,' he read. 'What does that mean?'

'It's a play on what Humphrey Bogart said to Ingrid Bergman at the end of *Casablanca*. It's another joke.'

Lionel didn't get it. 'Who sent them?'

'A man who doesn't make jokes,' she explained without explaining. 'Are there any details on the card for the florist? Address? Logo?'

He checked the card. '*Fast Flowers*. There's a local address.'

'Do me a favour and slip the card into a drawer? I don't want to lose it.'

The hands on the clock kept up their relentless motion. The date continued to advance. Two weeks was not a long time to recover from dying, but she had to make it enough. She wasn't prepared to live again only for it to get her killed again. That would be the worst luck, even for her.

The next killer wouldn't give her a lifeline. She wouldn't be able to bargain a reprieve.

Raven found she had little malice for the man who was her potential murderer and now tormentor. He had acted in self-defence, if pre-empted self-defence. But she was alive because he had changed his mind. She had convinced him she deserved a second chance. That second chance was proving an insurmountable challenge. This new life of hers was no life she wanted to live. It had to get better. It had to improve. She fought on because she wasn't one to give up. If there was the slightest chance she could improve, she would endure any agony, any setback to see it happen.

'You're pushing yourself too hard,' Lionel told her as he helped her back into bed.

'I don't care. I'll do whatever it takes.'

'You're making the pain worse by trying to run before you can walk.'

'I can't run, that's the problem.'

The two weeks were almost up. Once the cops had questioned her a second time, once she was fed into a database, she figured she would have maybe a day's head start. Her enemies would react fast and move faster. They wouldn't want to waste this golden opportunity. They would never have a better chance to end the problem that was once one of their own.

A day's head start. Not long. She had avoided her enemies with half that time, but at full health. She wasn't going to get far in her current state. Fatigued, weak, distracted by pain ... She had to mitigate those factors by making sure no one found her in the first place. So, she had to get well enough to slip out of the hospital unnoticed, before those questions were asked, before she could be fed into the system. She had to escape. She had three days before those two weeks were up.

She figured one day further for exercising and recovery. Plan and prepare on the second. Escape on the third.

It was going to be tight, but she could make it work. She had to.

She was awoken from her nap by a knock on her door and the cute nurse appeared and said, 'The police are here.'

FIVE

The instructor was one hundred and ninety pounds of honed muscles. He had been fighting since before he could read and write. First in the schoolyard, and then on the wrestling mat and then in dojos and rings, and he'd been doing so ever since. He was a national champion in Muay Thai, a third Dan in Shotokan karate; he'd fought in Pancrase; he'd mastered Russian Sambo; been taught Krav Maga by Israeli masters; studied Brazilian jiu-jitsu in the back alleys of Sao Paulo where there were no rules. He was born to fight and lived to fight, but a detached retina ended any hope of a career as a professional fighter, so instead he taught. He owned three gyms in Amsterdam and ran self-defence seminars across Europe and sometimes overseas. The rise of mixed martial arts meant he was in demand more and more, and had made plenty of money teaching cage fighters refinements to their techniques, new moves, and putting them through their paces. He had private clients too – rich guys and girls who wanted to be a badass or ready for one.

The new guy was different. He was no professional fighter, and no rich kid looking for bragging rights. The advanced classes the instructor ran weren't advertised. It was a word-of-mouth thing. You had to know someone who knew about them. Like a filter to ensure no time-wasters showed up. One glance at the new student warming up was enough to know he was no time-waster. He was too old, of course, to start any kind of career in the ring, but the way he moved, the way he fought, told the instructor he had done a lot more than just spar over the years. He hit the speed bag like a pro, but like a man half his size would, like a flyweight, his hands a blur of precision.

'How many fights have you had?' the instructor asked him.

'I've never fought professionally.'

A careful answer from a careful guy. He was an American, with one of those deep, coarse voices, and the instructor figured him to be a businessman on a transatlantic trip. Given the sharp grey suit he had come in wearing he was probably one of those hot-shot CEOs of a tech firm who liked to burn off boardroom steam in a cage fight, wherever his work took him. The instructor was good at guessing weights and body compositions, and put the new guy at a lean but strong one hundred and eighty pounds. There was nothing on his frame that didn't do a job. He was a natural light heavyweight in boxing terms, in the classic sense, but could maybe boil down as far as a middleweight and rehydrate back up on fight night.

'I didn't ask if you had fought professionally, but we'll move on,' the instructor said. 'So, what's your body fat? Seven per cent?'

'More like eight. I like to carry some extra fuel around with me.'

'In case of what exactly?'

The American raised an eyebrow. 'Just . . . in case.'

The instructor left him alone to continue his workout. The gym had a boxing ring and grappling mats, plenty of free weights, benches and squat equipment, Olympic bars and plates, but no machines. The instructor didn't believe in machines. He believed in compound movements and stabiliser muscles. More than that he believed in skipping ropes and flipping tyres, press-ups and pull-ups. He believed in functional strength. Boxing had proven again and again that building muscles wasn't the same as building strength. A boxer could move up the weight categories just by adding mass, but did his punching power carry up too, did his punch resistance? No, was the short answer. Almost never. The young guys didn't buy it. They wanted bigger guns to flex on social media. They didn't realise that having them meant fighting guys who might weigh the same but were really that weight, who were that weight thanks to nature, until they were crying in the changing room and the instructor was doing his best not to say 'I told you so'. It had taken the instructor twenty years to put on twenty pounds – twenty real pounds.

The new student worked out with bodyweight only. He performed handstand push-ups, one-handed pull-ups, plank bars and other feats of strength that made his fellow students' eyes widen. It provoked them. They didn't like being shown up by someone new, someone older.

The gym was small, but had high ceilings thanks to being formed under the arch of an elevated train track. It was a hot, sweaty establishment with no air conditioning save for large wheeled fans that were powered only on the hottest of days. The owner wanted everyone to sweat, all the time. He liked sweat. Sweat meant hard work. He wanted the body to work even while resting. He wanted sweat to pour like rain while exercising. Train hard, fight easy. It was said for a reason. The bare bricks of the arched ceilings glistened with perspiration, all day long and half-way through the night. Mould was a problem. He had developed his own mix of bleach and cleaning chemicals to deal with it. He had a telescopic brush used by window cleaners to reach. He made the prospects do it. They hated it, but it built character.

The place stank. That was the downside. No way to scrub the stench of body odour from the air. He was so used to breathing in the rank smell of stale sweat that inner-city air, choked with pollution, seemed fragrant and clean. Some people who tried out his classes couldn't cope with it. They didn't like to soak their own clothes any more than they liked to choke on someone else's pit stink. There was a word for people like that. The instructor tried to watch his language these days. He felt it was a nice coun-terpoint to the tattoos and shaved head, the muscles and the scars. People expected him to swear. It caught them off guard that he didn't. He liked that. He liked it more that in his mind every other thought was spelled with four letters.

28

It was an all-day seminar: strength and fitness in the morning, followed by lunch, then on to techniques, with sparring at the end of the day for those who wanted it. The new guy wanted it. He wanted it and then some.

'You either have it or you don't,' the instructor said to the American at the end of the seminar, once the sparring was over and people were resting and chatting.

'Have what?'

'Heart. You can't teach it. You can't train it.'

'You're talking about instincts.'

'Maybe. Whatever you want to call it, you got it.'

The new guy didn't respond.

'You tore through my best students.'

'I lost every spar.'

The American was a born fighter, the instructor could tell, even if his advanced students didn't get it. They thought they were kings of the mat when the new guy tapped out and they gasped in the corner, wringing the sweat from their shirts and trying to hide their pain. The instructor wasn't fooled, however. He looked at his best guys and knew none of them would be turning up for the next class – they'd all have bullshit excuses to cover their absences while they waited for their swelling to go down and the bruises to fade. The instructor looked at the American, tired but still standing after three spars back to back; rolling his shoulders and stretching out sore muscles; looking like he could go another three rounds with a fresh opponent and maybe another three after that, but had somehow lost every sparring session he was winning; somehow making a rookie mistake and finding himself in an arm bar or choke he couldn't escape from; forced to tap, to submit, to surrender to a man who needed help to stand.

No, the instructor wasn't fooled.

'None of the guys you sparred with will be in again this week. They might not be back next week either.'

The new guy didn't respond.

'You went easy on them, I know.'

'I lost,' the American repeated. 'Every time.'

'You know, I had just one pro fight, a boxing match,' the instructor said. 'And I lost. I was fighting some Mexican kid. A prospect, signed to one of the big promoters. They were looking to get him rounds, get him experience, but not put him at risk. They all do it. It's how the game works. Twenty fights against no ones to build them up, to make their résumé. Well, this Mexican kid was beating up the tomato cans they put before him so badly no one wanted to fight him, at least not for the chump change they were paying. So, I agree. I figure I can put him on his skinny ass because A, I was a stupid kid too, and B, I could actually fight. The promoter knew this too, so on fight night he takes me to one side and tells me that I'll get double my fee if I get stopped. That was a lot of money to me then, but I was so pissed that this was going on in the sport I loved that I went after that Mexican kid with everything I had. I was gonna punch his head clean from his shoulders. I was raging. I was Jake LaMotta and Marvin Hagler rolled into one. You know what happened? He put me down with the first shot he threw. Perfect left hook, right on the chin. I jumped up, madder still, ready to make him pay, and he spent the whole four-round fight beating me like a piñata, but he never landed that left hook clean again. By the time the final bell rang I had two blown ear drums, four cracked ribs, internal bleeding and a detached retina. Turns out, just before the fight his promoter had told him I was going to take a dive. And just like me, it made him mad as hell, so he did everything he could not to put me down again after that first punch. He made me suffer. He made me pay like I wanted to make him pay. And me ... well, I refused to know when I was beaten. I had heart – too much heart – and so I never fought again.'

'Why did you tell me that story?'

'I don't really know. It's not something I tend to share. Most people hear it and I can see in their eyes that they think *excuses, excuses*. But, and I could be wrong, I suspect you are one of the few people who can actually appreciate it for what it is.'

He nodded.

'Fancy sparring me?' the instructor asked.

It wasn't often he found another natural-born warrior like himself, and he had never encountered one who threw away a victory, because what separated a warrior from a fighter was the will to win; the will to answer the bell for the twelfth round when he had a burst ear drum, cracked ribs and couldn't focus; the will to climb off the canvas when the brain was trying to shut down and restart. That couldn't be taught. That was heart. He wanted to see how much heart the new guy really had.

He didn't hesitate, didn't think. He said, 'No, thanks.'

'How come? Because you know I'll kick your ass?'

The American smiled in good humour, showing he could take the joke, but he didn't respond.

'Or,' the instructor said, 'is it because you know I see through you and that you'll actually have to kick my ass to stop me kicking yours?'

He collected his things. 'Thank you for teaching the class today.'

'Funny you say that,' the instructor said, 'when we both know I didn't teach you a damn thing.'

SIX

It was the same two who'd come to see Raven the first time. One woman and one man. Both local cops in uniform. The man was short but had a big gut and fleshy face. He had a moustache – a dark hairy worm that covered his top lip. The woman was taller, and heavyset with broad shoulders and broader hips. She had a bruiser's posture but had the eyes of a thinker. She made Raven uneasy. This wasn't someone who would be deceived with ease. The woman was younger than the man, but she seemed to be the senior because she had done most of the talking last time, or maybe that was because of her youth – she was more interested in the amnesiac woman than the man, who had long since passed caring about the crazies he encountered.

The cute nurse left them alone.

'You're back early,' Raven said.

The short fat cop shrugged. 'Two weeks, ten days, what's the difference?'

'About four days, usually.'

He grinned at her. 'Give or take.'

The woman said, 'They say you're well enough to talk.'

'No point me arguing otherwise then, is there?'

She nodded. 'They know best, don't they? Doctors always know what's best for us. You look much better, I can see that. You sound it too.'

'Thanks.'

'A whole different person, almost. What about your memory? How's that? Better too? Must be.'

'Not really,' Raven said.

'That's a shame,' she said back, the thinker's eyes small and calculating.

The fat cop said, 'Bummer.'

'We'd better introduce ourselves again then,' the woman said. 'I'm Officer Heno and this is Officer Willitz. We're from the local precinct.'

'I remember your names from last time,' Raven said, too busy paying attention to their body language and the weapons at their belts to focus on Heno's words.

'Oh,' Heno said, 'so your memory is improving after all?'

It annoyed Raven to get caught out in such a simple way, but she smiled through it. She wasn't herself, after all.

'What else do you remember?' Heno asked.

Willitz was ready with a notebook. He licked the nib of his pen as if he enjoyed the taste of ink.

Raven shrugged. 'It's difficult. Before I woke up here, everything is blurry. Fragments. Shapes and sounds. I remember I'd had a few drinks. I can hear someone asking if I was okay ... That's about it.'

34

Heno glanced at Willitz. Willitz shrugged.

Heno said, 'That's what you told us last time. Anything further to add? Any details at all?'

'I want to understand this as much as you, Officer.'

She nodded in solidarity – a bad pretence of it, at least. 'What about yourself? Do you remember your own name?'

Raven shook her head. 'No.'

'Do you happen to know how rare complete retrograde amnesia is?'

'I'm not a doctor,' Raven said, then: 'As far as I remember.'

'You know, I've been reading up on amnesia since our last conversation. You're the very first person I've encountered like it, beyond someone drunk, I mean. My library card is practically ash it's been scanned so much. I've been trying to understand what could make a person completely forget who they are and what happened to them.'

Raven said, 'Try dying.'

Heno's smile was gone almost as soon as it had arrived. 'It's funny you should say that because almost all instances of complete retrograde amnesia are documented, and in most cases the person suffered a severe head injury or some other form of brain damage. Do you know how many cases resulted from cardiac arrest?'

She shook her head.

'Zero.'

They were both watching her for a reaction, and watching hard.

Raven showed a surprised and intrigued expression, which was genuine because she had more than a professional curiosity as to her condition and the neuro-toxin that had caused it.

She said, 'What about in cases of nervous system failure, oxygen deprivation to the brain, and poisoning?'

The glimpse-and-you've-missed-it smile returned. 'What I'm saying is that perhaps you do remember more than you're telling me.'

'Why don't you seem very interested in whoever poisoned me? Why do you only seem to care about ... me?'

Officer Heno took a step forward. 'We'd love to hear all about the person who poisoned you. You see, we'd like to catch him. But there's this little issue: you don't remember anything. You don't remember where you were, or who you are, let alone what actually happened. So, until we've established those little details, I'm afraid there isn't a whole lot we can do to trace the person who did this to you. Unless there is anything you'd care to share with us that you haven't already. Is there?'

'You'll be the first to know if I remember anything.'

Heno said, 'Sure.'

'Spend a lot of time in hotels?' Willitz asked.

'What does that mean?'

'Maybe it means a woman fitting your description was seen in a hotel bar downtown from here on the same night you came in.'

'I told you: I don't remember where I was that night.'

'Funny thing is this woman who looks like you was seen approaching a man drinking on his own.'

'So?'

'Doesn't that seem odd to you? You just happened to

pick out a guy to talk to who ended up spiking your drink. What does he do? Hang around in bars waiting for women to come to him? Is he that hot?'

'I don't know, do I?'

Willitz folded his arms. 'Maybe you do, maybe you don't.'

'I've read a lot about victim blaming,' Raven said after a moment, 'but experiencing it first-hand gives you a whole new perspective.'

'You remember what you've read,' Heno said, 'how interesting.'

'You must have a very dull life for all this to be so interesting to you.'

'Officer Willitz, please make a note that Jane Doe is answering in a hostile manner.'

Raven said, 'You have no idea what it means for me to be hostile. And you don't want to.'

'Officer Willitz, please add to your note that Jane Doe is now being threatening.'

She laughed and batted her eyelashes. 'You're not scared of little old me, are you? Don't worry, they've given me so many drugs my mood is all over the place. You'll have to forgive the occasional moment of frustration. I seem to have developed an incredibly low tolerance for BS.'

'I guess that's understandable,' Heno said after a moment, taking the bait and trying a softer approach.

It was all textbook stuff and Raven was playing along as expected. She didn't want to let the attempts to rattle her be ineffective and make herself into even more of a special case.

'Listen, lady,' Willitz butted in, losing his cool. 'What we're saying is that no one remembers nothing. No one doesn't know who they are. You must know something. You must remember something. And if you don't then that makes us think you have something to hide.'

Raven put a palm to her chest. 'You're saying I'm pretending?'

'I'm saying you might be lying, sure.'

Raven said, 'I don't like your attitude, Officer Willitz.'

Willitz laughed, as if her opinion had no consequence and to voice it was somehow ridiculous. Heno wasn't pleased with his reaction. She was trying to play it calm but menacing, and he was spoiling her rhythm.

Raven wasn't surprised when Heno said, 'Why don't you wait outside, Ken? Get yourself a cup of a coffee, yeah?'

Willitz clicked his tongue and sauntered out of the room. He didn't bother to close the door behind him. A pathetic act of defiance, but some people needed to fight the power however they could. Heno did so for him, easing it shut. Measured. Controlled. The thinker.

Raven said, 'I'm getting tired. Can we wrap this up?'

Heno said, 'In a few minutes. I have only a couple more things to go over.'

'Don't take offence if I begin to snore.'

Heno smiled a little. 'I have five brothers. There's nothing you can do or say that will offend me.'

'Six of you, wow. Your parents were busy. Latex allergy?'

'Seven of us in total, as it happens. I have a sister too.' She shrugged. 'Catholic family.'

Raven smiled as if she couldn't see through Heno's

attempt to humanise herself, revealing personal details to appear less threatening, trying to establish rapport now Willitz had gone, now it was two women talking together.

'I can't remember if I have any siblings,' Raven said. 'I've been lying here trying to think if I do. I hope I do. I want some brothers too. I want to remember us fighting and playing. Isn't that funny?'

Heno nodded and smiled, like they were having a chat – friends catching up.

'You know what's also funny?' Heno said. 'I can't find you on the system.'

Raven felt cold. 'System?'

Heno nodded. 'Yeah, system. Couldn't find diddly squat on you, which is more than a little odd.'

'Wait, what? I don't understand. Why have you looked? You only took preliminary notes last time. Surely you wouldn't have anything to input, anything to search with?'

'Why does that matter? We had your fingerprints. That's enough. But we couldn't find you, so you're obviously not a criminal, and you haven't been in the military on either side of the border.'

She didn't know she had been fingerprinted. It must have happened while she was unconscious.

'You don't look too good,' Heno said. 'Why does it bother you? What aren't you telling me?'

'I . . .'

She couldn't speak. She wasn't on any system because all of her records had been erased. But she was on systems Officer Heno couldn't access, systems that would recognise her fingerprints and send out all kinds of warnings and messages.

That they hadn't already found and killed her was itself a miracle. She guessed Heno hadn't looked for her straight away after that first conversation. There had been a delay. More pressing matters. Unless they were waiting for the right time when they could make her disappear. That made sense. They would struggle to do what they needed to do at the hospital. Not with all these witnesses and cameras. They couldn't hide something like that. Not their style. If she died here in suspicious circumstances, or vanished, it would only draw more attention to her and to them. Anonymity was everything to her enemies.

They needed to get her out of the hospital before they could kill her. They needed some excuse. Something to legitimise her absence and failure to return.

Heno said, 'Say, do you think you're well enough to take a little trip down to the precinct?'

Raven's pulse spiked. Heno and Willitz had seemed like real cops. They looked the part, and acted it. They had to be genuine. Raven didn't believe they could get away with impersonating officers on two separate occasions in the same place. Assuming they could, it was too risky to try. So they were on the payroll of her enemies, either long term or ad hoc. Her enemies had people everywhere. She knew this because she had been one of them. She hadn't realised their reach extended to Canada too, but she shouldn't be surprised by it either.

She tried not to stare at Heno too hard, but she failed.

'Why are you looking at me like that?'

Because she was assessing the threat, both posed by Heno in her room and Willitz outside, and their relation to her wider enemies. They had cops, spooks, politicians on their payroll.

'Why do you want to take me to the precinct?' Raven asked.

Heno said, 'We can go through mug shots. See if we can identify the man you spoke to in the hotel bar. No CCTV in the hotel got a shot at his face. Can you believe that? You can help us out. Let's get this guy. Let's find out what he did to you.'

'I'm sick.'

Heno seemed to shrug with her face. 'We can ask the doctors. You've been walking around the grounds, haven't you? They tell me you're coming on in leaps and bounds. A little car ride can't be more taxing. I'm sure they'll allow for a temporary discharge.'

'Temporary,' Raven echoed.

'We'll bring you straight back. Might do you good to get out in the fresh air. Change of scenery. We have decent coffee too. I'm not talking a drip machine here. We have an espresso maker. Coffee's so good it makes your hair stand on end.'

'I don't like coffee.'

'Doughnuts then,' Heno said with a big smile. 'Plus croissants and pains au chocolat. We have a fresh delivery every day from a local patisserie. Bet you have a sweet tooth.'

Raven was silent while she thought, and thought fast.

Heno looked towards the room's lone window. 'Don't you want to get out of here? Must make you all sorts of crazy, cooped up like this. I know it would me. It's a nice day outside. Sunshine. It's glorious out there.'

'My eyes are sensitive to light at the moment.'

'Bet you've never been inside a cop car, have you?' Heno asked. 'Could be fun.'

'I doubt it.'

Raven couldn't make a break for it. She couldn't run, even if she had the strength and energy for anything resembling a run. Any resistance would give them a perfect excuse to take her away. They might have hoped for just that situation. It could be the plan all along.

All they had to do was get her into a pair of handcuffs and it would be over.

She pictured a couple of square guys in suits and raincoats, with genuine IDs from south of the border to make them look official, to give them the unquestionable air of authority her enemies liked to operate within. Maybe Federal Marshals pursuing a fugitive. *We want this handled quietly.* Heno and Willitz were going to drive her out of the hospital grounds and pull over on a lonely stretch of highway where another car would be waiting.

Maybe the guys pretending to be Federal Marshals would be contractors with no idea who she was or why they had been hired to kill her. A couple of ex-military types with a whole string of bad things on their résumés. Or maybe she knew the two guys who would be waiting for her. Maybe they had worked together overseas in the days when she had been part of the intelligence community performing black ops. But that connection wouldn't stop them, just like it had never stopped her.

Nice to see you again, Constance.

Wish I could say the same.

However dangerous those two guys were, they were waiting on the side of a highway. Raven was in the hospital, protected by walls and distance and witnesses. She was safe here, as long as she stayed here. They must know that. In the same way they must know her guard would be up and she would be suspicious. So perhaps Heno and Willitz had been told to use force, to bend or break the rules to get her into custody if she didn't come along of her own volition.

Her throat was dry because Heno was inching closer with every word.

Raven thought of Willitz, waiting outside. The man. With him outside it gave legitimacy to anything Heno might have to do to control an aggressive witness. *She threw herself at me. I had no choice.*

She realised Heno had one hand out of sight by her side.

Raven said, 'What are you doing with your hand?'

'What hand?' Heno's expression changed. 'What are you afraid of? I'm just scratching my ass.'

Raven readied herself. She couldn't put up much resistance in her condition, but she wouldn't go down without a fight.

The door opened, surprising them both, and the cute nurse strolled inside the room, eyebrows rising in surprise when he saw Heno's proximity to the bed. Willitz followed the cute nurse into the room. He gave Heno a glance that said *I couldn't stop him.*

Lionel said, 'Hey ... sorry to interrupt but it's time to

see the physiotherapist.' He sensed the atmosphere. 'But I can come back later if you like.'

'That would be great,' Heno said without looking at him. 'Be a good boy and come back later.'

'No, no,' Raven said. 'Now's good. I'm ready. Perfect timing.'

Lionel helped Raven out of bed and into a wheelchair he had brought along while Willitz and Heno had a whole conversation between them with just facial expressions and gestures. Neither was happy and even Heno couldn't hide that fact.

'Excuse me,' Lionel said to the officers. 'A little room to squeeze by, please.'

'Beep, beep,' Raven said, smiling.

Heno didn't smile back. 'We'll wait.'

Lionel said, 'She'll be gone for a couple of hours, at least.'

Willitz rolled his eyes and stroked his moustache.

Heno checked her watch. 'We'll come back tomorrow. Please don't schedule any therapy until after we've gone.'

Lionel said, 'Then perhaps you'd better phone ahead next time and give us some warning, hadn't you?'

Raven said, 'You tell 'em, Tiger.'

SEVEN

The piano teacher was almost as tall as her student. She was a lean, graceful woman who had glided through seven decades of life with her back straight and her stride long. Her mother had been tall and her father taller, so it was no surprise their child had taken their height and added to it. She had dwarfed her female classmates and most of the boys too, and in adult life had turned heads wherever she walked. Now, age had taken away a little of her stature, but she still stood out in crowds and could intimidate men and women alike. She had straight grey hair that reached her middle back. She kept it tamed and smooth with daily treatments of raw coconut and jojoba oil. It was in a pony-tail while she taught or cooked, but untamed the rest of the time.

'In my youth, I dare say I might have been taller than you,' she told her student. 'In my heels, I would have towered over you.'

'I'm sure you would have,' he replied, polite and reserved.

She liked his careful manner and quiet personality. He wasn't shy, but he was not outgoing either. She had had her fill of loud and brash men. Her late husband had been such a man, and she had tolerated him when now she wished she had put him in his place. He had been a heavyset man, big but soft with it. Her student cut a lean silhouette in his grey suit but she felt the surprising solidity of him when they sat together on the bench. He tried to hide it, but he didn't like the intimacy of their closeness in front of the piano. She, who had spent more years teaching people how to play than he had been on this earth, detected this unease.

She would have enquired as to why he felt uncomfortable, but no doubt such a line of questioning would only further this, and she respected how he tried to fight down his discomfort. Manners were everything to her because there was no reward to them. They were done in selflessness. They were perhaps the truest indicator of character, and so she liked this student.

He was no master, but he was no beginner either. He had the natural dexterity of a classical pianist and within a few lessons had risen in skill at an exponential rate. Out of practice, he had told her at first, but there was something missing. Something that was preventing him reaching his potential. She tried to work out the cause.

'Music is not merely about notes, my boy,' she told him. 'It is about rhythm, it is about passion. Think of an orchestra. All the musicians can read music, all can play their instruments, but they need a conductor to really shine, to bring those instruments together, to harmonise and elevate. The conductor doesn't supply that passion, but harnesses that which is already inside them. Do you understand that?'

'I think so,' he answered, and she did not believe he spoke with conviction.

It took more than practice to master the piano. It was an art, and required talent. His hands were strong and his fingers long enough to glide in an effortless dance across the keys that was a joy for her to watch. He made mistakes, but only once. He never missed a key he knew to tap.

She was used to teaching young people bullied into learning by their parents and old people looking for hobbies. He was neither. He was a grown man who already knew how to play the piano, but a man who did not often play and missed it. She had been a concert pianist when she was young. She had fallen in love with the greats as a child. Her mother had been a patron of the arts and she had been nursed to Puccini and Mozart. She had fallen for B. F. Pinkerton the same way Butterfly had, and had cried the same tears. She had played in Paris and Rome, Warsaw and Sydney. She had loved music so much that she had never known true love outside of it. Music had spoiled her, but she would not have it any other way. Any love was better than none.

She taught from her home. It was a grand townhouse in Lisbon's artists' quarter. She lived alone in a house built for a family, but she had never had children and so the bedrooms had stayed empty of beds and the doors stayed shut but for the weekly dust and clean. A cat had kept her company after her husband passed, but she lived alone now. Acquiring another cat, like another husband, seemed too thankless a task to be worth the inevitable pain. She was content with music and her students and an afternoon daiquiri.

She told her student, 'Don't get me wrong: you're very talented. Reading and understanding music are one thing, knowing the keys and when to press them is another, but you need a rare dexterity to master this black and white maw. I call it a maw because not only do the keys resemble teeth if one looks at them in a certain way, but because they will bite you, they will hurt you, if you are not meant to sit before them. There are great pianists, revered and loved, who do not play certain tunes because their fingers are not nimble or their arms are short. They have all the skill in the world, but to be a true master you need the physical gifts. Look at my hands. They are slim but strong. My fingers have length. But when I flare my palm I lack breadth. This has always prevented me reaching the highest of heights. Your hands are powerful, but they have a lightness of touch. This combination is rare. So, I say again: you are talented. You have skill. You are out of practice, but that is easily rectified if you wish to put in the time. But,' she said, pausing for emphasis. 'And isn't there always a but when we are paid a compliment? Isn't there always a price to that small favour?'

He waited.

She said, 'The best concert pianists are animated. You could wear earplugs and still enjoy them, still be enthralled, because of that anima. They don't move as some sort of show, but because they must, because they ride the music, because they feel it. Now do you understand?'

'No,' he said, the honesty as stark as the disappointment that came with it.

'Herein lies the problem.'

He was silent. He looked at the piano, as if it would grace him with answers.

The piano they played on was older than her. It was older than the house around them or anything else inside of it. It had been built in Milan and had been restored to its former glory at great time and expense, but she had no one to leave her money to and to use and teach on an instrument with so much history and majesty made life worthwhile. The keys were ivory, which her environmental conscience disapproved of, but the ivory was part of the piano's legend. To replace them would be an insult to the instrument as much as the animal who had died to make them.

Her piano stood in the dining room, alone but for pictures on the wall she had painted in watercolour or oils when she had fancied herself as a painter first and musician second. Her student looked at each one in turn, but did not ask her about them. Most people did and she enjoyed talking about the follies of youth and ignorance. She took pride in her self-reflection as much as she did satisfaction that she had found her true calling.

She considered her student and the dilemma they faced together. It wasn't the language that was holding him back. His Portuguese was basic, but he knew enough to understand what she told him, and each time he returned for another lesson his language was improved. By the fourth it was hard to believe he had ever struggled. He learned fast. He was from Switzerland, but a well-travelled man of the world. His accent was soft and his manners befitting a Victorian gentleman. She presumed he was from a wealthy family who had sent him abroad for his education, maybe to England, maybe to America; then on sojourns far and wide, exploring, seeing, becoming. She didn't ask for exactitudes and he didn't offer. He was there to be taught and she was there to teach. She had too many students to get to know them all, and she had more than a passing knowledge only of those who had been coming to her house for years.

She was a cynic, she knew. She took money from anyone with the means to pay for her services, but she seldom cared. She loved music, and she loved it too much to care about the unworthy. If a deluded father insisted on enforcing piano lessons on an untalented daughter, who was she to argue? But with this student, she cared. She knew the talent was there. She could feel the enthusiasm in him, the will to learn and improve. She knew she would feel pride if someday he reached his potential, but more than that she felt there was a potential to make her efforts worthwhile.

Something occurred to her.

Once, between dabbling with painting and still finding her love for the piano, she fancied herself as a singer, although she didn't have the range or the lungs. She had a pleasant tone, her austere Hungarian singing teacher had once told her mother, and any talent at all was still a gift to treasure. She was more interested in the glamour than actual singing, which was ultimately what turned her away from yet another folly.

'Any talent at all is still a gift to treasure,' she told her student.

He nodded.

'Tell me about the pieces you love,' she asked him.

He spoke of Beethoven and Chopin, Tallis and Wagner. His knowledge was vast and intricate. He surprised her with his ability to dissect the merits of the most obscure nineteenth-century tune and how modern composers had both improved upon and devolved from the teachings of those who came before them. He could have talked for hours, had she not interrupted.

'I think I know the problem,' she told him. 'You can tell me the virtues of every great composer, of every piece of music; you can deconstruct anything I put before you and I would agree with everything you told me. But that's not what I asked for. I said tell me about the music you love. I wanted to know what moves you, what makes your soul soar. You can't do that, can you? I now know what is holding you back. There is no passion in your playing. You can't tell me what pieces you love because there are none. There is no love inside of you.'

It had been a foolish thing to say, so silly in retrospect, given his character, and she wished she had not had that second tongue-loosening daiquiri because she never saw him again.

EIGHT

Lionel wheeled Raven out of the room and along the corridor, nice and slow. It was almost relaxing. She leaned to one side so she could glance back. Officers Heno and Willitz stood watching her go. She couldn't help but give them a little wave. Juvenile, perhaps, but satisfying nonetheless. Her heart was hammering and she felt slightly dizzy from the stress of it all, so it was nice to get some release.

The nurse eased the chair to a stop outside an elevator and hit the down button. A light came on and glowed. She heard the whirr of machinery. It was faint. Lots of good insulation and background noise to mask it.

The elevator arrived and he waited for the doors to open then wheeled her inside. She heard him thumb a button behind her and the doors hissed shut a moment later.

'Why were those two giving you such a hard time?' he asked her as they descended.

Raven said, 'Who knows? Not enough sex. That's usually why people are in a bad mood, isn't it?'

He laughed. It seemed forced. A little nervous or uncomfortable with her humour. Which was funny in itself, because she was being serious. But it was hard to have a proper conversation when neither person could see the other's face. She was facing the rear wall. He stood behind her. She could see a blurred, distorted reflection of them both on the elevator's interior metal walls, but not clear enough to make out any details. In a way, she looked as she felt – unfinished.

Now the imminent danger was over, she thought back and was unsatisfied with her previous conclusions. The two cops who responded to the hospital's call about a poisoned woman with no memory just happened to be working for the bad guys? A thousand-to-one coincidence, at best. Her enemies were everywhere, but they weren't *everywhere*.

They could have been sent because they were on the payroll, of course, but that would have required knowledge of Raven's real identity from the get-go, before Heno and Willitz showed the first time. Impossible.

So they were just a couple of cops, as they seemed to be. But there was no precedent, no protocol, for taking an amnesiac woman recovering from being poisoned to a police precinct. That would never happen. Not in a million years. Not ever.

Heno and Willitz were real cops told some cover story, some lie, some order to get them to lure Raven out of the hospital. They didn't know who she was or why they had to get her out of there, but orders were orders.

Heno and Willitz, clueless but decent, would follow their orders and hand her over to someone, to a team maybe, and then she would never be heard from again. Willitz wouldn't care – *not my problem* – but Heno would be curious. She would want answers. She would pick holes in any spurious cover story. So it had to be good. It had to be convincing. It had taken time and resource to prepare, hence the delay. They had left her in the hospital while they put things in motion. *We have time. She's not going anywhere.*

Raven imagined there was some national security pretence behind it all, that maybe started with some pliable senator who got a call from an unlisted number with specific instructions, which were fed to an ally at the Bureau or Agency or other position of authority, who drummed up a report or file or actionable intelligence brief that was then fed through legitimate channels that went across the border and found its way to someone with power, someone who they trusted, who made sure it got to the right precinct to the right cop who wouldn't ask too many questions but would send out two cops on patrol to make everything look above board. It was how her enemies worked. It was what they were good at, disguising their movements under the pretence of legitimacy. She hated them as much as she feared them.

The doors pinged and opened and Lionel wheeled her out into a corridor. It was quiet. She couldn't hear anyone else.

'So, where are you taking me?'

He said, 'Physiotherapy.'

She said, 'Really? I thought you were just being a hero.

I figured you were coming to my rescue. I didn't think you were actually serious. The doc yesterday said it wouldn't be starting until next week.'

'Which doctor?'

She blew out some air. 'I've seen so many I've given up trying to remember their names. Anyway, he said physio would only start when I was strong enough.'

'You seem pretty strong to me.'

'Stronger than you, probably.'

Again the nervous, uncomfortable laugh. Again, she wasn't joking. She didn't find Lionel so cute any more. Had to have a personality to be cute. Dimples weren't enough on their own.

On a whim, she leaned to one side so she could glance back past him. She couldn't see what she wanted to see.

'You okay?' he asked.

'Never better,' she said, thinking hard. 'How long have you worked here?'

'Not long.'

Something in his tone.

She didn't respond to it straight away because they took a corner, a right angle, letting her look along the corridor they had just traversed to the elevator at the end and the single up button next to it.

She said, 'What does that mean? A year? A couple of months?'

He said, 'About a week.'

'Wow, you are new then. A real noob.'

He laughed, more comfortable. This time she was joking, but for a reason.

'Where are you taking me exactly?'

'Physiotherapy, of course.'

'Of course,' she echoed. 'Funny, because all I've seen are signs for the boiler, the incinerator and the morgue. We're in the basement, right?'

'It's a new facility,' Lionel said. 'Signage hasn't been installed yet.'

'Is that the best you can do?'

'I don't know what you mean.'

'You're a good actor,' she said after a moment. 'So I wonder why you said that?'

'Said what?'

'Come on,' she urged. 'You've stopped pretending so stop pretending.'

'Doesn't mean we can't still have fun? We've been getting along so well up until now.'

'This is fun to you?'

He said, 'Isn't it fun for you?'

She shook her head. 'No, not really.'

'I appreciate you saying that I'm a good actor. That means a lot to me, honestly. I lost character a moment ago, didn't I? I was too focused on the task at hand. Couldn't flirt back. That's why you became suspicious.'

Raven said, 'I didn't have a clue beforehand. You're terrific. You should be on TV. I only knew for sure because you stopped trying.'

'You know, I was Hamlet back in high school. I had dreams of Broadway, maybe the West End, but Dad wanted me to get a proper job.'

'I really wish you hadn't listened to him.'

'Me too, sometimes. But acting's a tough gig. Hard to make it.'

'Ain't that the sad truth. Easier to make it as a paid killer, I bet.'

'Much easier.'

'I thought the police were my biggest problem,' Raven said. 'That Heno and Willitz, I really thought they were going to hand me off to guys like you. Funny, isn't it? If I'd have gone with them, I'd have been safe. Ah, which is why you stepped in when you did.'

'That's right. I didn't want to risk it, but they left me no choice. Heno's a thorough police officer. It's taken a lot of work to keep her away. They took us by surprise this afternoon. We thought we had a few more days.'

'You and me both,' she said. 'Why have you waited so long? Surely it wouldn't have taken much to finish me off in the bed while I was barely conscious.'

'We found you too late. You were already a curiosity by then. Already famous, medically speaking. Had you died here they would have performed every test imaginable. They would have found the cause of death and known it was suspicious. So, things had to be arranged. Cover stories prepared. A whole new identity created for you. A criminal with a past. A charlatan, a fantasist. Someone with a history of claimed amnesia. An addict. It took effort. I'm sure you know how time-consuming a convincing alias is to prepare. Now, when you go missing, it will fit in with the pattern already established. No one will ask any further questions about who you are.'

'What about you? You're not a real nurse.'

'I go too. Tomorrow or the next day. The hospital's system will be updated and my contract status revoked. It's all taken care of.'

'You guys really are thorough, aren't you?'

'We have to be. Also, I can bluff being a nurse. I was a corpsman,' he explained, using the naval term for a medic.

'Teams?' she asked.

He nodded.

'Isn't doing what you're doing now the opposite of being a medic?'

He smiled. 'I like the irony.'

'Must be useful too. All that training in treating wounds must give you a lot of insight into how to make them.'

'Exactly,' he said. 'And it's good to know all that experience didn't go to waste.'

She said, 'Want to hear how loud I can scream?'

'We're underground. There's no one on this entire floor. There's three feet of concrete above our heads. Scream all you want. I won't try and stop you.' He stepped back and gestured for her to begin. 'Go on, knock yourself out.'

She didn't scream. It wasn't her style to do so, though if there had been any chance, no matter how remote, she would have done. But he was right, it wouldn't do any good here. And screaming would burn energy she couldn't spare.

When they reached their destination he stopped the wheelchair and applied the foot brake. She heard him lock the door behind them.

'Fitting that it's the morgue,' she said.

NINE

The mortuary had several rooms accessible through a swing door. He wheeled her past a wall of refrigeration units with their square metal doors and corpses beyond. He stopped in a room that had tiled white walls. He used the back of his hand to hit the lights. She squinted against the glare on the tiles and all the stainless steel.

On the wall opposite was a row of sinks and counters, all stainless steel. Cabinets lined the wall to her left, full of drawers and cupboards. Opposite the cabinets was a huge whiteboard with the marks and stains of a long life of usefulness. Between the whiteboard and the cabinet stood two dissecting tables, about two metres in length and a metre wide. Like the cabinets and the sinks and counters they were stainless steel. What made them different from regular tables were the drainage holes set at regular intervals and the narrow moats that framed the table edges to prevent blood and other fluids spilling to the floor. From the ceiling above each table was a retractable hose for cleaning purposes. Either side of the door were wheeled trolleys, a set of organ-weighing scales, cleaning supplies and a rack for coats and other belongings.

Raven said, 'I bet you bring all the girls here.'

He wheeled her between the two dissecting tables. In the chair, she found that the tables were taller than her. She felt tiny and vulnerable and trapped.

He stepped away and she pivoted her head to catch a look at him in her peripheral vision as he walked around the table to her left, to where the cabinets were located. Every time he looked away she glanced to take snapshots of her surroundings. She built a three-dimensional model of the morgue in her mind, highlighting any item that could be a potential weapon, every hard corner of metal that could hinder her or hurt him. She feared the floor the most. It was tiled. She didn't have good balance right now, and she would be slow to rise if she fell.

'Where is everyone?'

'The mortuary is closed for the rest of the day. My employers have arranged the specifics, which I am unaware of. The salient point is we are alone and will be for several hours.'

'I suppose begging won't do much good.'

A scrape of metal on metal as he pulled open a drawer. 'Not much.'

'I have a friend on the way,' she began.

He didn't turn back. 'Is that so?'

'He's a real badass. Best in the business. He's going to hurt you so bad you'll wish your mamma had strangled you at birth.'

Lionel said, 'He sounds terrifying. I bet he's just outside and if I run now I'll be able to get away. Something like that?'

'Something like that,' she echoed without any conviction.

'You're a trier,' he said. 'I'll give you that.'

'Well, I can't exactly put up a fight, can I?'

'No,' he agreed. 'I'm grateful for that. I was told you are quite something when at full health. Truth be told, I'm not much of a brawler.'

'Your arms say otherwise.'

'Thanks,' he said. 'But that really isn't me. I'm too slow. I prefer to outthink my enemies than outfight them.'

'Wise,' she said. 'You'll live longer that way.'

'And keep my handsome face in one piece in the process.'

'True enough. I like to think I wouldn't have been so easy to fool if you had a big ol' scar down one cheek.'

'They're disarming, aren't they?' He pointed to his dimples, smiling to emphasise them. 'No one with a face this sweet could be a threat. That's what everyone thinks.'

'I was even thinking about asking for your number.'

'You were? That's adorable. You're a little old for me, don't you think?'

'I would have knocked your world off its axis.'

'You should give yourself some credit,' he said. 'You weren't easy to fool. I'm just that good at this.'

'You know what gets you killed faster than arrogance?'

He waited, intrigued for the answer. 'No, what?'

'Nothing.'

He smirked. 'That's good. Is that why you're in that chair, because of arrogance?'

'In a way,' she explained. 'That badass I mentioned. He's the one who poisoned me. I thought we had moved beyond our differences. I thought he liked me. So, in a way, I was arrogant in thinking that.'

She remained in the chair while he walked around her and out of view. He was in no hurry. He thought she was bound to the wheelchair, weak and immobile. She was weak, but nowhere near as weak as he believed. She had to continue the ploy until the right moment. She would surprise him, yes, with ease, but she had neither the strength nor speed in her current state to capitalise in the way she needed. Wait, she told herself. Be patient. Pick the right moment because anything less than perfect means death.

She said, 'Do you actually know who you're working for?'

'I don't really care. They pay well, which is all that matters to me.'

'I call them the Consensus,' she said. 'They're like an insidious collective of the rich and the powerful, morally bankrupt and utterly ruthless. A shadow government.'

'Do they have a clubhouse?'

'You should take this a little more seriously. Once you're a part of it, you're a part of it for life. Which is dramatically shortened by association.'

He shrugged. 'I don't know anything about any consensus. I get phone calls every now and again. I don't know who is on the other end of the line. All I know is that they pay well, they pay on time, and they have the power to make my life easy as well as the power to make it hard.'

'That's why we should talk. I can help you make sure it's

not you sitting in this chair one day. Because they'll turn against you like they've turned against me.'

He ignored her and said, 'I'll give you a choice. I can make it quick, only a little pain, but I'm going to need your compliance. If you're going to struggle and make my life harder than it needs to be, then I'll have to hurt you in return. But I don't have to. Help me to help you. Can you do that?'

She nodded. 'I think so.'

'I'm going to lift you out of the chair and on to the table. What do you weigh?'

'One thirty,' she said. 'Usually. I might be a little less now. Muscle wastage.'

He squatted down and put his hands under her armpits. She let herself be slack so he had to do all the work. He grunted and pushed his hips back and straightened his legs, then back, until she was vertical.

He shuffled and pivoted before hoisting her up and setting her ass down on the dissecting table. He released her and stepped away.

'I think you weigh a little more than one thirty.'

'Do you really have to insult me when you're about to kill me?'

He was strong, but it was never easy to move a person. Even a little fatigue could help her.

He took a step back and nodded, looking ashamed, as if manners were more important to him than taking a life. He reminded her of someone else in that regard. Maybe it was a trait of male killers. Some last vestige of chivalry in the amoral.

He said, 'Lie down, please.'

She lowered herself with awkward movements, arms shaking. The table was icy cold against her back. He stepped away, out of sight. She tried to roll her head to keep him in view, but couldn't. She heard him open a drawer. She heard noises. Metallic.

He returned into view, pushing a wheeled trolley over to the table. She saw what was on the trolley: bone saw, scalpels, and other instruments of dissection. He saw her look, but misunderstood the calculation in her eyes for fear. She was afraid, but that was buried down because she couldn't afford to be scared.

He selected one of two scalpels and moved to the head of the table. When he looked down over her, he seemed upside down.

'I'll pierce the carotid,' he explained. 'An insignificant cut. You'll barely feel it. You're slim, so it doesn't need to be deep. Just a few millimetres. Over in a second. It won't hurt.'

'How do you know it won't hurt unless you've had your own throat cut? Maybe you should try it on yourself first to check.'

'Funny,' he said. 'There are very few nerves, and I'll keep the incision small. It'll be like a paper cut.'

'Paper cuts hurt.'

'Give me a break, okay? I'm trying to make this as easy as possible, as painless as possible. But I can't work miracles. And please remember I'm going out of my way to do you a favour here. Meet me halfway. You know as well as I do that you'll be unconscious in seconds. Are you ready?'

She swallowed. Nodded.

'Do you want to close your eyes?'

She didn't blink.

'Your choice.'

He brought the blade closer. It gleamed.

Now, she told herself.

She rolled to her right, using her left hand to push off with against the table and twisting with her hips. She dropped to the floor, crashing into the trolley, knocking it over. Instruments scattered across the tiles.

The fall hurt, bad, because she didn't have the reflexes or space to roll with it, to disperse some of the hurtful energy. She took the full force of the impact and the shocking pain that made her cry out.

He didn't get mad. He didn't yell.

He laughed. 'What the hell was that?'

She lay there, on her front, now as weak and immobile as she had pretended before. The pain in her face was as real as it had ever been.

He said, 'What happened to helping me help you?'

She didn't answer. She didn't look at him. Her eyes scanned her surroundings.

'I only have so much patience,' he said as he set the trolley upright again and collected up the instruments on to the tray and set it back in place. He frowned and looked around at the floor for a moment, then turned his attention back to Raven.

'I'm sorry,' she said, eyes pinched shut and her cheeks wet. 'I got scared. It won't happen again. I'll close my eyes this time. I think that will make it easier.'

He squatted down in front of her, ready to help her to her feet. 'Don't worry about it. It's hurt you more than it has me.'

Her eyes snapped open – 'I don't know about that' – and she drove the missing scalpel into his nearest foot.

There was no tough leather shoe for protection, to resist her meagre strength, just a pair of comfortable canvas pumps. She couldn't create a whole lot of force, but the scalpel couldn't get any sharper. It pierced straight through the canvas and the thin layer of skin and sliced through the metatarsal beneath and plenty of blood vessels beyond that. She had stabbed with the blade at a right angle to the foot, to do more damage to the bone and ligaments, making sure they were hit instead of the slim blade slipping between them.

He roared.

Pain and shock made him retreat. She managed to recoil the blade free before his movement ripped it from her grip. A brief geyser of blood followed it. The injury made him stumble. He had to go down to one knee. He looked confused. Everything he had believed about the situation – especially his control of it – had been shown to be false.

His eyes were red, bloodshot with rage.

'*I was going to make it quick*,' he spat. 'I was going to make it painless.'

She pushed herself to her knees with her left hand while keeping the scalpel ready in her right in case he lunged at her, but the weapon, coated in his own blood, was enough to dispel any such impulse. He reached out to the counters behind him to help him stand.

Raven used the dissecting table to do the same. She grunted, limbs shaking with the effort. She kept one hand braced against the table to keep herself upright, legs uncertain beneath her.

He snatched the other scalpel from the tray and held it out before him. 'Now we're even.'

'You said you weren't much of a fighter.'

'I was being humble. There's not much I can't do.'

'Except kill a half-paralysed girl.'

He smirked. 'There's still plenty of time for that.'

'Tell that to your foot.'

He tried to resist the taunt, but he glanced down anyway. Blood was pumping from the neat hole in his shoe.

'That's arterial,' she said. 'You're going to start feeling really cold and tired really soon.'

'This won't take long.'

He stalked towards her, shuffling because of the wounded foot, unable or unwilling to place his full weight on it. Blood soaked the shoe and left a smeared trail on the floor tiles. His face was creased and red in a combination of rage and pain.

'Big talk for a man who can barely walk.'

He gestured to her hand on the dissecting table, arm braced to keep her upright. 'Says the girl who can't stand by herself.'

'Oh,' she said, looking too. 'I'm not quite as much of an invalid as I've been making out.'

Raven moved her hand away. She stood without support, without needing support. 'Guess you're not the only one who's good at acting.'

The pain remained in his expression, but the rage became uncertainty, which led to a mistake because he tried to rush her. With the inability to get proper purchase with his right foot, he had to sacrifice balance for speed.

He whipped out the scalpel in a fast lunge aimed at her head, but it was a clumsy attack.

Raven backed out of the way, countering with her own scalpel and catching the outstretched hand. The blade split through the skin on the back of his palm.

The hit made him drop the weapon and it clanged on the floor. Blood pattered on the tiles a moment later.

He grabbed at her, and though his injured foot slowed him, she was also slow and failed to slip away from his reach. He fell forward into her because he had overextended, and though she sliced him again with the scalpel she couldn't stop him dragging her down to the floor, where she didn't want to be. His foot wouldn't hamper his groundwork and she couldn't match his strength and size.

Raven didn't need to, because that strength was fading fast as the blood drained out of his foot. He had her wrist tight in one fist, controlling her scalpel-holding hand, but he was slow and awkward in his attempts to wrest it from her grasp.

She tried to slip out from under him while his focus was on the weapon in her grasp, but he was too heavy and she too weak. As she thrashed beneath him, her foot nudged the second scalpel – the one he had dropped.

With his free hand he began prising back her fingers, one by one.

Raven contorted her leg and managed to kick the scalpel along the tiles towards her waiting hand.

He prised back the last finger and took her scalpel as his own.

His eyes glimmered.

She snatched the second scalpel up from the floor and drove it deep into the back of his closest knee.

He screeched.

She scrambled out from under him as he twisted to reach for the scalpel buried in his leg. She stumbled as she rose and slipped on the blood-slick tiles. Seeing her escaping, he tried to stand too, not knowing all kinds of tendons and ligaments in his knee were sliced in two, and his leg folded under him. He was going nowhere.

She fell into a dissecting table, but caught hold of it to stop herself falling all the way back to the floor.

She gasped as a hand grabbed the back of her gown.

She tried to pull away, but his grip remained strong.

'We're not done yet.'

Raven tried to anchor herself on the table to fight being pulled back to the floor, but this only gave him a secure base with which to drag himself towards her. He still had a scalpel in his hand, ready to cut her with just as soon as he was close enough.

She saw the wheeled trolley nearby. The tray of instruments sat on top.

She shot out a hand to the tray for another scalpel, but with no time to choose she made do with the first thing her fingers touched.

A bone saw.

With only one hand gripping the table, she couldn't hold on any longer.

As he dragged her to the floor, she twisted to face him and swung the bone saw down from the trolley and cleaved him on the top of his head.

The bone saw sliced his scalp in two and buried into his skull. Not deep, because the serrated teeth created friction and jammed in place, so when Raven tried she couldn't pull it free for another blow.

One was enough, however, to stun him in place as a single rivulet of blood ran down over his face. He trembled and his eyes watered, pupils dilating until no irises remained. The hand gripping her didn't weaken – strengthened even in the paralysis of shock – but the one holding the scalpel was just as paralysed.

She grabbed the bone saw's handle in both her hands to use all of her strength to pull it free from his skull. His grip on her gown kept her from flailing backwards with the force she generated.

She swung the saw down again.

The first blow caused him to drop the scalpel, the second was enough for his fingers to fall free from her gown.

She scrambled away, slipping on the tiles that became slick with spewing blood, falling to her ass and staying there, watching his face whiten and his mouth open, but instead of some final words escaping his lips, there was only more blood.

TEN

The English confessor; the Russian john; the American martial artist; the Swiss musician; now played himself – at least a version of himself; one of many masks that were interchangeable within a word or blink. All were variations and all incomplete because there was no whole. He had ceased to be himself long ago because the need to be someone else was always greater.

Victor was content in this moment to behave as a man of indeterminate origin. Caucasian, tall, with dark eyes and black hair he could have been from lots of different places. That hair was long for him, which at about two inches in length was at the upper limit of what he allowed. His skin was pale now, but was quick to tan given a little exposure to sun. He had a beard, as he often had, but he was often clean shaven as well. Under his overcoat he wore a good suit that was charcoal in colour, and which was perhaps the only consistency in appearance he adhered to when working, having long ago found the benefits of a suit out-weighed the liability inherent in maintaining any pattern.

For the last three months he had been living off the grid – Ireland, Bulgaria, the Netherlands and Portugal – keeping on the move; a few days here, a week there. No phone. No electronic communications. No credit card. Only cash. He travelled across borders by train or ferry. His credentials were never logged into any system. His ID was rarely checked.

He had begun the sojourn with just shy of one hundred thousand euros in jewellery in the form of his Tag Heuer, neck chains, a bracelet and a couple of rings. He had also started with ten thousand in cash, which was a lot to carry but compressed could fit into a jacket pocket. The money and jewellery was just enough to last him the duration at the rate he burned through it. Hotels, even cheap hotels, were not cheap. Neither was a new wardrobe of clothes every week. Trains, cabs, buses and coaches all drained his coffers on a daily basis. When he was over the next border he found a jeweller's or pawnshop and sold an item, providing him with a top-up of cash that would last until he reached another country. No need for banks, no electronic transactions. No traces. Victor sold the watch last because he had something of an affinity for Tags. The first one he'd stolen had fed him and his crew for two months when he had lived on the streets before he had stolen it back to much mirth and acclaim.

In the end, his funds lasted better than expected and he spent his final night in a fine hotel. By then he had travelled thousands of miles, crossed seas and borders, and stayed in dozens of hotels and guesthouses. He had started the journey without knowing his destination, using the randomness of the world around him to select his routes, to determine his choices. If he didn't know where he would be tomorrow then no enemy could either. He had not spent his time idly. Every waking moment was spent with counter surveillance on his mind. He had maintained his fitness in gyms, dojos and hotel rooms. He practised his shooting in gun clubs and on ranges. Every day he spoke in a different language.

He went off the grid whenever he could. He was running from no one in particular, but everyone at once. His last job had created new, powerful enemies and put his shadowy existence under more scrutiny than perhaps it had ever endured. Even with the extensive precautions he took he could still be found. There was no way in the modern world to avoid every CCTV camera, every watchful cop's gaze or street informant. If someone came after him they always had the advantage because they knew who they were looking for. He had to spot them before they were ready to strike. Better they not find him at all. Going off the grid ensured however close his enemies were, he would lose them. He'd once been told that no one could outrun a bullet, and he had never forgotten that, but it took time to aim the gun that fired it.

Tonight was different. Tonight he was back at work.

Life on the move, on the run, was a huge drain on his finances. Every contract earned him a small fortune, but the money never lasted long. Had he felt a compelling reason to retire – he didn't – and even if retirement didn't mean the inevitable erosion of his skills – it did – he had nowhere near the means. He had too many enemies to ever contemplate making himself a stationary target. If he retired, those he had angered or threatened, explicitly or implicitly, would not.

Besides, the only thing he really feared was boredom.

He approached an isolated cottage on the spur of County Cork in Ireland. A clear night sky bathed the cottage in silver moonlight. It was a one-storey house made of stone and topped in slate. It was a handsome building in Victor's opinion. Simple, yet elegant, and climbing ivy on one wall gave it a charmed appeal. The sort of place he could envision himself living in if it were possible to envision a time when he might live somewhere instead of everywhere. Even in that impossible future it would require extensive upgrades to make it more a fortress than a home. There were no cameras or motion sensors or other security apparatus because the occupant was a civilian, and that man partook in no security procedures beyond that which the average civilian took. He might look over his shoulder in reaction to a sudden noise if walking alone at night, but if he believed himself under threat he made no attempt to mitigate it.

Victor knocked on the front door – a heavy slab of riveted oak – because there was no reason not to do so and every reason to.

The occupant took a minute to open it. There was no spy hole and he didn't ask who was there first. A trusting man, living in a safe little world.

'Yes?' he said, when he saw Victor, examining him with a careful, but unworried gaze.

The priest was used to visits from his flock, if not so late at night, and there was nothing in Victor's appearance or demeanour to give him cause for concern. Victor's suit and overcoat gave him a respectable, civilised air. The priest didn't recognise him from their previous conversation.

'You'll need your coat,' Victor said. 'It's cold out here.'

His tone was neutral, if pointed. The priest frowned in a moment of confusion as he sought to pick apart Victor's words for meaning, for subtext; to deduce what he meant and what that meant because what people did not say was as important as what they did. Victor knew enough about him to know that there was no need to be explicit, and he didn't like to be rude. If he could do his job with good manners, he would.

The priest's confusion became understanding that settled on acceptance.

He managed to crack a small smile as he said, 'You know, I used to live in fear of this day. But I thought that was all behind me. All in the past. I haven't really worried for twenty years.'

'Worrying wouldn't have helped.'

'No, I suppose it wouldn't have.'

The priest broke eye contact, and Victor could read his thoughts as if they were printed on the man's face. He had seen such faces many times. It was the look of calculation. It was the expression of someone trying to work out the odds of success in a gamble they knew nothing about. The priest was thinking of slamming the door shut, hurrying for the phone, grabbing an improvised weapon along the way. He was trying to figure out if it could work; if it was worth trying.

Victor said, 'It's up to you, but whatever you try isn't

going to work, and I'm offering you the chance to come with me freely.'

There was no aggression in his voice or manner because he needed no show of dominance here. The priest was a small man, thin and weak even without the frailty of age. Victor wasn't going to hurt him any more than necessary.

'The end result is the same, right?'

'There's nothing you can do to change that now.'

The priest sighed and nodded. 'I guess I would prefer to come freely, wouldn't I?'

'You would.'

The priest collected his winter coat from a hook by the door. He fastened the buttons with hands that only shook a little. He was brave. Victor respected that.

'Okay,' the priest said when he was finished. 'Let's get this done.'

Victor moved to allow him to step outside. The priest locked the door behind him.

'I assume we're heading to the cliffs.'

'That's right,' Victor said.

It was only a short walk.

'Keep to the path,' Victor said.

There was no designated footpath along the cliffs, but walkers had forged their own with their tread, wearing down the grass so the rain wore the topsoil to a narrow, stony track.

The priest made his way along it at a slow pace. In part because of his age and limited mobility, but also because he was in no rush to reach the destination. Victor didn't hurry him because he was in no rush either. The priest's cottage was isolated. They were miles from any other dwelling. No one was watching. No one could watch. No one walked these cliffs at night. Too dangerous. The priest was no hard target but Victor was always thorough. He had made the same preparations for the priest as he would a warlord.

It was cold, as Victor had told the priest. Protocol kept Victor's overcoat buttons unfastened and his hands out of pockets. The priest was no threat, but every rule Victor had, every facet of protocol, had either kept him alive before or else might have helped one of the many who had died by his hand. Protocol became habit, habit became instinct, and instinct kept him alive.

'I've always liked the ocean,' the priest said as they neared. 'I'm not a good swimmer and I'm no fan of the cold, but it's the sound of it. The noise. If God speaks to us, it is through nature, and if He has a voice, it is in the song of birds and the crashing of waves.' He paused to inhale the sea air. 'That's why I came here. To find peace with myself and with God.'

'Take your time,' Victor said.

The wind howled, but the sea was louder. It was black and roiling; hungry waves foaming against the cliffs.

The priest said, 'Where will you go to find your peace?'

'I am at peace.'

'Then I pity you.'

Victor shrugged. The pity of others, or the lack thereof, meant nothing to him. He would first have to care about opinions. He would have to care about people. He allowed the priest to talk because it made things simpler. Not easier, because the priest was incapable of making things difficult for him. But a few minutes listening to what someone else thought of him cost nothing, and changed nothing. It kept things simple. It created acceptance. Chasing down a fleeing old man complicated matters when they didn't need to be complicated. Trying to run wouldn't help the priest, but it might leave footprints in the wet grass and an astute investigator might start to question whether it had been a suicide or accident, after all.

The cliff Victor had selected was about one hundred feet high. If the priest hit the rocks at its foot he would be killed in an instant. If not, the icy sea awaited and hypothermic shock and drowning would compete to finish off what the fall began. An excellent swimmer with youth and strength might survive those waves, but for an old man, the ocean was as certain a fate as a bullet.

The priest said, 'Can you tell me who sent you?'

Nothing could change the man's fate, so Victor answered, 'British intelligence.'

'But why?' he asked. 'I spied for them. I was an informer.'

'For both sides,' Victor explained. 'For every republican you gave up, you gave up a British agent too.'

'That's a lie.'

'You asked who sent me. You wouldn't have needed to if you weren't playing both sides.'

The priest didn't argue otherwise. Instead, he said, 'But it was decades ago. That's a lifetime ago. I was another person back then. I had no faith then, and no honour. I did what I had to do. I did what I did to survive. I had no choice. Both sides used me. You'd have done the same as me in my place. You don't understand what it was like back then.'

'I'm just the messenger.'

'But it's all over now. There's peace.'

Victor said, 'It's nothing to do with me and I don't know all of the details. If I were to guess, however, I would say that one of those British agents you betrayed all those years ago had a friend and that friend is now somebody and that somebody has a long memory. But maybe I haven't been making myself clear: I don't care.'

'You can kill an old man, no harm to anyone?'

'It's what I'm paid for.'

The priest recognised something in Victor's words, or maybe tone, and stared. '*You.*'

Victor nodded.

'The confessor.'

Victor nodded again.

'I thought you were making it up,' the priest said. 'I thought you were crazy.'

'I am, in a way.'

The priest was angry now. 'You're sick. You're twisted. What psychosis makes a man take confession from a priest who will become his victim?'

'I don't see the two roles as mutually exclusive.'

'Which allowed you to talk freely to me, knowing it could never harm you.'

Victor shook his head. 'I go to confession once every year. As I told you before, it's something I have to do. I'm always honest. I'm always candid. But like you, no priest ever believes me.'

The priest was silent. Far below, the sea was black like the night, crashing against the cliff. He stared down at his fate.

'I won't kill myself. Suicide is a sin,' the priest said. 'You'll have to push me.'

'That was always the plan.'

'You are a man of faith. I hope you're prepared for God's wrath.'

Victor said, 'If God made man, He made me. If God made me, He knew exactly what He was doing.'

'And why did British intelligence send you in particular?' the priest asked, now demanding, voice loud.

'It's a test from a new employer,' Victor explained, content to answer questions if that's what it took to keep things amicable. 'They want to see what I'm capable of.'

'Capable? And just what are you capable of? If you can murder an old man – a *priest* – where do you draw the line? Is there even a line?'

Victor did not answer.

The sea roiled below, ever hungry, black waves gnawing on the cliffs.

The priest was beaten down by the lack of an answer. Victor saw the will draining from him with each passing second, but the priest wasn't ready yet; he needed to keep talking a while longer. 'Okay,' he said, conceding, 'tell me why they needed to send a professional hitman to silence an old man like me. Weak. Frail. Any thug could have stabbed me in the night or throttled me in my bed. Why *you*?'

The priest was right. It didn't require a man of Victor's talents. He was perhaps as soft a target as Victor had ever been hired to kill. Clients used him to assassinate those no one else could: warlords, arms dealers, spies, mercenaries, terrorists and other professional killers; those too dangerous or too well-protected or too hard-to-find for anyone else. The priest was none of those.

'Because no one else would do it.'

The priest absorbed this and saw one last play to make. 'I'm not surprised that some killers would be reluctant. Not an easy thing, to take the life of a man of God, is it? If ever there was a sin that would be without equal, it would be that. Even for a non-believer, it would test their disbelief. It would weigh on the conscience, growing heavier year on year, until it became an unbearable, inescapable burden.'

Victor remained silent. In that silence the priest understood that he had failed, because he saw no conscience in Victor's eyes to appeal to; no humanity; no mercy; no pity.

'Do it,' the priest said.

Victor fed him to the waves.

ONE YEAR LATER

ELEVEN

Alvarez was no golfer. Sure, he could hit the ball four hundred yards, but he had to hit the ball first. He was more likely to take a chunk of turf from the fairway and leave the little ball unscathed. He'd done that before. He'd done that before several times. As a young man, he'd been banned from a golf club for the damage caused. Over time he had learned to rein in his strength and settle for a modest couple-of-hundred-yard drive that may or may not end up in the rough, but at least he didn't embarrass himself or the proper golfers in his company. He never chose to play golf himself, but Washington was a town full of men who liked nothing better than to discuss matters of national security out in the open. If he wanted to be kept in the loop, if he wanted to cement relationships and establish friends with power, he had to waste time in the way the powerful liked to.

It was a pleasant afternoon, at least. The sky was cloudy,

but the clouds were of the cotton wool kind that drift in a lazy way across the sky, allowing intermittent bursts of sun to brighten the grass and warm the back. Alvarez had left his suit jacket in the car and played with his tie in his trouser pocket and his shirt-tails loose, sleeves folded up to mid-forearm. His golfing partner had changed and looked the part: baggy slacks and polo shirt, canvas ball cap and those funny shoes. He looked a bit nerdy, and in truth, he was, but Alvarez was always respectful. He was respectful to most people, but he didn't always mean it. Here, he did.

'You're too stiff, Antonio,' his golfing partner said. 'You need to be loose. Like a piece of rope. You're like a chain.'

Alvarez tried to be more like a piece of rope than a chain. The ball, and a tuft of grass, sailed into the distance.

His swing wasn't improved by his bad shoulder. His right anterior deltoid had taken a nine-millimetre parabellum – a clean through-and-through – but it had never been the same since. Day-to-day activities were fine, but exercise could be problematic. He was never going to get close to his personal best in the overhead press. The scarring on the front was minimal and worse at the back where the bullet had come out again, tearing a chunk of flesh out with it. Alvarez couldn't see it unless he stood with his back to a mirror and near enough snapped his neck trying to look backwards over his shoulder. Christopher thought it was cool. Alvarez had tried to hide it from him, but his son was inquisitive and intuitive. He had sensed there was something his dad was hiding and therefore just had to find out what. His ex had given him hell over it. *He wants a scar too, just like his dad,* she had shrilled. *Is that appropriate? Is this your way of being a role model? Is this your way of being a good father?*

He was no kind of father because he didn't get the chance to be. Jennifer hated him for falling out of love, and even though she was married to another man – *happier than I ever was with you* – she still took delight in punishing him every chance she got. He tried to take it on the chin, for Christopher's sake. Alvarez had grown up with parents screaming at one another and he still wasn't over it. He wouldn't do that to his son, so he saw him every other weekend and tried not to show how much it hurt when the kid was picked up by his stepdad and gave him twice the hug he did Alvarez. He lived in the hope that one day things would be different.

'Ouch,' the other man said as the ball drifted wide and disappeared out of sight. 'Maybe I'm not giving you the right advice.'

'You're no golfing coach, that's true.'

'I'm a jack of all trades and a master of none.'

'That's a weird turn of phrase,' Alvarez replied. 'Was there a real Jack or is it a generic term?'

'You're an etymologist now?'

Alvarez shrugged. 'You're the one who used the phrase. It's got me curious.'

'I wouldn't know.' The other man gave him a look. 'The Queen of England told it to me.'

Alvarez chuckled.

'I shit you not.'

Alvarez nodded. 'I know you'd never shit me.'

Maryland had many such golf courses to cater for the

rich and powerful's insatiable need to hit plastic spheres with metal clubs. He understood the appeal, though he didn't enjoy the game. It was exercise, but gentle. Competitive, but not demanding. A game for those who didn't want to break an ankle or put their back out. There was a certain irony to the game and the players. To relieve the stress of politics and business and seventy-hour working weeks they went outdoors to get some fresh air and have a walk, maybe even a little fun with it. A simpler life, maybe spent outdoors, maybe fewer hours, maybe with exercise, and they wouldn't need to get rid of the stress in the first place.

'What's on your mind?' the other man asked. 'You look pensive.'

'I was just thinking about something the Dalai Lama said: Man ruins his health to make money, then spends his money to regain his health. Or something like that.'

'Try not to get too existential on me, Antonio. I get enough of that at home. Come on, the balls won't find their way to the promised land without our guidance.'

They played a while longer. Alvarez's golfing partner was going easy on him – mis-hitting his shots now and again so as not to embarrass him. It was a kind gesture, and Alvarez appreciated it. Had they been in the gym, he would have left a few plates off the bar, doing a few less reps. They weren't friends, but they were friendly. Pals, perhaps. Acquainted through work, and only work, but theirs was a mutual fondness. Alvarez didn't like many people. He didn't have many who he could rely on.

His golfing partner was some ten years older and though

in reasonable shape and reasonable health he was starting to look old. Alvarez hadn't worn his hair in anything but a buzz cut since leaving the Marines, so it was hard to tell how many grey hairs there were amongst the black stubble. He didn't care. He cared about his health, not his looks.

The other man said, 'How are you settling in to your new role? Everyone treating you well?'

'Too well. It makes me nervous.'

A chuckle. 'You're not regretting it already?'

'Not at all. I'm in the transitional phase. It's a big change to be steering the ship instead of in the engine room.'

A wry smile. 'I know exactly what you mean. Just watch out for icebergs. They can, and will, come out of nowhere.'

'I'll add that to the list.'

'List?' The other man regarded him. 'You mean the list of useless bits of advice all and sundry have given you to tell you how to do your job?'

'That's the one.'

The laugh was brief, but genuine. 'What's the first order of business?'

'Taking down bad guys. One in particular. The one that got away.'

'You make it sound so simple.'

'This won't be, but I have faith in myself.'

'Confidence gets you everywhere.'

'Ain't that the truth?'

His golfing partner nodded along with him, then said, 'I'm hungry. I skipped breakfast. Are you hungry? Wanna get a bite at the clubhouse once we've finished up here?

They make an incredible off-menu Sloppy Joe. Just for me. Privilege of the position.'

Alvarez said, 'I'm not big on red meat or refined carbs.'

'They have a salad bar,' the other man said, a glimmer of tease in his eyes. He glanced back over his shoulder, hearing something, and said, 'That looks ominous.'

Another man approached. He was taller than both the golfers and broader even than Alvarez. He was dressed in a black suit and wore sunglasses with impenetrable lenses. He spoke to Alvarez's golfing partner.

'Sir, I need to ask you to come with me.'

'I know that tone well, Terrence. Credible threat?'

Terrence nodded.

'I'll see you at the car in one minute.'

Terrence nodded a second time, almost robotic, and left them alone.

'Duty calls, Antonio.'

He gave an understanding look. 'I have somewhere I need to be anyway.'

'You know, we almost got through a whole game this time. Had you not spent quite as long in the sand trap, we might have actually finished.'

'I was giving you a false sense of security,' Alvarez said. 'I had you just where I wanted you. I think you gave Terrence a signal because I was on the comeback trail.'

His golfing partner grinned. 'It won't be long before I have plenty of time on my hands. Then, we might actually finish a course.'

'When that time comes,' Alvarez said, 'I won't need to pretend to like golf.'

Another laugh. Deeper. 'I will miss your frankness.' He offered his hand. 'Good to see you, Antonio, and all the best in your future endeavours.'

Alvarez shook it. 'And to you, Mr President.'

TWELVE

Procter settled into the armchair. It was comfortable, but he wasn't. His hip made it hard to sit down. The right angle was the problem. The bone didn't sit in the socket as it should. He had to brace his hands on the armrests and lower himself with his triceps. It was the same standing again. He had lost around 50 per cent of the muscle mass of his glutes, hamstrings and quadriceps as a result of the accident. He had never been a fit man. He had never been into exercise or eating right or even caring as his waistline expanded at a steady rate, year on year. The accident had changed all that. Being immobile for so long had made him reliant on Patricia. Patricia had hit her half-century and exploded into life: Pilates, yoga, interval training and some Olympic lifting. She counted calories and macros. She had a fruit basket's worth of smoothie every morning. She took so many supplements she had an entire kitchen shelf just for the bottles. The pea protein, spirulina, wheatgrass and chia seeds took up a whole cupboard. She had halved her bodyweight and never felt better. Procter had felt better too because, while immobile, while reliant, he had to eat what she prepared for him. Steak and fries became tofu stir fry. Barbecue ribs became beans and vegetables he hadn't known existed. She assured him the healthy eating would help him recover. Maybe it had. Maybe he would be in a worse state otherwise.

The thought must have shown on his face because Alvarez said, 'Are you all right? Can I get you anything?'

He shook his head and waved a hand to halt the younger man, who was already rising to assist in whatever way was necessary.

'Would you like some water?'

'I don't need babying, Antonio. And I don't want to have to empty my bladder any more than necessary.'

Alvarez relaxed again. He wasn't offended or insulted and he didn't pester Procter with questions about his condition. Procter liked that about him.

They were sitting on the long porch of Procter's house, facing west. Procter had taken a wicker armchair, padded with two cushions. Alvarez was perched on the bench swing. He planted his feet so it didn't move. Procter never used it for that reason. Too much effort just to stay still.

The sky was pink with a low sun that flared orange through the trees. The light was perfect.

Procter said, 'When it's like this I don't need a book. I can just sit out here and that's enough. It's the magic hour. That's what they call it in the movie business, when the light is like this, just before sunset. They'll spend all day preparing and rehearsing to shoot a scene during the magic hour. If you see a film and the light is like this, then the director is a perfectionist and the producer hates him for spending so much money. But, you can't beat it. You can't fake it. Everything and everyone looks better in this light. You and me sitting here look the best we're ever going to look. This, my friend, is as good as it gets.'

'Maybe we should take a selfie.'

Procter chuckled.

The silence settled over them. Procter was in his chair on his porch on a warm evening. He could wait as long as it took. He had nowhere to go and nowhere he'd rather be. Alvarez knew it too, which was why he spoke before long.

Alvarez said, 'You've lost a chunk of weight since I last saw you, Roland. You look good for it. I always used to worry about your health.'

Procter laughed and cupped his jaw. 'I have a chin now, see? But it's hard to take any comment on my weight loss seriously when you turn up at my door looking like someone carved you out of clay.'

'I try to keep in shape.'

'I'll say. What's your secret?'

Alvarez said, 'You really want to know?'

Procter nodded. 'Hit me.'

'Two-fold,' Alvarez began. 'One, eat clean – no sugar, no processed food, no added sodium, no alcohol – and watching macros – 40 per cent protein, 30 per cent carbs and 30 fat. Two, exercise. That means five hours of weight training – alternate push/pull split resistance – and three of cardio – interval training on the rower or bike, plus Bikram yoga and some Krav Maga – each and every week without fail for twenty years now.'

'Is that all?'

'I find it hard to break a habit once it becomes one.'

'Any time for fun between working and working out?'

'I enjoy working out.'

'You'd get on well with my wife,' Procter said. 'She's similarly obsessed.'

'She's looking great these days. I see her around now and again.'

'I'll tell her you said that. She'll appreciate it. But you didn't have to come all this way to have a chat, did you?' Procter paused. 'A phone call would have done.'

'I was in the area. It was a good excuse to check in on you.'

'Check in on me or check up on me?'

Alvarez shrugged, as if he didn't know the difference.

Procter said, 'How's Christopher?' so he could delay the inevitable.

Alvarez let him. 'He's good. Growing fast. He calls me Antonio.'

'It's a phase.'

Alvarez shrugged again. It seemed an awkward movement. He was lean but broad, and the big shoulders looked heavy. 'What about Patricia?'

'She keeps me honest.'

Procter showed a wry smile. Alvarez matched it. Neither man blinked.

It was all a game, of course. The same test of wills

Procter had participated in a thousand times throughout his career. Alvarez had spent more time in the trenches than he had in a war room, and he hadn't learned the same tricks, the same subtlety. He thought it was about patience, about who cracked first. It would be another ten years, when he was Procter's age, by the time he realised that he had failed this first contest.

Procter said, 'You're a month into your new job working for the Director of National Intelligence. You have no need to visit your old CIA boss, especially a retired cripple like me.'

'Semi-retired,' Alvarez couldn't help but correct. 'You don't work from Langley, but you're still in the game.'

Procter didn't react.

'You know my remit?'

Procter nodded. 'To liaise with foreign and domestic agencies in the pursuit of terrorists, criminals and those who offer a direct threat to the United States.'

'Foreign *and* domestic.'

Procter nodded for a second time. 'And CIA, NSA, DIA, FBI, and everyone else has to bow beneath you. Am I close?'

A lesser man would have smiled, or even nodded, given the incredible power in his hands, but Alvarez, although no spymaster like Procter, showed no reaction. He saw his role as a duty, an honour, and so his ego took nothing from it. He was a better man than Procter had ever been.

'How can I be of assistance?'

'Do you remember the particulars of what happened in Paris? The Ozols Operation?'

'It rings a bell.'

Alvarez smirked at the understatement. 'Then you remember how you ordered me to back off when I was getting close to the assassin who killed my source and the man who hired him?'

'I remember how you disobeyed me, yes.'

Alvarez looked away. He peered out over Procter's immaculate lawn, and the fields beyond that. 'Someone once told me that to be satisfied all we must do is try our best.'

'That makes a certain sense.'

'I wasn't allowed to try my best back then.'

'If you want me to justify my actions, you're wasting your time. I have to talk to you because you're the Jesus of the intelligence community, but don't expect me to apologise for doing my job.'

'You know what I think about?'

Procter waited.

Alvarez continued: 'I think about all those dead people that were a direct result of that op. Most of whom deserved to die. But not everyone did. Two American citizens died and no one paid. There was no justice.'

'The man responsible paid for what he did by putting a gun into his own mouth.'

Alvarez said, 'At Nuremberg, it wasn't only the generals who were charged for their crimes.'

'I think I see where you're going with this.'

'Let's not pretend. You saw where I was going with this the moment my car pulled up outside.'

Procter didn't react. 'You're going after the killer.'

'I've always been after the killer. The guy who killed Ozols and started it all. The assassin who disappeared into the night. Vanished.'

'That trail is years old now. We never came close to him. We never got a name. How do you even begin going after someone like that?'

Alvarez said, 'Have you heard of something called the Minsk Tape?'

'Excuse me, but did you ask if I've heard your mix tape?'

'Funny,' Alvarez said without humour, 'but that's not what I said. I'm talking about a tape – a video recording – from Minsk, dating back a couple of years now. It's a water-cooler talking point. Almost an urban myth. Some junior analyst will brag to his colleagues that he's seen the Minsk Tape, but he won't tell them what's on it. He'll tell them that they have to see it for themselves. Of course, that junior analyst hasn't seen it and probably never will, but he's sure as shit heard of it. I'd heard of it too. Like I said: water cooler. But, eventually, I got to actually watch the video itself.'

'What is it?' Procter asked, as if he didn't know, as if he didn't care.

'I'm glad you asked, because it's relevant to the larger conversation. The Minsk Tape is a short CCTV recording, shot in a hotel suite with covert cameras. It's only a couple of minutes long, at most, but during those short hundred or so seconds a whole crew of Belarusian mobsters along with some Lebanese gun runners are massacred by a single man.'

'I see,' Procter said.

'Yeah, I saw too. But the human eye ain't great, really. No offence to us humans, but we've peaked. Technology, though, is still evolving. Gets better all the time. So good in fact that between facial recognition software and body composition algorithms the lone shooter in the Minsk Tape is an eighty-seven per cent match for Ozols' killer.'

Procter said, 'What are the odds?'

Alvarez said, 'Eighty-seven per cent is a good ten per cent from a home run, but it's good. It's close. It was enough for me to analyse that footage, to find out who the other people – the victims – were. And more importantly: who made the tape and why did they.'

'The Israelis. Mossad.'

'Then you have seen the Minsk Tape?'

'Of course.'

'Turns out our boy is wanted by Tel Aviv as well. They passed the tape to CIA. They asked for our help. But they never found him. My source in Mossad tells me a Kidon unit was dispatched to Eastern Europe a few weeks later and not all of them came back, but I'm sure that's just an amazing coincidence.'

'Why are you telling me this?' Procter said.

'Because I believe the killer has protection. He's avoided CIA and Mossad, all on his lonesome? I doubt that. Someone tipped him off. Someone's helped him.'

'Someone,' Procter said.

'Maybe it was fate that I was running the Ozols Operation back then. Maybe it was bad luck that I never got the guy who killed him. Maybe it's serendipity that I now have the opportunity to correct that luck.'

Procter was careful of his tone. 'You have a lead?'

Alvarez, to his credit, nodded. 'The killer was in Ireland a year ago. I think he was on a job. A priest died around the same time. Accidental death, but this priest was an informer during the Troubles who worked both sides.'

'You'll need more than just a coincidence like that to get this guy.'

Alvarez was unfazed. 'I have a lot more than that.'

'Forget about him, Antonio. This is someone you don't want to find.'

THIRTEEN

Victor saw the glow of a cigarette in the darkness before he saw the man smoking it. Tall and wide, the bodyguard wore a cheap suit and an overcoat of marginally better quality. His head was shaved down to the skin but he had a week's worth of beard growth. He heard, then saw Victor approach, but only because Victor allowed himself to be noticed. The bodyguard looked tired. It was almost three a.m.

The meeting place was an old hunting lodge at the end of a valley, accessible by a single-lane road that led to a gravel drive. The lodge was a grand Bavarian building of thick timbers and a low peaked roof. A single vehicle was parked out front. Victor had parked his rented Audi half a mile away and had traversed a stretch of trees to come at the lodge without using the road. Doing so would only have foretold his imminent arrival, and he never liked to announce his presence until the moment of his choosing.

The bodyguard tossed the cigarette away and it glowed from the gravel. He was startled by Victor's presence, which was good. The man had been expecting a car. He had expected to have warning. He didn't like that he had been caught out and he held forth a hand before Victor could get too close, even though Victor's hands were empty and obviously so, down at his sides.

'*Passwort?*' the bodyguard demanded.

Victor said, '*Nicht mit einer Schere laufen.*'

The bodyguard gestured and Victor raised his arms so they were perpendicular.

Victor wore a navy suit, white herringbone shirt and brown brogue boots. The latter were dirtied from the wet ground, which was regrettable. He had no coat and nothing in his pockets. It didn't take long for the bodyguard to pat him down and know he had no gun or knife on his person. Victor heard the crepitus cracking in the man's knees as he squatted down to check around Victor's legs and ankles. The bodyguard was slow to stand again, putting a hand to one thigh for balance.

He seemed satisfied, but when Victor lowered his arms he changed his mind and did another check. As amateurish as the first, but it gave the bodyguard peace of mind. Victor imagined the man had been told to be thorough, but he wasn't used to performing such checks. Which was interesting.

Another gesture, this time for Victor to enter, and the front door was opened for him. Victor didn't like people holding open doors for him – it meant giving them his back as he passed through – but the bodyguard gave him no reason to be concerned. The man was still red-faced from performing two whole bodyweight squats.

Victor wiped his boots on a doormat that said *Willkommen geehrte Gäste* and stepped inside.

There was no entrance foyer or hallway. Instead, the front door led straight to a large open-plan living area and kitchen. Victor put it at about a thousand square feet of floor space covered in polished wooden flooring. A huge stone fireplace dominated one wall, with sofas and armchairs arranged before it to create a living space. In the other half of the room was the kitchen and a long dining table that could seat sixteen people. The far wall had patio doors and windows that looked out to the grounds, but were now covered in drawn curtains. A lattice of timbers supported the roof above.

'It's a beautiful building,' Victor said to the man waiting for him.

He stood near to the fireplace, which was lit, and seemed to have been staring into the flames before Victor entered the room. A leather briefcase rested flat on a coffee table.

'I'm glad you like it,' the man said with a faint accent. He sounded a little more German than either his nationality or heritage suggested. 'Although it is wasted somewhat for our needs, don't you think?'

He stepped towards Victor, manoeuvring between armchairs.

Victor moved to meet him halfway. Neither man offered their hand.

The broker was a man named Wilders, a Belgian

national of Dutch descent, but of no address known to Victor. Wilders was a short man, out of shape and well dressed. His hair was equal parts white and gold and cut into a neat, timeless side-parting. It was thin at the crown. His face was tanned and his cheeks reddened by high blood pressure and heavy drinking. From the lines around his eyes and a sag to his jowls, Victor put Wilders' age in his late fifties. He had a gold chain around one wrist. He had removed his wedding band, and although it was too dim to see any change in skin tone, Victor noted the indentation in the skin. A careful man, but no one in this business should be married. No professional should have dependants. It was as unfair as it was dangerous.

'It's a private hunting lodge once owned by a Bavarian aristocrat. Some duke or archduke or such,' Wilders explained, holding out his arms. 'Now rented out for vacations and excursions. The occasional odious team-building retreat. Can you imagine a worse horror? No? Me neither. Tonight, it is purely for our purposes.'

Victor nodded. No doubt hired through a shell corporation registered in Switzerland, Luxembourg, or the Bahamas. In turn that company would be owned by yet another offshore organisation, registered in another part of the world. The web of ownership could be stretched out even further, and at the end of it there'd be no sign of Wilders or his associations. Nothing that happened here could ever be traced back to those involved.

As Wilders had said, the lodge was excessive for a discussion between two men, but it was remote. It was isolated.

He gestured to a staircase that led to a mezzanine floor.

'Feel free to stay the night if you have no other arrangements. Or the whole week if you need to. Make yourself at home. There's plenty of room. Schnapps in the fridge. Steaks in the freezer. There are pretty Bavarian girls in the town in yonder valley who are likely to be mightily impressed with such an abode. Do they all have those cute little outfits in their wardrobes?'

Victor remained silent.

Wilders seemed pleased with Victor's lack of reaction, or maybe he had amused himself. 'Oh, I should add that I don't expect you to take me up on the offer, but I thought I'd ask nonetheless.'

'Why?'

'To see how you responded, of course.'

'And did I do as expected?'

Wilders nodded. 'Not that it matters to me what you do.'

'But it matters to someone.'

The broker inched closer. 'Doesn't it always?' His breath smelled a little of brandy.

Trophies hung from some of the horizontal beams overhead: deer, wolves, bears, boars. Wilders saw Victor looking.

'Are you a sportsman?' Wilders asked.

'There's no sport in shooting at something that can't shoot back.'

'Is it really a surprise that we prefer to play games stacked in our favour?'

Victor didn't respond. The small talk was boring him. Talking on the whole tended to bore him. *Remember, it is what we do, not what we say, that defines us* someone had told him.

Victor adjusted his footing.

Wilders sensed his lack of interest. He offered him a seat near the fire. Logs burned, sap crackling and spitting, embers rising. A guard caught the sparks. Victor watched one that almost made it over the top, then faded from searing yellow to matte black in an instant.

He perched on the sofa closest to the hearth. In part because he could see the front door from there, as well as hallways that led off to the rest of the lodge and the large staircase without too much head movement, but also so he was within reach of the poker that hung from the fireplace. It was a solid piece of metal, cast iron, and a blow to the temple or brainstem would mean death to the recipient. A hard strike to pretty much anywhere else on the body would result in incapacitation – broken femur; shattered ulna; crushed jaw.

He needed no weapon against a man like Wilders, but it was always better to have a weapon within reach than not.

The broker sat opposite him, falling into the seat in the way some people did. He lounged back and crossed his legs. Victor sat on the edge of the sofa, knees above his ankles and head above his hips.

Wilders said, 'I appreciate that this is not something you would normally do.'

It wasn't, but Victor asked 'In what sense?' because he wanted to hear Wilders' interpretation of the meeting.

'Meeting a stranger, alone and unarmed, in a place not of your choosing. I'm not sure if I really expected you to show. So, thank you for coming.'

'Thank me when we have parted ways amicably,' Victor said. 'Not before.'

Wilders looked over one of his shoulders, towards the front door. 'I hope my friend outside was suitably courteous.'

'He didn't touch anything he didn't need to.'

Wilders smirked as Victor's expression remained the same. 'So, what do I call you?'

'You don't need to call me anything.'

'You don't have a name?' Wilders asked.

'None that is my own,' Victor answered.

'How about Tesseract?'

Victor didn't react.

'Or would you prefer Cleric?'

Victor didn't react.

'I'm well informed,' Wilders said. 'As I've demonstrated, I know a lot about you, which might be enough to fill a sheet of paper if one were to write in an inefficient prose.'

'What's your point?'

Wilders shrugged. 'Only that you've protected your anonymity well over the years, and in managing to do so your reputation has skyrocketed.' He raised a hand above his head in demonstration.

'It's a double-edged sword,' Victor admitted.

'But that's why I want to hire you. I need a professional.' He paused, considering for a moment. 'No, I don't simply need a professional, but someone exceptional.'

'You'll make me blush,' Victor said without inflection.

'I'm not here to merely flatter. I have a serious offer for your consideration, I assure you.'

'Good,' Victor said. 'Because I don't like wasting time. There's not enough of it as it is.'

'I wish to hire you, obviously. I have a contract that would suit your skill set and one worth a considerable purse.'

Victor said, 'I'm listening.'

'May I open this briefcase?' Wilders gestured to the briefcase resting flat on the table. It was alligator skin, polished dark. 'Or do you want to do it yourself?'

Victor lifted the case from where it sat and took it over to the dining table, where he placed it down. 'You can do it from here,' he said, because a bomb could be small enough to kill the person who opened the case and leave a bystander alive. 'But I'll stand behind you as you do.'

'Why?'

'So that if I don't like what's inside I can tear your throat out before you can remove it.'

Wilders' eyes narrowed. 'I do hope you're joking.'

'Not even a little bit.'

FOURTEEN

Bagels were surely the universe's way of saying life wasn't random, that there had to be a point, a plan, a design to it. And if that were the case then cream cheese was the universe's way of saying it wasn't soulless, it cared. Janice Muir felt that love with every huge bite. She wasn't sure what role coffee played but she felt the universe's benevolence there too. It was part of her morning routine: a run, then breakfast on the way home. She had awoken while it was still dark and the sun was only beginning to rise over Arlington. The air was cold, but thanks to the coffee and the run, she couldn't feel it.

She had spent most of the last couple of years behind desks, but she knew the Lincoln was going to pull up alongside her long before it did. She knew the vehicle, though she hadn't seen it in person for a while. Muir knew its owner in the same way.

'Good to see you out and about,' she said as the window buzzed down.

Procter said, 'Get in, please, Janice.'

'I'm sweaty. I'll make a mess of your seats.'

'Don't make me stretch across and open the door for you.'

Muir tutted. 'Still playing the invalid card, I see.'

She held the bagel between her teeth so she had a free hand to open the door, and climbed into the passenger seat. It *thunked* shut.

'Warm in here,' she said.

'Do you always dress like that when you run?' Procter asked.

'What are you trying to say?'

'You're not leaving a lot to the imagination.'

'It's called aerodynamics, Roland.'

He said, 'It's called something all right.'

'Since when did you become my dad? Because I'm owed a ton of back-dated allowance.'

Procter smiled and pulled away from the kerb. 'It's good to see you again, Janice. It's been a while.'

'This vacation of yours is certainly an extended one.'

'Sabbatical. I'm not on vacation, Janice. I'm convalescing. I've had three major surgeries in the last two years.'

'Whoa, back up. I'm teasing. Since when did you become so uptight?'

'Since Alvarez swung by to see me yesterday.'

She sipped some coffee. 'I'm surprised he still has time for you. Isn't he rubbing shoulders with the great and the good now?'

'That's precisely my point.'

'Talk to me, Roland. What's up?'

'He wants Tesseract.'

'Okay,' she said so Procter would continue.

'He's still salty about what went down in Paris. He's still bitter I had him back off. He never got his man back then and now he's been promoted he can do what I didn't allow him to do before.'

'What does he know about our involvement?'

'He suspects. He knows Tesseract showed up in Minsk. He's seen the footage. He knows about Mossad. He could know a lot more he didn't let on.'

'Why did he come to see you?'

'For help. At least, under the guise of asking for my help.'

'He was trying to rattle you?'

'Alvarez isn't the kind of guy who plays mind games. He's the guy who stares you out.'

'What does that mean?'

'It means I don't know why he came to see me. If he believes I know more than I've told him – and of course he would – then it makes no sense to show his hand so early.'

'So he's fishing. He doesn't know for sure if there are any fish in the pond but he's throwing out the line just in case.'

'Maybe.'

'It's not like you to be shaken. I don't think I've ever seen you shaken.'

'I'm limited in how I can respond. I'm stuck at home. I'm not in Langley. I can't so easily cast my own lines in response. I don't like that. I feel like I need to sew on a button when I'm wearing oven gloves.'

'Okay, I've caught up. This is why I'm sitting here in your

Lincoln. You want to make use of my unburdened fingers.'
She waggled them.

'I need you, Janice.'

'To do what, exactly?'

'Make contact with Tesseract. You need to warn him about Alvarez.'

Muir's eyebrows arched. 'Oh God, are you serious? You can't think that's a wise course of action. That's what Alvarez wants you to do.'

'There's a risk, Janice, I understand that. But Alvarez has something, else he wouldn't have come to me. As long as Tesseract stays out of his way, then there is nothing that can hurt us, but Tesseract needs to know who to be looking over his shoulder for.'

'If you contact him, you're helping Alvarez get closer to apprehending him.'

'He needs to know who he is dealing with. He needs to know what's at stake here.'

'I want no part of this.'

'You're already a part of this. You can't change that. But we can work with what we have. We have to. If we open a line of communication with him, then we can make sure he stays one step ahead of Alvarez. He must have something. He has something we don't know about, but it emboldens him enough to show up at my house and threaten me.'

'He doesn't,' Muir said. 'That's precisely why he showed up at your door. He's shaking the tree and hoping something falls out.'

'He wouldn't dare play that game with me. I know him.

He worked under me for years. I know how he thinks. I know how he operates.'

'And he knows that too. He's playing you, Roland. He's playing on your expectations of him to rattle you, and it's working.'

'If I could leave you out of this and get hold of Tesseract myself, I would. But I don't have any way of getting hold of him personally. It's been too long. And if there was a way, I can't do it myself with this sort of scrutiny. Alvarez will be watching my every move.'

Muir said, 'Yet you want me to expose myself while Alvarez is watching? What drugs do they have you on?'

'He didn't mention your name, Janice. He's not looking at you. He came to see me. He knows I was involved. He doesn't know about you.'

'You can't know what he knows and what he doesn't.'

'What I know is that Alvarez is a relentless son of a bitch with the scent of blood, but now he's leading the pack too. This is a serious situation. We need Tesseract to keep a low profile until this heat passes.'

'That's what he does, remember? That's who he is. The guy is a walking dictionary definition of paranoia. He can't be any more cautious than he is already. He can't be any more anonymous.'

'Then we need to establish a channel of communication with him, to keep him updated on developments. If Alvarez has something, or finds something, or gets closer than we think he is . . . Well, better Tesseract knows what's coming for him.'

'The more contact we have, the more exposure there is.'

'I don't argue that point. But let's just say that Alvarez gets hold of Tesseract, which is not beyond the realms of possibility, then Tesseract will give you and me up in a heartbeat. He's an assassin. He's a killer. He has no loyalty to us. We're just clients to him. We're just people he's worked for. There's a good chance he hates our guts.'

'I'm very well aware of that. But we used him for a reason. You had me use him for a reason. Even we don't know who he really is. So he's on a couple of video recordings? So he's a wanted man? Who exactly is Alvarez going to look for?'

Procter said, 'You don't know Alvarez like I do.'

'And maybe you don't know Tesseract like me.'

Procter was silent for a moment, then asked, 'When did you last have any communication with Tesseract?'

'About a year ago,' Muir said. 'He turned up out of nowhere to grill me on a job I'd passed him. He thought I set him up.'

'Did you?'

'I'm alive, aren't I? So, no. I didn't set him up. Someone did though, and he wasn't best pleased, as you might expect. Then, with you out of the game and given the job I passed to him didn't go so well, I figured maybe a little breathing room would be good for the both of us.'

'Do you know what he's been doing since?'

She shrugged. 'Your guess is as good as mine. He's not exactly what I'd call a sharer. I expect he's been working. For whom? Who knows? Maybe that's why this has all come about. He's popped up on someone's radar. He's left some evidence.'

'That doesn't sound like him, does it?'

'He's good, but he's human. We've cleaned up for him before. What if he's been operating without that sort of backup?'

Procter nodded. 'It's a possibility. But that's not what's driving Alvarez. Before, when I first decided Tesseract could be useful, I had Alvarez back off from the hunt because I knew that if left to his own devices he would pull down anything I tried to build. That was then. That was when I was his boss. When I could control him.'

Muir said, 'That was when he was on the inside. Alvarez had a link to Tesseract back then. That's the only reason you got to the guy yourself, because there was already a link in place. Alvarez doesn't have one now. That's why he came to you. He has no starting point. He wants you to create the link for him. If we try and reach Tesseract, then we're doing exactly what Alvarez wants us to do. What he needs us to do.'

'Maybe.'

'No, not maybe. Roland, you're not seeing the obvious. If Alvarez had something, he wouldn't have come to you at all. That he did turn up at your door shows he's looking for help, only not the sort of help you think he wants. You're not giving him enough credit. You've played him once so you think he can't play you in return. I hate to say it, but you're being arrogant, and a little stupid, which isn't like you.'

'I know what I'm doing, Janice.'

'I'm sure you really think that, but you want me to make contact with Tesseract to give him the heads-up on Alvarez and I'm not going to do it. No chance. No way.'

Procter struggled to find his words. 'You know, my only naivety in this is that I didn't think for a second you'd refuse to help me.'

'I'm not refusing to help,' Muir said, 'but I want to protect myself well before this spirals out of control, and I want to protect you in the process. Even if that's from yourself. Now take me home so I can shower. I'm starting to hum. Tesseract doesn't need our help. He's good at keeping his head down all on his own.'

FIFTEEN

Victor waited for Wilders to rise. He did so with the same slowness the bodyguard had shown while squatting. He didn't understand why anyone allowed themselves to degrade to such an extent. The Belgian approached the table, eyeing Victor with suspicion. Wilders stood before the briefcase, paling as Victor circled around him.

Wilders said, 'There's a dossier inside. That's all.'

'Then there's no need to be afraid of me standing behind you, is there?'

'I'm starting to understand how a man such as yourself stays alive with so many enemies.'

'You cannot begin to understand.'

Wilders was several inches shorter, so Victor had no trouble peering over his shoulder as the briefcase was unlocked, then opened. Inside was a slim manila file.

'The target's dossier,' the broker explained.

'I can see that. Take it out and hand it to me.'

Wilders did as Victor said. Inside was an A4 photograph of a man. Maybe fifty. Maybe Middle Eastern. It was a black-and-white shot, a covert head-and-shoulders photograph taken at long range. Behind it was a few dozen pages of biographical information. Victor didn't waste his time with it.

He looked at Wilders for a moment. 'You know, I wasn't sure how far you would take this, but I really didn't think it would get this far. A lot of work went into this dossier. It looks genuine.'

The broker was confused. 'That's because, naturally, it is a genuine dossier. He's a Jordanian. He sits on the board of one of the largest natural gas pipeline developers in the whole—'

Victor held up a hand. 'Spare me. Who's coming?'

'I'm sorry, what?'

'It's not the bodyguard. He's too big and too obvious. I've never come across a competent professional who would struggle to get off of the toilet.'

'What are you talking about? Who are you expecting?'

'It's not you either. No offence, but I could kill you just by making you run up a few flights of stairs. So we're talking about a third party. Given, as you put it earlier, my reputation, it's going to be someone like me or it's going to be a team. And the last time your boss sent someone like me it didn't end so well, so if I had to pick one or the other I'd say a team. How am I doing?'

'I'm afraid I have no idea what you're talking about.'

Victor regarded him. In Wilders' eyes he saw only confusion.

'Ah,' Victor said. 'You haven't been told what this is, have you?'

'I have no idea what you are talking about.'

'Let me explain it then. You work for an independent broker who goes by the handle Phoenix. You take these face-to-face meetings so your boss can remain anonymous. He gets the rewards while you take the risks. This particular meeting is an illusion, because Phoenix doesn't want to hire me. Quite the opposite in fact. There's an open contract out on me. A big one, worth a considerable amount of money to whoever kills me. Phoenix is the broker. He's tried to earn that purse twice before in the last year. That's why I'm here. I'm not here to get hired, I'm here to get to Phoenix.'

'I work for Phoenix, yes, but I know nothing about any of that. I'm here to hire you. As I said there is a Jordanian businessman we need eliminated—'

'Again, I believe you, but that's not why you're really here. Your orders were to discuss the contract in detail, yes?'

He nodded. 'The point was to be thorough. To make sure we could work together going forward.'

'No,' Victor said. 'Those were your orders. The point is to keep us talking, to allow the team enough time to move in undetected. This is a trap for us both. I'm afraid I'm more valuable to him dead than you are to him alive.'

Wilders said, 'I don't believe you. You're wrong.'

'Phoenix couldn't know for sure if I'd actually show,' Victor explained. 'If you weren't certain I would, then he definitely wasn't. He wouldn't want the team in close proximity to see me coming in case I spotted them in return. Therefore, he needs confirmation I'm here before the order can be given to execute. So, how will he know? Are you going to call him? Is he going to call you? If I'm wrong, then there's no way he can know I'm here and you have nothing to worry about.'

Wilders said nothing for almost thirty seconds but his expression said everything. He walked back across the room towards the fire, towards where they had sat. He reached a finger and thumb into the bouquet of dried flowers and removed a coin-sized audio receiver. He held it up for Victor to see and then tossed it into the fire.

'What do we do?' he asked, sudden urgency in his voice.

Wilders may have done business with killers, but he had never found himself in a position like this before. His earlier confidence was gone. He had lost control of the situation, but in truth it had never been under his control. He had come here to arrange a contract, not be part of one. It was a struggle, catching up with the turnaround. He was numb. He couldn't think. He didn't know what to do. Victor had seen it before. He had seen it many times before. The fight or flight reflex, going back and forth between the two, undecided. The end result was panic.

Victor didn't panic. Victor never panicked. He had been expecting this. He had wanted it, to an extent. He had wanted to get closer to Phoenix, whatever the danger, because he was in danger regardless. He was calm because he was always calm. Unlike Wilders, Victor was used to such situations. Making enemies was an inevitable side effect of being paid to kill people. He couldn't hope to neutralise all threats. He couldn't hope to know of all threats.

'I'll make a deal with you, Mr Wilders. It's a one-time, yes or no offer, and it's the best offer you've ever had. There's no time to negotiate. Help me get to Phoenix and I'll help you live through this.'

'How?'

'Leave the details to me. Yes or no?'

'I'd love to say yes but I'm afraid I don't know how to get to Phoenix.'

'You do,' Victor said. 'You just don't realise it. You know something after working for him all this time. No one is perfect. No one is invisible. Everyone makes mistakes. He slipped up. He gave something away or you worked something out. Think. Think hard and think fast because I'm the only hope you have and I'd as soon gut you as help you for nothing in return.'

Wilders put his hands to his pinched face. His brain had never worked this hard in his life. Victor watched. Waiting. Counting down the seconds Wilders had left alive.

'If you knew it was a trap, why did you come here?'

'I knew Phoenix wouldn't show in person, but I knew he would send someone in his place. Someone who could be useful. If you're useful, then you get to live.'

The broker said, 'We need to get out of here.'

'Answers first. Who is he?'

'I don't know his name.'

'You've met him, though? You know his face?'

Wilders shook his head.

'You're running out of time. Talk to me.'

'But I have information. I have lists. I have data. Calls. Numbers. Contacts. Times. Places. Email addresses. Bank accounts. Companies.'

'I see,' Victor said. 'In case he ever turned on you. Which is almost certainly why he now wants you dead. He found out you've been gathering intel on him. I hope you can see the funny side.'

Wilders could not. 'I've been collecting it for years, but I don't have the resources to make use of it. I've never been able to put the pieces together myself.'

'Where do you have it stored? Can he access it?'

'No,' Wilders said. 'He can't know where I have it. I have a safe, in an apartment I own, but not in my name. I owned it long before I ever came to work for him. Everything's in the safe.'

'Where's the apartment?'

'Get me out of here and I'll tell you.'

'Tell me and I'll get you out of here.'

Wilders didn't hesitate because he didn't have time and he didn't have any bargaining power. He may not have been as good at this as he thought, but he knew when he was out of his depth. He said, 'Zurich.'

'The address,' Victor demanded.

Wilders supplied details for an apartment in the Enge quarter, near to the Arboretum Park.

'Okay,' Victor said. 'Give me your gun.'

'I don't have one.'

'Now's not the time to start being coy. You need to give me your weapon if you want to survive who's coming.

Unless you think you're a better shot.' Victor gestured. 'In which case, by all means, after you.'

'I'm telling you, I don't have a gun. That was our agreement.'

'Then I'll need your bodyguard's instead. You'll need to order him to hand it over, unless you don't like him very much.'

'He . . . doesn't have one either.'

'You're joking.'

'Those were the conditions of the meeting. No guns.'

Victor sighed. 'Typical. For the first time in my life some-one actually played by the rules when they shouldn't have.'

'Phoenix insisted we follow the terms.'

'Then let me take a guess: the bodyguard is freelance, paid in cash, and more used to keeping the paparazzi away from pop stars than he is fighting off killers.'

'He wasn't my first choice for that very reason.'

'But Phoenix insisted.'

Wilders could only nod.

'Then he wants you dead as badly as me,' Victor said. 'You're not very good at this, are you?'

'I thought I was, until now.'

'Be glad I'm here to show you the error of your ways. Who's coming?'

'I told you, I don't know that.'

'Again, you do, you just don't realise it. You've hired them for something recently. Like I said before: not an indi-vidual, but a team. You hired them for a job that's coming up soon, either in this country or a neighbouring one. Only thing is, Phoenix switched the targets without your knowledge. He likes to keep things clean. There'll be no traces back to him because you've hired your own killers.'

If Wilders was pale before, now he was white. Everything Victor said made sense. Cold, hard, lethal sense.

He struggled to speak now his sympathetic nervous system went into overdrive. 'They're ... Greeks. Well, Macedonians. A five-man team.'

'I don't care where they're from. What's their background? Are they sitting out there with sniper rifles and thermal imaging or will they assault with SMGs?'

'I don't know any of that.'

'Why would you?' Victor said. 'Can you at least tell me if they're any good?'

The broker said, 'They were expensive.'

'That's not the same thing.'

'I ...'

He heard a noise. A crunch of gravel. Outside.

'Forget it,' Victor said. 'We're about to find out.'

SIXTEEN

The bodyguard was waiting outside of the car, as he was instructed. He was supposed to keep his distance, but to stay close enough to offer aid should it be required. He couldn't imagine the guy in the suit being much trouble to anyone. The bodyguard could snap him like a twig if it came to it. He played with his phone to pass the time, swiping young chicks he liked the look of and playing the slots with a casino app. He was supposed to be working. He was supposed to be on guard, but what was the point? He was hired for show, to intimidate, to scare. He hadn't so much as punched anyone in months, and then it had been some smug little photographer who sneaked too close to his camera-shy client. It was the most boring job in the world, hence his increasing dependency on dating and gambling apps. Had to pass the time somehow.

He didn't see the shadow approach. He didn't hear the

footsteps. He didn't feel the knife. He was dead before the pain could register.

Victor thought about the lodge. It was a great place for an ambush if only because of its remoteness. Even if things got messy and loud, there was no one nearby to see, no one to hear. Plus, the size of the building and the grounds meant a team could approach without being detected, and enter unnoticed. There was no way to watch every door, every window. Phoenix had chosen well. This was no surprise to Victor. He knew next-to-nothing about the broker, but as Wilders had said of Victor, anonymity only enhanced Phoenix's reputation.

He didn't know the building's layout, but he didn't need to see blueprints or perform a walk around to know there would be multiple entrances and exits. The Macedonians would have done their homework. They had chosen the best approaches, the best points of entry. They knew their target and wouldn't all come in the same way. They couldn't risk Victor slipping away out of the front while they crept in through the back. That cut off any chance of escape, but it split them up. It made them vulnerable. He couldn't fight off a whole team by himself, but one-by-one he had a chance, especially considering he had a single, significant advantage: he knew they were coming.

The problem with the room was it was too big and too open. There were no real blind spots to hide out of line of sight. He could duck behind the U-shaped worktops in the kitchen, or use the blocky island for cover, but he couldn't hope to take an enemy by surprise from there if they entered from the far side of the room.

Phoenix was smart, so he would have briefed the team on Victor's capabilities and his history, but they were expecting to catch him by surprise. They were expecting to ambush him.

That the lights were on cemented this fact. If they cut the power, he would know they were coming. So, lights on. Which meant they didn't have night vision.

Wilders stood still and silent as Victor approached the touch screen by the front door. It was a master control panel for the whole building. Every electronic device – sound system, television, climate control – could be operated from here. A few taps and swipes and he had access to the lights. He could select by room and by individual fixture. He could also select them all.

The whole building went dark.

The screen glowed; more taps and swipes and he had access to the sound system. There were genres and playlists and albums and artists and individual songs. He selected genre, chose metal, then tapped the first band listed. He pressed the volume control until it maxed out.

The five Macedonians were already spread out inside the building when the lights went out. If this was unexpected, the blaring music that followed a few seconds later was a shock. There were speakers throughout the building and no escape from thumping drums and wailing guitars. A singer screeched and screamed.

They had no thermal nor starlight scopes or goggles,

so the darkness was a problem. They did, however, have tactical lights fixed to their weapons, just in case. That foresight paid off now. They paused a second to switch these on, giving them concentrated beams of light to illuminate their path.

There were two targets: an assassin and a broker named Wilders. The latter was to be killed only once the first was dead.

The darkness and the screaming music told them that they were expected, but it didn't matter. The Macedonians still had a significant numerical advantage, and they had been assured both targets would be unarmed. The assassin was making things difficult for them, but this was going to end only one way.

The first gunman to reach the main room picked out Wilders with the tactical light. The broker was terrified, his hands held high and obvious.

The gunman had to yell to be heard, '*Where is he?*'

Wilders yelled back and pointed. '*Above you.*'

The Macedonian's head snapped up, and he saw Victor – hanging upside down – but in doing so exposing his neck for Victor to reach down and loop his right forearm under the man's jaw, wrapping around his throat in a choke hold. Victor locked off on his own left wrist, left hand braced against the back of the man's head, squeezed and lifted him off the floor.

Extreme pain, panic and airlessness made the Macedonian drop his gun to free up his hands in a desperate attempt to save himself.

Victor hung upside down, the backs of his knees against the horizontal support timbers while his feet were crossed around one of the verticals. Not an ideal position to be in for lots of reasons, least of all because supporting his own weight and that of his enemy meant considerable pressure and pain in his legs where they met the beams, but his options for surprising an armed enemy were limited.

The choke shut off the Macedonian's carotid arteries. The toes of his shoes scrambled for purchase. After three seconds his legs jerked and thrashed. Six seconds later they swung back and forth.

Victor lowered the unconscious man a little to ease the strain, and to make it easier to adjust his hold to break the man's neck. He released the corpse and contracted his core to raise his torso back up so he could grab the timber and lower himself down again. The resulting drop wasn't far.

He retrieved the dead man's gun, which was a pistol, but it had a vertical fore grip and folding buttstock. It was a Beretta 93R. The R stood for *raffica*, or burst. Each squeeze of the trigger fired off three bullets, making it a deadly close-range weapon, but it needed the grip and buttstock to help control the recoil generated by that rate of fire. The tactical light was useful, but it was attached to the right-hand side of the gun because the folding vertical fore grip was in the way underneath. That meant the focus of the light beam wasn't quite where the muzzle pointed. Insignificant at point-blank range, but that difference could put a shot wide at range if the shooter used the beam to aim.

It would never be Victor's first choice of weapon, but he preferred his enemies armed that way. The weapon wasn't suppressed, which was unusual when dealing with professionals. It probably wasn't the team's first choice either, but Victor knew as well as anyone that it was almost impossible to operate with the best gear. The most effective weapons were the ones hardest to obtain. More often than not he had to make do. The Beretta was what an associate of his had once referred to as a spit gun – because spitting distance was about as far as it could be shot with any accuracy.

He made sure it was loaded and a round was in the chamber, but didn't frisk the body for more magazines or comms equipment. The others were close and he couldn't afford to have his gaze anywhere but sweeping the entry points.

That diligence meant he was ready when the next guy entered. A single squeeze of the trigger put three subsonic nine mils through his cranium.

The next was harder to kill. He entered through the north doorway a second later than his team mate, catching Victor off guard while his gaze was elsewhere, but the man was as surprised seeing two corpses on the ground and both targets still alive. He didn't hesitate, but the surprise threw off his aim. He shot too soon, before he had Victor in his sights, the torch beam working against him.

He had the same model Beretta and put a three-round burst wide of Victor, shattering a window. The recoil was fierce, even with the fore grip and buttstock, making the second burst slower; correcting his aim took longer.

It gave Victor enough time to twist and fire off a snapshot.

The burst hit centre mass and the Macedonian staggered and cried out, but didn't go down. Victor saw no mist of blood or bloodied clothing, and was able to aim his second shot for the head before the gunman could recover. A red splash hit the wall behind him.

Three squeezes of the trigger. Nine rounds fired. The Beretta had eleven remaining.

Victor switched the selector to single shot. He preferred accuracy to firepower.

The music ceased.

One of the Macedonians had found another control panel and killed it. Victor had expected they would, sooner or later. The lights followed, bathing the room again in a warm glow. It didn't matter. He had a weapon now. He was armed. He didn't need to hide himself any longer. It was time to finish this on his own terms.

Wilders was cowering behind a sofa.

Victor said, 'Where else in the lodge are there control panels that affect all rooms?'

Wilders was silent. He was terrified.

'For the music,' Victor prompted. 'For the lights.'

Wilders snapped out of his panic. 'Master bedroom. Mezzanine.'

Victor changed position, rushing to cover the staircase, reaching it in time to see a shadow on the landing above and squeezing the trigger when that shadow became a human form. A double-tap left nine bullets in the 93R's magazine, and dropped the gunman, who slid on his back down the stairs, coming to rest at the foot of the staircase, at Victor's feet.

He swapped out the half-empty mag for a full one from the dead guy's gun.

Footsteps.

The last Macedonian tried stealth. He attempted to be quiet. He crept along a downstairs hallway with slow, careful footsteps, but like the rest of his team, like Victor, he wore boots. He couldn't be silent on the hardwood floors. But he expected his enemy to be as noisy, to be as detectable.

Victor slid across the floor on his stomach, the highly polished floorboards letting him slither with a decent amount of speed, just using his left palm and right elbow to pull himself forward while he kept the weapon clear. He was down behind the kitchen worktops, hidden, when the gunman entered the room.

Victor popped up behind him and shot him in the back of the head.

Wilders was still behind the sofa after Victor had swept the lodge to make sure the five-man team really had consisted of five. He found their various points of entry, but no evidence there had been anyone else. Wilders had been right about something, at least.

He stood. He was sweating. He was out of breath. He was shaking. Victor could see it on his face – he'd never felt more invigorated, more alive.

'I did okay, yes? I stood where you told me to,' Wilders said. 'I can't believe I'm still alive.'

Victor said, 'I can't believe it either,' and shot him twice in the face.

SEVENTEEN

There wasn't an inch of CIA headquarters that Muir didn't know. She had been in many briefing rooms, situation rooms and conference rooms. She had even spent time in the hallowed halls of the seventh floor, where the royalty of espionage held court. This particular conference room on the fourth floor could have been in any office in the country. It was nothing special. Just a room. Maybe that was why it had been chosen.

Alvarez said, 'Would you like a glass of water?'

Muir nodded. 'Please.'

He poured her some from a glass jug. He filled it half-way. She didn't get the point of that. Fill it up or not at all. Waste of a glass otherwise.

'Shall we get right to it?' Alvarez said. 'Skip the small talk?'

She took a sip. 'Suits me. I have a busy day ahead.'

'I won't take up too much of your time. I just have a few questions for you.'

'That's what your message said.'

'I'm looking to apprehend a professional assassin. Someone who you know quite a bit about, as I understand it.'

She resisted the urge to take another sip of water, to stall, to hide her nerves. Procter had said nothing about Alvarez knowing of her own involvement.

'I'm going to be straight with you, Janice,' Alvarez said. 'I'm a stickler for justice. I can't like a movie if the bad guy gets away with it, you know? And I've never gotten over the fact there is a piece of shit hitman out there who was allowed to just slip away from my grasp. That irks me. That keeps me awake at night. It's kept me awake at night for years. Now, I think I can get this guy. Now I think I finally have a chance to sleep like a baby again. Maybe banish these bags once and for all.'

'What does this have to do with me?'

'You and Procter are close. When he got busted up by that Hummer you visited him in the hospital more than anyone else. In all, you were there nineteen times.'

Muir sat back. 'You checked the hospital visitor logs?'

'I'm thorough, Janice. It's what I do. Now, bear with me on this because it's going to take a moment, but I have very good reason to believe that not only did Procter allow the killer to escape when he ordered me to stand down, but he then employed that very same assassin to do all manner of black ops work directly for him.'

'I'm still waiting for what this has to do with me.'

'So, not only did Procter allow a criminal to escape

justice but he then used and protected that criminal for his own personal benefit.'

Muir huffed. 'If you think you can convince me that Procter is some rogue operator, out for himself, then you're wasting your time.'

'I'm making very good use of my time, Janice. It's how Procter had you use your time that is the important point here. There's no name for this assassin, but he's been spotted now and again over the intervening years. I call him Mr Eighty-Seven Per Cent for reasons Procter can explain if you care to ask. He's tall, white, dark hair and eyes, and that's all anyone can say for certain. He's like an apparition, appearing now and again; a rumour, a myth. Hearsay. Not verified. Not real. You have to want to believe in him to see that he exists at all.'

'Where are you going with this?'

'I'm glad you asked. There's a name I've heard, a codename. Tesseract. I had to look up what it meant. Some weird geometry term. Four-dimensional object. I don't really understand it, but it's a nice-sounding word, right? I've come across it a couple of times over the years and whaddya know, this Tesseract and my Mr Eighty-Seven Per Cent are one and the same.'

'So?'

'So, I believe he was here in the States last year. I believe he was in New York. For the briefest time everyone was looking for a tall white guy with dark hair. And then, like magic, they weren't. No one cared. Eliminated from enquiries. No longer a person of interest. From suspected terrorist one minute, back to no one the next.'

'Happens all the time.'

'Sure it does, but I checked it out because I check out every potential sighting of Mr Eighty-Seven Per Cent, and you know what happened?'

'I'm sure you're going to tell me.'

'I met resistance.'

'What does that mean?'

'It means people didn't answer phones. It means I was fed BS. It means someone was getting in my way.'

'And you think that was Procter? You think Procter was sitting on his porch giving you a hard time?'

'Funny, but no. I think it was you.'

Muir smiled. 'You know what, Antonio? You have to be careful with all these assumptions and suppositions you're flinging around the place, because sooner or later you're going to tell me something I didn't already know. You're going to put two and two together and come up with five, and the very fact that you do is going to give me something you don't want me to have.'

'You can't make me doubt myself. Don't bother.'

'Good,' Muir said. 'Hold on to that unshakeable confidence. That always works out so well.'

'I think you were the one Procter asked to liaise with his assassin while he was out of action.'

'Do you have any proof of that?'

Alvarez sat back. 'You know I don't.'

'Then we're through.'

'But you also know the proof is out there, just waiting for me to find.'

Muir went to stand.

Alvarez said, 'I don't want you, Janice. You were doing your job. At least, I can believe you thought you were doing your job. And, frankly, I don't care if you knew you were breaking the law, because we've all done it. But Procter doesn't get the same pass.'

'You only want Procter because it'll look good. He's a big score. People will pat you on the back and say good boy.'

'Hardly. Truth is, that assassin of yours – did you ever stop to ask yourself what he'd done for Procter before the accident, before your involvement? Now, I'm sure you've been told some of it.'

Alvarez opened the folder and took out a series of A4 photographs. He set them on the table, one by one.

'American citizens. Dead. This guy here was a CIA officer. He was working directly for me. Look at the mess your killer left him in. This woman here was a former analyst.'

Muir was shaking her head before Alvarez had finished. 'No way did Procter have current or former CIA killed. It's hilarious that you would believe it, and even funnier that you would expect me to.'

'Did I say that? I don't think I did. But Procter knew about them. He knew who killed them and not only did he let that person get away with it, he employed that very same murderer. Do your diligence. Check them out. Both deaths are unsolved. First one was put down as a mugging gone wrong, and I swallowed it at the time because I had other things to take care of. But the muggers left no evidence. They've never been apprehended. The second death, in Greece, made the news. It was a bomb. Two people checked into a hotel room, a couple. Man and woman. The woman never left, but the man was never found. Tall. Dark hair. What are the odds?'

Muir sat still and maintained her concentration on the images.

'I know you're telling yourself that this can't be true, that I'm bluffing, I'm lying, but there's a simple way to know.'

Muir met his gaze.

'That's it, Janice. That's all you have to do. Just look me in the eye, and then make sure you look Procter in the eye while he lies to you. Procter used you, so don't protect him now. You don't owe him anything.'

'He's my friend.'

'He's your boss. He doesn't care about you. Why do you think he came to see you already?'

'You can't rattle me, Antonio. I don't care if you're tailing Procter, or me for that matter. It's not a crime for me and him to meet.'

'That's not my point. He came to see you under the guise of warning you, asking for your help, yeah? Whatever, it doesn't matter what he told you. The point is, he didn't have to see you, did he? But he did. Because he wants me to see it. Because, if it comes to it, he's going to set you up to take the fall for everything he's done.'

'Now you're just being childish.'

'Am I?'

'It's borderline ridiculous that you're trying to make me turn on Procter by making me scared he'll turn on me first. Which isn't going to work. That you could think it might work shows you have nothing. And it shows me that the only reason you got this job is because you play golf with the president.'

Alvarez couldn't hide his surprise.

'Yeah, I know about that, or did you forget I'm CIA? So before you make me doubt myself, maybe you should be asking yourself those same questions.'

He leaned forward, jaw flexing. 'You're wrong. I have plenty. You want facts, Janice? Fine. You want proof, then you can have it. I know for certain that your boy – Tesseract – he's worked for MI6 too. This same Eighty-Seven-Per-Cent-er – tall, dark hair, no name – their people have heard of him. Only they call him Cleric over the Pond. I think I prefer that. Tesseract don't mean squat to most people. Whereas Cleric is emotive, it's got some imagery with it. Word is he's been on the books in a more official capacity for our British cousins. They haven't tried to hide him to the same extent you did, because he's not wanted for any crimes over there. There are no dead Brits attributed to his handiwork – at least none anyone cares about.'

Muir said, 'What would I know about any work he's done for another nation?'

'Are you trying to tell me you didn't broker that arrangement? I know you were at a meet-and-greet with Cleric's former handler and I know you have another shindig coming up with his new handler. Or are you telling me that's purely coincidental?'

Muir said nothing. She looked at the grooves between Alvarez's eyebrows to keep her mind empty, lest her thoughts show on her face.

Alvarez said, 'I know you're a good person, Muir. But I also know you care about the end result more than you care about how that's achieved. Which is a judgement call, and I'm not judging you for that. But if I have to challenge those judgements to get what I want, then I will. If I have to put everything you've done under a legal microscope to encourage your cooperation, then that's what I'm going to do.'

Muir said, 'And if you can't get Procter then you'll settle for me instead.'

'It never needs to get that far.'

'You're asking me to betray my mentor.'

'I'm asking you to do the right thing. Answer me this: if you found out that one of your colleagues was murdered and I not only allowed the murderer to escape justice but then employed him, how would you feel?'

She stood.

Alvarez said, 'We're not done here.'

'Yeah,' Muir said, 'we are.'

EIGHTEEN

The bank didn't look like a bank. There were no ATMs outside, and there were none inside either. The foyer was laid out like the lobby of a grand hotel. The receptionists were beautiful women and the clerks were handsome men. Every front-of-house employee wore a black suit. No hair was out of place. No tie was off centre. The bankers themselves weren't actually bankers. They were accountants and lawyers.

The bank offered no interest. It took only fees. There were no savings accounts. No current accounts. Just accounts. A customer could have as many as he or she wished, and the more money they had at the bank, the more fees they paid. Those fees were high, but they were far cheaper than any tax rate. Which was the point.

Raven had been in many such places – in Switzerland and Panama, the British Virgin Isles and Singapore. The business of hiding money was the fastest growing of all. As the world economy grew, the desire to mitigate tax liability rose with it. For those like Raven, whose primary desire was to hide the source of the payment and the reason for it, the proliferation of such establishments made her life a little easier. She was able to move funds and access them. She could cover her tracks and hide her future movements. She had powerful enemies but she was liquid – mobile, unpredictable, impossible to grasp.

She'd had an account with this particular bank for six months. She had a sizeable amount of money in her account; no sum of note compared to the bank's other customers, but enough for her to get a meeting with one of the associates at short notice, enough to receive polite treatment when she waited, but not enough to be remembered. Today's disguise was a wide-brimmed hat to hide her hair and large-lensed sunglasses to disguise her eyes. The dress and the heels did the rest – Chanel and Louboutin. Elsewhere they would make her stand out. Here, she was just another woman with expensive tastes.

It had taken weeks to regain her fitness and lost strength, and months to claw back her dexterity, her speed. She had seen many doctors and therapists, in many countries, never the same one twice, always lying and holding back details. This served to protect her anonymity, but the downside was it prevented the specialists from helping her to their full capabilities. Maybe that was why it had taken so long to recover from the pain that required her to sit down, else fall down. She still dreamed of paralysis, inescapable torment, longing for death.

The poisoning, the hospital, the assassin disguised as a nurse had all helped to bring her here to Rome.

Twelve months before she had been sitting on the hard floor of the mortuary, her back against the cold steel of the dissecting table, her chest heaving from the exertion, trembling from the adrenaline and pain. The cute nurse – cute assassin – lay before her in a lake of blood that spread further in perfect straight rivers between the floor tiles. She sat there for a while, watching the ever-slowing crawl of those lines of blood, wondering how far they would reach as she rested from the crippling exertion of the fight.

The blood was coagulating by the time she felt strong enough to stand. It was harder than climbing back into bed after exercising, but she did it. Then she rested again. Only a short rest this time, because walking wasn't too bad. It wasn't as stressful on her weak muscles and weaker nervous system.

She considered the corpse. A problem, because there was no way she would be strong enough to move it, even cutting it up first. The incinerator was on the same basement level, she knew. But it was out of the question, given her weakness. So the body would be discovered just as soon as the mortuary reopened.

That it was shut down made her think. The assassin's employers – the Consensus – had arranged that. They had managed to get him a job at the hospital. Their pervasiveness was her advantage here. They wanted her dead. They didn't want her questioned by the police, or worse, detained. There would be another cover-up here. They always covered up their mistakes. She had helped them often enough.

She explored the mortuary until she had found gloves and galoshes, bleach and alcohol, magnifying glasses and tweezers, and set about sterilising the scene of her presence. It was exhausting, it was time-consuming, and she doubted she could erase all traces, but anything was better than nothing. The Consensus would do the rest on her behalf.

She bagged up all the clothes and other items she had come into contact with and used the showers meant for morticians and pathologists to wash the blood from her hair and body. She changed into hospital scrubs and a pristine white doctor's coat she found hanging on the back of a door. There was no convenient ID badge to clip to the pocket, but she found a pair of reading glasses and a couple of pens to complete the look.

In the drawer where she found latex gloves was a similar box of disposable hair nets. She bunched her hair inside one and checked out the disguise in a mirror. She looked as though she belonged here. The drawn face, bags under her eyes and tired complexion of her recovery all helped. She was just another overworked hospital employee. Busy, harried, not to be stopped or hassled by security, not to be noticed by inquisitive cops or anyone on the Consensus' payroll.

The dead assassin had a few coins in his pocket – for the vending machines dispensing soda and peanuts – and a set of keys, but nothing else. She checked the keys. The one for his car was obvious, as was the small key for a padlock. The latter was for his locker, no doubt. His wallet would be inside. A fake ID, of course, but that in itself could prove useful. The risk of getting to the locker was huge. It would be near the ward where the other nurses and doctors would recognise her face, or worse, where the cops might be waiting for her to return. It might be inaccessible in a room protected by a punch-button lock. She couldn't take the risk. It was frustrating to know she was close to perhaps invaluable intel on her enemies, but it was out of her reach.

She rested again before heading to the elevator, because she was feeling lightheaded from being on her feet so long and needed to be at her best when she made it out of the basement. She would have ignored the elevators and taken the stairs had it not been for her condition. A few flights of stairs now seemed an insurmountable obstacle, a mountain she couldn't hope to climb. The elevators increased the risk of discovery, of exposure, but she had no choice. She could bluff her way past almost anyone with a smile or a shrug, but her basic disguise wasn't going to fool someone who had treated her.

In the foyer she felt dizzy and had to fight to maintain not only her equilibrium but her guise of balance and poise. The disguise worked. She passed by dozens of people. No one gave her a second look. She found the section of the parking lot reserved for hospital staff and walked through it with her hand in her pocket, pressing the button on the key fob until she heard locks thunk.

The car was a Prius, common enough in Canada. She climbed behind the wheel and shut the door.

Sitting in a comfortable car seat felt good. Encased in a steel and glass shell, she felt safe. She could relax for a moment, resettle and rethink. Just for a moment, because she had to get as far away as possible. But she favoured a tactical withdrawal over an out-and-out retreat. There was nothing to run from at this moment. Better to take a few minutes and work out her next move instead of hurrying into doing the wrong thing.

She checked the glove box. A cell phone sat inside. It was an old handset, blocky and heavy. Plenty of marks and scratches. Well used, sold and resold and traded in; multiple owners, a long life. Her pulse quickened. She knew a burner phone when she saw one. A new SIM card, prepaid credit. Untraceable.

There was no pin to unlock it because it contained nothing. No call history. No messages. It might never have been used.

She used it. She called Fast Flowers.

'I'm wondering if you could help me,' she began. 'I received a lovely bouquet of lilies last week in hospital ... Yes, I know that's unusual, but the man who sent them has a bizarre sense of humour. Anyway, this joker is something of an admirer, but he didn't leave his name on the card ... No, he's not exactly a secret admirer, but I'm hoping I can appeal to your romantic sensibilities and you'll give me his details, because here's the crazy thing: I've lost my memory ...'

One minute later she had a name, address and phone number. All fake, she knew, but left for her to find, so that she could find him. After all, she owed him.

The only question now that she needed answering regarded the burner phone itself: was it here so the assassin could call his employers or so they could call him?

The phone rang.

NINETEEN

Switzerland had once been Victor's country of residence. Not home, because although he had lived for some years in a chalet near Saint-Maurice, he had never felt settled. It had been a house, and he had been quite fond of it, but nothing more. He wondered if it had been rebuilt after the explosion and fire that had destroyed it and any trace of his existence there, or else if nature had reclaimed the land. He would never go back to find out. He was curious, but not nostalgic.

He arrived in the country via a flight from Madrid, having first travelled from Holland, and Germany before that. As usual, he avoided travelling in a straight line if possible.

There was a delay landing in Geneva and as they circled overhead the cabin crew offered complimentary food by way of apology. Victor declined. He avoided the food served on flights. He had little concern his meal would be tampered with – an assassin would have to predict he would eat, as well as his chosen option, and slip poison inside without detection – but food poisoning was a legitimate risk. The statistics were shocking. Besides, eating kept him occupied, and he didn't like to be so confined and immobile with people all around him. There were many reasons why no killer worth concern would make an attempt on board an aeroplane, but it was impossible for Victor to switch off the instincts that had kept him alive thus far.

In Geneva, he spent several hours rotating through taxis, trains and trams, choosing destinations at random, doubling back on himself, and pausing at intervals to make sure he wasn't being followed. He took an afternoon train to Zurich and was the last person to board before the doors locked. He selected a seat in a carriage with few other people. One of whom was a woman. She had short dark hair cut in a choppy style. He looked at her longer than he should because she reminded him of someone, and she noticed. She looked back. She mistook his intention and smiled. He couldn't bring himself to do the same.

The journey was a little under three hours and he slept most of the way in a series of naps that were no substitute for proper sleep, but that ensured he arrived without too much fatigue. Zurich was cold. It always was when he visited. A thin layer of early snow coated the pavement and rooftops. A lazy shower of flakes turned hats and shoulders white. It was the kind of snow that people liked, but wouldn't like tomorrow when it had formed ice, blocking their driveways and waiting to slip them up.

Wilders' apartment was where he'd said it would be. It was located inside a handsome block in a nice, quiet neighbourhood of the Fluntern district, with tree-lined streets and polite pedestrians. Victor kept his coat open and his hands free of his pockets regardless of the chill or that these details would make him stand out to a careful observer. Some precautions just couldn't be ignored.

He spent a day observing who came and went and looking out for surveillance until he was satisfied that no one working for Phoenix was waiting for him. The building was accessible by a heavy door and intercom system, easy to bypass – *Delivery for apartment twenty-three* – but he waited for the morning and rush hour. It was a simple enough trick he had used before. He loitered outside until he heard the door begin to open and thanked the harried, but polite, commuter for holding it open for him.

There was a decent lock on Wilders' door, but nothing that Victor hadn't picked countless times. He was inside before any neighbour could grow suspicious. The apartment wasn't lived in, that was clear. It was furnished, but there was a large pile of circulars behind the front door. There were no letters addressed to a named occupier, Wilders or otherwise. The fridge was as bare as Victor had expected, with nothing but condiments.

The safe wasn't set into a wall, but in the walk-in closet. Victor had graph paper, pencils and a stethoscope with him in case it had a dial, but the safe was electronic. For that he had a compact laptop and software to deliver a brute-force attack of combinations and the safe clicked open within a minute. He had expected a hard drive or thumb drive, or maybe even a disk of some sort. Instead, he found paper. The safe was empty except for a two-inch-thick stack of documents: files, receipts, handwritten notes, some sketches, photographs, brochures, purchase orders, invoices, fliers and other correspondence that seemed inconsequential or unrelated. A quick flick through showed that Wilders had indeed been collecting information for some years. The collection seemed haphazard and random, which made sense because Wilders hadn't known how to get close to Phoenix. He'd been gathering anything that could be useful, but hadn't found any links. Victor could see why. It made little sense to him. Paperwork had never been his strong point – he didn't need to be good at record-keeping to be an effective killer – but he knew someone who could sift through Wilders' haul and maybe find something the broker could not.

He left the apartment and took a five-minute stroll to the nearest high street and to a mobile phone retailer.

'I'd like to buy a handset,' he said to the awkward teenager who served him. 'Whichever one has the best camera.'

TWENTY

It had been a shrill sound. A polyphonic ringtone, electronic and crass. Raven let it ring in her hand, looking at the little LED display and 'unknown' in place of a caller ID. Should she let it ring? Would they leave a message? She had only a few seconds to decide one way or the other before the call ended. She turned the car key and started up the engine. The dashboard instruments came to life and she tapped on the radio and increased the volume. She pressed one hand flat against one ear while bringing the phone up to the other and accepting the call.

'Yes?' she said, lowering her tone in imitation of the assassin's.

It was never going to be perfect, but with the loud music as background noise, it was enough to convince the voice on the other end of the line to say, 'Is it done?'

'Yes,' she said again.

'Confirmation code, please.'

She squeezed her eyes shut. She had no idea what it could be, or perhaps just asking was a test and silence was the answer. She thought back to her own time working for the Consensus without her knowledge, under the guise of government work, but she had never communicated with her handlers in this way.

In the end it didn't matter. She took too long, because the voice said, 'Miss Stone, I presume.'

She switched off the radio. There was no point in pretending. 'No one calls me Miss Stone. How about *Ms* Stone? Sounds sexy, right?'

'Not quite as sick as your hospital records suggest.'

She produced a weak cough. 'I'm so very poorly. Please send help. I'm all alone and defenceless.'

'I wouldn't feel too smug if I were you. We have many men at our disposal.'

'Great,' she said. 'I'll take them down one at a time. Or send a team. That would be better. It would save me a lot of time.'

The voice on the end of the line said, 'You need to know that we're never going to give up. You're never going to be safe. We're going to keep looking and we're going to find you again.'

'You won't have to look very hard,' she said.

A pause before the voice said, 'Why's that?'

'Because I'm coming for you. Like I came for the others. Like I'm going to keep coming until every last one of you is a corpse.'

'What do you think you can achieve through threats impossible to realise?'

'You say impossible, I say improbable – let's agree to disagree. As for right now, as for this conversation, I've already achieved what I set out to.'

'Which is?'

'Hearing your voice.'

He said, 'My voice tells you nothing.'

'You're a man, obviously. American. You're in your fifties. You have a deep voice, but it has a raspy quality. So you're out of shape. A smoker. A long-term smoker, so it's going to show in your face. Your skin will be thin, your eyes washed out with dark circles underneath. You fumbled and took a while to transfer the phone from one ear to the other, so you're lacking in dexterity, you're not a shooter, you're no field operative. You're a middle-aged, out-of-shape manager. Someone important. Someone who's going to be missed.'

He huffed. 'Do you honestly think it matters that you know some generic details about me? You've just described millions of men.'

She kept watch over the lot as she talked, wary of people leaving the hospital or cars arriving.

She said, 'Yes, I do, because if I were wrong you would do your best to make me believe I was right. Assuming you have any intelligence, and I'll take it as given you're competent. The Consensus have already vetted you in that department. If I were wrong then you would let me lead myself in the wrong direction, but you're not doing that. You're challenging the value of what I know, because it has value. But I lied when I said what I wanted was your voice. It wasn't your voice. I got all that in the first few words.

What I wanted was for you to keep talking so I could listen to what was going on in the background. You've let me talk because you've been trying to learn something about me, something you can pass up the food chain, something of value to cover your failure to kill me. You think you've been playing me but I've been playing you, and whereas you've learned nothing, I've learned plenty.'

There was a long pause as he decided whether she was bluffing or not, whether continuing the conversation would only give her more, but ultimately he needed more now. He needed to know.

He said, 'What have you learned?'

'There's a lot of background noise, so you're speaking outside. I can't hear voices, so you're not on a populated street. You're on a balcony then, because something is amplifying the sound of your footsteps as you pace around, so you're overlooking a back alley with a building only a few metres across the street. That church bell chimed four times, so it's four p.m. where you are. And that's a small engine with a high rev, obviously a moped. It's going a little fast for a back alley, so it's not really a back alley but an actual street. So you're somewhere warm enough to be standing on a balcony at this time of year, in a city where mopeds are common, because what are the odds of an unusual vehicle driving past your balcony? And that rhythmic thump of tyres is caused by paving stones. So, in summary: warm, with lots of churches, narrow paved streets where mopeds are common. I hope you're not just there for work and you have time to see all of the sights. I have to see the Sistine Chapel every time I visit. I just have to.'

She heard him inhale and exhale in a loud, angry breath. 'I'll be gone long before you get here.'

'Ah, so you are just in Rome temporarily. Thanks for confirming that, and that you're there for some business activity. I'll be paying very close attention to what makes the news in the coming days and weeks. How ironclad is your operation, exactly? Because either I'm going to find out what you're doing, or you're going to have to cancel it and explain to your superior how you screwed it up. You'll probably get a second chance, right? These guys are forgiving. Ah, but you've already spent that second chance, haven't you? Because this is not today's first balls-up: your assassin failed to kill me as well. Wow, two failures in the same day. Man, I wouldn't like to be you right now.'

There was a long silence. She heard no background noise so she pictured him with his hand over the phone. Maybe a mouthed expletive or snarl of rage before a moment of calm thought and deliberation, which would lead to panic because there was no way back from what he'd said and she'd learned.

Except one way out, which he came to of his own volition:

'I can help you,' the voice said, 'if you help me in return.'

She smiled at herself in the rear-view mirror. 'How can you possibly help me?'

'You want to know more about them. I have information.'

'And who are we talking about here?' she asked.

'The Consensus – that's what you call them, isn't it?'

'I'm glad that name is finally catching on. What can you tell me that I don't already know?'

156

'You'll help me?'

'What do you need my help for?'

The voice said, 'To stay alive, of course. Like you said: I've already blown my second chance. Now, I either wake up in the middle of the night with a pillow over my face, or I do what you did. I turn against them. I use what I know to protect myself. But I'm no spy, like you. I'm no field agent. I'll need help. I'll need protection.'

Raven said, 'And what do you know in return for that?'

'There's a bank, here in Rome. Roma Investimenti. That's why I'm in the city. They launder money. I have three suitcases of dirty cash to deposit.'

'That would never have made the news.'

'It would next week because the banker who laundered it is going to commit suicide.'

'Why would he do that? Is he depressed?'

The voice said, 'He's going to die because they want to bring down the whole bank. The money is mob money, stolen mob money. The banker is going to leave a suicide note detailing what he's been doing. The bank won't survive the fallout. The corruption goes too deep. It'll land half the board of directors in jail.'

'Why do they want to bring down the bank?'

'How would I know? But I guess they want to destabilise the markets, affect currency prices, you name it. It's above my paygrade. You know how they work.'

'All too well, unfortunately.'

I could have been the one helping the banker to commit suicide.

The voice said, 'So you'll help me?'

'To stay alive? That's not going to work, I'm afraid.'

'But you said—'

'I said nothing. You let yourself think otherwise. Maybe if you were like me and didn't know what you'd landed yourself in I might go out of my way to keep you breathing. But you're no clueless foot soldier. You're a lieutenant. You're an officer. You're like the man who sent me out to do the dirty work.'

'I'm just following orders. That's what we all do.'

'Not me,' she said. 'Not any more. Now, I follow my own orders. And you know what? It feels *great*.'

'They'll kill me. Please.'

Raven said, 'I have more sympathy for the assassin who tried to slit my throat than the man who gave him his orders. I'm glad they're going to kill you. Then it's one less asshole of theirs I have to kill myself.'

'I'll tell them about this conversation. I'll tell them you know about the bank, the banker. They'll be waiting for you.'

'Even better,' she said. 'That would save me tracking them down. But if you did do that, they'd definitely kill you and then you'd blow your only possible option for staying alive long enough to see Christmas. I'll tell you what to do, what I'd do: take all that money and run. Three suitcases full, you said? Wow, that's a lot, isn't it? Probably enough to set you up anywhere in the world with a new identity. Must be a difficult choice: bags of cash or certain death. Jeez, what would I do in your place?'

Silence on the line.

'Shame about your physical condition, though. All those smokes and the spare tyre around your waist are really going to slow you down out there. Rest assured I'll be checking the internationals for an article about a fat American middle-aged businessman who died in Europe under suspicious circumstances.'

'*You bitch.*'

While he screamed obscenities down the line, Raven said in her best cheery tone, 'Great chat. Really good catching up. Take care.'

He hung up before she could.

Despite what she said on the phone she hadn't been in a rush to go to Rome. She didn't know who she was looking for and was nowhere near well enough to travel to a foreign city where Consensus assets could be waiting for her. It would take weeks to recover, to get back her strength and fitness. She didn't know about the long-term consequences. Maybe there would be nerve damage, brain damage, or damage to her cardiovascular system. She was still in pain from the encounter with the assassin, still exhausted from it. She couldn't go after her enemies in Rome in her condition, but she had killed another one with just a phone call. If the guy on the end of the phone line told his superior about their conversation, either freely or under duress, or if he ran with the money, the plan against the bank would be forfeited. The banker wouldn't die in an apparent suicide. The bank wouldn't collapse. No currency or stock or market would be affected. Another scheme destroyed because of her, because of a phone call.

Raven had felt pretty pleased with herself. She still did, a year later.

She would take her revenge, however she could, one bone saw or phone call at a time.

That banker had been most surprised to learn he was going to die, that his former business acquaintances were planning on having him killed. He had taken some convincing, but what she told him about the fifty-something chain-smoking American male she'd spoken to was an uncanny match for his business partner who had drowned while sailing in calm weather. He had thanked her by revealing everything he knew, which included the name of the lawyer who had brokered the deal in the first place. A man named Samuel Cornish.

Echoing heels focused Raven's gaze.

A well-dressed woman approached her.

'Mr Cornish will see you now.'

TWENTY-ONE

Bankers, Raven could handle. They were all the same, pretty much. But Cornish wasn't a banker in the same way no one in the whole bank would qualify as a banker. Cornish was a lawyer, or a solicitor as he would be called in his homeland. British by birth, but holder of an Italian passport, he had been in Italy almost the whole of his adult life. He had an Italian wife – ex-wife – and his kids spoke English only because of Hollywood movies and their favourite singers. Cornish was nationalised, and integrated.

He was also huge, in width as well as height. His face was so round and his jowls and chin so distended that he seemed to have no neck at all. His torso was the shape of a barrel. His elbows were flared because his arms could never hang straight at his sides. He wore a pinstripe suit. Which had to be custom-made, because Raven doubted anyone produced clothes so big that weren't made to order. It must have taken half a cow to make his shoes.

'Good morning, Miss Coney,' he said, standing up from his desk.

He spoke to her in English because she wasn't disguising her own nationality. He had a British accent. Not the classical aristocratic one nor from *Landan* but one of the many others she couldn't hope to identify. She once read that there were more accents per square mile in the British Isles than anywhere else on the planet.

She looked up as he approached to shake her hand.

'Jeez, they build you guys big in England, huh? Must be all that rain making you grow like a plant in a pot.'

He responded with a stilted smile. 'Take a seat, please.'

She did, crossing her legs and resting her hands on one thigh. Cornish returned to his chair behind the desk. She felt sorry for the chair.

In the same way that Cornish wasn't a banker, the room didn't look like the soulless room where a mortgage would be discussed or repayments on a loan negotiated. There were no veneers, no plastic, no grey carpet or magnolia walls. The office was more akin to a study in some grand old villa. The desk was oak with a leather protector. The lamp resting on it was solid brass, as were all the fixtures. He even had a brass letter opener. Neoclassical paintings and sculptures added tasteful, if unnecessary decoration.

This was a room where tax evasion, secret wire transfers and money laundering were the order of business. She could smell it in the air the same way she could read it in Cornish's smug, fat smile.

'How can I help you today?' Cornish began.

'Hard to get a sit down with you guys,' she said in return.

'You've made me wait my turn and then some, haven't you?'

The stilted smile returned. 'We are very busy, yes.'

'I'll say. Took several large deposits just to get through the door.'

'We have an exclusive clientele. What may I do for you?'

'Your website says your aim is to make me as much money as possible.'

'I believe it says that we will endeavour to assist your goal of growing your assets.'

She nodded. 'Yeah, that's it. By helping me evade tax.'

'We describe it as mitigating your tax liabilities. We can do that by assisting with the creation of offshore accounts, investments and other strategies.'

'Yeah, yeah. Other strategies. That's what I'm mostly interested in. What are those, exactly?'

'Miss Coney, I'm afraid we don't really offer such services. We merely help you make the most of the services you require. We help you choose wisely and assist in the implementation, but it has to be your own choice.'

'You're telling me you can't show me a list of what you can do, but if I tell you what I want you to do then you'll do your best.'

He nodded. 'Exactly.'

'I get it. You can't offer an illegal service, because that would be, well, illegal. But if I bring you dirty money then you'll provide the soap to give it a good old-fashioned washing.'

He shrugged with his palms. 'Something like that.'

'Thing is, Sam, what I'm really after is information. To

pay for it, I'm going to leave that money in my account and never take it out again.'

'I don't understand.'

'A year ago, give or take, you had an arrangement with a banker who works at Roma Investimenti.'

Cornish, like a good lawyer, had a great poker face. 'I don't know what you're talking about.'

'Of course you don't, but I can help you remember, don't worry. We're starting off at the legitimate end of your operation, and you'd already made deposits with this bank on behalf of one of your clients. Now, said client was due to give you another few mil of dirty money that was supposed to be deposited like the rest. Only, this cash was traceable, and it was going to bring down the bank when the authorities received a juicy tip-off. Well, that never happened for reasons you don't want to know, but let's just say it involved a bone saw.' She paused while Cornish's eyes widened. 'I know, right? *Messy.* Anyway, I'm doing a little bit of private eye work. I'm a regular Sherlock Holmes in high heels. I want to know the name of your contact. I want to trace the money that you never received. I want to know where it came from.'

'I don't know what you're talking about.'

'You already said that. Word for word, in fact. I imagine it's your go-to line for when someone quizzes you on your work. I call it work, but let's face it, you're a criminal. Criminals don't really work, do they? They lie and cheat and steal, but not work. I know this because I'm a criminal too. They say don't bullshit a bullshitter, but I say don't scam a scammer, don't fight a fighter. *Capisce?*'

Cornish took a moment to respond. She had a bet with herself: if he sat back in his chair she could wear him down, make an offer, bribe, lie, or negotiate an answer; if he sat forward then he was going to take some more ... *convincing*.

Cornish sat forward.

Raven said, 'And here was me thinking it was going to be another boring day. Glad I opted for the sports bra.'

He frowned in confusion, but ignored the comment and said, 'You need to go now, Miss Coney.'

'Done already?' she asked.

He nodded. 'I don't believe I can help your money grow.'

'I'm not looking for it to grow. I'm offering it to you. Grow it for yourself. Stick it in that plant pot where they grew you.'

He stood. 'If you please.'

Her lips turned upwards. 'I don't please easily.'

'Time to go, Miss Coney.'

She twisted her head around, looking at the walls and ceiling. 'No cameras in this room, right? That would violate your clients' privacy. More to the point: no one is going to talk about money laundering if they're being recorded. All the security is in the lobby.'

He stepped around the desk. 'What's your point?'

'My point is that it's just me and you here. All alone. Total privacy.'

'I don't think I understand what you're trying to do. Are you attempting to intimidate me? Because you would have had far more success flirting with me.' He smirked. 'And by far more I mean negligible instead of zero. I think you should leave now.'

'Nah, I'm good.' She shifted in the chair to get more comfortable. The leather squeaked.

'I'll call security.'

'For me? You're three times my size. At least. Won't that make you look like a big pussy? You don't want the security boys making fun of you over coffee, do you? *Sam's scared of girls . . .*'

Cornish stood and rounded the desk. He towered over her, gesturing with his right hand – big and fleshy. 'The door. Please use it.'

She stood too. The hand was too big and too inviting to ignore. Be rude not to accept.

Her own hands snapped out in a blur, grabbing Cornish's and twisting it anticlockwise and back against the joint into a wrist lock. Savage. Sudden.

'Ah,' she said, 'you don't know how good it feels to have full grip strength back.'

Given his size and obvious power, she used both hands, but it was unnecessary. He was a civilian. He was untrained and he was slow. He understood what was happening only when the agony exploded up his arm and he was forced over the desk, taking a good hard shot of oak to the gut in the process.

He was a man. He didn't want to scream. She kept the pressure on the joint to keep him immobile and compliant, but not enough to induce a noise that would draw security.

His teeth were gritted and his fingers red and swollen with trapped blood. Raven scooped up the brass letter opener in her left hand while she controlled the wrist lock with her right.

She had to shuffle her feet to get in position so he could see the blade and Cornish's other hand, braced flat against the desktop, fingers spread.

She spun the letter opener in her palm so the point faced down from her grip.

'We're going to play a game.'

She positioned the letter opener over the desk, over his braced hand.

'I haven't done this for a while,' she said. 'And I don't think I've ever done it with my left hand, but I like a challenge, don't you? What could possibly go wrong?'

She eased the pressure on his wrist enough for him to say, 'Don't.'

'Don't what?'

'Cut me.'

'I'm going to *try* not to, but I make no promises.'

He went to speak again but she turned up a notch on the wrist lock, and only a grunt escaped his lips.

She said, 'Here goes nothing.'

She started from outside his little finger, stabbing the blade down to strike the desk, lifting it fast and bringing it down again, this time in the gap between the little and ring fingers, then the next and the next until she reached the outside of the thumb, then back again, each strike faster than the last.

Raven said, 'This is harder than I thought. How am I doing?'

Cornish's eyes were wide at the blurring golden blade. Panic, fear and pain. He couldn't speak, even had he wanted to.

'Whoops, that was close,' she said. 'Want me to stop?'

She eased the pressure enough for his grunts to become a single word, '*Yes*.'

'Then tell me what I need to know. Who's the bag man? Who brings the money?'

He took a breath, composing himself. 'Paolo Totti.'

'You say that name like it's supposed to mean something.'

'Mafia.'

She shrugged. 'Makes sense. Where can I find him?'

'Anywhere. Everywhere. He's not the sort to keep a low profile.'

'Are you expecting another delivery of cash?'

'I've not been informed.'

She said, 'Don't lie to me,' and increased the pressure on the wrist.

His teeth clamped shut with such force she heard a crack.

'*I'm not*,' Cornish managed to hiss.

She believed him. It was a shame there was no delivery to exploit, but not a disaster. She released him.

For a moment, he didn't react. Surprise. Fear. Pain. All held him back. He didn't know what was about to happen. When he had caught up with the idea he was free of the vicious wrist lock, he let out a gasp that became a sigh. He sank backwards off the desk until he was sitting on the floor, cradling his wrist, the fingers of his right hand in a frozen grip he couldn't open.

'You're insane,' he said.

She nodded. 'But I'm cute.'

'Totti is not the kind of enemy you want to make.'

'Don't worry about me. I can take care of myself.'

'Who *are* you?'

'Someone you would do well to forget,' she said, and then as she approached the door: 'Hey, I know you're divorced, but do you have a girlfriend?'

Cornish hesitated, unsure, but said, 'No. Why?'

'Then I really hope you're ambidextrous.'

TWENTY-TWO

It took some effort to meet. Muir wanted it soon, but it had to appear organic. They didn't imagine Alvarez had a full twenty-four-hour surveillance detail on either of them, let alone both, but precautions had to be taken. Because she ran almost every day, sometimes multiple times a day, it made sense to sync up during one of those. Procter lacked her mobility, but between them they knew how to be discreet. Muir made sure her run took her through a textbook Surveillance Detection Run, that ended up at the right kerb at the right time to get into Procter's Lincoln unobserved.

'No one's following me,' he said as soon as she had closed the door.

She wasted no time. 'Alvarez isn't just after Tesseract, he's after you. And he knows I'm involved.'

She summarised their conversation, leaving aside a significant part, whilst Procter drove. He listened, concern increasing on his face with every passing mile.

'Pull over,' Muir said, 'into that lot.'

'Why?'

'Because I said so.'

Procter did. He stopped the car in front of a strip mall. 'What's going on, Janice?'

'Alvarez also claims not only has Tesseract killed active and former CIA officers, but that you knew about it and covered it up.'

Procter hesitated. That was all she needed.

Muir said, 'Go to hell,' and opened the passenger door.

'Janice, wait. Let me explain.'

'You lied to me, Roland. I told Alvarez *he* was lying.'

She began climbing out. Procter reached for her arm.

She grabbed his hand before it could reach her, and shoved him away. 'Watch it. You do not want me to break your hip all over again.'

'Please, hear me out. It's not what you think.'

'Why should I? You used me.'

'Used you? You're my employee, for God's sake. Did I tell you everything? Of course I didn't – and you knew that.'

Muir paused.

Procter said, 'Tell me otherwise and I won't try and stop you. Tell me you were young and naïve and I exploited you, made you do things you knew were wrong. Tell me that, Janice. Tell me.'

Muir hesitated, like Procter had done, but then she shut the door again. 'You have two minutes.'

'Tesseract was – is – a piece of work, and we've never

pretended otherwise. Can we agree on that? Good. To my knowledge – and I swear to you I'm telling the truth – the only killings of CIA or former CIA agents were in self-defence, barring one: a traitor responsible for all the other deaths, who I helped him kill. Anyone else Alvarez is talking about is nothing to do with Tesseract. I promise you that. Either Alvarez is wrong or he's trying to turn you against me.'

'Roland, you had better be square with me now, because if Alvarez provides the slightest shred of proof that contradicts you, I will tell him everything I know about Tesseract, about you, about what we have done. I mean it. Everything.'

'I can tell you mean it, Janice.'

Muir exhaled to relieve some of the pent-up rage and fear. Procter reached to comfort her. She leaned away, shaking her head. 'I don't need a hug, Roland. I need you to fix this. Alvarez made it very clear. If I don't help him and he doesn't get you, then he'll be happy to settle for me.'

'I will fix this,' Procter promised. 'Don't be afraid.'

'Afraid? I'm terrified.'

'Don't be.'

'Don't tell me not to be scared when I'm being investigated for crimes I actually committed. I'm looking at life without parole just on the charges I can think of, let alone what a DC lawyer out to make a name for himself will drum up.'

'It won't come to that. I swear it.'

'You can't swear it.'

'I'll do everything I can, I can swear that at least.'

'I wasn't made to wear a jumpsuit. Orange is not a good colour for me and it definitely isn't yours.'

Procter said, 'I can handle Alvarez, but I'm going to need your help.'

'I don't know right now if you deserve my help, so I'm not going to sit here and lie to you.'

'I don't expect you to. I just want you to hear me out. I just want you to consider what I propose.'

'Which is?'

'Same as I asked before: meet with Tesseract. Warn him. Convince him to go underground until this blows over.'

'Why? Why me? We're both in Alvarez's crosshairs.'

'You know Tesseract better than I do.'

'You were the one who recruited him.'

'And that was the only time I've ever been in his company. You, you've met him several times. When I spoke to him, he was at my mercy, so to speak. You've spoken to him on his own terms.'

'And I was terrified every single time. Not because he was trying to scare me, but because I never forgot who I was dealing with.'

'That's why I brought you in. That's why I believed you could handle him.'

'I don't think I could say that I ever managed to handle him.'

'He didn't kill you, Janice. That means you handled him just fine.'

'And now? What happens when we do get hold of him, assuming we do? Because this won't be the first time we've put his life in danger. If he wasn't happy about us putting him at risk before, how unhappy will he be now? The first thing he's going to think is that the best way to distance himself from Alvarez is to eliminate us.'

'He won't do that.'

Muir said, 'You just told me that I know him better than you do.'

'I know him well enough to know that even if he doesn't care about doing the right thing, morally, he cares about doing the right thing, tactically. He kills me, you're going to go straight to Alvarez and give him everything because you know you'll be next.'

'But that's not going to happen, is it?' Muir said.

'Why not?'

'Because I'm the one who has had most contact with him. You keep telling me I know him better than you. And I will be meeting him, won't I? I'll be the one most exposed. If he feels threatened, I'm the first problem he's going to solve. If he's going to kill anyone first, it's going to be me.'

'He's not that reckless, Janice.'

Muir sucked in air between her teeth. 'Don't do that. Don't talk down to me. Don't treat me as though I'm over-reacting. I'm not, and I'm not naïve. I'm speaking plainly, that's all. I'm saying it like it is. We're not going to get through this by hoping for the best and we're not going to get through it by being anything less than straight with one another.'

'I'm sorry,' Procter said. 'It won't happen again.'

They were silent for a time.

Muir said, 'If we do nothing, Alvarez is going to find a link to Tesseract eventually, isn't he?'

'Careful as we were, we've left enough of a scent that he's never going to stop until he can put one of us behind bars.'

'And if we inform Tesseract, we expose ourselves to the possibility he'll kill us to protect himself.'

Procter nodded.

'Jesus, Roland, how did it come to this?'

'It's my fault. I reined Alvarez in when I should have let him loose. He's never forgotten that and he's never forgiven me for it.'

'You're saying he's doing all this to get back at you for giving him a hard time?'

'I'm saying that he's blinded by personal anger. That makes him relentless. He might have let this go otherwise. He might have left it to someone else. Someone we could handle.'

'Does anything involving men come down to anything else but ego?'

'Ego's all we have, ultimately. All we are is ego. If we don't protect that, what do we protect?'

'So that's a yes, then.'

Procter said, 'We need to find a way of contacting Tesseract that Alvarez can't intercept, and can't discover after the fact. Any electronic communication we send, no matter how careful, is bound to trip us up. I'm sure that's what he's waiting for. When I thought it was just me he was looking into I figured you would be safe to make contact. Now, after your conversation with him, I think it's too much of a risk.'

'Agreed.'

'So we need to sift through everything we know about Tesseract. Every associate he has. Every place we know he's been. We need to find him first. It's going to be a nightmare, but we don't have a choice.'

Muir buzzed down the door window to get some air and said, 'I already know how to do this.'

Procter said, 'I'm listening.'

'Alvarez slipped up when he threatened me. He told me that Tesseract has worked with MI6. He didn't say how he knew, and I didn't ask, because he wrongly assumed I had made the introduction. He revealed that I've been at a social event with Tesseract's former handler and I will be at one coming up with his current handler.'

'You're sure about that?'

'I deliberately pissed him off and he tried to knock me down a peg, and in doing so he told me something I didn't already know because he figured I had been part of it.'

'So you've never had personal contact with Tesseract's MI6 contact?'

'No, never. Had it not been for Alvarez, I wouldn't have even known he worked for them. And similarly he wouldn't share that information with me even if we'd had contact since I got him in trouble. And we haven't.'

'That's what I thought. But Alvarez seems to think so.'

'He's wrong.'

'Then this is the first thing he's got wrong so far. I would dearly like to know how he's come to this conclusion. But besides handing us a minor victory, how does it help us make contact with Tesseract if we don't know who his handler is?'

'Alvarez said nothing about the former handler being at the next gathering. Which seems telling, don't you think?'

'I follow you. So you're going to check the guest lists for the events in question and find out who was at the previous one but not the one coming up?'

Muir nodded.

'But it's unlikely to leave us with just two people.'

'I know.'

'We're probably going to get several for each.'

'I know.'

'But two of those people are going to have a connection – they'll share a reason as to why Tesseract moved handlers.'

Muir said, 'Now you're in danger of making the same sorts of assumptions as Alvarez.'

'My only assumption is if there is a connection, you'll find it.'

'Create a difficult objective, but show faith in the other person's ability to complete the task ... You taught me all these tricks, remember?'

'Sometimes they're not tricks, Janice. Sometimes I'm just telling the truth.'

'But isn't that the problem for people like us? We spend so much of our time telling lies we can't see the truth when it's staring us in the face.'

Procter regarded her for a moment, then said, 'You've already done all this, haven't you? You've already worked it out.'

Muir nodded. 'I wanted to see if Alvarez was bluffing, so I went over the guest lists of both social events. Earlier this year I was at a reception of some 209 other people. I was there with thirty-three representatives of US intelligence or our affiliates. Cross them off and we're left with the Brits and other foreign nationals. Strike off the latter, obviously. Now, another ninety-seven were British intelligence but not MI6: they worked for MI5, the Ministry of Defence or GCHQ. That leaves us with those that were certifiably MI6. Of those, nearly half are not on the guest list for the next event. If we discount junior roles and the most senior positions, we have just four individuals: two men and two women, nice and egalitarian. I've neither the time nor the resources to pick their lives apart, but one name stands out of those four. His reason for not coming to the next event is just about as good as it gets.'

'He's dead.'

She nodded. 'Shot dead outside his home, in fact.'

'Not by Tesseract, we can assume, else they wouldn't still be using him.'

'Unless it was an internal job. Anyway, it doesn't matter. But if we go with this guy as Tesseract's former handler, that allows us to jump through the entire guest list for the next event and zero in on a single name: Monique Leyland. Oh, I forgot to say they have their own codename for him: Cleric.'

'How did you work out she's Tesseract's – or Cleric's – new handler?'

'Because she now has the dead guy's old job. Which is far too much of a coincidence to be a coincidence. I don't know how long he's been working for them, or even if they're still in contact, but if anyone can get hold of Tesseract without Alvarez knowing about it, it's going to be her.'

'When is this event? Tell me it's soon.'

'Next week.'

Procter exhaled. Relief. Hope. 'It could be a trap. You warned Alvarez against jumping to conclusions and you're doing it yourself.'

'Everything could be a trap, Roland. We'll be as careful as we can be.'

'Then you are going to help? Help us both?'

Muir said, 'I've never shied away from a fight. I'm not going to start now.'

TWENTY-THREE

Victor had the taxi driver drop him off outside the hotel. It was not the usual way he did things – he preferred to take routes less obvious and not share his destination with anyone – but the hotel was set on a hill unnegotiable in a suit and shoes, and the winding driveway was long and steep. Any potential advantage to be gained by hiding his intentions from the taxi driver would be more than offset by arriving at the hotel in a wet and soiled suit, or taking a long walk up the driveway, giving any waiting threats plenty of time to line up a shot.

He gave the man a modest and forgettable tip and bade him good day. As Victor was in the UK, in the historic city of Bath, he adopted an appropriate English accent – something as common and forgettable as the tip he had given.

It was an old hotel that had lost a little grandeur over the years, but there was a stubbornness in its weather-beaten façade that Victor liked. He liked buildings that had endured. It gave them personality. He didn't like modern hotels built for functionality, especially with windows that didn't open, wardrobes that couldn't be moved to barricade the door, and cameras in every hallway. Maybe that was why Leyland had chosen it. She couldn't know how he used wardrobes, but maybe she had deduced his shyness for CCTV. He didn't like that. He didn't like anyone understanding him.

He kept this from his expression as he entered the hotel lounge, which joined the lobby via an open double-doorway. The lounge was a pleasant space to relax and read the papers, else drink coffee or take tea, as he saw Leyland was doing.

She stood to greet him as he neared. Victor shook her hand because that's how normal people behaved and his goal was always to seem just like them. She smiled at him with a certain warmth, as though they were close, as though she was happy to see him. She wasn't playing the same game as Victor, but hers was still a game.

Neither behaved in a way to suggest they knew the other person was acting, nor that they knew the other person knew.

She had a model's height and a gymnast's figure. She wore a knee-length tweed skirt, white cashmere sweater and suede boots. Her black hair was straightened as it had been the last time he had seen her, but it was longer now. The length suited her.

'Sit down, please,' she said.

Two sofas faced each other across a glass-topped coffee table. She swept her skirt as she sat down. He took the sofa opposite. She had already taken the sofa facing the door, so Victor had to break protocol to face her, but he sat in such a way that he could keep watch of his back in the reflection of a nearby window pane. Not ideal, but it would do. There was little chance of an assassination attempt in a busy hotel lounge at eleven a.m.

Leyland asked, 'Can I have anything brought over? Tea? Coffee? Something to eat? The avocado sandwiches are little triangles of pure heaven.'

He was hungry, but he said, 'I'm fine.'

He didn't want to be here any longer than he had to be.

She had chosen to sit as far from the door as possible, in a corner to further isolate them. There were other people in the lounge, but none in earshot.

He had been in her company only three times before today. He had only known her as Monique in their first encounters, but he had since learned her full name to be Monique Cynthia Leyland. She was thirty-two and single, and held two degrees. She spoke French, German, Italian and Latin. Her role as Victor's handler for British intelligence had been inherited from the man who had recruited his services, and Victor didn't trust her any more than he had trusted him. Like her predecessor, though, she had gone out of her way to encourage trust and cooperation.

He had once avoided any personal contact with those with whom he did business, but with his more recent employers he was forced to break that rule. He kept face-to-face meetings rare, and held them only when necessary. All other communication was done via electronic means.

Leyland poured tea from the china pot. It had a swirling

glaze of flowers and birds. The cup and saucer were decorated in the same pattern. She used little tongs to select a sugar cube from a bowl and dropped it into the tea. She stirred with a spoon until the sugar had dissolved, then added a splash of milk and stirred again. She put everything back in its proper place.

'I'm not really a fan of tea, truth be told. But I'm a stickler for tradition.'

Victor couldn't remember the last time he had drunk tea. He quite liked it, but he liked coffee more. The last time he had ordered tea it had been to use as a weapon.

She said, 'How did it go in Bavaria?'

Victor said, 'It worked out as planned, to an extent. Things were a little messy, but Wilders is – was – a subordinate of Phoenix as we suspected. He handled personal interactions. Also as expected the meeting was an ambush, but Wilders wasn't in on it. The kill team were there to assassinate him too. He'd been collecting intel on Phoenix for years as an insurance policy, which I suspect was the ultimate reason Phoenix wanted to get rid of him.'

'Ironic.'

'Isn't it just? Wilders had the information stored in a safe in Zurich.' He removed a thumb drive from a pocket and presented it to Leyland. 'Everything's on there. It was all hard copies so I took pictures.'

'You left the originals?'

He nodded. 'Wilders told me Phoenix didn't know about the apartment, but I'm sure he's looking for it. Wilders wasn't anyone special. He'll have left a trail, and I can't see Phoenix targeting him unless he felt confident he didn't need to extract anything from him personally. So, it's only a matter of time before Phoenix finds the apartment. If he finds an empty safe he's going to think someone – no doubt me – got to the information before him. If Wilders really did collect enough to track him down, then I don't want Phoenix to know I have it. At best, he'll disappear and reinvent himself and I'll never get this close to him again.'

'At worst?'

'He'll double his efforts to protect himself.'

Leyland thought about this as she took possession of the memory stick. 'Yes, then that's especially wise. I'll get cracking on this and see what correlates to our own intel.'

Victor said, 'Do you know the gentleman by the window? The one with the grey jacket.'

She shook her head. She didn't look. 'No, why?'

'He's been glancing at you the entire time I've been here.'

Her expression didn't change. 'You get used to it.'

The sofas were comfortable and low. The padding was soft, made softer as the sofa was old and the material covering the padding had stretched over time. It was a sofa to lounge on, to sink into, to fall asleep on. That made it awkward for Victor to perch on, ready to spring to his feet should it be required. It made him look awkward and uncomfortable, but he would rather that than sit back and be vulnerable. Monique sat back. She was comfortable.

One long leg was crossed over the other and she held the saucer in her left hand while two fingers and the thumb of her right hand gripped the cup of tea. She looked at him through the steam. It was no hardship to look at her in return.

She glanced at a flag flying outside the window. 'They always look so dirty, don't they? Like the flags are ashamed. Like a metaphor for the grubbier side of patriotism, or maybe here we don't have anything to be patriotic about?'

Victor didn't answer. There were many things he didn't understand because he was beyond them or had never experienced them. He would first need to belong somewhere to feel patriotism. Besides, Leyland wasn't looking for a discussion. She was just voicing her thoughts, as people were apt to do. Victor tended to keep his own thoughts to himself. Even those that could do him no harm he was reluctant to share. Sharing was for civilians.

'I hope you're reassured that I'm delivering on my promises,' she said.

'Promises you wouldn't have had to make had one of your organisation not sold intel on me to Phoenix in the first place.'

Leyland sipped tea. 'You're not going to let that go, are you?'

'I want you to maintain focus, yes.'

It was only half the truth. He didn't hold Leyland responsible for another's corruption, but he wanted her to think he did. He wanted her to think so because he didn't want her to know he felt indebted to her, because she had done him a favour when she hadn't needed to do so. He couldn't tell her that without revealing more of himself than he was willing for anyone to know. It was another game of sorts, only this one had far higher stakes.

She said, 'I can promise you this has my every focus. I'm

185

a laser beam of focus, in fact. I want to put you back to work. The world, in case you hadn't noticed, is fuller than it has ever been with tyrants and villainy. Every day you're out there looking for Phoenix, they're out there multiplying like bacteria.'

Victor said, 'I thought you were too clever to be an idealist.'

'A clever idealist is but an optimist. Once we've put this Phoenix business to rest then I can put you back in the field. The sooner the better.'

In a way, she was like Wilders. The only difference being she worked for an intelligence agency and therefore had some legitimacy behind her. Victor had never fooled himself into believing the actions of governments were any more just than those of private individuals, even when he had worn a uniform. Killing was killing, however it was marketed. Defence, regime change, intervention were all terms used to make the unpalatable less so for general consumption. The only real difference between Wilders and Leyland was Leyland made maybe five per cent of what Wilders had earned.

'I trust that eagerness will not result in rushed work.'

'Tut, tut,' she said with a smile. 'You really need to have a little more faith in your friends. Now, if you'll excuse me, I need to catch the train back to London. I have a party to attend in a few hours.'

TWENTY-FOUR

Muir had never been a party girl. She had studied and exercised through her youth and figured fun would come once she had put her career in order. It had, but only through a series of bad choices and regrets. Maybe she should have gone to more parties along the way. Maybe she would feel more comfortable in a sleeveless dress and modest heels and some colour on her lips. Maybe she wouldn't feel so out of place now.

The British intelligence community liked their gatherings, or soirées, as they were fond of calling them. At first, Muir had thought they were a waste of time and had gone along to them only when she had been compelled to by a higher power. She had been naïve then. The Brits just did things their way, in the way they had always done. The gatherings were social occasions – no secret work could be done between quaffing champagne and nibbling smoked salmon canapés – but it was all a distraction. Smoke and mirrors, as they also liked to say.

They held the parties to sniff out the weak links in their allies. They wanted to see who drank a little too much, whose eyes were a little too roving, whose lips were a little too loose. It worked, because the junior analysts and assistant cultural attachés and first-time-in-the-field operatives loved an embassy party. It was the reason they wanted to work in intelligence. They wanted their slice of the juicy glamour pie and it took enormous resolve not to gorge upon it and choke.

Muir had been immune. In part, she knew, because of her natural aversion to parties, but she had never been easy to fool, even as a fresh-faced newbie. The Jedi mind trick only worked on the weak-willed, after all.

'Ah, Janice, how lovely to see you again.'

Air kisses were exchanged. After all these years, Muir still found such Europeanisms weird and awkward. She was good at hiding it, however.

'And you, Donald. I like your tie pin.'

'Oh, thank you. How charming of you to say so. It's quite bourgeois, isn't it? A gift, obviously. Do be a good chum and help us get through all this fizz. I've only gone and ordered too much again.'

Again. She had heard that one before. She had heard all the lines before. She had a few of her own, of course, but she preferred to be the recipient of the lines. It told her far more about the speaker than they could ever hope to learn from her responses.

She played the game a few more times. She did quite

enjoy it, she had to admit. A form of dancing, she thought. The moves were well practised, rehearsed and implemented. But improvisation, rhythm, was everything.

The US Embassy was the venue, even if the party was hosted by the Brits. The special relationship at work. The embassy was a monstrosity of blocky concrete in one of London's most charming and beautiful neighbourhoods. It was almost as if it had been constructed as a deliberate insult to the surrounding buildings. There was a message in its ugliness, in its harsh lines and dark colouring. The building said: *I'm strong and I don't care that I don't belong here.*

Muir didn't like that. It was a bullying posture. Friendship was about respect, not power. But were allies anything more than friends of convenience?

She had no more time to think about it because she saw Monique Leyland had entered the room. She couldn't have been there long because she was hard to miss. London was a diverse city, but the intelligence community was not, despite recent initiatives to change that. Leyland stood out because she was one of the few people in the room who could not be described as pasty. She had dark skin and her impressive height was made taller still by lethal heels and a long evening gown that Muir would consider too risqué for the bedroom. Leyland somehow managed to stand both rigid and relaxed. Her neck was long, made longer by her black hair fixed up with clips and a backless dress.

Muir felt shorter and more plodding just looking at her.

She waited until the right moment and approached, wasting no time in an effort to look casual. If Alvarez had someone watching, there was no way to avoid that gaze, and any preamble only gave that watcher more opportunity to gain an advantageous position.

Muir introduced herself, formal and full: 'Janice Muir, CIA.'

She offered her hand and the other woman took it. Her grip was light and their handshake fleeting.

'Monique Leyland, Secret Intelligence Service.'

Muir smiled to herself.

Leyland asked, 'What is it?'

'I just wonder why I used the acronym while you used the full title?'

'I wonder why too.'

'It's nice not to have to say Department of Justice or suchlike. What do you normally say, Ministry of Defence?'

Leyland nodded and showed a small smile of her own. 'It helps though, doesn't it? To stay in practice. Lying, that is.'

'It's a skill like any other. Use it or lose it.'

'How are you enjoying the party?'

Muir held up her glass, untouched. 'Trying not to get too drunk, you?'

'I sip only if it seems impolite not to do so.'

'I like the way you said that.'

'I thought you might. I recognise your name, I think. A report on terrorist financiers in Europe, I believe.'

'God, that was a long time ago. In my early days at the Agency. I'm amazed you remember it let alone who wrote it.'

Leyland said, 'I'm good with names. I'm even better at remembering those who impress me.'

'I would have come over earlier if I'd known you would be this nice.'

'And there was I, thinking this was simply happenstance.'

'Is anything?'

'In this business, probably not. But I can but hope that there is life outside of it.'

'Do you see much of that?' Muir asked. 'If so, please tell me where it's hiding.'

'I wouldn't want it any other way.'

'Me neither.'

'So, given that we are both married to our work, and that this conversation is not mere chance, perhaps you could tell me what you're after, Miss Muir?'

'Please, call me Janice.'

'Only if you call me Monique.'

'Sure.'

'Then, Janice, what can I do for you?'

Muir said, 'I don't suppose it would do much good to pretend this is just an informal chat?'

'Not much,' Leyland agreed.

'I'm hoping we can work together,' Muir said.

'Of course. That's what our agencies do on a daily basis. But as for you and I, I'm not sure how our responsibilities align.'

'I'm talking personally.'

Leyland positioned herself a little closer. 'What sort of work?'

'Data sharing, you could say.'

'And what data would we share personally that our larger organisations do not?'

Muir said, '*Would* not.'

'Go on.'

'I need to know whether you're in.'

'The answer is no,' Leyland said, 'unless I know a lot more.'

Muir said, 'I can't tell you any more unless you're onside.'

Leyland was silent for a moment. Muir said nothing further. Around them the party continued. Chatter. Laughter. Leyland looked at Muir with an analytical gaze. Muir let her.

'Of course you won't say more unless you have assurances from me,' Leyland began. 'I fully expected you to say that, and at the same time you must have known I couldn't agree to what you asked of me. You're hardly fresh out of the Farm. Which makes me wonder what possible reason you could have for asking. It's a waste of time for both of us, but you've done it anyway. Which leads me to believe someone made you do it, which would have to be a superior, so they are hugely incompetent to force you into doing something you must have argued would be unsuccessful. But, as much as we Brits like to joke you guys are a bit dim, it's no truer than the idea we all love fish and chips. And that leads me to think your superior sent you all the way here just to keep you out of the way. But that seems extreme, and again incompetent, because you would see through that in the same way I would, negating the rationale. Hence, there must be some other reason why you asked me a question when you already knew how I would answer.' She thought for a moment. 'You never expected me to say yes, which means you never needed me to say yes.'

Leyland thought for a moment more.

'But that doesn't really ring true, does it? So, the only possible reason behind this charade is that it's played out as you expected, as you wanted, which is meaningless unless that matters to someone other than me or you or your superior. We're talking about someone else. Someone not here. Someone who is going to ask me about this conversation. They're going to want to know what you asked and what I said, and you want them to hear the truth.'

Muir produced her card and passed it to Leyland. As well as her formal contact details it had a phone number scrawled in pencil on the otherwise blank reverse side.

Leyland said, 'So this someone else is going to tell me what this is all about, and after they do I'm going to want to contact you. I see. Then this affects me as well as you, because why else would I want to call you?'

Yes, Muir thought, it was exactly like dancing.

She said, 'Enjoy the rest of the party,' and backed away into the crowd.

TWENTY-FIVE

Yvette told people she was alive only because she drank so much gin the alcohol in her blood killed off every microbe, virus or parasite before it could take hold and do any damage. She said it to make people laugh. At most, she drank a couple of glasses of Hendrick's at the weekend, and always with plenty of tonic. Indian tonic, of course. And lime. Lots of lime. When she told the customer her joke, he smiled. Which was unusual. She told the gin joke so often she could say without hubris that she had mastered it. Everyone laughed. Maybe not always a gut-bursting roar, but at least a chuckle. Not this customer. No laugh. Just a wee smile.

The customer was a short, sweaty man, overweight and ugly. An American in his forties, dressed smart, but in cheap clothes. Yvette could tell a suit with more polyester than wool just from the way the jacket hung from the shoulders. She could see the low thread count of the cotton shirt even without the semi-transparency caused by his perspiration.

His smile was the sickeningly polite, fake smile people used. Yvette had been on this fair earth long enough to know how fake and phoney people could be to her, to one another, to themselves.

A sweaty, phoney man. She disliked him immediately.

Unlike him, Yvette could fake it. She was polite and courteous because she had good Scottish manners. She had been raised well, had lived well and was approaching her final years with that same wellness.

Given the disappointing response to the gin joke, Yvette decided to put an end to the small talk and skip the conversation ahead to business. Not because she wanted to make a sale, but because she wanted to get rid of this sweaty man as soon as possible.

'How may I help you today?'

'I read a lot,' he said. 'I need some more books.'

'Well,' she began with just the right amount of sarcasm, 'you've come to the right place.'

Her little bookshop overlooked a wide swathe of Aberdeenshire greenery. It was called The Bookshop on the Green, which she had named after a long-ago holiday with Harry. They had visited a small town in rural France where they had been surprised to find a book store with that name, run by a retired English couple, who had named their shop in English just to annoy the patriotic French locals. After Harry died and Yvette sold up their marital home and downsized, the money she made on the sale was enough to start her own bookshop, which she named after the shop in that French village because Harry had found much humour in that small act of rebellion, of provocation. He had been English too. Maybe his only imperfection.

Yvette sold used books and plenty of oddities too – maps and classic movie posters, decades'-old board games and forgotten collectables. The shop didn't really make any money, but she owned it outright and her expenses were minimal. It generated some pocket money and kept her busy during her retirement. Except on Thursdays and Sundays, when the shop was closed. On Thursday she played cards and on Sunday she went to the local church, if not to pray – *sorry, Lord* – then to flirt with the widowers. Most of them were too prudish or too dim to realise, but persistence was a girl's best friend. Faint heart never won fair gentleman, or whatnot.

The sweaty American was no gentleman. He didn't have that air. Yvette had learned over a long life that it was in how a man carried himself that she could read his personality. A man in a rush was unreliable, he was lacking in attention, he was unperceptive and often rude. A man who took his time was aware of himself and his surroundings and his place in the world. That was the man who made a good husband, as her Harry had been. He was never late. He was never impolite. He considered other people at all times.

The customer couldn't have been more different to Harry. This was a man who wasn't polite, was in a hurry and lacked anything resembling class. She couldn't help but notice the cheap suit jacket was too big for him too. She remembered her mother's wisest of words: If you have any spare room you're only going to end up filling it.

'Like I say, I read a lot, but I don't keep up to date with what's new or good. I tend to go off recommendations. So, I was wondering if you wouldn't mind picking some books out for me.'

Yvette loved to recommend books, and in other circumstances would happily name some of her favourite authors or novels. But she did not waste her time or passion on this phoney man.

She said, 'How many would you like?'

He shrugged. He hadn't thought his request through.

To expedite the process, she suggested, 'How's five sound?'

'Perfect.'

She shuffled from behind the counter and moved around the store to find the five books she hated the most. This took some time because Yvette had been putting her knees through their paces for pushing eight decades. The customer, as impolite as he was sweaty, didn't offer any assistance.

He said, 'You know, my sister is the big reader in my family. She loves books, that girl. Always got her face buried in the pages of some story.'

'Women read more than men, I'm sorry to say. Boys are missing out.'

He nodded in quiet thought for a moment. 'I expect you wouldn't guess from my accent that I came from these parts, once upon a time. Moved to the States when I was a boy.'

She didn't care, but her manners meant she couldn't be rude so she said, 'I never would have guessed.'

She rang up the purchases and he paid in cash. Everyone did because she had no electronic payment methods, but most folk these days wanted to pay with a card and were annoyed when they had to fish around in their pockets or purses for cash.

'I was born over in the next town,' he said as he took his change. 'Haven't been back for years though. I went to Saint Augustine's Comprehensive. Truth be told, I'm hoping to bump into my high school sweetheart, Suzanne. Don't suppose you know anyone of that name?'

Why he insisted on making small talk was beyond her, but she decided it was his innate crudeness, his lack of manners, his lack of class. He was doing his best to imitate a gentleman, but failing miserably.

Yvette hid her thoughts as she said, 'I don't know any Suzanne, but I know the school. I mean, you can't miss it, can you? But I can't say I've had much to do with it.'

The customer's sweaty face changed, as if that imitation was now too much effort to maintain in his disappointment. 'Oh, I see.'

Now it was Yvette's turn to fail to hide her true feelings. She was agitated because he knew what she meant: she had no children. She did not like the sympathetic tone people were apt to use. She wanted no sympathy. God had chosen not to bless her in this way.

There was an awkward silence.

The customer said, 'I'll be on my way. Thank you for these.'

She watched him leave and as she watched him stroll along the street some curiosity made her leave the counter to move to the window so she could continue to watch him.

He reached a parked car – some showy thing that didn't impress Yvette – and opened up a rear door to toss the books on to the back seat in a manner that showed no respect to literature and angered her more than his misplaced sympathy.

Yvette hoped to never see him again. There was something about the man that she didn't trust. It wasn't just his fake smile or his cheap clothes. It wasn't his sweatiness or his phoniness or his Americanness or even the misplaced sympathy or the way he treated his purchases. It wasn't just that she disliked him.

There was something about him that made her afraid.

TWENTY-SIX

Monique Leyland lived in that darkest of dark zones, known as South of the River. London was north of the Thames, according to Londoners who lived north of the Thames. On the other side was a no man's land few dared venture into. A semi-civilised apocalypse, as one of her colleagues was keen on claiming. It was all bollocks, of course. Except that London, like the United Kingdom as a whole, was rooted in classism. Leyland came from a bad stretch of the south-east named Deptford. Her parents had moved there way back when there were only three channels on the television and some pubs still carried signs reading *No Dogs, Blacks or Irish*. They had sweated and laboured with the odds stacked against them to give her and her siblings the best chance they could. She had resisted the teenage temptations that waylaid many of her classmates and charged through higher education with the fever of purpose that would not be bridled by money, background or skin tone. She still lived south of the river, but she had moved on from the crowded urban melting pot of Deptford to the leafier suburbs of Greenwich. A stone's throw away, geographically, but a world apart otherwise.

She had a terraced house that she couldn't really afford, but her outgoings were small beyond the essentials, and with a steady government job she had been able to get a mortgage back in the days when London was still affordable to young singles. She couldn't imagine living anywhere else. She loved her job, her family and the city.

Except on days like today. A humid day in London was a hellish thing. The English, and their nation, were simply not designed for it. Air conditioning was some futuristic utopian dream impossible to realise. She sweated on the tube. She sweated on the overland train. She sweated on the bus. Sod the Indian summer.

The walk up the hill from the railway station almost became a water slide back down.

By the time Leyland had showered and dressed and cracked open that first bottle of beer the evening had cooled to something tolerable. She had her French doors open and along with the warm evening air, the occasional mosquito buzzed inside that she was happy to swat with bare hands. Her neighbour had a pond.

She had a couple of pork chops frying on the stove next to a pan in which corn on the cob boiled. Sweet potato wedges roasted in the oven. It would have been easy, and satisfying, to ignore her ringing house phone, but she had been in the business too long to let a ring go unanswered for long.

She said, 'Yes?'

Leyland never gave her name. The person calling should know who to expect, and if they didn't then she would be hanging up pretty fast.

She didn't recognise the voice at first, because it had a neutral accent. Something middle class and austere, quintessentially English, yet modern and relaxed – an average kid done good; well educated and well travelled. Worldly. She heard such accents all the time in her job. The old boy network had almost been phased out. The Oxbridge mafia days were over. Progress. Diversity. Thank God.

But this accent, common enough and ordinary as it seemed, was different from the one she had heard the first time they'd spoken. Then it had been Eastern European, Baltic. Something harsher, but at the same time subtle. It was the tone she had heard before, the tone she recognised.

The man she knew only as Cleric said, 'I apologise for calling you unannounced.'

She replied, 'You've never struck me as a man who is sorry for his actions.'

'Manners cost nothing.'

'But I was expecting you to be in touch.' Leyland felt the urge to shut the French doors. 'How did you get this number, by the way?'

'You gave me your card a long time ago, if you remember.'

'My card had my work details only. This is my home number. It's unlisted.'

'I have ways and means.'

She said, 'I assume this call relates to the message I sent you regarding the visit I had from your former paymasters.'

'Naturally. You need to turn your food, by the way.'

Leyland said, 'What?'

'The chops are burning. You need to turn them.'

She would have said, 'How do you know that?' but she realised he was in the room.

She turned to face him. He stood in the living area, close to one wall so he wasn't exposed by the large window. There was no light on in that room, but she recognised his silhouette. Her first instinct was to look at the hands, which she was relieved to see held only a mobile phone.

She hit the end-call button on the handset and set it down. 'Do you make a habit of sneaking up on people?'

'It's in the job description.'

He was right. The pork chops did need turning. She checked the wedges too. They were done and she used oven gloves to take the tray out and shake them into a bowl.

'Did you wreck my alarm?'

He said, 'You're going to need to call out the engineer.'

Leyland sighed. 'It was an expensive system.'

'That's why I had no choice but to break it.'

'The point of an alarm like that is to stop someone like you, not cause you some difficulties.'

'No alarm is going to stop someone like me, but I did my best to disable it without causing irreparable damage. I didn't want to leave you with the cost of replacing it. I don't imagine SIS pays all that well.'

'How thoughtful. And accurate. I dare say it takes me a year to earn what you do from a single contract.'

'I don't want to sound conceited, but it probably takes you more like ten.'

'Fancy paying off my mortgage?'

'I give a lot to charity as it is.'

She drained the corn and took a homemade dipping sauce from the refrigerator. The sauce was made from pureed spinach, raw garlic and olive oil and went well with the wedges. She slid the pork chops on to a plate and set the food down on the kitchen table.

'That smells good,' Cleric said. 'It's been a long time since I had a home-cooked meal.'

She gestured to the bowl. 'Would you like a wedge?'

'Very much so.'

He stepped out of the lounge and into the kitchen. His actions were slow and unthreatening but she couldn't help feeling a little nervous having a hired killer in her home.

'Beer?' she asked.

He shook his head and picked a sweet potato wedge from the bowl on the table. He took a bite before she could say, 'Careful, they're a little spicy.'

He coughed. A lot.

She poured him a glass of water and placed it on the table before him and tried not to laugh.

'If I didn't know better,' he said, 'I would think you're trying to kill me.'

'I assumed you could handle a little fire, but I suppose I grew up with jerk-spiced food so what I think of as spicy isn't on the same scale as yours.'

'It caught me unawares.'

'Sure it did.'

She finished assembling her meal and sat down at the

kitchen table. It was too big for the space, but an impressive piece of furniture. The oak was so thick she fancied its chances of stopping a bullet should things turn bad.

'I'm going to eat,' Leyland said. 'I've had a long day and I'm starving. There's not enough to share, because you didn't tell me you were coming.'

'I'm okay with keeping the skin of my throat intact.'

She smiled and ate for a moment. He looked through the window. In part to check for threats, she could tell, but also because he was trying to be polite and not watch her eat.

After she had swallowed she drank from the beer bottle. 'Look at us, meeting again so soon. People will start to talk. I take it you're suspicious of Muir's warning to keep your head down.'

'The last time I worked for the CIA it led to a huge mess. I was happy to wash my hands of them when your old boss tracked me down. I'm not happy that they're still making my life difficult. I'd like to know your take on it before I decide how to handle it.'

'Muir seems like a straight arrow to me. I don't think she's setting you up, if that's what you're thinking. As for Alvarez, I've done a little homework on him. He was CIA, working in Clandestine Services for Roland Procter, but he's recently taken a role for the Director of National Intelligence, which puts him above his old boss. He's a big deal now, and seems to have made catching you a priority, given the heat he's putting on your old handlers. They're in his sights too, according to Muir. They want you to disappear as an obvious precaution.'

'They want to protect their own skins.'

Leyland nodded. 'Who doesn't? But Muir was gracious and clever enough to give me plausible deniability.'

'Alvarez made contact with you?'

She shook her head. 'Not directly. It would be a foolhardy play on his part to try and beg or barter with a foreign intelligence officer, but he put in an official request with SIS for information on you. And given that our association is sensitive, that might have put me in a difficult position. I can't very well lie to my director, can I? But Muir ensured I wouldn't have to. She was nicely vague about why she needed my help. Of course, when the request came in it was easy to discern the reason. I had a diplomatic attaché from the DC embassy courier a secure burner phone and she filled me in on the rest of the details.'

Cleric was quiet for a time. She left him to his thoughts while she continued with her meal. Eventually, he said, 'Why are you helping them?'

'We're allies, for one. And we have a shared interest in you.'

'Are you saying that you'll be similarly in trouble if Alvarez catches up with me?'

'I'm saying that I don't want a useful asset to be thrown away without a key. And if I can avoid any difficult questions in the process, then that's an added bonus. But, whatever my interests, they align with your own.'

He was quiet for a while. She carried on eating, then said, 'Do you know why?'

'Why?'

'Alvarez has made you a priority. What have you done to warrant this?'

'I'm a bad person.'

206

'I suppose I don't want to know,' Leyland said. 'What you've done in the past is none of my business. I'm interested in what you can do. Maybe you are a bad person, but maybe you're necessary. We all set out to do the right thing, but some of us realise the best way to achieve that isn't always by doing the right thing. Your handlers across the Pond knew that. My predecessor knew it. I know it. Alvarez isn't of the same mindset, apparently. He's – how do they put it? – a boy scout. But this is personal to him too. I know how you boys don't like to lose.'

'How did Muir know to contact you in the first place?'

'I was curious too. It transpires that Alvarez inadvertently tipped her off to our arrangement. So yes, it would seem that the file on you that ended up in Phoenix's hands also found its way to him.'

He didn't get angry, as she had expected, to learn that his involvement with British intelligence had given him not one, but two, powerful enemies. Instead, he asked, 'How is that even possible?'

'I have no idea. But it's another reason to get to Phoenix.'

'Has Wilders' stash been of any use?'

'Not yet, I'm afraid. There's a lot to go through. I'll contact you as soon as I have anything.'

He nodded. 'I understand. How did Muir seek you out?'

'Embassy party,' she explained. 'Pre-planned, which was fortunate.'

'So you're not likely to meet her again.'

'Our paths aren't due to cross.'

Cleric said, 'Can you find out any other travel arrangements she has?'

'I already know. She's due in Helsinki in a week or so for a few days to give a series of lectures at the university. She told me in case I needed to talk to her in person. Why?'

'Because I want to know more about the threat Alvarez poses.'

She put down her knife and fork. 'Is that wise? Alvarez is bound to have her under surveillance. He probably had her shadowed at the embassy party. It's not a stretch to imagine him anticipating a face-to-face between you and Muir. Could very well be a trap.'

Leyland wasn't often surprised, but what Cleric said next couldn't have been more unexpected.

'I certainly hope so.'

TWENTY-SEVEN

Kevin Sykes didn't hear the doorbell at first because he woke up hungover. The piercing shrill of the bell permeated his unconsciousness and triggered waking, but his alcohol-ravaged brain was slow to power up and slower to understand. He felt terrible.

He didn't have a headache – not really – but he had that feeling in his stomach, the nauseating sickness that only booze could produce. It seemed to pulse out from his core, infecting his entire body with gut rot, making him feel in the clutch of some lab-created pathogen. The nausea made him woozy; made him breathe hard; made him feel like his insides belonged outside.

Sykes drank to sleep. He drank to forget. All the classic reasons. He would spend these early waking hours regretful as he nursed his self-inflicted sickness. He had to stop, he knew. He told himself every time. He was killing himself, for sure. He was no longer young or fit and healthy. He had never taken care of himself beyond a youthful vanity. He had nightmares of looking in the mirror and finding his skin had taken the yellow tinge of jaundice. When the gut rot was at its worst he wondered if this was the day his liver gave up on him. Every irregularity in his mouth and throat was the beginnings of a tumour.

He hadn't yet begun drinking in the day, but he knew it was coming. Once, he had waited for it to get dark, but in the summer the wait was too damn long. So, the evening had been the boundary. At first, anyway. Because when did the evening begin? After six p.m.? After five? Five was the cut-off point, he had concluded after much careful thought. It was almost about the time he had shrugged off the day's hangover to such an extent that tomorrow's inevitable repeat didn't seem so bad.

The doorbell rang again. This time there was no mistaking the sound. It hurt his brain as much as the gut rot hurt his stomach.

He dragged himself off the sofa. It was slow and hurtful to do so. He couldn't remember the last time he had slept in the bed. The sofa had a woollen throw that he had bought for decoration in the days before he drank every night. Now, he sometimes used it as a blanket, but only when it was cold outside.

'*All right*,' he yelled, as he neared the front door.

He didn't bother to get dressed because it was Saturday morning – afternoon, when he checked his watch – he had on a pair of boxers and an undershirt. He looked a state, but no one would judge him for getting shit-faced on a Friday night. It was only the rest of the week he had to be careful. He didn't want his colleagues or superiors picking up on his problem. He carried around eye drops to ease the bloodshot appearance and would slap his cheeks before interacting with people to put some colour into them. For the same reason he used a different store each night, and never shopped only for alcohol. He bought food too or cleaning products, spreading out his weekly needs in case anyone was observing him and to hide his habit from those serving him. Even so, it was tough to pretend he needed all those limes.

He figured it would be the postman with something to sign for, but when he heaved open the door he saw Alvarez on his doorstep.

'Hey, Kevin,' Alvarez said. 'May I come inside?'

'What do you want?' Sykes said when the surprise had worn off.

'I want you to put some trousers on. You'll scare the neighbourhood kids with those legs. How do they manage to hold you up, anyway?'

Sykes frowned, and sighed, and swallowed. He gestured for Alvarez to come inside and he led him to the lounge.

'Party for one?' Alvarez said, wincing at the smell while Sykes fished his trousers from the floor and pulled them on.

'Why are you here?' Sykes asked, zipping himself up.

Alvarez's gaze passed over the collection of empty bottles of booze – too many scattered around the coffee table to be explained away – and the fast-food containers.

'You need to sort yourself out,' Alvarez said.

'Who are you to tell me what I need?'

'I care about your well-being, even if you once pointed a gun at my face.'

211

Sykes looked away. 'I didn't pull the trigger.'

'Hey, no hard feelings,' Alvarez was quick to add. 'But, let's face it, you'd have probably missed. You're no shooter.'

Sykes headed to the kitchen in search of coffee. Coffee with a hangover was all he could handle. He couldn't stomach the thought of food just yet. He was in the hangover paradox: he was ravenous, but the very idea of eating made him want to throw up. It was a familiar sensation. It would pass. The first step was caffeine. Then in an hour maybe some dry toast. By lunchtime he would be okay to eat something substantial. Something greasy. At one time he had kept orange juice in the fridge to help fight off the hangover – long experience had taught him its benefits in such a capacity – but long-term alcohol abuse had irritated the lining of his intestines to such an extent orange gave him worse nausea than the drink.

'I'm over the whole gun-in-the-face deal,' Alvarez added. 'But it's still hard to believe that you got away with it. Some of us are just lucky, I guess.'

'Yeah,' Sykes said without commitment.

'And what good did it do you?'

Sykes settled on a glass of water because he'd forgotten to refill the drip machine and it now seemed like far too much effort. 'I made a mistake back then. I'm paying for it. What's your point? Why are you bringing this up again?'

'Because whatever prison you've created for yourself is a hell of a lot roomier than a cell in a supermax. Not so easy to get hold of Johnnie Walker and Domino's behind bars.'

'You can't threaten me. I have protection.'

'I know, I know. All those lovely documents proving you

were following orders. A regular hero, working undercover to root out corruption.'

Sykes didn't try to keep the smugness from his tone when he said, 'That's what it says in black and white.'

'Irrefutable, I know. Bulletproof.'

'That's right,' Sykes said.

'Didn't you get some sort of medal?'

'A commendation.'

Alvarez sniffed one of the empty whiskey bottles. 'What you are is a mess, Kevin. These people you work with now over at that lobbying firm didn't know you before. They didn't know the Sykes I knew. You look like dog shit. You look ten years older.'

'Stop talking about how I look.'

'I'm telling you to give you some perspective, not to make you feel bad. You may think you have it together because no one sees all this, but you don't. You need to get yourself sorted out.'

Sykes said, 'Your concern is touching.'

'I have your best interests at heart.'

'Only because you've been using me.'

Alvarez nodded. 'I don't want you to drink yourself to death when I might need you again. You're right about that.'

'I've told you what I know. I can't tell you anything beyond that.'

Alvarez nodded again. 'And I'm grateful. You filled in plenty of blanks for me about your boy Tesseract and all that other good stuff. It's really helped me put pressure on Procter.'

'I'm delighted for you,' Sykes said.

'But you had better not have held anything back,' Alvarez continued. 'I had better not find out you know more than you've told me.'

Sykes shook his head. 'I wouldn't. I told you what I knew to keep me out of this, not to get myself in deeper. I'm done with all that. I just want to get on with my life. I want to move on.'

'What life are you talking about exactly?' Alvarez asked, not expecting an answer. 'This?' he toed a pizza box. 'Tell me about Poland.'

Sykes was hesitant. 'What about Poland?'

'Since our agreement I've found out that you were once in charge of an enhanced interrogation at a black site outside of Warsaw, correct?'

Sykes didn't answer.

'You don't need to confirm it and it's pointless to deny. I've spoken to one of the contractors you were there with. Nice British fellow. Such a character. Salt of the earth, you know? I've a signed statement from him swearing you were there. You see, that's what happens when you use freelancers for your dirty work. They got no loyalty.'

'If you had such a statement, if I was there, then I was following orders.'

'That's my point, Kevin, and that's something you didn't tell me. I'm giving you that one pass because I like you. I feel sorry for you.'

Sykes didn't respond.

'The thing you need to remember about Procter is that he's been getting away with this kind of thing his entire career. I'm going to bring him down for what he's done and he knows it, so he's doing exactly what your first instinct is to do: deny everything. Which means he's not going to back you up about what happened in Poland because that's only going to expose him more than he is already. He's not going to admit to sending you there because he's got to explain *why* he sent you there. Are you following where I'm going with this or do I need to spell it out?'

'I got a C in English.'

Alvarez smirked. 'I can't come after you about your association with the killer or what you did while you were "undercover", but those bulletproof documents of yours do not protect you from what happened since then. Only Procter can do that, and you're just about the last person on this planet that he would risk himself to protect. So, if I come after you about what you did in Poland, then you're all on your lonesome when it comes to the unauthorised rendition and torture of an American citizen. A piece of shit, granted, but still a citizen. He still had rights that you violated the hell out of.'

Sykes said, 'What do you want from me to leave me alone?'

'There's the Sykes I know. That Sykes gets a gold star for interpretation. You know what I want: I want Procter and I want the killer.'

'Not me?'

'Maybe I was premature giving you that gold star. I don't want you, Kevin. I don't care what you did. I don't even care you pointed a gun at me. You were just an errand boy. You're a no one. You were nothing then and you're nothing now. You're less than nothing.'

Sykes looked away.

Alvarez said, 'I want you to think. I want you think real hard. If there's anything else you know, anything that can help me, now's the time. If I find out you've not been honest with me then I'll ask Procter about Poland just to get my revenge. I'll record him so I can play you his denial. I think he'll say something like . . .' He lowered his tone in imitation of Procter. '"I have no knowledge of Mr Sykes' activities in Poland at that time. Anything he did, he did without my orders." That sounds like him, right? That sounds like something he would say.'

Sykes said, 'I don't know anything else. Like you said, I'm nothing.'

'Okay. I'm going to believe you because I want to. I want to believe you've changed. You've made a lot of bad choices, but you're capable of doing what's right too. I hope that's who you are now.'

Sykes answered with a weak nod. 'I'm trying to get back on the right track. I really am.'

'I know,' Alvarez said. 'Everyone deserves a second chance. Even you.'

TWENTY-EIGHT

Tiger stripes of colour filled the sky above Rome – the clouds forming thin strips of black silhouetted over the orange sunset. Not twilight, Victor thought, but not yet night either. The slim period between, only visible when facing what was left of the sun, where it could still colour the sky, darkness elsewhere. The rooftops blurred together to form a jagged horizon between. A glimmer of light from a faraway aircraft was almost star-like. He tried to imagine the passengers on board, their lives and relations, connections. Impossible to understand, beyond his experience and comprehension. He could smell perfume on the air as she neared.

Raven looked the same as Victor remembered. She was tall and slim, but not weak. He knew, again from experience, that she could handle herself and handle herself well. Like Victor, she was deceptive in her strength. She carried herself with grace and poise, her posture straight yet relaxed; always ready to explode into action. Unlike his, her clothes were more stylish than practical. The cut of her suit was a little too flattering to offer the best manoeuvrability. The heels of her shoes were a little too high for running at maximum speed.

He understood the reasoning. She was a woman, an attractive woman, and if she dressed down too far it would draw her the wrong kind of attention. *Why didn't she make the most of herself?* She didn't want potential threats identifying her that way. She would rather turn all heads than only the wrong ones. There were changes, though, from when he had last seen her. The hair was different. It was shorter than it had been. Then, shoulder length. Now, it reached the nape of her neck. Her skin had a darker tone too, nearer the colour of caramel than the cappuccino shade he remembered. Her eyes hadn't changed. They were as black as his, if not more so. Even in the dim light it was hard not to stare at them.

She smiled at him.

'My, my,' she said as she stopped before him, 'if it isn't the man who killed me.'

'You look good for a corpse, Constance.'

The smile disappeared. She sighed. 'I'm more annoyed about your insistence on using my given name than the whole killing me. Please, call me Raven. Call me anything but Constance. I've told you I don't like it. I've never liked it. I don't mind Connie. Call me that, if you insist on ignoring my wishes.'

'You're not a Connie,' he said.

She blew out some smoke. 'And is that a good thing or a bad thing?'

'It's no thing,' he explained. 'Connie is a nice name, but it's not you.'

'Neither is Constance,' she said. 'But that doesn't stop you. Why here?'

It was a small square, with few people nearby, but lots of ways in and out. There were bars surrounding it. A hot-dog stand in one part.

Victor gestured at it. 'These are hard to find in Rome.'

She turned up her nose. 'With good reason. Just seeing it here is an insult to Italian cuisine.'

The young guy serving the hot dogs was dressed in red, white and blue. He handed Victor his order – extra onions, extra mustard, extra ketchup.

Victor took a huge bite from the hot dog. Raven looked on with untempered disgust.

He chewed for a short moment – between the soft dog and softer bread it didn't take long – and wiped his mouth with a serviette.

He said, 'What?'

'Do you actually know what's in one of those things?'

He nodded. 'I do, and I choose not to think about it.'

'You spend your entire life just trying to stay alive, and yet you're happy to kill yourself a little at a time. I don't get it.'

He gestured to the hot dog, said, 'This may not be good for the body, but it's great for the soul,' and took another bite.

He smiled at her as he chewed.

She looked away. 'I think I'm going to vomit.'

He swallowed and motioned to the young guy. 'I'll have a second one of these when you're ready.'

Raven said, 'Cancer and heart disease aside, you should

be more careful. I think you've put on some weight.' She glanced at his midriff.

Despite himself, Victor glanced too, and before he could utter a hasty defence he saw she was smiling, not because she was right but because she had made him look, because she had made him doubt himself.

'Still annoying then,' he sighed.

She grinned. 'And you're as boring as ever.'

'That must be why we get on so well,' he said without inflection.

She ignored the irony. 'Yes, indeed. Imagine what it would be like if I were as humourless as you? We would never need to worry about our various enemies. We'd kill each other with dullness.'

'We would be more successful with more professionalism, I agree.'

She laughed. 'See how well we bounce off one another.' She paused and her eyes sparkled.

'Just don't,' he said before she could speak.

She raised an eyebrow. 'So you were thinking the same thing I was.'

'Only because I know you.'

'Oh, but you could know me so much better.'

'You're relentless.'

'You have no idea.'

He rolled his eyes. 'This is exhausting.'

'Hmm, if you're tired already, perhaps I've been giving your stamina too much credit.'

'My level of endurance is exceptional, I assure you.'

She chuckled, pleased with herself. 'Despite the

emotionless persona, you're still human, still very much a man. Can't let even the slightest slight to your masculinity go unchallenged, can you?'

'What are you hoping to achieve with all this?'

'I think it's safe to say that I've achieved it.'

'Good,' he said. 'We can finally get down to business.'

He realised what he'd said and grimaced before she had begun laughing.

Victor didn't respond. There were some fights he couldn't win, so he concentrated on finishing his hot dog. He paid for the second one the young guy had wasted no time in assembling. Raven looked away while he ate.

'Thank you for the flowers,' she said, now genuine instead of glib. 'They were beautiful, even if you only sent them so we could establish a means of communicating. But they helped me to forgive you.'

'It was the least I could do.'

'Do me a favour and tell me what you poisoned me with? It's been driving me insane not knowing. Tedrotoxin?'

He said, 'A synthetic variant that I picked up on a job a while back. I was saving it for a special occasion.'

'I'm flattered you felt so threatened by me.' She looked him up and down. 'Have you got taller?'

'People always ask me that.'

'People? You make it sound like there are those out there who actually know you.'

'No, but there are those out there who believe they know me.'

'Had you been anyone else, that would be one of the saddest things I've ever heard.'

He finished the second hot dog and cleaned his hands.

Raven said, 'Feel better now?'

He nodded.

'Walk with me. There's a fabulous little bar nearby. They do excellent pudding wine.'

She winked at him, and he did as she requested and they made their way out of the square, side by side, but with more distance than the couple they appeared to be from a casual observation.

She said, 'I take it you came here to cash in on your IOU.'

He nodded again. 'I saved your life so I want you to do the opposite for me.'

'You're not making any sense.'

Victor said, 'I want you to kill me.'

TWENTY-NINE

Samuel Cornish had a suit for every day of the week. Navy was the colour that saw him through Monday to Friday, two pinstripes, a three-piece, one double-breasted and a single; he had two stone browns for the weekend, when he could relax. He had a black suit too, for ceremonies and funerals. He was a very tall man, once in shape in an almost forgotten prototype version of himself, and had never worn anything but an XL. Now, he didn't know what size he wore. *It's like ironing a tent*, his dutiful sister remarked on a recent visit, when trying to get the creases out of one of his custom shirts. All his clothes were hand-made, not because he was so tall, but to accommodate his ever-expanding breadth. He was scared to check, but feared the circumference of his waist wouldn't be far off his height.

He had been called handsome in his youth, though he could never see it himself, and in middle age, no one called him handsome. His hair was thin and grey and not even a sky-blue tie could bring out the colour of his eyes, now pale and lost in the red around them. His cheeks were sagging into jowls and his forehead never stopped frowning despite all the fat to plump out his features. He would look ill if not for the pinkish tinge of health in his cheeks, but it was a sign of high blood pressure. He didn't feel stressed, but he hadn't worked up a sweat by choice in decades. He sweated all day long just in his skin. Exercise was for the vain or those afraid of mortality, and he was neither. His doctor implored him to take better care of himself. *Too late now*, he always retorted. He would rather live another two decades eating cheese and drinking wine than three spent miserable on a treadmill.

He popped a couple of painkillers on his way to pick up his evening coffee. It was awkward opening the bottle with one hand pretty much out of action, but he had adapted fairly fast to the injured wrist. He had bluffed his way through the conversation with his doctor, claiming he had fallen, he had been clumsy, a silly accident, being stupid, just give me some pills, okay?

The doctor, a good and decent little old Italian who wasn't averse to patching up the occasional mafioso, had fixed Cornish a wrist support. It was badly hyperextended and swollen. Keep it elevated. Rested. Be careful.

Yeah, yeah. Cornish wasn't stupid. He knew how to be careful.

Which was why Paolo Totti wouldn't be hearing of Cornish's encounter with the bitch from hell. No one had, in fact, and no one would. He hadn't told his colleagues at the bank. His ego, though as bruised as his wrist, had nothing to do with that. It was bad for business for word to get around that Cornish's lips could be prised open with little more than a letter opener. He had binned the letter opener. He couldn't bear to look at it any longer.

Whoever she was, whatever she wanted, it was someone else's problem now.

Totti's, to be specific. But regardless of her jiu-jitsu or whatever it was, she wasn't going to be able to do that with a proper gangster and get away with it. Those guys were *all* about ego, all about reputation. Totti being bent over a desk by a girl would bring down his whole outfit. He'd never live it down. He'd rather do a stretch than take that kind of hit to his street cred. The bosses would never trust him with anything again.

Not. My. Problem.

Cornish slurped from his espresso, after blowing away steam. It took a triple shot to get Cornish's motor running in the morning, and he liked to have the same later in the day to ensure he didn't fall asleep the second he flopped onto the sofa. Since he had moved to Italy all those long years ago the popularity of proper coffee had exploded back in his homeland. There were more coffee shops in London than pubs by a factor of . . . well, he didn't know. It would be a lot, he was sure, if anyone bothered to count. But the best Italian coffee in London wouldn't touch the worst of Rome. It was something beyond the beans, beyond roasting and grinding. Maybe it was the water.

Whatever, it was good and he made the espresso last while he strolled home from the office. He lived a couple of miles from the bank and walked every now and again when the weather was nice but not too nice and he had a low-hassle morning. The espresso bar at the midpoint gave him a chance to rest and recharge for the second leg, which he needed to do.

He saw an old man approaching on the pavement. He was well dressed, and had an innocent, almost juvenile, smile – the kind that arrived with ease and lingered long after the moment had passed – as if he took humour in all things, because life was a gift and every experience could be positive if only the person allowed it to be so.

Cornish smiled too, despite the soreness in his wrist. Considering he laundered mob money for a living, which carried plenty of dangers worse than he had suffered, life was indeed a gift. He should be more grateful.

'Excuse me,' the old man said in English as they neared, 'Do you happen to have the time?'

Cornish stopped and extended his left arm to reveal his platinum Rolex and looked at the watch face. 'Three minutes after eight.'

'Thank you,' the old man said. He was an American.

Cornish said you're welcome but made no sound. He felt faint.

There was a tickle on his neck and he realised the old man was holding a hypodermic syringe. Cornish rubbed at the source of the tickle and saw a smear of blood on his fingertips.

He would have fallen had two sets of strong hands not steadied him. Two men he hadn't even seen guided him to a parked SUV and into the back seat.

The last thing Cornish saw before he blacked out was the old man's innocent smile.

THIRTY

The evening air was warm and dry. They waited until there were no passers-by before they continued their conversation.

Raven said, 'You're joking, of course.'

'I'm not suicidal, Constance,' Victor said, 'if that's what you're suggesting.'

'So you're saying that you want me to appear to kill you?'

He nodded. 'That's right.'

'Well, I can't pretend that I'm not surprised. I never expected you'd want out. I never thought you would be the one to retire first. I never thought you would retire, at all. Ever.'

'I'm not retiring,' Victor explained. 'I'm resetting. My life is becoming more complicated than I can manage, so a simple way for it to become less complicated is if certain people out there were led to believe I'd met with an unfortunate, but deserved, end.'

She pursed her lips. 'I see. Reset. Unburden. Start again.'

'It's a temporary solution, perhaps. I don't imagine it will fool people for long, but for a good head start, at least. Long enough for priorities to have changed, promotions and demotions to have taken place, maybe the odd heart attack. It might be a different world before anyone realises what really happened.'

'Why now? What's happened in the last year?'

'New York is part of it, of course. That's kicked up plenty of fallout, as is to be expected. There's also an open contract out on me, brokered by someone named Phoenix, presumably at the behest of your pals in the Consensus. I've been trying to track him down, but it's a long process. I'm not sure how close I am.'

'I know of Phoenix. The Consensus have used him before, so I can't say I'm surprised by this. They know me personally, so they've never needed to go via third parties. You, however, are a different case. Why not lie low for a while? It's good policy every now and again. I wish I had that luxury. But that still doesn't explain what's happened recently to make you want to disappear, especially if you're still trying to find Phoenix.'

'That's not all,' Victor said. 'One of my previous employers has been in touch. There's a guy looking for me. He's trouble. Some big shot working for the director of national intelligence.'

'A double whammy then. Poor baby.'

'Which is further complicated because this ex-employer delivered this message to me via my current employer.'

'You don't like that they know about one another?'

'No, I don't. But it's more than that.'

'And if they're chatting with your other employer then it's another intelligence agency closely allied to US interests. So are we talking Mossad or MI6?'

'The Brits.'

'Then I can't say I'm following your problem.'

'Why does my CIA handler need to pass a message to me through my SIS handler? Because they're in trouble too. They can't contact me directly because the guy after me is watching their communications. Therefore I'm on my own. No assistance. No intel.'

'So you've been doing black-bag jobs for a faction of CIA under the rest of the intelligence community's nose, but now that nose has caught a big old whiff of your scent.'

'Seems that way, doesn't it?'

'It must be dire straits if your old handler can't even risk contacting you directly. I take it you haven't tried to contact them?'

'I have no wish to expose myself without help.'

Raven pursed her lips. 'I'll help you expose yourself.'

Victor didn't react.

'Hey, sorry, you seemed so serious I figured you would appreciate a little light relief. And yes, that is another offer.'

'Could you be serious for a minute?'

'I'm only serious in the bedroom, so . . .' She shrugged with her hands.

'If I don't respond then you can't turn it against me.'

'Shrewd tactic,' she said, then: 'Here we are.'

She had taken him to another square, larger and busier. The last of the tiger-stripe sky could be seen to the west.

Multiple sets of tables and chairs sat outside bistros, restaurants, bars and cafés. Diners and drinkers chatted and laughed. It was noisy, and therefore a good place to talk.

She picked out a table for them both and they sat down. A waiter was quick to arrive and take their order. He saw they were not locals and so spoke in English, 'Do you know what you'd like?'

Raven glanced at Victor. 'I know exactly what I'd like.'

The waiter chuckled.

'Only he doesn't want me back.'

The waiter gasped at Victor. '*What?* She's beautiful.'

She slapped the table. 'You see, even the waiter knows what's good for you.'

Victor said, 'I'll have a sparkling water. The lady would like a Scotch, no ice. An Islay, if you have one.'

'Very good.'

When the waiter had left them, Victor said, 'Must you draw attention to us?'

She didn't answer, but she looked particularly smug, even for her. 'I know you like me because you remembered my drink.'

'I can have the waiter bring us some pudding wine instead, if you'd prefer.'

She pursed her lips. 'Ouch.'

They were silent until the waiter returned with their drinks.

Raven said, 'Perhaps you should tell me where this heat originates.'

'A few years ago I had a contract. The target was a Latvian named Andris Ozols. It was a kill and collect, which should have been a red flag, but the years before that had been quiet. I'd been successfully freelance. A few cuts and bruises, but nothing serious. The contract itself was simple. Easy, in fact, which should have been another red flag. He was flying to Paris. I knew which flight he was on, which hotel he was staying, where and when he was meeting his contact to make the exchange. I ambushed him en route. He never saw me coming. I took the flash drive he was carrying with the plan to stash it later that day and arrange a pickup, but when I returned to my hotel there was a clean-up crew waiting for me, sent by the broker to protect the client. Turned out Ozols was selling secrets to the CIA, so I was on the run from them and other killers looking to pick up where the crew in Paris left off. In the aftermath I ended up working for the CIA. At least, one guy there had me doing black-bag jobs for them. Now, the CIA officer who was trying to track me down back then has got a new job and is coming after me again. But instead of taking orders, he's the one giving them.'

'And he hasn't forgotten about you.'

'Something like that.'

'You do tend to rub people up the wrong way.'

Victor nodded. 'It's an unfortunate side-effect of the profession, yes.'

'It doesn't have to be that way.'

'Some Americans lost their lives in the aftermath. I didn't kill them, but their deaths have been attributed to me.'

She regarded him, detecting something in his voice he tried to hide but there was no glib comment, no follow-up question. He was thankful for her rare tact, but he didn't like the fact she could read enough in his tone to elect to apply it.

She said, 'So, you have a serious problem.'

'Yes,' he agreed.

'And the fact that we're discussing it tells me there's some reason you don't want to end the problem in your usual manner.'

He nodded. 'There are reasons why that is not the most viable course of action.'

'Such as putting yourself in the crosshairs of the entire US intelligence community?'

'That's certainly up there.'

'And going on the run won't work, even with my help. Posing as a couple would only throw them off in the short term. Eventually, they would work it out and the benefit would be lost, but we wouldn't know, so it would end up as a disadvantage.'

'Correct.'

'That's the first and best two options right there. Faking your death isn't going to be easy.'

'I never said it was going to be.'

She sipped her whisky and thought. 'You're going to need something loud, something messy. Something that leaves lots of evidence behind for the right people to discover. A pre-established narrative: two assassins who have crossed paths before. It's a story that tells itself.'

He nodded. 'There's a potential opportunity coming up with my old CIA handler, which I think will be a good one. But before I go, I need to know whether I have backup or not. So, will you help me?'

'What did I tell you? I'm the only person out there who can have your back. You gave me a second chance at life. The least I can do is give you the same.'

He nodded. 'Thank you.'

THIRTY-ONE

The old man's innocent smile was the first thing Cornish saw upon waking. His eyes were slow to focus, but blurred colour became blurred shapes became that smile. A headache from hell caused Cornish to grimace and groan. His mouth felt tarry. His lips were dry. He struggled to swallow.

The old man said, 'I expect you'd like some water.'

Cornish was confused. He didn't know where he was or what was going on, but he had never been thirstier. He nodded.

The old man moved out of view and a tap squealed. The noise was claws scraping down Cornish's spine. Water rushed. A glass filled. The old man held it to Cornish's dry lips and he drank the whole glass down, minus the inevitable spillage. Cornish didn't care. He'd never tasted anything so refreshing, so delicious.

'I expect you're wondering where you are,' the old man said.

Cornish didn't answer. Beyond the old man, all he could see was a bare brick wall. It was the same wherever he looked. Not that he could rotate himself, because he was secured to a chair with duct tape. It was wrapped around his wrists, pinning them to the arms of the chair. His ankles were fixed to the legs.

'I expect you're wondering what this is all about.'

Cornish managed to say, 'What's going on?'

'It's very simple. Recently you were visited by a woman. She was the one who hurt your wrist, I don't doubt. She asked about the Totti arrangement, did she not?'

The fatigue and the disorientation were wearing off because fear was replacing them and the accompanying adrenaline washed away the fogginess of waking from drug-induced unconsciousness. Cornish was terrified.

'Did Totti send you?'

The old man seemed amused. 'Totti? I'm afraid Mister Totti is little more than a courier. He doesn't know for whom he works, so how could he send me? He doesn't know I exist, let alone why I exist.'

'Who are you?'

'My name is immaterial,' the old man said. 'As is any other answer you might request. All you need to know is that what happens in this room is both my profession and my passion.'

The old man moved out of sight once more. When he returned, he held a long thin instrument. Stainless steel, like a needle only much longer, but unlike any Cornish had seen before.

The old man said, 'We think of pain as a reaction. We

235

think of it as a response to injury. But it's not. It's a message. It's a warning. It's the most powerful warning there is, because we have no power over it. We can manage it. We can ignore it. But it's still there. It's the unconscious telling the conscious that the source of the pain is going to kill us if we do not get away from it. It's evolution's way of silently shouting *run*. Pain is the body's way of saying *I know best*. It's humbling. We think we are so very in control of ourselves, but we are merely passengers on this journey.

'What I like about pain,' he continued, 'is that it is imperfect. A paper cut can hurt worse than a broken bone. We don't even have to be injured to feel pain.'

Cornish's heart was hammering. His face gleamed with sweat.

The old man said, 'This is an acupuncture needle. It's incredibly thin and sharp, so that it can miss nerves altogether, so that it does not hurt, so that you cannot feel it. See?'

He used a light jabbing motion to stab the needle a matter of millimetres into the skin of Cornish's exposed left forearm. The needle was so light it remained protruding straight and true when the old man took his hand away.

'Doesn't hurt at all, does it?'

Cornish swallowed and nodded. Scared, but agreeing.

'It can feel good, if used correctly. The benefits of acupuncture are well documented. With half a dozen of these needles I can make you as blissful as you've ever felt. Peaceful. Like being awake and asleep at the same time. Like you're weightless. Like you're floating on a dream. You'd like that, wouldn't you? I know you would.'

Cornish said nothing. He couldn't take his gaze from the needle.

The old man removed the needle with a slight, waving motion of his hand. Effortless.

His lips pursed and the needle shone white under the glow of a bare bulb overhead as he continued the waving motion as might the conductor of an orchestra; a melodic movement to guide a tune only he could hear and appreciate.

He said, 'Push the tip of your tongue against the roof of your mouth, please.'

Cornish managed to say, 'Why?'

'So you do not bite the end off, of course.'

The answer seemed so reasonable, so concerned, that Cornish did not understand. Could not understand. He did not do as instructed.

The old man's hand stopped the waving motion and the needle plunged downward to again pierce only a few millimetres into the skin of the forearm, but this time near to the pit of the elbow.

Cornish's teeth clamped together in a frozen spasm. His face was painted red with rushing blood. Ligaments and veins stood out from the skin of his hypertensive neck. Knuckles whitened. He roared and bucked against the restraints.

'The median nerve,' the old man said as he used the tip of his little finger to manipulate the long needle with slow, circular movements. 'It needs to be highly sensitive to carry measures from the hands, for touch is so very important from an evolutionary perspective.'

Cornish thrashed in the chair. Saliva and blood frothed and spattered his lips.

'It's like fire, isn't it? It's like your whole body is on fire on the inside, but it's a cold fire. Ice and lightning coursing through you. Amazing, isn't it? What the body can do. What we can do to it. I like to write the alphabet,' the old man said as his fingertip continued to guide the needle with tiny, almost imperceptible movements. 'The skill is keeping the letters small, so the nerve is not damaged by the needle, only stimulated. Q seems to be the letter that causes the most pain. For reference, we're currently at E.'

Cornish's face glowed in the light of the bare bulb, coated in sweat and tears and mucus and blood.

'Would you like me to stop?' the old man asked.

Despite the thrashing and spasms, Cornish could nod.

The old man lifted his fingertip from the needle's end.

Cornish vomited over himself.

'Look there,' the old man said, gesturing. 'There's the tip of your tongue. I did warn you.'

'Whatever you want to know,' Cornish slurred despite the pain, despite the injured tongue, despite the retching, 'I'll tell you.'

'I know,' the old man said. 'Please tell me every detail about the woman's visit. Every detail about her accounts at the bank.'

Cornish spoke for several minutes. Everything he could think of. Every shred of information that might be relevant. He left out nothing. Every word. Every thought.

'That's it,' Cornish said. 'I don't know why she wanted to know about the money, about Totti. She never told me. I swear it.'

The old man nodded, 'I know, I can see,' and moved the needle again.

Cornish screamed.

The innocent, almost shy, smile returned. 'Remember when I said this was not only my profession, but my passion? That's why I'm going to continue hurting you. Not because I need to, but because I want to.'

THIRTY-TWO

Victor had the waiter bring them both a second drink. He resisted Raven's pressure to order something alcoholic. She ordered some olives too.

'Something to nibble on,' she said.

Victor said, 'I take it you are still on your crusade.'

'Someone has to fight the good fight. Which is why you had to meet me here and why I can't rush to your assistance here and now. You might have to wait a day or two.'

Victor shrugged. 'A few days is fine. I have something to take care of myself too.'

'Good,' Raven said, 'because I have a hot date coming up.'

'Who are you after this time?'

'I don't know, but I'm going to find out, obviously. After you killed me in Canada, someone else tried to do the same while I was still learning to walk again. I mean, where is the chivalry in that? I've been working my way through this particular cell of a-holes and, a few missteps along the way aside, I've done a pretty good job too. Stopped a major operation going down, took out some bad guys, and now I think I'm close to a top boy. I don't know who he is, but I've found someone who has to know more.'

'What did they do to you?'

'I told you before. They betrayed me. Turned me into a fugitive.'

'And yet instead of running away from them, you keep running at them. I'd like to understand why.'

She didn't reply straightaway, but Victor could see she was working her way around to saying something from the way she toyed with the olives. He used the moment to scan the square for new arrivals, for anyone who looked out of place. He saw nothing that made him look twice.

Raven said, 'I never really told you about Yemen, did I?'

'You told me a little. You told me you were close to a team member who died there. Because of bad intel, if I recall correctly. And I've put a few pieces together from what you just said.'

She nodded. 'We were there for a long time and had lost people already when we shouldn't have. Me and Stephen, we were more than close. He was more than a team member. A lot more than that. We had worked together a number of times over the years, but didn't become lovers until that particular operation. In hindsight, it was inevitable we would be together. It's such an isolated world we operate in. The only people who really know us are those we work with. Have you ever been with anyone who got to see the real you and didn't mind what they saw?'

He said, 'No.'

'Then you can't really know what I'm talking about, but I'll try and explain anyway. With Stephen, I could see a life beyond that which I had, but a real one because we would both be starting that life, not one person joining the normal life the other already knew. I saw the end to death and chaos. I could see calm for the first time since I was a kid. I could see a white house on the beach. Matching surfboards. A dog. A big, fluffy one. All that good stuff. I never thought to ask: do you like dogs?'

'Yes.'

'Ever had one?'

He shook his head.

'Me neither. But that's what I wanted. Dog walks on a beach. Making a fire from driftwood. He wanted it too. We would be on surveillance and would be planning these little details. I used to look forward to those long nights keeping track of targets. I couldn't wait for the operation to be over. I couldn't wait to quit.'

She was silent for a moment and Victor didn't press her. He knew she would speak in her own time or not at all.

'But then I found out he was a double agent,' Raven continued eventually. 'He was working for the enemy all along. I was nothing to him. He was using me the whole time, and when I'd served my usefulness I would have ended up as one of his other victims. It was him. He was the reason we had lost people. He'd been killing them.'

'So you killed him.'

'I had no choice,' she explained. 'But as I told you: it was bad intel.'

'Ah,' Victor said.

Raven said, 'I don't know at what point they found out Stephen was getting close, but that's why they fed me the lie about him being a rogue operative. That's why they had me kill him. I killed the only man I ever loved to help the rich get richer.'

'No wonder you want revenge.'

'It's more than revenge. They took everything from me. They took away my future, all my hope. They took away my soul. So every one of them I kill, every plot I destroy, I take back a little piece of what I lost. What I'm doing is beyond revenge. It's beyond justice even. It's salvation.'

Victor was silent.

'For a time I was obsessed with who supplied that bad intel, who fed us the lies. I don't know. I never found him. I doubt I ever will. I've killed lieutenants but I've never knowingly got close to a general. And a part of me hopes I never find out who is responsible, because then it *would* be about revenge. Then I would only care about that one man or woman, that one person. But they're all responsible, if not for Stephen, for others like him. So, they all deserve my wrath, and they're all going to suffer it. I'm not going to stop until each and every one of them is in the ground. Then I'll stop. Then I'll rest. I'll get that house on the beach and the dog to go with it. But not before. I can't. I won't.'

Victor said, 'How did you know you had been lied to?'

'Stephen being Stephen, he had foreseen they might come after him, and had left me everything he had discovered. I found out the rest on my own, hoping to find the source, the one giving the orders, but that's impossible. That's why I call them the Consensus. It's not an organisation. It's worse than that. It's an alliance of interest, and the collective desire for wealth and power and willingness to do absolutely anything to maintain and increase it. What happened in Yemen was the result of one branch of that, one cell. The Consensus isn't run by a single man stroking a white cat – its leadership is shared by the billionaire who funds the senator's campaign in return for a favourable vote on beneficial legislation, and that senator's chief of staff who wants a promotion ... and the CIA case officer who supplies the intel to one of his contacts, now a private security contractor, who hires a bunch of mercenaries to kidnap the daughter of the rebel leader to extort that intelligence, and the black ops operative who kills that rebel after the event to ensure they can never tell the tale. How do you destroy something like that?'

'I don't know,' Victor said.

'You can't,' Raven said back. 'It's the hydra, but at least the hydra was a single beast with many heads. This is many hydras.'

'You said you'd only get the house on the beach once they were all dead.'

She smiled, briefly, sadly. 'Whoever said it was a perfect plan?'

He didn't answer because there was no answer. Instead, he said, 'I trust you'll take every care in your pursuit?'

'Aw, that's sweet,' she replied, 'and I'll pretend you're actually concerned for my safety and not simply worried I'll get myself killed before I can help you.'

'Perish the thought.'

'But seriously, I don't expect any trouble. He's not exactly holed up in a fortress with a private army. If anything, it'll be a walk in the park.'

'That doesn't seem likely for a serious player.'

'I've been watching him long enough to know all I need to know. If he has anyone worth worrying about then they're invisible or ethereal or both. There's no one else. Trust me.'

'I don't trust anyone.'

'Then see for yourself, he's sitting over there.'

Victor followed her gaze, turning his head only a little and only when absolutely necessary.

'Table by the tree, reading the newspaper.'

Four young men sat where Raven referenced. Three were laughing and joking amongst themselves while the fourth sat cross-legged, with a broadsheet open and holding his attention. He was smiling to himself and checking his phone at the same time. They were dressed in expensive but casual clothes. All Italians by the shade of their skin and their hair. Not professionals.

'Who are they?'

'Newspaper Boy is Paolo Totti. He might not look it, but he's a made guy. Local mafioso. The others are part of his entourage. I need to find a way of having a quiet word with Don Totti. Seems he's been a bag man for everyone's favourite multinational syndicate of death and destruction. I've got it all planned out and will be executing – not literally, unless he forces it – in the next couple of nights. Fancy helping out? Could be just like old times.'

'Even if I were feeling uncommonly charitable,' Victor

said with a shake of his head, 'I'm sure you can handle it. And I have something to attend to myself, as I said. Meeting you in Italy is a good excuse to see someone else.'

She looked disappointed, not because she needed his help but because she wanted it. 'You are such a spoilsport. Which reminds me that I need to think of a new name to call you. Something appropriate. Something annoying.'

'I'll leave that to you,' he said, standing. 'I'll be back in a day or two.'

'Can't you stay for one drink? Don't tell me this someone else is easier on the eye than I am.'

He shook his head. 'I have a train I need to be on soon and a friend who might take some time to track down.'

Raven's eyes were as big as he had ever seen them. 'Wait, I didn't hear you correctly. You said you have a friend. *You* have a friend?'

'Acquaintance is probably a more accurate term.'

'Phew,' she said, hand on chest. 'You almost gave me a heart attack and killed me a second time.'

THIRTY-THREE

It was cold because it was always cold. The bookshop had no central heating – at least, none that worked – and a fan heater didn't do a fat lot to combat the fine Scottish weather. Suzanne Mayes was used to the cold in that she could tolerate it. She dressed for it. She wore lots of layers, and kept her hands in fingerless gloves. The heating was on her list of things to improve, but that was a mighty long list when the bookshop was nowhere near breaking even. It was a labour of love, but one she hoped – prayed – would one day turn a profit. The bank, after all, didn't care for literature. It cared about the repayments.

Money was tight because the farm struggled to make a profit and the bookshop did its best to take that profit and throw it away. Ben wanted her to be pushier, but she refused to hard sell. She didn't have it in her and she didn't believe it worked. Might result in the odd sale, sure, but was that person who felt compelled or embarrassed or forced or tricked into buying a novel they didn't really want really going to come back to buy another? That's the question she posed to her husband when he made those little condescending remarks about maybe needing to try harder.

Can't force people to read. They either had it in them or they didn't. She saw her job as helping those that did to discover it, and if they already had it, to keep it.

She had a comfortable stool perched behind the counter where she sat and read while letting those people – few people – who came through the door browse and decide. She had a nice demeanour, she knew, and was content to let them look and read and think and dwell and approach her or not. They would if they needed to and if they didn't then they wouldn't.

Why can't you get that through your caveman skull? she would ask He of Little Faith.

This afternoon's potential customer was a man she had never seen before. The man did the dance, as she called it when someone entered the shop for the very first time and kind of waltzed. There was a certain rhythm to their footsteps. They didn't so much turn as pirouette.

'Chilly in here,' he said when he was near.

'Yeah,' she replied.

Not much else she could say, other than plead poverty. And that never sold anything, least of all a book.

The man was an American. Sort of short. Sort of fat. Forties. He had one of those faces that looked both young and old at the same time. He was bald and unshaved. He had an open leather jacket and his T-shirt had a band's name she didn't know. She didn't listen to much music these days. All the new songs sounded too produced, too fake, and she had grown out of the artists of her youth. That his jacket was open told her he didn't mind the cold, whatever he said. It even looked like he was sweating. The type of man who would be a boiler to sleep next to. Her own hubby had feet as cold as her own.

'Man,' he said, 'you don't see many of these places any more.'

She looked up from her reading. 'Bookshops, you mean?'

'Yeah, not so common these days.'

'We're a dying breed, I'm sorry to say,' she said, nodding. 'I'm guessing you're not from round here.'

He shook his bald head. 'My accent, right?' He pointed, like people did. 'I'm from the States. I love it here, though. I love Scotland.'

'Oh, thanks. What brings you over here?'

'Just business.' He shifted his feet. 'You know.'

'Well, I hope it was worth the trip.'

'It's been tough, but I think my boss will be pleased with the results.'

He paused and she wasn't sure what to say.

'Anyhow,' he said after one of those big sighs, 'I thought I'd pop in and pick up some reading material. You know, for the long flight home.'

She nodded her understanding. 'What books do you like?'

'I ain't never been much of a reader, I'll tell you that. But you can only watch so many of those in-flight movies. And I can never sleep on a plane, so seems like a good excuse to get into reading.'

She nodded. She understood. He was sweet, in an awkward way. 'What do you think you might enjoy?'

'I don't rightly know. Maybe something about aliens and such.'

'Speculative fiction?' she asked.

'Yeah, that might be my thing. I like those movies.'

He waved his arms in some vague mime she couldn't quite get her head around, but she nodded anyway.

'I've got some Asimov and a short story collection by Dick.'

His eyes widened. *'Excuse me?'*

'Philip K. Dick, I mean. He's an author. Was.'

'Oh, I see. Like I said, I'm pretty damn ignorant of books and writers and such. But never too late to learn, is it?'

'No,' she said, 'it really isn't.'

She left her stool to help him pick out a selection of books to keep him company on his flight. She rang up the sale and bagged the books.

He said, 'Thank you for all your assistance ...' He glanced down for a name tag that wasn't there. ' ... uh ...'

She smiled. 'Suzanne. Suzy, really.'

His face pinched as he thought. 'Say, you wouldn't happen to be related to a guy named Ben?'

She was a little surprised and said, 'Yeah, I'm his wife. How did you know that?'

He grinned and rapped his knuckles on the counter. 'See, I had a hunch you might be. I was at the convenience store. I told 'em I was looking for somewhere that sells books. They said Suzy Mayes owns a place. See, I used to go to school with a kid named Ben way back. I heard he'd moved to Scotland.'

Suzanne Mayes' eyes were huge. '*No way.*'

'Yes, way. Haven't seen him in years. I heard he'd scored himself a pretty Scottish girlfriend and moved to Aberdeenshire with her, but I didn't know your name.'

She blushed. 'It's sweet of you to say so, but did you really hear that about me?'

'Swear down I did. How's Ben doing these days?'

'Good. Working hard. He took over my dad's farm.'

'Yeah, I can imagine him as a farmer. Tell Ben I said hi. He might not remember me, come to think of it. It was a lifetime ago and I wasn't exactly one of the cool kids.' He looked away.

Suzanne Mayes said, 'I'm sure Ben wasn't either, whatever he thought. And, just between the two of us, he still isn't, not really. But I'll be sure to tell him you stopped by. What's your name again . . .?'

'I'm Jimmy.'

'Jimmy . . . what?'

'He'll know me by Jimmy or not at all.' The man smiled. He had crooked teeth. 'Thanks again for the recommendations. I do appreciate your insight.'

'I'm just sharing my love any way I can.'

His smile broadened. 'What a nice way of putting it.'

'I like to think so too.'

The customer who called himself Jimmy left the bookshop with his purchases and strolled along the wet pavement, still with the easy smile, still with the buoyant step. When he reached his car he threw the books in the boot, not caring how the pages creased and the spines broke because he didn't care about books. He hadn't read a book in his life. He climbed behind the wheel.

A cursory glance was all that was required to know there were no observers, and he took out his phone, thumbed his contacts and dialled. The smile faded, replaced by a blank expression that hid his excitement, his success.

'This is Niven,' he said once the line connected. 'Second store checked out. I've finally found them.'

THIRTY-FOUR

Victor had known Alberto Giordano for years, dating back to his early days as a freelance assassin and Giordano's first forays into the realms of professional forgery. He had been young then and had somehow maintained that youth and impossible good looks, if ageing at all then ageing in reverse. He thought of himself as an artist and lover, and could have conceivably gone into a career in forgery just to satisfy some revolutionary sentiment. It had been a while since Victor had had any contact with him, which was normal. He would turn up unannounced for a new brace of documents to create a perfect legend like no other available in the world.

Then, Giordano had been hard to find. He had built up a small but effective operation with a multi-faceted defence. Victor was forced to go through several layers of contacts before reaching the man himself. He expected the same this time. He expected to spend a day or more on the streets of Bologna, asking questions, gaining trust, finding the next person who revealed a little more and the next, all the while watched by Giordano's people or those who owed him, liked him or sought a favour from him.

This time it took Victor a matter of hours.

He found an osteria he had been to before and asked questions – subtle but pointed questions. He had been surprised by the bluntness of the answers.

The barman knew where he could find Giordano, as did a patron who overheard the conversation. Both seemed surprised to discover who he was looking for, as if such a thing was unique and unnecessary. He didn't ask why. He would find out for himself.

Bologna was one of Victor's favourite cities, and he had visited enough to know the difference between a place that was good for sightseeing and good to explore. Bologna was the latter. It had everything except trees, but in their absence gained something else, something pure. A city all of brick, of stone, was its own forest, man-made but could be as hostile as any wilderness.

Victor wasn't expecting trouble, but he identified its potential within seconds of entering a second osteria where he'd been told he would find Giordano. The potential trouble consisted of three men who sat together in the centre of the room, drinking and making a lot of noise. It was not their rowdy behaviour that made his threat radar hum, but the fact one of them had a gun. The grip of a pistol was protruding from his waistband.

They had similar features, and Victor made them as brothers. Criminals, but not professionals. Not here for him.

He discounted them as threats, but he didn't ignore them.

Victor never forgot a face. He spent his days analysing them for signs, for tells, to distinguish civilian from target, citizen from combatant. He had been taught how to read what facial recognition software now did automatically. Some features of a face could not be changed without surgery and those were what he had always focused on first – how he spotted Giordano, anonymous in a crowd he would have once stood out from.

His blond hair was long and greasy, and hung over a face further hidden by an unkempt beard. Women who would have once gazed adoringly at him now walked by, eyes averted. There was no splendour in his clothes, no ostentatiousness in his mannerisms. In some ways he acted like Victor – blending in, attempting to go unnoticed.

There were no pleasantries. None of the playfulness Victor had been expecting. When Giordano realised who was standing over him, he looked up once to acknowledge Victor's presence, then looked away.

'What happened to you?' Victor couldn't help but ask.

Giordano smirked. 'What happened? You happened.'

Victor was silent.

'You, Vernon, my dear friend of all these years. Ally. Compatriot. You did this to me. You took a flower and stripped it of petals, and now you ask why it is no longer beautiful?'

'Tell me what happened.'

'I don't know who they were. All I know is they came out of nowhere, a month, maybe two, after we last met. They kidnapped me. They took me somewhere I didn't know. I was so scared. That was not my life. But it was your life. You had led them to my door because you are you and the things you do without consequence have consequences for me.'

Victor didn't know what to say. He began establishing a timeline from what Giordano said, working out how it slotted together with his own actions and movements. He knew exactly who had taken Giordano.

He continued, 'I spent two days hanging from chains while they questioned me continuously. They would take it in turns: a man and a woman. Non-stop, no breaks, no sleep. They gave me water so my throat didn't dry out and stop me speaking. Every question I answered led to more questions. They wanted endless clarifications and ever more details. I never thought I would leave that place.'

'Did they hurt you?'

He lifted up his shirt, past his navel, to reveal a long, vertical scar that ran the length of his abdomen.

'I'm sorry.'

'That's not all.' He unfastened a few buttons of his shirt so he could open it up to show Victor his shoulder and some of his back. There were more scars; thumb-sized, discoloured and wrinkled. Burns.

'I'm sorry,' Victor said again.

Alberto didn't seem to hear. 'I gave you up as soon as she cut me.'

'Good.'

'It didn't stop them using a blowtorch on me. Israelis, right?'

Victor nodded.

'What did you do to them?'

'I killed some of their people. They got between me and a target.'

'Have they caught up with you yet?'

'Maybe a month after they tortured you.'

'How many more did you kill getting away?'

'It doesn't matter. I've only got one life for them to take revenge upon.'

'So many enemies. Is it worth it?'

Victor ignored the question because Giordano's shoulder was bumped by a passing man, and bumped hard.

There was no apology. Giordano made no reference to it.

The man said, 'Say hi to your sister for me,' as he walked away.

Victor saw it was one of the three men he had identified as trouble.

'You know those guys?' he asked.

Giordano nodded.

'What's their problem?'

'That was nothing. Just a reminder to pay my debts.'

Victor didn't ask anything further because he understood. Giordano had borrowed from the wrong people. The brothers were loan sharks.

'I can help you, Alberto. I can set you up wherever you want. Any country. Just name it.'

'I'm happy where I am. Or, as happy as I could hope to be, given the circumstances.'

'Money then. However you want it: cash, jewellery, transfer—'

'I don't want your money. Who knows who will come looking for it someday.'

'Then what can I do to help you, to make amends, Alberto? Anything, just name it.'

The younger man exhaled as he thought. He fastened the buttons of his shirt. 'Give yourself up to Mossad.'

'I don't understand.'

'Yes you do,' Alberto insisted. 'You're just trying not to. You can't magic my scars away, any more than you can erase the memories of how I got them. But what you can do is ensure no Israeli spy gives me any more of them. While you're still out there, they'll still be looking. Who knows where or when they might spot you. Maybe they'll trace you here and they'll want to know the name on the passport I arranged for you. But this time I won't be able to tell them and they won't believe me. They'll have to make sure I'm telling the truth. Will they let me go twice? But none of that will happen if you take a flight to Tel Aviv. There'll never be any need for them to come looking for you then, will there?'

'Alberto, I . . .'

'Don't worry, Vernon – or whatever your name really is – you don't have to say anything. I know you're not going to do that. That's why I can say it. I'd never ask anyone to sacrifice themselves for me, regardless of what they'd done. But I can ask you to, can't I? Because there's not a chance in hell you would. You're not going to sacrifice yourself for anyone, least of all for a nothing like me.'

THIRTY-FIVE

Cornish had been accurate in everything he had told Raven. He had told Raven Paolo Totti wasn't trying to hide, and he wasn't. Totti didn't keep a low profile. He kept the opposite, in fact. He was something of a minor celebrity in the region. Paparazzi snapped his picture whenever he had a new girl on his arm or whenever he pulled up outside a premiere in a gleaming Rolls. He was one of the new mafia, the son of an old boss in the Cosa Nostra, who had followed in his father's footsteps in principle only. He was a brash club owner and playboy who had a large following on social media thanks to his lavish lifestyle and flamboyant personality. Every day he uploaded selfies showing off his wealth.

Raven scrolled through his updates with a sense of bewilderment. At first it was almost impossible to accept the Consensus had ever considered using such a man. He represented everything they went out of their way to avoid.

Totti's infamy and pursuit of even higher celebrity seemed in direct competition to their philosophy of anonymity. It didn't take long, however, for her to understand his usefulness. Totti's reputation provided perfect misdirection. No one was ever going to question for whom he worked, because he made it so very clear he was his own man, his own boss. He spared no opportunity to brag about this whenever he could.

She had spent a few days learning all she could about his operations, which was easy enough. Because of his celebrity, people wanted to share what they knew. Totti didn't seek to punish those who spoke about their connections to him. He revelled in it. When she had enough background, she posed as a reporter to ask questions of the local police, who were more vague but didn't seem all that interested in pursuing a known mafioso. There was a simple reason for this: Totti wasn't involved in narcotics. He might be rich, brash and arrogant, but he wasn't poisoning kids. There were no political points to score going after him and diverting efforts away from the drug trade. Totti knew this, and thought himself invincible, but the truth was there wasn't the will to bring him down. No one was interested in him enough to put in the groundwork. There were worse criminals out there to be dealt with first.

The connection to Cornish and the Consensus as a whole made more sense when she discovered local business owners had been intimidated and coerced into signing away assets to Totti at below-market rates. It made even more sense when these businesses proved to have high cash turnovers. The clubs, bars, restaurants and cafés all seemed profitable, but only a few hours with a calculator and the numbers didn't add up. It wasn't hard to work out his main source of income was laundering money for other criminals, doctoring the books of those businesses to legitimise dirty money.

So it made sense that the Consensus would use him as a go-between. Totti no doubt imagined he was doing deals with the same mobsters he always dealt with; he'd have no idea he was being used by a foreign collective with more power and influence than he could imagine. But, as with Cornish, Totti would know a name or a have a phone number or *something* that would take Raven one step closer to her enemies, to salvation.

Totti had some personal protection, but nothing serious enough to give Raven cause for concern. His crew was small and seemed to be comprised of his closest and oldest friends. None of them had been in the military. None of them had any security training. There was a good chance that none of them had ever drawn a weapon in anger. However, with paparazzi and groupies, hangers-on and fans everywhere he went, getting close enough to Totti to have a chat with him was a serious challenge. Raven would have preferred dodging the bullets of battle-hardened mercs than trying to avoid having her face snapped by swarms of cameras.

She found she wouldn't have to because, as with many of the fame hungry, Totti placed extreme value on his privacy. The glamorous lifestyle he led and revelled in only had appeal when it could be switched off again. Celebrity had no worth if it couldn't be controlled. He had several residences in his name – apartments in the city – but the home where he spent the most time was an out-of-town villa in Fregene. The villa stood alone in countryside, surrounded by vineyards on three sides and the sea on the other, accessible via a mile-long driveway guarded by his crew. No photographer, or cop for that matter, could get anywhere near him when he wanted to step out of the limelight.

It would have been time-consuming to get close enough for decent recon under normal circumstances, but Totti posted so many photos of his villa, gardens and private beach to his social media accounts that Raven didn't need blueprints to have an accurate plan of both the villa's interior and surroundings. There were even videos to give her a better sense of scale and proportion. She had identified every member of his crew from these photos and videos, and knew his personal retinue numbered four – one friend who acted as the designated driver and PR officer, two who were around to look tough and give him street cred, and his best friend, who was also the business manager/accountant. She also knew that there could be anywhere between two and six young women present at the villa; they weren't prostitutes, and all seemed to be there of their own volition, attracted by Totti's wealth and fame and hungry for their own, updating their own social media with their exploits.

The most useful revelation that came from analysing the various uploads was that Totti had a sophisticated security system comprised of top-end motion sensors and cameras. They would have been a challenge had Raven not been able to learn exactly where they were positioned.

She reminded herself to thank him for doing the hard work for her.

Given the proliferation of security measures in and around the villa, Raven decided on an approach from the west, to the back of the house, where she had to cross the least open ground. Which meant coming from his private beach.

For this, Raven acquired – stole – a small pleasure boat that she took from Fiumicino down the coast and anchored three miles off the shore. She waited until two a.m. and dropped backwards off the boat. The water was cold, but the neoprene dry suit took the edge off. She had an oxygen tank and breathing apparatus, goggles, fins, and a waterproof bag strapped to her waist containing what she would need on dry land.

She needed no light as she swam close to the surface and had studied the topography and currents of this part of the coast. There was a cloudless sky but no moon, so plenty of starlight reached the surface, but not enough to make her rethink her approach.

She was a strong swimmer but swam at a slow, comfortable pace and reached the beach in twenty minutes, her heart rate still low and her breathing even. The beach was short and narrow, but for Totti's exclusive use. There were sun loungers, a fire pit and barbecue equipment. The beach was beautiful white sand under the night sky. Black water lapped against it. Deprived of the sea's support, the scuba equipment was awkward and heavy. Her feet sank into the sand.

Clear of the water, she removed the goggles and stripped

off the fins, tank and breathing apparatus. The dry suit came off next and she hid it and the scuba gear amongst the rocks. From the waterproof bag she took a change of clothes, rolled up tight – trousers, long-sleeved shirt, climbing shoes, beanie hat and gloves, all black. She dressed, and emptied the final items from the bag – a Heckler & Koch P7 pistol, suppressor, magazines, a shoulder rig to hold the gun and ammo, and a multi-tool.

She would have liked some night-vision equipment, body armour and various other useful pieces of kit, but logistics were always an issue for her. As she was a lone gun, she had no assets to smuggle weapons and equipment, no limitless funds to purchase what was needed in a country, on site. She didn't have backup or supporting intelligence. It was commonplace to be unprepared, but no one said it would be easy.

There were narrow steps carved from the rock that led up the cliff face, but Totti was security conscious and it was covered by a thermal-imaging camera. Not impossible to disable without giving herself away, but far easier to avoid. The cliff face was only 56 metres in height.

Raven had been a climber long before she had begun considering a career in intelligence work. She had climbed trees instead of playing with dolls and spent every spring break in the Rockies; while her peers fantasised about fairytale weddings she had dreamed about the Eiger and K2.

A little bottle in the waterproof bag contained liquid chalk. She coated her hands and began her climb. She was a stronger climber than she was a swimmer, and had taken it easy in the water to save energy for the climb. A free climb – she couldn't swim with all the equipment necessary – was always strenuous.

She found her starting point, took a deep breath, then leapt up to take her first handhold. She pulled with her back and arms as she swung her legs up to find purchase. The cliff face was damp from proximity to the surf, but the liquid chalk helped mitigate that and the starlight reflecting off that dampness helped her to better see the texture of the rock.

Despite the exertion and the danger of falling, she enjoyed the climb. It had been a long time since she had scaled any kind of natural rock face. In recent years she had scaled more walls than she had cliffs, and reached more rooftops than she ever had mountain peaks.

At the top of the cliff she lay on her back until her breathing returned to normal and then surveyed her surroundings. The villa lay some 200 metres away, illuminated by the starlight. She saw no lights on, no glow from windows or outside lighting. It was a home, not a fortress.

A long swimming pool and lawns lay between the cliff and the villa, but with enough trees to provide a covered route to close the distance. There were cameras, but they had been installed by civilians to protect against gangsters, who were still civilians. They covered perhaps 90 per cent of the villa's exterior, but Raven was a lot smaller than the remaining 10 per cent. She crept through the gardens to the immediate rear of the villa, detecting no one patrolling. Totti's crew was far too small to provide twenty-four-hour protection on a building this size. The isolation, the cameras and his reputation had formed enough of a barrier until now that nothing stronger had been required.

No one really expected an assassin to turn up where they lived.

Raven had the multi-tool to help gain access via a window or patio door, but there was no need. French doors had not only been left unlocked, but open. Maybe to allow a pleasant sea breeze inside.

She couldn't help but shake her head.

The climbing shoes were good for deadening the sound of her footsteps on the tiled floors she found inside. With the P7 in hand, she swept the ground floor, expecting to find no one and finding no one. All the bedrooms were upstairs, after all. She had to be thorough, regardless. Assumptions were always dangerous.

She paused in a small utility room that housed monitors linked to the security cameras as well as the more traditional white goods. There were no cameras present in the bedrooms upstairs, but the landing leading to them was covered, as well as the main rooms and hallways downstairs. Raven used the multi-tool to unscrew the apparatus and gain access to the hard drive where the footage was recorded. She slipped it into her small rucksack.

Raven ascended the stairs, taking extra time to lighten her footsteps and cancel out the amplifying echo of the stairwell.

At the top, she paused to listen. She heard nothing but the faraway surf seeping through open windows. Totti's bedroom was at the end of the hallway, accessible through a heavy door that stood ajar. The other rooms housed his crew. For now, she ignored them.

She eased open the door to Totti's room enough for her to slip inside and, gun leading, approached the bed.

It was a huge, circular bed, draped with silk sheets the colour of pearls. Drapes rustled in the breeze from open windows that stood behind. Two figures lay in the bed. One female. One male.

The lack of snoring or heavy breathing was the first clue.

The absence of rising chests the second.

Raven was already spinning on the spot before she had seen the blood on the sheets.

A voice from the darkness said, 'Drop the weapon.'

THIRTY-SIX

She didn't. No way. Not her style. Raven had already begun her turn, already committed to action, and shot towards the voice and a blurry shape of darkness as she continued her movement – dropping low to make herself a smaller target, then dodging laterally to throw off an enemy's aim.

The P7 was a small weapon, compact and concealable. It had no real range, but at point-blank she couldn't miss.

Two shots. Always two. She never fired only once.

The blurry shape across the bedroom changed; distorting; falling, hitting the floor and going slack.

Where there was one enemy there were likely more, so she kept moving, knowing the villa's layout and the probable points of hiding, such as—

The en suite bathroom, which she pivoted towards, sights lining up on the expanding line of smooth blackness as the door opened from the inside; firing when that line of blackness roughened.

Another man. Same clothes. Same approximate shape. Another gunman. Another killer sent by her enemies.

A trap.

No time to consider how they knew – although it wasn't hard to guess – and nothing to gain by distracting herself over such inconsequential questions as how and why.

Live first, evaluate later.

She put another two rounds into this latest gunman, because he didn't go down as expected; then, as he did drop, she pivoted back to land another two on the first guy, because like the second he was wearing body armour she hadn't seen in the darkness, and he had recovered enough to be trying to line up his own shot from the floor.

The bullets struck his cheek and eyebrow. The floor tiles became a mess of ejected brain and bone fragment.

A decent ambush, but not a great one, because she was still alive. She had been faster, her instincts tipping her off before she had crossed the threshold.

Hidden in place, the two gunmen couldn't know her movements.

Surveillance then, outside, passing on her whereabouts.

Target has reached the villa ...

Her focus had been on Totti's security, not external threats. She knew better than that.

A poor ambush, she re-evaluated, even if she had helped them out a little. Then she realised: it wasn't just an ambush, but a set-up.

They wanted to blame her for Totti's death, hence the attack in the bedroom instead of gunning her down else-where, making use of their numbers.

Always a narrative. Always someone to take the fall.

She had done the hard work for the Consensus: from Canada to Rome, from Cornish to Totti.

She checked the first guy's gun: it wasn't a firearm, but a tranquilliser gun.

Drop your weapon, he had said.

Surveillance outside, but the set-up had failed. The plan hadn't worked. They had no need to stay hidden any longer. There was no need for stealth. She readied herself for an assault.

Raven thumbed the mag release, tucked away the released clip, and slammed home a second. If there were two shooters, there were more, and she wanted a full clip before she faced anyone further.

If they killed her it wouldn't be because she was two rounds short. Oh, the indignity.

She dashed across the room to stand with her back flat against the wall as she knocked the half-open door with her heel, hard and fast.

A sudden movement, enough to encourage a storm of bullets in response.

She turned her face away as splinters thickened the air.

Another two shooters, based on the rhythm of muzzle reports. She let them waste rounds and damage their hearing. The gun smoke in their immediate vicinity would also be a hindrance.

The firing stopped and the door sizzled. The burnt polish stank.

Raven looked at the windows leading to the balcony.

*

The two shooters in the hallway were cautious. They had shot in haste, high on adrenaline, but were now controlled. Calmer. The woman was inside the master bedroom, still alive; so they were down two, but she was as good as trapped. They were a freelance mercenary outfit, all battle-hardened and experienced. They had worked together as a team many times, with roles determined at random, not by merit, because they were all competent. Once they had been part of a legitimate private security outfit with action in all the usual places. Now, they weren't on anyone's books. They were hired out by cartels and warlords, multinationals and individuals. They went anywhere the money was good. They didn't ask too many questions and never expected to finish a job with a clean conscience. They brutalised and tortured, assassinated and massacred. As such, they were in demand. They had a good rep. Which was why a mysterious old American had hired them to clear a villa of whomever was present, and then to wait for a woman – a pro – to arrive. Alive was the preferred condition, but dead if not. The old guy had supplied them with a location and orders to stand by and not much else. She would show up there to interrogate the home owner, a man named Totti, and wouldn't be expecting much resistance. He left them alone after that. They were mercs, not soldiers, and put together their own tactics. They had an objective, but they didn't take orders. Money had been paid up front, based on their reputation. All cash. No traces.

The two men had been there primarily for surveillance, to provide intel to the designated shooters. They had been positioned in the villa's grounds to keep watch on the target's movements – they couldn't predict her approach – and to secure the perimeter. The surveillance had supplied the two inside the master bedroom with constant updates.

They had listened to the gunfire, knowing the ambush had gone wrong. Now, they were no longer surveillance. They were no longer securing the perimeter. They were clean-up.

Two choices: wait for her to come out, or breach?

Those were the only options. The two shooters had the advantage if she emerged from the bedroom, but they gave that away to her if they tried to gain entry. Always easier to defend than to attack. Two-to-one odds in their favour, sure, but a good chance one of them would take a bullet or several in the process of breaching. They both wore good-quality armour, but better not to test its effectiveness. Especially given it hadn't saved the previous couple of guys. The two gunmen were no strangers to a firefight, but they weren't reckless and they weren't braver than they were paid to be.

They glanced at one another. They were thinking the same thing: stay put. Let her come to them. She had to, sooner or later.

One gestured to make clear, and the other nodded. Same page.

Glass smashed. Then more followed.

'*Balcony*,' one whispered.

They rushed forward along the hallway, rushing into the bedroom, rushing past the corpses on the floor towards where the French doors to the balcony had been shattered.

*

Raven, lying on the floor in the shadow of the first corpse, shot the two new gunmen in the back of the head.

She could take an extra split-second to make sure her aim was true, because even in the darkness she had nice clear targets as they silhouetted themselves against the night sky.

She rose to one knee as they dropped, then stood, gun trained on the open doorway as she listened for more. She heard nothing, but she had heard nothing the first time. These guys knew how to stay quiet.

Two fire teams of two men. One primary, one secondary. But each was hidden in place, attacking only when she had reached the designated ambush point – the master bedroom – and the second revealing themselves only after the first had failed. Good tactics. Four guns were better than one, but not possible for them all to hide in Totti's room, and it was too small to accommodate them; a stray bullet from a crossfire was just as fatal as one intended.

She searched the bodies, finding weapons and comms equipment, and night-vision scopes on the second two, which would have been used to track her approach to the villa.

She used the balcony and the first-floor windows to peer out into the night, utilising the vantage of higher ground. The night-vision scope was state of the art and amplified the available ambient light to enable her to spot a vehicle parked on the periphery of the villa's grounds, on a lane some 400 metres away. She could even make out a figure sitting in the driver's seat.

That the driver was still there told her he hadn't been

in direct communication with the other four, otherwise he wouldn't still be there. So he couldn't be any kind of commander. He needed updating only when the job was complete. He might not even have an earpiece. He might not know about the operational specifics.

But he would know where he had driven and where he had driven from, and where he would be driving to.

'We're going to play a game,' Raven said as she rose out of the darkness next to the van.

The window was down and she aimed the P7's muzzle at the driver's face. He stayed cool, despite the inevitable surprise and panic. His hands rose, slow and obvious.

'Do I need to explain the rules?'

He shook his head.

'Good,' Raven said. 'In which case, you might just survive this.'

THIRTY-SEVEN

The three Italian brothers had a car parked a short walk from the osteria in a narrow side street with parking restrictions they were happy to ignore. The vehicle was a classic Jaguar polished to a perfect sheen. Victor waited, leaning against the boot so he would see them coming and they would see him.

He heard them long before he saw them, because they had been drinking all day and all evening and were loud as they sauntered back to the Jag. They slowed when they saw him, not because they recognised him from the bar, but because he was leaning on the car.

'Hey,' one shouted as they drew near, 'get off, get away from my baby.'

Victor didn't move. He checked his watch.

The speaker was enraged, but his two brothers thought this was funny. They laughed and mocked him.

'It's a beautiful vehicle,' Victor said. 'XJS. Classic.

Racing green, cream interior. Probably my favourite combination. I almost stole it, just to take it for a spin, but I didn't have the heart. You can't steal a car like this without damaging it.'

The speaker came forward. He was the eldest brother, and had a solid build, almost squashed. His neck was so thick it appeared as one with the head and blended without seam into his trunk. His elbows jutted out, unable to fall in line with the shoulders with so much underneath competing for space. He walked with an awkward gait. Victor reckoned the man went through trousers fast, worn threadbare by rubbing thighs. His clothes had all been chosen to show off the physique to best effect. They were tight and restrictive. The sleeves of his T-shirt pinched his arms so hard that veins looked fit to burst down his forearms. Intimidating to some, maybe, but to Victor those veins formed a roadmap of how to kill the man in record time and with minimal effort if he had a blade.

'Do you know who I am? Do you have any idea who we are?'

Victor nodded. 'Do you know who I am?'

'You're the idiot who is going to get his head caved in,' another said.

'Giordano's debt,' Victor began. 'I'm clearing it.'

This surprised them and confused them in equal measure.

The third brother said, 'We don't want you to pay it off. It's his debt and his alone.'

'We're reasonable,' the first said, 'we let him pay in instalments.'

'You mean you want to keep the debt as leverage over him,' Victor said.

The second shrugged. 'He's a useful guy to know. What's this to you? Is he your boyfriend?'

'I'm not unreasonable either,' Victor said. 'So I'll tell you what: cancel the debt and I'll let you have the car back. That's the best I can do.'

None of them answered, but it didn't matter. They all stepped forward, until they were standing about a metre away – a show of strength, unity in case he was serious, which they still couldn't quite comprehend.

Victor said, 'The debt is cleared. You need to leave him alone, and his sister. One last chance to take my offer.'

'No way,' the third said.

The second added, 'Not in a million years.'

Victor's gaze passed over the three. They were a crew, but they were also brothers. Family. They were close. It didn't seem like anyone was in charge. They had all spoken to him. No one had looked to either of the others for guidance. No one had contradicted another. They were a democracy. They were a collective. There was no leader.

Victor said, 'Someone pick a number between one and three.'

'Why?' the first said. 'What are you doing?'

'One of you has to pick. It would be unfair if I did it for you.'

'Three,' the third one said with a grin, playing along because he didn't care.

'That's you,' Victor said.

'So?'

'I hope you're paying attention,' Victor said to the two others.

He walked away from the car and towards those two brothers so that when he pivoted on the spot and whipped out the edge of his palm, the third brother was caught unawares, too surprised to block or even flinch.

He staggered back a step. The other two hadn't seen the blow strike. They didn't understand what was happening.

The third brother clutched at his throat and his face reddened. He gasped and sputtered and made a soundless cry. The other two rushed to his aid.

'What's wrong?' the first shouted.

The third brother's face flushed from red to purple as his eyes turned the colour of blood. His lips became blue.

'His trachea is crushed,' Victor said. 'He's suffocating.'

'*Call an ambulance*,' the second screamed to the first.

'They won't get here in time,' Victor said. 'He's got less than a minute.'

The third man became limp in their arms. They called his name and tried mouth-to-mouth. He shuddered and trembled and was still.

'Now,' Victor said, 'about that debt.'

The gun came out, fast and in sure hands, but Victor had been expecting it. He intercepted the weapon before the muzzle was anywhere near him, twisting and ripping it from the man's hands, tossing it away because he didn't want the sound of gunshots alerting nearby cops or witnesses. Besides, he didn't need it.

Two swift elbow strikes put the disarmed man on his knees. A third, downward elbow to the temple dropped him face-first to the ground. A stamp to the back of his neck made sure he would never get up again.

The first brother, the eldest and the biggest, was also the slowest to react, overcome by shock, and could think about fighting back only as Victor's arm wrapped around his throat. By then it was far too late to make a difference.

A quick and easy way for Victor to pay off Giordano's debt and in some small way pay off his own. At least it would have been, had Victor waited against the boot of the car.

He hadn't. He had stood nearby, just watching them. He had mentally rehearsed the encounter as they approached the Jaguar, imagining how the failed attempt to get them to agree to cancelling the debt might go; then the moves necessary to disable and kill.

They were joking amongst themselves as they neared the car. They had no idea he was close to them. They had no idea he could kill them all in seconds. But they weren't targets and weren't threats. He had no reason to kill them and every reason not to. They were connected to Giordano, and so was Victor. His goal was to stay unnoticed, not attract further attention. Giordano was right: Victor wasn't going to put himself at risk, whatever debt of honour he owed.

When they reached the vehicle, the brothers were near enough to see him, if not his face. They paused, eyeing him with suspicion.

The eldest brother said, 'Get lost, creep.'

Victor did.

THIRTY-EIGHT

Sykes didn't like to drink in social situations. He liked to drink to get drunk. It wasn't acceptable in polite company to get shit-faced and pass out like guys at a bachelor party, like teenagers after prom. So he had a seltzer or a Coke, because one drink was a waste of his time and he could never stop at two. A soft drink meant he could maintain his façade of sobriety and then leave under the pretence of an early night. That was acceptable. People couldn't judge what they didn't know.

But he'd had a crappy day and had found himself with colleagues at a bar. So he had a drink to take the edge off, to wash away the stench of kissing ass. Then another. Then the inevitable third. Then everyone had made their excuses and gone and he had found another bar because he couldn't wait to get home to have the fourth drink he needed, and then lose count of those that followed.

The bar was some corner-block dive he had never set foot

in before. Warped linoleum lined the floor and the bar itself hadn't been polished in years. There was a poor selection of draught beers and a limited range of spirits, but they all contained alcohol so were all good with Sykes. He started with beers. Going into a bar and ordering bourbon seemed too eager, too needy, even a few drinks in, so he began with a cool glass of something imported. Then, when he asked for something stronger next, it made it look as if he had worked up to it; a natural progression, not desperation.

He hadn't planned on staying, but then again he had no plans. Plans were things he used to have and care about. There had always been some goal to work towards, something to achieve; promotion, recognition, wealth or power. That was the Sykes that Alvarez had talked about, had mocked the current incarnation for its weakness, its imitation.

Worthlessness and failure. Regret and longing. Darkness awaiting.

He realised both his elbows were on the bar and he had been talking for a long time. Drinking alone meant he didn't have the problem of oversharing, except maybe to the mirror or the idiot who read the news at one a.m. There was no comeback to that. They didn't remind him the next day what he'd said. They didn't remind him of what he couldn't take back.

Sykes stopped talking.

He had spoken in generalities only, he was sure. He was drunk, but he wasn't stupid.

'I hear what you're saying,' a voice said.

The man sitting nearby – the man Sykes had been talking, not to, but at – was maybe twenty years older and had a face marked by weariness, but his eyes were full of energy and mischief.

'You know, friend, this is why you shouldn't drink.'

'Explain,' Sykes said, trying to push himself back towards vertical.

'Makes you sad when you don't have to be,' the man said.

'Not if you're already down. It can't make you sad if you're not.'

The man shifted his stool a little closer, as if in conspiracy. He said, 'A man over fifty can pick and choose his reasons to wash away the melancholy because they are legion. A man under fifty has no real reason to be down, but that young man with a drink will believe any problem he has is both unique and insurmountable.'

Sykes listened.

The man continued: 'He will believe each inevitability of life is a cruel twist of fate engineered purely for him.'

Sykes stared.

'That young man with a drink will convince himself not only of his own insignificance, but paradoxically of his own exception, because he cannot comprehend that everyone else is just as trivial, their problems equally as ordinary.'

'What's the solution then?' Sykes asked after a time, seeking further wisdom.

'I would have thought that was the most obvious thing in the world,' the man responded with a wry smile. 'Have another drink.'

*

Sykes puked his guts up in the alleyway outside. It was over fast, however; a sudden and unexpected unleashing. A good deal of snot and tears followed. He wasn't crying – he wasn't the sort – but once one tap was turned they all were. He had staggered outside with the intention of going home when the need to urinate had compelled him into the alley instead of back into the bar, which had seemed beyond acceptable levels of effort.

'Ah, shit,' Sykes said, seeing his right shoe.

Without thinking, he raised his foot to wipe the toe of his shoe on the back of his left trouser leg.

'*Shit,*' he said again, when he realised what he was doing.

He stepped – stumbled – away from the splatter of yellow vomit on the ground, and found that staying upright was an incredible tax on his energy and balance. Better to take a seat.

He slumped on the asphalt, back against the exterior wall of the bar, opposite the vomit. It was steaming in the cool night air. He couldn't look away. The steam was a ghost, his ghost, ascending into blackness . . .

Sykes heard footsteps. He looked away from the mouth of the alley, trying to hide himself. He didn't want to be seen like this. He wanted the ground to open and drag him beneath.

It didn't.

'You okay over there?' a woman said.

He grunted and shooed with his hand. He didn't want help. He didn't want the ruin that was Sykes to be witnessed, to be made real, accountable.

'Need me to call someone? Get you home?'

'I'm fine,' he said without looking at her, breathing hard.

She stepped towards him and he attempted to shuffle away from her, but he found himself far too heavy to move with any effectiveness. Leaning was the best he could manage, until he realised he would tip over, and shot out a palm to steady himself.

Sykes spluttered, 'I don't want your help, lady.'

She positioned herself so he had no choice but to look at her. She lowered herself to her haunches, so her ankles became her legs, then body and then face. He found her attractive in the same way he found pretty much any woman attractive when he was hammered. Not that he remembered the last time his dick worked as it should.

'Are you sure?' she said. 'Are you sure you don't want me to call someone?'

'Leave. Me. *Alone.*'

She reached into a pocket of her coat. 'Here, you can use my phone. You can keep it if you like.'

Sykes didn't feel quite so drunk all of a sudden. He watched as the woman took a mobile from her pocket and held it out towards him. Now he understood.

'Take it,' she ordered.

Sykes obeyed.

THIRTY-NINE

The driver wasn't just the driver. He was the go-between. The bag man. He knew who had hired the team of shooters to wipe out Totti and his crew and lie in wait for Raven. That man was a foreigner, an American. *He's old. Distinguished. He never gave a name, but I know where he's staying ...*

That old man was staying in a rented apartment. It was the penthouse of a small tenement that occupied a corner in Rome's old town. The converging streets were narrow; plenty of room for horses and the occasional carriage, but now part of a one-way system. Traffic was rare. Residents in this part of the city didn't own cars. There were no garages and no room to park on the streets. There weren't even any kerbs. It was quiet as a result.

Raven had done her homework, and found nothing interesting or concerning. After the ambush at Totti's villa she had taken no chances with her preparations. She had risked losing her window with the old man instead of risking her life rushing into another trap.

To her surprise, there was no evidence of one. Whoever the old man was, he wasn't scared of reprisals. He had to know she was getting close to him. But he hadn't fled. He had stayed put, despite the massacre at Totti's villa. She couldn't help but wonder why.

A day was plenty of time to make an escape, but not a lot of time to assemble more shooters. The Consensus had no standing army of people to draw upon.

The old man's bodyguard was a local from a security firm. He was a different man from the one who had been keeping the old man company during the daytime. They worked twelve-hour shifts to provide him with round-the-clock cover. Both were competent, from Raven's observations, but after posing as a prospective client to scope out their firm, it was obvious they were no real threat to her. Both were big and intimidating, the sort of guys who were hired out by visiting pop stars. They were good at pushing away over-eager fans and carrying luggage, but they had no military background. Neither was a serious operator.

Which was interesting. Raven knew something wasn't right, but she didn't know what.

She needed to question the old man regardless. She couldn't waste this chance to learn more about her enemies, and if there was nothing to learn in this instance, she could still remove another one of them. Maybe eliminate this entire cell's operational capabilities.

It was too good an opportunity to miss.

She decided on a rooftop approach. No need to bother any of the neighbours in the apartments below that way. Aside from borrowing their balconies to scale the building, that is. In the late afternoon the neighbourhood was almost silent. Siesta time.

The penthouse's balcony had terracotta tiles and wrought-iron railings. Some plants provided greenery around a bistro table and two chairs. She imagined it was a pleasant place to enjoy a glass of wine in the evening. French doors provided access to the rest of the apartment.

They were locked, but the lock was as quaint and charming as the neighbourhood, built in a quieter time.

She eased the doors open and stepped into an open-plan lounge and kitchen. It was bright, with plenty of ambient light from the sunshine outside flooding inside, and a flickering glow came from further inside, along with faint sounds of conversation. She pictured the bodyguard watching TV to pass the time while his client did whatever.

She kept close to the walls as she made her way over the floorboards. They looked solid and well-maintained, but it didn't hurt to be careful. In the hall, she could hear the sound of the television enough to make out the laughter track of a sitcom.

It was a two-bedroom apartment, with a clear master bedroom and a second, smaller one, suitable for a 'single bed' or 'home office', she had learned from an old listing. As far as she could tell, the apartment was rented by an off-shore company. There would be a spider-web of ownership behind it that would take forever to link to any individual.

There was no noise or any sign of activity from the

master bedroom. The old man could be having a siesta. A decent parabolic microphone could have told her for certain before she had committed to entering the property, but she had no such luxuries.

She caught the bodyguard napping – literally. He had fallen asleep in front of the TV.

Raven shot him with one of the dart guns she had taken from the shooters in Totti's villa.

It made a *pop* sound. Loud, like a balloon exploding.

The bodyguard woke up, wincing because he had a big dart in his shoulder, but he didn't know that. His eyes struggled to focus on Raven as she reloaded the gun with another dart and shot him again. He was a big guy.

He said, 'Who . . . ?' and passed out.

He had a gun, which she collected. Like the dart gun, like the night-vision scope, she looted what she could to utilise on the next mission. Spoils of war.

The old man was ready by the time Raven entered the master bedroom. He was sitting on an armchair with a pistol in his right hand, pointed at her.

She glanced at the desk next to him. 'I don't imagine you're much of a shot without your glasses.'

'They're for reading.'

'So go ahead, let's see what you're made of. Dare you.'

'And why haven't you shot me, Miss Stone?'

She rolled her eyes. 'What is it with people refusing to call me Raven?'

He didn't answer. 'Is Luca dead?'

'He's sleeping. He's going to wake up feeling like crap, but he's going to wake up.'

'How merciful of you.'

Raven said, 'I'm not big on collateral damage, and I'm not going to kill innocent people just to get to the bad guys. That would make me a bad guy too, wouldn't it?'

'I'm afraid I'm not qualified to judge your motivation, Miss Stone. Perhaps I could recommend a psychiatrist to you.'

'You're funny,' she said. 'But do you know what's funnier? I told someone once about you guys. I tried to explain what you were. I said you were the old white men who ran the world. I wasn't being literal. Yet here you are. Old. White. Male.'

'I don't rule the world, Miss Stone.'

'You work for those who do.'

'Maybe I work for no one. Maybe, like you, I serve my own interests and only my own interests.'

'Then your interests must align with the others or they wouldn't let you do what you do.'

'You give them too much credit. You're creating phantoms to explain what is very real, very human.'

'I know all too well how real you guys are, and I like to demonstrate that you're all too human.'

The old man said, 'Then perhaps you could tell me why you haven't yet demonstrated my humanity. Why haven't you killed me?'

'I'm a traditional kind of gal. I like to get to know a person first.'

'You can't hope to learn anything from me. You must have realised by now that we operate with next to no knowledge of one another's activities.'

'Yeah,' she said. 'You Consensus guys have got a good

289

thing going on there. Doesn't make my job very easy, I'll tell you that.'

'We're not called the Consensus, Miss Stone. We're not called anything. We have no name.'

She shrugged. 'You're the Consensus to me. I had to name you something. When you say "they" or "them" all the time, people think you're a conspiracy theorist in a tinfoil hat.'

'We wouldn't want anyone to think you're crazy, now would we?'

'I have a hard time convincing myself otherwise, let alone anyone else.'

The old man gestured with his pistol. 'I'm going to set this down. It's getting heavy.'

He did so with an exaggerated slowness. She watched, confused. Then she sidestepped towards the window, still keeping her own weapon aimed at him while she glanced outside. The street was empty. No sign of any backup.

'You have nothing to fear from me,' the old man said. 'In fact, I've been waiting for you to come and see me.'

'Don't think you can convince me you mean me no harm. You've already tried to have me killed.'

'That's not my goal.'

'It's not? Because there's a whole lot of corpses who would argue otherwise. I mean, if they could argue. They can't, being dead. That's part of the condition.'

'I have sent only one team after you, and they were tasked with your apprehension, not execution.'

'Then why the guns?'

'Backup,' the old man explained, 'in the event the

primary objective failed. A contingency is useful when dealing with a dangerous individual such as yourself.'

'Stop it, you'll make me blush.'

The old man said, 'Killing you has been a goal of ours for a long time, given your insatiable desire to do us harm, but I'm of the belief that there are other, better solutions to the particular problem that is you. It is a problem I have inherited and thought carefully about. I believe my predecessors lacked imagination. I believe they misjudged you.'

'Go on.'

'Why do you think I put down the gun?'

'Because you're a weak old man with about as much chance of hitting me as we both have of being struck by lightning at the same time?'

'Amusing,' he said. 'I had read about your glibness. I told you I don't want to kill you and I know, once this conversation is concluded, you won't kill me either.'

'Keep dreaming.'

'Your parents are both dead, correct?'

'Thanks for reminding me of that particular pain. But, please, give me even more reasons to dislike you.'

'You have no family at all, do you? No dependants?'

'No one for you to use against me,' she said, and then regretted it.

'That's what it says in your file, otherwise we would have exploited that by now. However, when I said my predecessors lacked imagination, I wasn't just talking about their desire to kill you. You see, no one looked beyond your CIA file, and why would they? Because you would have been thoroughly vetted. But the Agency was only looking at you as a person, as a potential threat. They weren't looking for leverage. They weren't picking apart your young life to find any potential weakness that could one day be used against you. Your file listed blood relations, naturally. But not those that would be considered family by any other name.'

Raven felt cold.

The old man said, 'How's your brother Ben getting on these days?'

FORTY

Raven hid her rising nausea. The old man was bluffing. They didn't know about her brother. No one did. Maybe they found out the name, but he was her stepbrother in everything but name. They had grown up together. Her mother had taken Ben in when his junkie mom had abandoned him. It had never been official. No papers, no adoption, because the junkie mom had got herself cleaned up in the end and wanted Ben back. By then he didn't want to go back. He never changed his name. He stayed with them, where he wanted to stay. He was her brother but not via biology and not on paper.

'It took considerable time and effort to find him,' the old man explained. 'Ironically, had you not gone rogue, had you not turned against us, we would never have known about him. Only in our hunt for you did we stumble across his existence. There's no legal document linking the two of you, but plenty of your old high-school year who never moved away knew about Constance and her "brother", Ben. All the algorithms in the world couldn't discover what legwork and small talk could. Of course, it helped you that he moved to Scotland, which certainly slowed the process. I dare say much of the trouble you have caused us might have been averted had my predecessors known what I know.'

She was caught in a moment of indecision: deny the connection or pretend it didn't matter. They already knew Ben was real so she said, 'He's nothing to me. I haven't seen him in years.'

'I thought you might say something like that. But you must know you can't bluff your way out of this. If there is even a one per cent chance you care about Ben, then we will act on that. If you haven't seen him in years then you might not be aware he's married now. He has a lovely Scottish wife, Suzanne. She runs a book store. It's losing money, but it means a lot to her. Ben has taken over her father's farm. The father's too old to run it himself, but he thinks of Ben as a son. Ben and Suzanne seem happy. I wouldn't be surprised if they were thinking of starting a family.'

Raven couldn't speak.

'I see you didn't know about the wedding. Must hurt not to have been invited.'

It did hurt. She hadn't seen Ben since she began doing black ops, not since they were kids, when they were still close. They had been the same age, brought together by chance, two lost souls without siblings. Their bond had been like no other. Which was why she hadn't seen him for ten years, doing everything she could to keep him secret, to keep him safe from what she was doing for her country, then safe from her enemies. She kept wanting to seek him out, to ask how he was doing, to hug him, but the more she learned about the Consensus, the more impossible that hug became. She thought it had worked too. It had worked, but no longer.

'You should have known this would happen one day. Everyone can be found if one knows how to look.'

She had no choice but to ask, 'What do you want?'

'I want you to work for us again, Miss Stone. I want you to work for me. The team at Totti's villa were there to drug you and bring you to me so we could have this very conversation. There is nothing personal between us. I care about very few people, least of all those you have killed to expedite my progression in – what did you call it? – the Consensus. I want to bring you back on side, to make use of your talents in the way they were designed.'

'And in return you leave Ben and Suzanne alone?'

'A simple arrangement that benefits all parties involved, wouldn't you say?'

'How do I know you'll stick to the deal?'

'If you have reservations, I'm happy to kill Suzanne first, just to prove to you that we're serious, just to incentivise you to do as we ask. And, naturally, we will make sure Ben knows that you could have saved his lovely wife but chose not to.'

'You're a monster.'

'I'm whoever I need to be. Now, I'm your new boss.'

Raven said, 'What do you want me to do?'

'What you're good at, what you're best at. I want you to kill for me.'

'Who?'

'All in good time, but, naturally, someone whose death we would benefit from.'

'You mean someone who is a threat to you,' she said. 'Like I am.'

The old man smiled. 'Like you *were*.'

Raven understood. This target would be someone important, someone who would be missed, and they wanted her to do this particular job because she was already a wanted woman, already a rogue assassin. No need to create a narrative for the assassination when there already was one. Then the Consensus could pass the baton to the whole US intelligence community. They would come after her with everything they had.

'So I'll be on the run and too occupied to come after you. Clever. I like it.'

'That's correct, Miss Stone. But Ben and Suzanne will be safe. They'll be alive.'

'What's stopping me killing you right now and going straight to Ben and Suzanne?'

He checked his watch. 'Because tonight you need to be in Prague. There's a man-made beach along the river. There'll be a bank of payphones near it. One will ring at midnight. The one on the east edge. You're going to answer it. You will be provided with another city, another address, another deadline. I'm sure you can see the merits of this. If you don't pick up by the third ring, your brother and his wife die.'

'What if the phone is being used?'

'Get there early. Make sure no one is using it.'

'My flight could be delayed.'

'Miss Stone, if you want your brother to stay alive, you will find a way to pick up that phone when it rings. And please note that we are closely monitoring Ben. If you attempt to contact him, that will be the last time you hear his voice.'

'What happens if I make all the calls? You can't keep me bouncing around indefinitely.'

'At some point you'll end up in the right city and you'll receive your assignment.'

'How do I know this isn't a trap to kill me?'

'If I wanted to kill you, this would be the trap. But, unlike my predecessors, I don't wish a bloodbath. You're not the type of girl who goes quietly, are you?'

'That almost sounds like another compliment.'

'Take it how you wish, but don't forget what's at stake here. There is an odious gentleman in Aberdeenshire right now, awaiting my call. It's up to you what he does next. He's the one who managed to track down Ben and Suzanne. He's dependable. He's efficient. He's not as refined an operator as yourself, but his enthusiasm for such tasks makes up for his lack of finesse. You would be sent to assassinate a warlord, for example, while he would be sent to massacre the village. He has assembled a team of similarly unpleasant gentlemen. They're waiting for my call. Or . . . not my call. Right now, they're on a leash, and it's a tight one. But I can release them at any time if you don't work for me exactly as instructed.'

'Work,' she echoed. 'You make it sound so ordinary, when you want me to be an assassin again.'

'That's who you were, who you trained to be, who you still are. It's all you'll ever be.'

She was silent.

'In return,' he continued, 'Ben will be safe. Suzanne will be safe. They'll continue with their lives and you'll be able to thank yourself for that.'

'And live with the ghost of who I killed for you.'

'He's no innocent. No one is in our world. The only innocents in this are Ben and Suzanne. Your family. Wouldn't it be nice to be an aunt some day? Work for me and you can have your life back. You might one day even be able to go home. You do remember your life, don't you?'

'I remember how you people took it away from me.'

'You didn't have to go rogue. You didn't have to betray your country.'

'I killed innocent people for you. I was made to believe I was doing the right thing. I thought I was doing good.'

'The right thing for the people I represent is the right thing for America.'

She laughed. 'Do you know how ridiculous you sound?'

'What's ridiculous is that you still don't understand you have no choice.'

Raven said, 'Oh, I've got that. But, answer me this: are you in the Consensus for life? Do you stay a member in retirement?'

'What are you asking?'

'Because after I've done this, after I'm long forgotten, after Ben is long forgotten, I'm going to kill you. And it won't be quick.'

He smiled. 'Even if this absurd fantasy ever came to fruition, I didn't make this decision. I'm merely a messenger.'

'But you're enjoying this, aren't you?'

'I take a certain satisfaction in a job well done.'

'I'll remind you of that when I'm peeling the flesh from your face.'

'Careful, Miss Stone. I don't have as much at stake in this as you do. I cancel this mission with no comeback, no fall-out, and no regrets. I can ensure neither Ben nor Suzanne come to a pleasant end. There is a flight to Prague at seven p.m. You can make it, but not if you delay.'

Raven thought.

The old man said, 'What is your decision?'

FORTY-ONE

The drive back to Rome was pleasant and uneventful. Victor didn't drive often. He didn't like being boxed inside a small vehicle with his attention distracted by driving. The Jaguar was a joy to drive, however, and he was sad to leave it unlocked in a bad part of the city. He could only hope the thief who stole it next would treat it with some respect. Two buses, a taxi and a long walk to draw out any surveillance brought him back to his hotel. It was approaching dawn, but he wasn't tired. For his current sleep pattern, it was about midday.

Victor liked the hotel. It was a grand old building with uneven walls and skewed floors that made him feel drunk as he walked along them. He didn't remember the last time he had been drunk. The room was perfect. The room's sash window was stiff and required plenty of upward force to shift. There would be no sliding it up from the outside even without the catch fixed. The door was big and old and heavy, and the handle didn't turn as it should; the door required a good heave to open inwards. There was no way anyone could do so without making noise. A heavy desk was positioned on the wall next to it, which was simple enough to drag, but formed an excellent barricade when Victor positioned it before the door. The thick carpet and uneven floor combined to ensure that even the strongest and most determined assailant would struggle to get the door open far enough to enter with the barricade in place.

It wasn't, of course, because he hadn't been in the room. He unlocked the door and stepped inside, knowing he had an uninvited visitor before he checked any of his indicators because she was standing waiting in the centre of the room.

Raven said, 'Where have you been?'

He recognised the distress in her voice. 'What's wrong?'

'Is there any reason you can't leave this moment?'

'No.'

'Then let's move.'

He heard the urgency in her words, and respected her opinion enough to do as she requested without argument. She handed him his attaché case – already packed because he always had his things ready to go at a moment's notice – and led him out of the room and through the hotel. He didn't ask any questions. Now wasn't the time. She would explain when she could.

She had a car parked a few streets away. He climbed into the passenger seat.

She told him what had happened at Totti's villa and then in the old man's apartment. She explained about Ben and

Suzanne and the flight she needed to be on as she drove to the airport.

'There's more,' Raven said. 'This old man knows about you. He doesn't know that you're here in Rome. I didn't tip him off, but he told me you were being taken care of.'

Victor thought about this. 'So, he knows about the open contract. About Phoenix.'

'He didn't say any more. I don't know if he's the one who put the contract out there.'

'If he knows about it, then either he's the client, or he knows who the client is.'

Raven nodded. 'Probably.'

'The guy running the crew in Aberdeen,' Victor began. 'Did you get a feel for how close he is to the old man?'

'He used words like dependable and efficient.'

'So, they've worked together before. There's a connection there. He's more than just a contractor.'

Raven said, 'That's my take on it.'

'Then he could lead me to the old man, who could lead me to Phoenix.'

'You know what I'm going to ask, don't you?'

He did. He had known early. He said, 'I'm not a body-guard, Constance. I've done that exactly one time and I made a mess of it. That's not who I am.'

'I'm not asking you to be a bodyguard. I want you to intervene. I wouldn't ask you if I could do it myself. But there's just no way. They've got me in a corner. If I try and get to Ben, it won't work because in a few hours I need to be in Prague to answer a phone call. If I try and get to Scotland myself, I'm going to be sat on my ass at 31,000 feet when that phone rings. I'm going to be somewhere in the clouds when the old man hangs up and calls his guy in Aberdeenshire. I'm going to be hundreds of miles away when my baby brother and his wife are butchered. But you can go for me.'

'And I'll still be unable to help because I'll be just as far away as you would have been.'

'He said there would be another location, another phone call to answer. Think about it, whatever they're planning can't be ready yet. This is the plan, but they didn't know when they would be able to put it into motion. He said the crew is waiting to go into action. That means when everything is in place, that crew is going to go in and take Ben and Suzanne hostage to make sure I kill the target. But I'm not where I need to be yet, so the crew is still waiting.'

'The target could be in Prague.'

'No way,' Raven said. 'They're not going to show their hand so readily to their worst enemy. They're not going to reveal anything until they know for sure I'm going to comply. That's only going to happen when Ben and Suzanne are at their mercy. They want me hopping from city to city, answering these phone calls to keep me out of the way, not only so I can't get to Ben but so they have time to put things together. You know how a hit works. You can't just have a plan and expect it'll work whenever you choose. You have to wait until the timing is right. That's not always up to you.'

'You're making a lot of assumptions.'

'What choice do I have?'

Victor didn't answer because he didn't have one.

Raven said, 'Will you help me?'

'It's already you who owes me.'

'You only care about yourself. I get that. I don't care. So do this for yourself, because this is a chance to get one step closer to Phoenix, and the only way I can help you is if you help me first. You want to die and be reborn, well I'm your minister. If anything happens to Ben or his wife then I'll be no good to you, because I'll be dead too. Whoever is out there watching Ben and Suzanne, deal with them. There's a crew. I'm asking you to do exactly what you're good at. Nothing more. I'll pay you, if that's what it takes. Think of it as a job. This is a business transaction. I'm hiring you to kill whoever is planning to kill my brother.'

Victor said, 'There's no guarantee I can get there in time.'

'Try.'

'I'm rushing in blind. That's not what I do.'

'No, you've got it the wrong way around. You're not rushing in blind. They are. They have no idea you're coming.'

She was right. Whoever was in this crew had been hired to kidnap and murder two civilians. They weren't expecting exterior threats. There was no time to prepare, but the element of surprise was perhaps the best advantage he could have.

Raven said, 'They don't know we're still working together. You're my ace in the hole.'

'What are you asking me to do exactly?'

'Keep Ben safe, temporarily. The old man told me the guy running the crew is waiting for a call. Stop him. I want you to buy me some time.'

'For what purpose?'

'I want to find out who the target is, and I want to keep him alive. If he's a threat to the Consensus, then he's an ally of mine.'

'You can't keep Ben safe forever.'

'Maybe not, but I don't have much choice right now. The old man kept talking about his predecessor – he never spoke about a superior. I don't believe anyone else knows about Ben. These cells operate largely independently from one another. If we can get rid of this particular cell, the others might never find out I have a brother. Which is why I need you and I need you now. Do this for me and I'll do whatever it takes, whatever you need.'

'You have Ben's address?'

She nodded. 'Of course. He runs a farm in Aberdeenshire.'

'It's going to take time to reach him.'

'You can be there by the afternoon.'

Victor spent a minute thinking it through. He said, 'We know you'll arrive first, but they're going to keep you busy because, as you said, however much you've played into their hands, they couldn't have known when you would show up. And you're right that even if they have a whole crew watching Ben, they can't just move on him instantly. He could be at the store. He could be hosting a braai for the whole neighbourhood.'

'What's a braai?'

'South African for barbecue. Anyway, they're sending you to Prague, where you'll receive more instructions, which may or may not take you to your final destination. When you do, there'll be someone waiting for you. Someone who will be keeping an eye on you until everything else is in place, and then to make sure you actually follow through.'

'A babysitter.'

He nodded. 'Even when they have Ben and Suzanne hostage – they can't control you otherwise. He'll make sure you stay put while they do whatever else they need to do. The more I think about it, the more I'm convinced that even with the most meticulous planning, this is something that is going to take at least a couple of days to put into motion. There are too many moving parts to fall into line.'

'That gives us more time. That gives you more time to get to Ben.'

'Just because they'll need to hold your brother and his wife for two days, it doesn't mean I can get to them before the crew does.'

She knew this too. 'And what if you don't?'

'Then I'll need to improvise.'

'Be careful. He's my brother.'

'If they get to him before I do, he's dead anyway. You need to accept that now.'

She took a huge inhale and nodded.

'I'll do what I can,' Victor said. 'But whatever happens, they're not letting him go. If you do exactly what they want, Ben and Suzanne are loose ends they won't leave alone.'

'I know you'll do what you can. I won't blame you if you can't save them.'

Victor was silent.

Raven said, 'This is my fault and mine alone.'

He said, 'You need to concentrate on your own task.

Don't get yourself killed because you're distracted by what's happening in Scotland.'

'Since when do you care if I get myself killed?'

'Because you still owe me that favour. I need you alive.'

'Do you ever think about anyone but yourself?'

'Now really isn't the right time to bait me, Constance.'

'You're right. I'm sorry. I'm freaking out here.'

'And that's precisely what will get you killed, and probably Ben and Suzanne too. You can't help them if you're dead.'

'What if I am? What if they send me on a suicide job before you can rescue them? Will you still help them if I'm not around to pay my debt?'

'Keep yourself alive and the answer is irrelevant.'

'Tell me you'll still help them.'

'Stay alive, Constance, for me, for Ben and Suzanne, and for yourself too.'

FORTY-TWO

Boxing had two benefits: it kept Leyland fit and kept her calm. It was impossible to feel anything beyond the physical when exercising above 70 per cent of maximum heart rate and trying not to get hit in the face. Her dad had got her into it, and though he was long gone, she carried on his obsession like a good daughter. She didn't train every week – work could be hell – but sometimes she trained more than once per day. Today was one of those days. She had managed to get an hour at the boxing gym before heading to the office, but hadn't felt like going home at the end of the working day. Which for Leyland often ended closer to midnight than not. Her gym was open twenty-four hours and was accessible only through a key-card entry system, which was why Alvarez was waiting in the car park instead of inside.

She recognised him from her research. He looked older in person. More weary.

'It's late,' she said as she approached.

He was sitting on the bonnet of his hire car, which was parked next to hers. A street lamp made his scalp glow.

'Plane landed a couple hours ago,' he explained. 'Didn't much fancy tossing and turning in a crappy hotel bed. Thought it would be good to say hello.'

Leyland said, 'Hello.'

'Would you like to know why I'm here?'

She used a key fob to unlock the boot and dropped her gym bag inside. 'I'm guessing you're going to tell me.'

'How was the embassy party last week?' Alvarez asked. 'Have a nice time?'

'I love an official party. They're always good value, even when they're not. If you know what I mean.'

'I'm not sure I do, Miss Leyland. But I'm sure you would be good company.'

'If this is your way of asking me out on a date, you're going about it in the worst possible way.'

'Forgive me.'

'What can I do for you that couldn't wait until tomorrow?'

Alvarez said, 'I'm not going to be here tomorrow. This is just a pit stop. I'm in the air again first thing.'

'Terrible shame,' she said, stony-faced.

'Look,' he said. 'I'm sure you and Muir were acquainted at the party. I'm sure you've been in contact since. Thick as thieves, I bet.'

'We swapped numbers.'

'So you're all up to speed,' he said. 'And I'm guessing that you're of the opinion that this is nothing to do with you and you can stay out of it. Am I close?'

'You may continue.'

'This is a CIA problem,' he continued. 'An American problem. But I would appreciate the cooperation of our very close allies.'

'Funny word, allies,' Leyland said. 'It's kind of friends, isn't it? Except an ally is only a friend while they're useful.'

Alvarez shrugged. 'We can be useful to each other, sure.'

'How so?'

'Because when Tesseract – or Cleric as you call him – is brought down, everyone who has used him is going to have to answer for that. Heads will roll, as they say.'

'I see,' Leyland said. 'And you'll be grateful to those who helped sharpen the axe.'

Alvarez nodded. 'Something like that.'

Leyland leaned against her car. 'And what, pray tell, might I receive in return?'

'You'll have a close personal friend in the upper echelons of the US intelligence community.'

'I'm overwhelmed with Christmas cards as it is.'

Alvarez folded his arms in front of his chest. He was frustrated, but trying to hide it. In doing so it was only more apparent. 'I'm sensing you're not going to cooperate with me on this.'

'As you said before, this is a CIA problem. It's not my business what has transpired before my time. This Tesseract you speak of – even if I did know him, whatever he did beforehand is irrelevant to me. A useful asset is a useful asset.'

'You're going to lose that asset, Miss Leyland. That's going to happen with or without your help. It'll take a little longer without, granted, but this is only ever going to end one way. When it does, your asset is gone and you've had the chance to make a new friend and chosen not to. That doesn't seem like the smartest play to me, does it to you?'

'I think we're operating with a different playbook here.'

'Tell me about it. While I'm trying to do the right thing, you're employing a professional killer wanted on four continents.'

Leyland smiled, polite, and opened the driver's door. 'Good night.'

'Wait,' Alvarez said, reaching out a hand to catch the door. 'I have no problem with you, personally. I know you're just doing your job in the best way you can.'

Leyland stared at Alvarez's hand and he released it. He backed off a step.

'We're on different sides here,' she said. 'But we don't have to be enemies.'

He nodded. 'I agree.'

'So, let's just stay out of each other's way. Okay?'

He nodded again. 'I shouldn't have come here. I'm sorry. It wasn't necessary. It was just something I ...' He didn't finish. Instead he said, 'Good night.'

Something in his voice made her curious. *It wasn't necessary.* 'Can I ask you a question?'

'Sure. Shoot.'

'You seem pretty confident you can catch Tesseract.'

He shrugged, like admitting to confidence was something embarrassing.

She continued: 'This is a man who has been on the run for years; a man whose name no one knows; he's a mystery, a ghost; the only trail that leads anywhere near him is the line of corpses of those who have tried. He's avoided CIA, Russian intelligence, half the police forces of Europe, and he even slipped through the net on US soil. Yet somehow, despite all of this, you're going to be the one who catches him.'

'Yes,' Alvarez said.

Leyland didn't know whether to laugh or sigh. She said, 'If you don't mind, and this is purely to satisfy my own curiosity, please tell me what makes you believe you are going to do what no one else has managed? What makes you so special?'

'Remember that rogue agent you had, the one selling secrets a while back? Well, he sold me a file on the killer. A real bargain at twice the price. It's been a big help, but even without that I was the one on his trail once upon a time. Put the two together and I've found out something about him that no one else knows.'

Alvarez stood and backed away a step. He removed his car keys from a pocket and thumbed the remote unlock. He made Leyland wait.

Leyland waited, but she cracked first. 'Well, what is it? What do you know?'

She couldn't see Alvarez's eyes because he had turned to get into his rental car, but she sensed a glimmer in them as he said, 'I know who he really is.'

FORTY-THREE

The call came right on schedule. Niven listened to the short confirmation of his orders and passed them on to the crew he had assembled. They were all veteran criminals. One had even been a police officer. Niven had been one too, way back. He had worked in narcotics, busting dealers and going after gangs. Good times, until he had been forced out of the police when Internal Affairs had come sniffing around on account of one too many infractions. The list of felonies while in uniform they were after him for was extensive and included fraud, extortion and excessive force, but what they didn't know was he had done far worse. They didn't know he had been a career criminal with a badge, who had hijacked, beaten, stolen and murdered. He had tried to fight the mounting pressure, but Niven could only intimidate, coerce and kill so much, so he had quit before IA found anything that would put him in a cage. He had put plenty of lowlifes inside, some legit and some he had set

313

up, but either way he knew he wouldn't last long in prison. The Consensus liked people like him. People who appeared clean on paper, but were dirty to the core; men and women who had broken the law and were more than willing to break it again if it meant sizeable donations to offshore accounts or a briefcase of cash left on their back seat.

There were no women for this job, though. It had been deemed inappropriate. The five men had been selected as individuals. They were from all corners of the British Isles, all used before by Niven's shadowy boss, but they hadn't operated together until now and they wouldn't afterwards. No one used their real name. It kept exposure to a minimum. Loyalty was non-existent as a result, but loyalty didn't matter when those in question were expendable. They were not like Niven. They were foot soldiers. Just thugs. Useful for messy jobs like this, but not for anything more. If necessary, they were disposable.

Niven's orders were simple: make it look like a home invasion. Common enough to imitate, if not as common in Scotland as they were back home. Home invasions almost always ended the same way, and this one would go by the established pattern. It would be bloody. It would be brutal. Niven had been chosen because he had proven himself without compunction. The crew were the same. They had done awful things before the Consensus had started hiring them to do even worse. They were hired because they were animals.

The fate of Ben and Suzanne Mayes was set in stone, but that end might not come for a while. So far, Raven – who Niven had been briefed on – was going along with the plan, so Ben and Suzanne were to be held hostage, not killed outright. From what Niven knew about Raven, he hadn't been sure she would be manipulated with just threats. He had figured there was a good chance it would all be over pretty fast, and he'd be rushing in and butchering the Mayes right at the get-go. Now, there was a good chance Niven and his crew would be there for a couple of days, if that's what it took. Some had hoped it would last. Some were sadists.

Their vehicle was a Ford Explorer. It was stolen. An old vehicle that was as disposable as the men inside. They made sure to stop longer than they needed at a stop sign they knew was overlooked by the CCTV camera of a convenience store at the lonely intersection. The camera's angle was such that it wouldn't see the occupants, but the licence plate would be visible. They wanted the local police to find the footage and match the vehicle to one that belonged to a local heroin addict, a man who had been in prison for aggravated robbery, who associated with degenerates and thugs with records. Jewellery from the Mayes' house would be stashed at the house where the junkie lived. DNA would be planted. The case would solve itself. Justice would be done for the Mayes, and the community could sleep easier knowing their brutal murder had been avenged.

That's why Niven was so essential to his boss, to the wider organisation. He knew how to handle these kind of jobs in such a way that they didn't look like these kind of jobs at all. He had been doing them his whole life, in one way or another. Without a badge, he started off working for mobsters and dealers, running protection for small-time crooks to keep other small-time crooks from ripping them off. He used what he had learned as a cop to maximise his criminal activities, both in who to target and how to avoid getting caught.

He had built up a reputation as being uncompromising and brutal by the time he started receiving anonymous phone calls from unlisted numbers. He hadn't known who hired him, apart from the fact that it was always the same voice on the end of the line. One of those slimy DC types from the way he spoke. Niven was fascinated by the secret world he had been brought into. They always paid on time and well over the going rate, but Niven wanted more. He wanted in.

'I can do more for you than just odd jobs,' he implored. 'I can be a real asset.'

'Keep doing the work I send and doors will open,' the voice told him.

You don't want me to take your job, he thought. *One day I will. One day I'll be kicking back with a cold one while someone else throws away another ruined shirt.*

He had gone from being someone called upon only to hurt to an all-round go-to guy. He had found Suzanne and Ben, after all. He had been trusted with sensitive intelligence, trusted to make use of it. He was earning his way inside, a little at a time.

And he had an edge the guy on the phone didn't know about.

Niven was sly. He was an ex-cop. He had friends and he had leverage and he put both to use. All electronic communication was traceable with enough time, enough effort and enough resources. Niven knew who was calling him. He wasn't supposed to. He reckoned it would get him killed if they found out, but it was his way in when the time was right, and until then it was his bargaining chip if they ever turned on him.

It had been a cold day and the evening had taken that cold and doubled it. The five guys were shivering because Niven wouldn't let them put on the heater. He could sweat in a snowstorm. When they were only a few miles out, they stopped the vehicle and disembarked. In the trunk were six sets of black synthetic trousers, black T-shirts and sweaters, gloves, shoes and beanie hats. They stripped to their underwear, shivering hard, and Niven ignored their complaints while he checked them for personal effects or anything else they shouldn't have on their person. Then he bagged up their day clothes, handing out the right set of black clothes to each man. Niven's own outfit was a little tight because he had been less honest when supplying his waist size to their employer. No problem. It wasn't as if he was going to be getting physical. That was what the others were paid for. He was paid to run the job. He was looking forward to it. To promotion. To being the guy on the other end of the phone. He didn't want them thinking he was fat and lazy. He wanted them to think of him as a good investment.

The Mayes' farmhouse was isolated. Grazing pastures surrounded it. There was only a single-lane dirt track that led from the highway to the home, weather-beaten stone and tile, classic Scottish, rugged and decent. The perfect location for indecency of the worst kind, thought

Niven as he directed the driver to kill the lights and drive slow.

It was three in the morning. No lights glowed at the farm.

They parked the Explorer half a mile from the front door. Niven handed out guns, one to each man – pistols that were stolen and, like the clothes, supplied for him. Hard to come by in the UK, but Niven's employers always delivered. He didn't think they would need the firepower, but always better to be over-armed than under.

When everyone was loaded, Niven led them forward.

There was a dog, they had been briefed. No way to get to the house without alerting it, but by the time the dog – a thirteen-year-old German shepherd – heard them, they were at the porch. It barked, as expected.

Niven shot it with his pistol as they hurried into the hallway, the busted front door hanging from a single hinge behind them.

Ben Mayes had woken fast and armed himself and put a shotgun blast down the stairway – a warning shot, panicked and scared.

'There are six of us, Mr Mayes,' Niven called, out of sight and safe from the shotgun. 'Think of yourself. Think of your wife. Don't do anything stupid.'

Mayes called down from the landing, 'What do you want?'

'We're here to rob you, Ben. We want your TV, we want your wife's jewellery. This can all be over in ten minutes. You don't have a choice. Take a moment to think this through. You're a farmer. We're criminals. You're outnumbered. This is what we do.'

Mayes took the moment and threw his double-barrelled shotgun down the stairs.

'A wise choice.'

Niven gestured and his men raced up the stairs, overpowering Mayes and going to the bedroom to fetch his wife, Suzanne. Niven ordered the others to check the ground floor to make sure there were no surprises, and spent the waiting period nudging the dead dog with his shoe.

'She's not here,' one of the crew called from upstairs.

Niven frowned and trudged up the stairs, out of breath when he reached the landing. He entered the master bedroom. Two of the crew held Mayes, who was on his knees. The bedroom was big and had all the expected furniture, but there was no place for a woman to hide.

'Where is Suzanne, Mr Mayes?'

Ben Mayes swallowed. His eyes were wide. 'She's ... she's at her sister's house.'

Niven said, 'Why is she there, not here?'

'She stays there two or three times a week. Sometimes more. They're close.'

Niven frowned again and wiped his brow with the sleeve of his sweater. It was an oversight on his part. He should have been more thorough, but there was only so much one man could do.

He saw the other men were looking at him for answers. They knew only what he had told them. They assumed he knew what he was doing.

He didn't want to look ignorant in front of them, so he said, 'Then we're going to wait for her to come back.'

Mayes's expression changed. 'Why?'

'My reasons are my own.'

Only Niven knew why they were staging a home invasion. That was privileged information, not to be shared with the grunts. Only Niven knew the significance of Ben Mayes and the identity of his stepsister.

Mayes said, 'Take all the jewellery. I have cash too. I also have—'

Niven put a finger to his lips. 'Stay quiet, Mr Mayes. There's plenty of time for that. First, I need to make a call to find out if your sister is still playing ball.'

'Wait, what? My *sister*?'

Niven nodded. 'Yes, I'm afraid all of this is Constance's fault.'

FORTY-FOUR

Prague was still busy approaching midnight. Raven hadn't slept on the plane from Rome. She hadn't slept for more than twenty-four hours. The old man had given her plenty of time to get to the city and plenty of time to get to the phone, but not if anything went wrong. Not if there was a problem. A delayed flight, bad traffic, could mean missing the call. It was always on her mind. Impossible to forget. Impossible to ignore.

She had been to Prague many times before. The last time, just over a year ago, had been her first encounter with the assassin who was now her ... ally? She couldn't be sure what they were. She loved the city, but there was no time to see the sights. No desire to look in any direction except forward.

The plane landed on time. There were no holdups in taxiing or at passport control. Her alias was good. Her funds may have been limited, but she never skimped on documentation. She could make do without all the fancy tech, she could improvise weapons, but she could not operate with second-rate forgeries. The world was changing too fast and technology becoming too sophisticated to risk anything but the best.

She took a calming breath. Her mind was racing at a hundred miles an hour. She was coolly professional when she operated, but the long career doing black ops for the Agency had not been conducted while her brother was under threat. That changed everything. She knew she would make mistakes. She knew that, because she was distracted by worrying about Ben, she couldn't operate at her best. She could only hope her nameless partner was at his best.

Like the plane, the metro was running on time. A drunk guy tried to chat to her. It took every ounce of willpower she could muster not to break all the bones in his body. Instead, she made polite small talk in return. The kind every woman had to perfect, to master, just to get through the day with a minimum of harassment. The guy was determined, and not without charm, but he realised eventually this was a battle he couldn't win. He didn't say goodbye when he alighted.

She was making good time. She took a cab to the river. She made sure the driver knew that she was in a hurry and she'd be happy to tip well if he spared the scenic route. He was offended by the implication. She figured she had spent too much time in cities where taxi drivers were just thieves in cars.

The taxi dropped her off and she had to continue on

foot down a pedestrianised street, and then to a narrow promenade. Here she could see the dark waters of the Vltava and hear the gentle lapping of waves on a man-made beach. A soothing sound at any other time in any other place.

She saw a bank of payphones and approached with caution. She told herself that this was all pointless and unnecessary if the old man wanted to kill her. The team at Totti's villa didn't need tranquillisers for that. The old man had sent her here to keep her away from Ben. That mattered only if the threat was real, and the only reason to threaten her was to force her to do something she wouldn't otherwise. All superfluous if her death was the priority. Even so, she couldn't stop herself looking for threats.

There were plenty of people out having a good time, but not so many as to deter an assassin or interrupt a carefully selected line of sight. The payphones were exposed. The strong breeze from the river offered a modicum of protection, but a good marksman would have no trouble hitting her from any number of potential sniper nests.

She checked her watch. A few minutes to spare, so she hung back. She didn't want to spend any time she didn't have to waiting at the phone itself. That would mark her out. That would only play into any potential surprise she hadn't been able to anticipate. With one minute to go, she walked towards the phones.

There were six in total. They did a lot more than just make calls. They were mini internet terminals. Tourists could check maps and see local attractions and a host of other things to justify the existence of the payphones in an age when almost everyone had a phone on their person.

Six phones-cum-terminals and none were being used. She was only interested in one of them. *There'll be a bank of payphones. One will ring. The one on the east edge.*

It was the one furthest from her, and she saw as she neared that someone else was approaching from the opposite direction.

A man. He looked in his thirties, normal build, casual clothes. He could be a regular no one or an exceptional assassin. As the distance closed and she had a better look at him she saw he had a cell phone in his left hand and his attention was on the payphones, not her. A dead battery then, or poor signal. When they were only a few metres apart she saw he was going for the closest phone to him, the one on the east edge.

He was nearer to it than Raven.

She quickened her pace to a jog, then a run, not caring about losing any guise of normalcy because maintaining that illusion was a secondary consideration.

The man noticed her, because a woman walking towards him was suddenly running towards him, but he didn't realise what she was doing because she ran past five other phones so it would only seem natural for her to run past the sixth one too. Instead, she came to an abrupt stop before it, a second before he did.

He had to make an abrupt stop too, so he didn't collide with her.

He was not happy.

'Sorry,' Raven said.

He looked at her, brow furrowed at the narrowly avoided collision over a payphone she wasn't using. She just stood before it, blocking its use.

'Excuse me,' he said, angling for the terminal.

'I need this one,' Raven said.

'You're not using it.'

'I will be in a moment.'

Her responses did nothing to reduce his annoyance. 'What's special about this one?'

'I'm awaiting a call.'

He sighed. 'Then why didn't you say so?'

He stepped around her and headed along the line of phones until he reached the one on the west side, the one furthest away, and she wondered herself why she hadn't explained at the first opportunity. She tried to relax, to act casual again, to be—

The phone rang.

She snatched it from the perch and said, 'Hello.'

The voice that replied was the old man's. She would recognise it anywhere. It had a deep, but nasal tone. Weak, but superior.

He said, 'How was your journey, Miss Stone?'

'Relaxing,' she answered. 'Best flight ever. Who cares? I want to know that Ben is safe.'

'Miss Stone, if you want your brother to live then you will do any- and everything I ask of you.'

'That's what I am doing. You told me to answer this phone and you'll tell me where to go, so tell me. Let's not waste time chatting when I can be moving.'

She thought of what her nameless partner had said. They

needed time to put things in motion. They had to keep her out of the way while they captured Ben and Suzanne.

'That's the spirit,' he said. 'Here's where you're going next . . .'

FORTY-FIVE

Ben Mayes was handling his captivity well, or as well as could be expected. He was meek and subservient but his terror was in check. He kept his cool. He wasn't begging or crying. He wasn't trying to establish rapport with his captors. He wasn't even showing any signs of – *what do they call it?* – Stockholm syndrome. In fact, he was the perfect prisoner, or was he a hostage? The guy watching him in the master bedroom wasn't sure. He didn't know what was going on beyond the basic details. The boss had explained that this was going to look like a home invasion. It was going to be messy. It was going to be the type of crime that made the news, that they made documentaries about. The guy watching Mayes had done things – *bad* things – but he wasn't thrilled about hacking up some poor dickhead and his wife.

Still, the job was worth a whole chunk of change. The cash would go a long way to paying off his bookie. The guy guarding Mayes was called Gaffney, and he liked to bet on horses, and when he won, he liked to spend his winnings on coke and underage prostitutes. Trouble was, he didn't win too often and his bookie didn't much like to hear his excuses. The bookie was bad news. It was almost as though he wanted his clients to lose so he could hurt them. Gaffney had cleared some previous debts by helping show others that it was in their best interests to pay what they owed, and pay fast.

Gaffney liked all of his fingers and toes and wanted to keep them.

He used to be a cop, but he hadn't lasted long. He spent a whole eighteen months in the Met before he was fired for lifting drugs out of evidence. He wasn't prosecuted because the drugs were part of a big case against a big trafficker and the barrister would have thrown a shit-fit had he found out because the defence brief would have torn the case apart. Chain of custody was sacred for a reason.

Turned out Gaffney wasn't cut out for being a cop. All he wanted was some respect, some power. Turned out that could be achieved a whole lot easier out of uniform. Fewer rules that way. Fewer laws. More fun.

He didn't know the guys he was working with, but this wasn't the first time he had received a call from an unlisted number with instructions to meet someone he had never met before and carry out a job like this. It was all a little strenuous on his nerves – the fear of walking into a sting operation was constant – but he always needed the money. He figured he was working for the mob. Not the classic mafia, but the real organisations that ran the criminal underworld. Russians, or whatever. The city firms that no one had heard of because it was their business not to make noise. Hence people like him. Hence the anonymous crew.

Watching Mayes was boring. The man had no fire in him. Gaffney almost wanted him to try something. Then Gaffney would have an excuse to vent some of that nervous energy. But he wasn't going to provoke. The boss was explicit. Mayes wasn't to be hurt, he wasn't to be marked – until the time was right. Gaffney didn't understand why, but he knew to do as he was told.

He stroked his nose, thinking about a big bag of blow, and scratched his crotch, thinking about something else.

Niven waited downstairs, making the most of Ben Mayes' reclining armchair. It was one of those automated chairs, and was just about the greatest thing Niven had sat his ass on. Period. He was waiting for a callback. Waiting to be connected to someone in the know. He had reported the absence of Suzanne Mayes.

'I'll get right back to you,' the voice had said and hung up.

There was a guy upstairs watching Mayes, who had been secured with cable ties and left sitting on the bed. No need to go to town with him. It was supposed to look like a home invasion by heroin addicts, not a hostage situation orchestrated by professionals. Niven had seen the aftermath of the former enough times. The invaders didn't use handcuffs. They kept things basic. Simple.

The other members of Niven's crew were ransacking the house for anything of value, to add to the narrative.

They were turning the place upside down, making a lot of noise and a lot of mess in the process. Things like TVs and computers were ferried out to the Explorer, which had been brought closer to the house. The Mayes household wasn't overflowing with value items, so Niven had his guys take whatever they found that could be sold on. He left it to their own discretion. A bunch of junkies wouldn't be too thorough or discerning.

He had no one on guard, no one doing laps or checking the perimeter because they were in the middle of nowhere. There were no neighbours. No one was going to pass by. And if they did, better they see lights on in the middle of the night than a stranger patrolling the property.

That was why Niven went outside himself when he thought he heard something.

He eased open the busted front door and stepped on to the porch that ran around the house. The night air was icy. He heard the rustling of nature in the breeze and nothing further. Could have imagined it, or could have been some critter.

Nothing to worry about.

One of the other crew members came into the master bed-room. Gaffney had plenty of warning because the stairs couldn't have creaked any louder. It was the same with the floorboards. The farmhouse was in fine shape other-wise – clean windows, pristine paint, no missing roof tiles. The floors were polished and there wasn't a speck of dust anywhere. Kind of place Gaffney might retire to, once he'd found a wife who knew her place. Women like that were a rare breed. He'd been married twice so far and wasn't going to go through it again for anyone less than perfect.

'Hey,' the guy who came in said, 'found beers in the fridge. Here.'

He handed a cold can to Gaffney, who said, 'We allowed these?'

'Who cares? Boss stepped outside. I won't say a word if you don't.'

Gaffney grinned at their illicit behaviour and said, 'Cheers.'

He waited until he was alone and used his teeth to open the can so he could keep his weapon in hand.

Niven circled the house just to be sure, because something was bothering him. Something didn't seem right. It wasn't just the noise – imagined or real – or the absence of the wife. It was something else. Something he couldn't put his finger on. He was nervous, which wasn't like him.

He wasn't a tall guy, but he was tough, he was strong. He was out of shape, but that didn't matter. Nine times out of ten, a fight was over with the first punch. Even as a cop he hadn't been one to chase after a fleeing perp. He didn't like to exert himself. He didn't like to sweat any more than he did anyway, standing still. He'd been in his share of danger. He'd had his share of muzzles pointed at his face. So why the nerves?

Maybe it was the waiting that was the problem. He didn't have much patience. That was why he had become a criminal, he supposed. He was never satisfied. He always wanted more. It seemed like too much work to actually work for anything. Easier to take it. Simpler to steal. Quicker to hurt. He found he liked to hurt people.

He re-entered the house.

One of the guys supposed to be tossing the place was descending the stairs.

Niven said, 'What the hell are you doing?'

'Nothing, chief. Just checking.'

'Do what I told you to do,' Niven said. 'That's all you need to do. Leave everything else to me, okay?'

The guy nodded and Niven dropped himself back into the recliner, waiting for the next call.

FORTY-SIX

Helsinki was the second, and final, destination. A two-hour flight from Prague touched down in Finland at nearly five a.m. Again, Raven had a payphone to reach. This time it was at a metro station in the city centre and quick analysis at the airport showed public transport the fastest route to the city. A metro line ran from the airport straight to downtown. It was a regular system too, even in the middle of the night. She sat among Finns going home from night shifts and those heading to the office for early starts. No one tried to chat her up. No one tried to make conversation. Her fatigue and fear let her blend in with the tired and the stressed. She was in disguise without trying.

She wasn't familiar with the city or the country and had to ask directions, but there were no issues with language. She knew from past experience that Scandinavians spoke excellent English. She knew Finland wasn't classed as a Scandinavian country technically, but most people considered it to be, geographically, at least. She was on time to answer the phone without interruptions.

The old man said, 'You'll be glad to know there are no more planes. No more phones to answer. Ben is safely in our custody and cooperating.'

'He had better be safe. What am I doing here? Who's my target?'

'All in good time. For now, I want you to liaise with an associate of mine.'

'You told me I was here to kill someone. Now you're telling me I'm here to meet someone instead?'

'For the time being, that means syncing up with a man who will provide you with further details. Your contact is a fellow professional assassin who will be your partner for this job. He has the operational details. He will provide you with support, surveillance, and backup.'

'You mean he's here to kill me if anything goes wrong.'

'Let's not allow paranoia to interfere with the task at hand.'

Raven said, 'I want proof of life before I do the job. I want to speak to Ben on the phone. I want to ask him a question that only he will know the answer to. I want to hear him say it himself. That's my condition, my only condition, but it's non-negotiable.'

'That's acceptable to me.'

'Good, because you don't have a choice.'

'I believe it's the other way around.'

'Nuh-uh. You've gone to a lot of trouble for this, to get me here to do your dirty work, so it's important to you. It's vital. I don't want you to hurt my brother, but you want me to kill your target just as bad.'

'Don't delude yourself into doing – or not doing – something you'll regret.'

'I'm telling you the same thing.'

The old man said, 'I'll keep my side of the bargain if you keep yours.'

'Well,' Raven said back, 'we're each about to find out if the other is telling the truth.'

The old man gave her an address: 'This will be the location of your safe house. Sync up with your partner there and I will arrange for you to speak to Ben. Good enough?'

'If he's been hurt . . .'

'Get to the safe house, Miss Stone. You don't have time for any more threats.'

The address turned out to be an old apartment building on a quiet, leafy street. The building was grand and imposing, but had fallen into disrepair and was being renovated. It was six stories tall and surrounded by scaffolding. A rubble chute descended from the top level of scaffolding down the back of the building. The apartments were unoccupied while the building was gutted and refurbished. The front door was unlocked and Raven made her way up the stairs to the penthouse, where the babysitter was waiting.

He was a man, but not a native. He didn't say where he was from but Raven had a good ear for accents so could tell he was Estonian. He had a wide face, with dense, prominent cheekbones and a jutting chin. He wasn't old, but the lines in his face were deep. His eyebrows were constantly pinched together. His eyes always squinted.

His neck was thick and his hands large and calloused. He had the straight back of a military man, and the patience to go with it. In a reasoned tone he told her to wait and not cause any trouble. He said there would be a call, and until then, there was nothing to be done.

He wore boots, loose khaki trousers and a T-shirt. His sidearm was worn at all times in a shoulder holster, safety off, ready to be drawn at speed; fired without hesitation. He looked like an operator who enjoyed his work. He looked like he couldn't wait to shoot her. He had a knife too, sheathed to his belt.

This wasn't someone sent in to do a subtle job. This wasn't someone who shadowed a target for days or weeks, hiding in plain sight, picking the perfect time and the perfect method to minimise exposure. This was a guy who would happily open fire in a restaurant with an assault rifle. This was a guy who would shoot down a passenger plane to kill a single target.

The penthouse was large, but rundown. There were few items of furniture, and anything of value was covered in a dust sheet while the renovations were being carried out.

Raven watched as the babysitter sat cross-legged on the floor, with an oil-stained cloth laid out before him. On top of it were weapons, which he stripped one at a time, methodically cleaning and oiling and reassembling. He was smooth and fast in his hand movements, graceful in the small, intricate actions required. He knew his guns. She made a mental log of this, of his familiarity with weapons, of his dexterity and precision, but most of all she made a mental log that he could strip these weapons, clean and oil and reassemble them, and all without looking, because he never took his gaze from her the entire time.

She imagined the sorts of jobs he had done. Loud, messy, but effective. She couldn't picture him waiting patiently behind a rifle. She couldn't imagine him analysing wind speed and adjusting for the Coriolis effect. But she could see him fearless in a firefight, unflinching in hand-to-hand combat. Relentless. Deadly.

No way to reason with him, no chance of convincing him to deviate from his mission, no way of distracting or bluffing. An automaton.

He said, voice low and monotone, 'Why are you looking at me like that?'

'I'm getting to know you.'

'Don't bother. We're not here that long.'

'Long enough,' Raven said.

The babysitter's phone rang. She stared at the glowing screen. He picked it up and answered it, never taking his gaze from Raven.

Niven's phone rang too. The guys downstairs with him all heard the phone ringing and were all looking at Niven for orders. Niven took his time answering it. He pulled out the phone slowly, pretending he couldn't feel their expectation, pretending he wasn't a lackey to a voice on the end of the phone, pretending he was really in charge, really somebody.

He heaved himself out of the recliner to take the call. 'Yeah?'

The voice said, 'Put Ben on the line.'

'One minute.'

He made his way up the stairs, fast but not hurried, to the master bedroom and entered to find things as they should be: Ben Mayes sitting on the bed, Gaffney watching him nearby, but not too near. Niven approached Mayes and held out the phone.

Niven said, 'The phone's on speaker. I'm here with Ben. Ben, your sister wants to speak with you.'

A woman's voice spoke. It was distorted a little, but clear. 'Ben? Are you there? Are you okay?'

Mayes said, 'Constance, is that you? What's going on? What's happening?'

'I don't have time to explain, but I will. I'm sorry. This is my fault. Just stay calm. Do what they say. Don't cause any trouble and this will be okay. I promise. Ben, I need to know you're okay. If you are, tell me the colour of the old swing we used to have out back. The one you broke. Remember?'

Niven watched Mayes closely.

Mayes said, 'Blue. It was blue.'

There was a huge sigh of relief that came through the speakerphone.

A disconnect sound followed it, and the voice told Niven, 'Take it off speaker.'

Niven did as he was told and listened to his orders. He said, 'Okay,' and hung up. He slipped his phone away and turned his attention to Mayes. 'You see, Ben, everything is going to be fine. Your sister is going to do what she's been asked to do, and when that's done we'll be on our way. You just need to keep calm for a day or maybe two, okay? Can you do that, Ben?'

Mayes nodded.

'Good boy,' Niven said, and left the room.

The Estonian lit a cigarette and peered at her through the smoke. The cigarettes were strong. A French brand Raven recognised. She had smoked herself, before the poisoning, before her recovery. Coming back to life and struggling to move again had killed any nicotine addiction. Now the thought of inhaling tobacco smoke again made her feel . . . not ill, but foolish. Such a waste of time and health. She preferred dodging bullets to emphysema.

'You see,' the Estonian said. 'Your brother is safe so you can now get some sleep. We'll start work tomorrow.'

Raven coughed and gestured to the balcony doors. 'Do you mind if I open these?'

The Estonian said, 'Why?'

'Because you stink.'

He frowned, then shrugged, and when she approached the balcony and he thought she wasn't looking, quickly sniffed one of his armpits.

'The cigarette smoke,' she said as she opened the French doors and took a deep breath of fresh air. 'I can't handle it. Makes me lightheaded.'

'Whatever,' he said, agitated. 'Get some rest while you still can.'

'There's no way I'll be able to sleep,' Raven said.

He shrugged. 'That's up to you, but you might not get much chance later. You don't want to fail because you're asleep, do you?'

'What if I try and run?'

'You won't. Your brother is safe for now. If you run . . .'

'So you don't need a gun then, do you?'

He didn't answer.

'How many people have you killed?'

He hesitated, and said after a time, 'A lot.'

She said, 'How does it make you feel?'

'Like life is a precious gift, and mine is more valuable than anyone else's.'

'You know, if you really think that, then you should cut your losses and sit this one out. Whatever they told you about me, they didn't tell you the half of it. I'll give you the benefit of the doubt. You're just a foot soldier. You don't know who the voice on the end of the phone belongs to. You're ignorant, if wilfully. But I'll spare you because of that ignorance, but only if you back down right now.'

'A generous offer.'

'But it's a one-time deal. You only get a pass if you go this instant.'

'That's not going to happen.'

Raven said, 'I knew you wouldn't listen to me but I had to try.'

He smiled at her. 'They assure me you'll cooperate fully. They always know how these things play out. You'll do as asked. I'm not worried about that.'

Raven said, 'You won't mind if I use the bathroom, then?'

The Estonian looked at her as if she were crazy.

'I take it that's allowed,' she said. 'I take it you don't want me to go pee-pee here.'

She began lowering herself into a squat.

He frowned and shot to his feet, thinking she was serious. 'At the end of the hall.' He pointed. 'Don't take too long.'

'That's up to nature.'

She took her time walking along the hallway, using the opportunity of being unwatched to examine more of the penthouse, to peer into rooms with the doors open and to ease open the one door that was closed. She figured it was closed for a reason and she was right. This was the Estonian's room. A sleeping bag was draped over the single bed and she glimpsed other items – a rucksack, clothes and so on.

There was no time for a thorough examination as she heard floorboards creak behind her and closed the door before he could see what she was doing.

She heard him enter the hallway and glanced over her shoulder. 'Do you want to watch?'

He didn't answer. He didn't come any closer. She entered the bathroom.

It was like the rest of the apartment – in need of some serious attention. Tiles were cracked. There was an infestation of black mould. Limescale was everywhere. The door had a catch and she engaged it. Not strong enough to stop the Estonian, but strong enough to slow him down.

She heard his voice call to her: 'Don't forget that your

brother is trapped at home with a team of very unpleasant men.'

'You've got it the wrong way around,' Raven called back. 'They're trapped in that house with him.'

FORTY-SEVEN

Gaffney had been given a piece, same as everyone else. The boss had distributed them from a case in the Ford Explorer's boot. His was an old Beretta, scratched and worn. The serial number hadn't just been filed off but a groove had been dug into the metal where it had once been – to prevent acid bringing it out at a microscopic level, Gaffney knew. He remembered some of the useful stuff from being a cop. That the people he was working for were that thorough said a lot. It reassured him they knew what they were doing, because he sure didn't.

He was the youngest by some way, and he figured the least experienced. That was why he was tasked with watching Mayes while the others were tossing the joint downstairs. Babysitting was the short straw because he was the baby of the crew.

Mayes said, 'I need to use the bathroom.'

Gaffney said, 'So?'

Mayes gestured with his chin. 'It's just through that door.'

He didn't know what he was supposed to do in such a situation, but he didn't want to ask. He wasn't supposed to take his eyes off Mayes, so he would have to yell down the stairs, which he didn't want to do. But he didn't want to get into trouble by letting the captive use the loo if he wasn't supposed to.

'You'll have to hold it.'

Mayes said, 'I've been holding it in since you guys got here. I can't hold it much longer.'

'Not my problem.'

'I'm going to make a mess.'

Gaffney thought of piss-stained bedclothes, or worse. That might be against the plan. He didn't want to screw up. He feared the people he worked for more than any bookie.

He approached Mayes. 'You think I'm stupid? You think I'm going to let you in that bathroom alone? Don't make me mad, don't make me hurt you.'

Mayes recoiled, tense and scared. He couldn't take his gaze off the gun pointed at his face.

'You hold it in, okay?' he hissed. 'You make a mess and I'll make a mess of your head, you got that? I will *annihilate* you.'

Gaffney was breathing hard. Waving the gun around had got him pumped. He loved that feeling of strength, of dominance. He liked making others afraid. He was neither big nor strong, so those moments didn't happen without a weapon in his hand. He paced about, heart racing, enjoying the surge of adrenaline.

'Do you know what the problem is with cable ties?'

Mayes was sitting on the end of the bed, as he had been the whole time. His head was bowed. He was too scared to look up. Gaffney revelled in that power. This was what life was about. He was a king and Mayes was just a farmer, a peasant. He didn't quite catch what Mayes had said.

'Hey, what? What did you just say?'

Mayes repeated himself, 'The problem with cable ties . . . do you know what it is?'

'Do I look like I care? Do I look like I give a shit? You are a fool if you think you can find some common ground with me. I am the antichrist. I will beat you to death just to see what your corpse looks like. Don't make this hard for yourself. Keep quiet and keep prayin'.'

He was surprised by his own performance, his confidence – or the imitation of it. Hell, it would've convinced him, had their roles been reversed. But he wasn't dumb enough to get caught up in . . . whatever this was. Mayes was just a farmer, not a king.

Funny then that Ben Mayes didn't look much like a farmer, come to think of it. He looked like he spent his days throwing hay bales, but he seemed too lean, too fit, too *clean* to be the kind of man who worked on the land. It wasn't Gaffney's job to think much about these inconsistencies. He was just the hired help. Don't ask questions, was the first thing he had learned when working for the people on the end of the phone. A simple yes or no was all they wanted to hear. Anything else was superfluous to requirements. More than that, and it got dangerous.

Gaffney was here to make money, to pay off some of his debts, and go back to his flat in one piece and scrub away the memories of what he had done in a cleanser of blow and booze and young arse.

Mayes said, 'The problem is that the tighter you make them, the easier they are to get out of.'

Gaffney smirked. He had to admit, he was intrigued. 'What are you, some Houdini wannabe? What are those guys called?'

'Escapologists.'

'Yeah, that's it. That what you wanted to be instead of a farmer?' He was smiling now, grinning his way through the adrenaline surge. 'I love magic shows.'

'I studied Houdini, as it happens,' Mayes said. 'Self-education, you might call it.'

'What's that got to do with cable ties?'

Mayes raised his hands. 'Would you like me to show you?'

'Show me what? What are you talking about?'

'I can show you how to get out of cable ties.'

'I already know, dickhead. With a knife.'

Mayes said, 'That's the best way, sure. But you don't actually need a knife.'

'Really?' Gaffney said, all the hyped-up rage gone now and only curiosity remaining.

'Really,' Mayes said. 'With enough force, you can pop them open. If you extend your arms then pull them back hard enough against your abdomen' – he did – 'they'll pop open.'

'But they didn't.'

'Yeah, it's like forcing a locked door,' Mayes said as he continued to demonstrate. 'If you use your shoulder, some of the force you generate is absorbed back into you. You don't transfer it fully into the door. If you use your foot, all that force travels through a smaller area and breaks the lock. You could say there is more resistance. Of course, it helps if you have good core strength, but it's not essential. It just means you don't have to bring them down as hard against yourself.'

Gaffney couldn't help but step closer to get a better look. The rhythmic action of Mayes raising his bound hands then bringing them in a slow arc to his stomach was almost hypnotic.

'What on earth does that have to do with cable ties?'

'Localising the force is the key,' Mayes continued. 'If the cable ties are fastened like this, with a slight gap. Tight, but not too tight, then the ties themselves absorb some of this force. But if we tighten the ties' – he used his teeth to do so – 'until they're really, really tight, then the next time I try to pop them open, all the force will be delivered straight at that lock. Like this—'

Pop.

It was a handsome house, Niven thought. He liked that it was old and weathered. He liked its character. Tough and resilient. Like Niven himself. A family home, but no family. Just Ben and Suzanne Mayes. There were two other buildings making up the property. A barn stood to the east, tall and strong. Outbuildings lay between the house and the barn. Niven knew nothing about rearing cattle or growing crops, and he couldn't imagine how anyone could lead a life so dull, so uneventful.

He was thinking how thankful he was to be doing something he enjoyed when he heard a noise. But it wasn't from outside like earlier. It was from upstairs, directly above him. The noise was a thump sound, like something heavy had dropped hard on the floorboards. Another noise followed it. Not as loud, but more organic. Hard to place, but worrying.

'What the hell was that?' Niven gestured to one of the crew – a thin man with a moustache. 'For the love of God, find out what that idiot is doing to Mayes and make him stop. Shoot him if you have to. Mayes is not to be harmed. Yet.'

'Sure, boss.'

The thin man with the moustache climbed the stairs. In his hand he gripped a pistol. A Smith & Wesson. It was big and heavy and didn't feel right. He wasn't a strong man. He had never even shot a gun before.

He swallowed as he neared the top of the stairs. He turned around as he reached the landing, looking to the leader for guidance. Niven, impatient and concerned, gestured for him to get on with it.

The thin man pushed open the door to the master bedroom and stepped inside.

Niven watched him disappear out of sight. He heard the hard shoes on floorboards.

Then a thud and a clatter, something solid striking the floorboards and skidding away.

A scream.

More clattering, scrapes and thuds. More screams. A snap, and the scream became a piercing shriek.

Then silence. An awful, heavy silence. Niven could hear nothing but his own panting.

He overcame his shock and yelled, 'Go,' to two of his other men.

They bolted up the stairs, guns out, eager and angry, hyped into action. They reached the landing.

Rapid gunshots sounded, light flashed from inside the bedroom, highlighting the two men's faces – grimacing and contorting.

They staggered and fell, bullets punching into their chests and heads. Blood and flesh spattered the wall behind them.

Niven and the two remaining men backed away. The two looked at him for guidance, for *leadership*. Instead, they saw him turning for the front door, flinging it open and rushing outside. They followed.

Niven made it to the Ford Explorer first, not because he was the fastest, but because he had a head start. A gunfight wasn't part of the plan. He was no soldier. He had no more courage than he needed.

The two men behind him didn't make it to the Explorer at all.

More gunshots. Niven glanced back to see them drop to the dirt behind him, and the shooter – Mayes – stood at an upstairs window, pistol smoking in the moonlight.

How the hell a simple farmer had escaped his bonds and massacred Niven's whole crew was a question that would have to wait. For now, Niven wanted only to get away.

The job had gone bad, way bad, and he only knew that whatever had gone wrong it meant he needed to be gone.

Niven rounded the vehicle to the driver's door and climbed in. His shaking hands started the engine.

Another gunshot. Hissing air from a plugged tyre. The vehicle tipped forward and left.

Niven put the Explorer in reverse and drove.

The front right tyre went next. The vehicle shook and rubber flapped and frayed as he tried to spin it around.

Bullets took out the headlights.

Both back tyres were blown before he made it on to the dirt path. The tail lights were next. He made it another 50 metres before the wheels had shed the tyres and the rims were spinning uselessly as they failed to grip the dirt.

'Come on you piece of shit,' he yelled, thumping at the wheel.

He glanced at the mirrors. It was almost pitch-dark. He couldn't see more than a few metres behind the Explorer, but no one was there. Mayes hadn't followed. He would be calling the cops or his wife or shaking with relief, glad to be alive, high on the post-action adrenaline buzz. He wouldn't be chasing. He wouldn't be pushing his luck.

Niven calmed down, thought. Evaluated. He had to continue on foot. Hurry to the main road, flag down whichever vehicle came by first, take the driver hostage and go as far as the tank of gas would get him.

He took his gun in his right hand and gripped the lever with his left, glanced behind him to double-check no one was there, and went to open the door—

Glass shattered, the window collapsing as a pistol was driven through it and smashed into Niven's face.

The Estonian was checking his watch every few seconds. He knew the woman was dangerous. He had been well-briefed on her capabilities, on her history, on her relentlessness. After a minute he made his way to the hallway to see the bathroom door closed. How long did it take a woman to use the bathroom? How long did it take a dangerous woman to fashion some weapon or trap?

To his mind, there was nothing inside the bathroom that could pose any real threat. A strip of shower curtain could be torn away and rolled tight into a noose; the cistern lid could be employed as a club; a floor tile could be prised away and broken into a shiv. All lethal in the right hands, but none of them would give her enough of an edge to best him. He had guns, after all.

After a second minute his patience was failing. He drew his sidearm and made his way along the hall, the bathroom door growing larger and occupying more of his vision with each step. He could hear no toilet flushing, no tap running, no woman urinating.

He tried the door handle. Locked.

He tapped on the door with the gun's muzzle. 'Hey, what are you doing in there?'

No answer.

That was all the justification he needed. He kicked the door open.

The bathroom was empty.

There was no space to hide behind the door. There was no space to hide anywhere.

The window was open.

Do you mind if I open the balcony doors?

He spun around, moving back out into the hallway, and there she was: standing before him, her bare feet red and dusty from climbing out of the bathroom window and along the building's exterior, window ledge to window ledge, then on to the balcony and into the lounge.

She pulled the knife from his belt sheath.

He had no time to react or fight back because the blade had already pierced his chest, slipping horizontally between ribs to find his heart.

His gun fell from his fingers and she guided him back into the bathroom while he still had the strength to stand, then as that last strength failed, lowered him backwards into the tub.

He saw her step away, then retrieve the fallen gun from the floor in a spiral of blending colours that faded to black.

FORTY-EIGHT

Head injuries were problematic. Knocking someone out wasn't an exact science. Different people reacted in different ways. It was difficult to get a precise result. Making someone lose consciousness wasn't the problem. Waking up again was where things became awkward. Some people didn't. Swelling and bleeding on the brain could cause serious complications. The person might not wake up at all. They might wake up again but not as the same person. Niven woke up, which was good. When he did, he seemed awake and alert, despite the pain and disorientation, which was better.

Victor watched as Niven assessed his surroundings and realised he was restrained. He was slumped on the floor of the Mayes' barn. It was a large building, made cavernous because it was almost empty at this time of year. Niven's face was bruised and swollen from the blow that had knocked him out, and his eyes were squinting against the barn's lights. They were bare bulbs hanging in strips, trussed up between beams. Niven's hands were roped together and a vertical support post was between his elbows. He could stand, but didn't.

Niven was trying to process the situation he was in and what had led to it and he was struggling. Victor helped him out:

'All of your guys are dead. You're concussed. You're not going anywhere. And I want answers.'

Niven said, 'You need to let me go, Ben. You need to let me go right now. If you don't let me go, then other people will come for you. They'll kill you. They'll kill Suzanne. You need to think about what you're doing. You're making a terrible mistake. You need to fix it before it's too late.'

The barn was cold. The only heat was provided by a wood-burning stove. It was an old bulbous thing made of cast iron, almost a relic of another era. Victor fed it another piece of wood. He held his hands before it.

'You're out of your depth,' Niven said, adjusting his seating position on the floor. It was hard without use of his hands. 'You're stepping into a world you can't hope to understand. If you could, you'd run. You'd be running now. You should run while you still can.'

Victor opened a large leather sports bag he had found in the Ford Explorer. 'Let me see ... a multi-tool, claw hammer, belt sander, pliers, nail gun, morphine, and epi-nephrine. Quite the collection.'

'They were just to scare you if you didn't comply.'

Victor said, 'Do they scare you?'

'Don't do anything you're going to regret.'

'Trust me, I won't.'

Niven said, 'If you let me go, I'll tell you anything you want. I can tell you who I was working for, what they want with your sister. Everything.'

'You've got that right, but the wrong way around. You're going to tell me all of that first.'

Niven managed to get up to his knees, but it made him grimace. 'Ben, listen to me. You have no idea what's going on here. I'm just a guy doing a job. The people I work for are the worst of the worst. It's your sister they want. They're just using you to get her to do what they want. Let me go and I can help you, and I can help her. I know things.'

Victor said, 'You haven't figured it out yet, have you?'

Niven was silent. He was confused. Maybe it was the concussion. Maybe he was dumb.

Victor ran a hand over his fresh buzz cut. It was enough to make Niven understand.

'You're not Mayes.'

'Finally,' Victor said. 'So, maybe this realisation will help expedite this conversation. I'm an associate of Ben's sister. You know, Raven. She asked me to assist in resolving this matter. She's not very happy you came here to kill her little brother and his wife.'

'I was following orders,' Niven was quick to say. 'We were only threatening him. We were never going to kill either of them. We're not barbarians. We're not monsters.'

Victor said, 'It takes a monster to know another monster.'

Niven was silent. Victor warmed his hands on the heat from the stove.

'The people you work for,' he began, 'the people who

355

are doing this to Raven, put out a contract on me. It's been quite the nuisance.'

Niven stretched out his arms so the rope binding his hands was braced against the vertical beam. He used that leverage to stand up. 'You're the hitman. I've heard of you.'

'I'm really not fond of that term,' Victor said. 'There's no need to romanticise what I do. I'm just a killer.'

'Whatever you are, you're messing with the wrong people by siding with Raven, but it's not too late to back out. It's not too late to pick the winning side. Let me go and I can get you a seat at the table.'

Victor stared into the flames. 'Men with a seat at the table don't end up captive in an isolated barn in the Scottish countryside.'

'I'm a man who gets things done. That's why they use me. That's why you can use me.'

'It's in your best interest to tell me everything you know as succinctly as possible.'

Niven said, 'No way. I know how this shit works. I'm alive because of what I know and what you want to know. I tell you what you want, I lose my bargaining power. Ain't gonna happen, pal. I've been in your shoes too many times. I know exactly how this goes.'

'Ignorance is bliss.'

Niven stared at him. 'You don't have any idea who you're dealing with.'

'You're right,' Victor agreed. 'I don't know who you are and I don't care who you are. But you need to start caring about who I am, because, whatever you've done, whatever you're capable of, I've done worse.'

'You can't scare me,' Niven said.

'Fear is but one aspect of what I can do, but I understand why I can't scare you. You don't really know me. But you know your employers. You know what they'll do to you if they find out you've talked.'

Niven's arms were locked out because he was trying to get as close to Victor as possible. 'You're right about that. And it'll never happen, because I won't talk. I don't know much about you but I know who I'm dealing with. I can see it in your eyes. You can't scare me because you're not going to do anything. You're trying to make me think you'll do it. All the talking is just that: talking. You'll get frustrated eventually and slap me around a bit, but torture? Are you kidding me? You don't have it in you.'

Victor said, 'In a way, you're right, because the best tor-turers enjoy what they do. That gives them an edge over me because I take no pleasure in hurting people. I am, however, very, very good at it.'

'You think I can't take a beating?' Niven spat at Victor. 'Try me.'

'Pain, like fear, is one aspect of what we can achieve here. The fear of pain is as effective as the pain itself. Usually, you're restricted. Time, facilities, pressure all affect the process. Here, we're all alone in the middle of nowhere. There are going to be no interruptions. I am, however, on a limited time frame. I have to be on a plane in the morning. We don't have all that long.'

Niven didn't respond because he thought he had been given an advantage. He thought the limited time frame helped him.

'We've mentioned pain,' Victor said, 'and we've mentioned fear. As a man who is experienced in these matters, you will know the third, and arguably most powerful, aspect of what I can do to convince you to be veracious with me.'

Niven said nothing. He was confused. He didn't know.

'Horror,' Victor said. 'If pain doesn't work, if fear won't work, then horror will.'

He pointed to the wood stove. 'That fire has been burning for a while now. It's about as hot as it's ever going to get. The stove itself is like a cooking plate right now. I bet you could fry bacon on that.'

Niven couldn't help but stare.

Victor approached a pile of logs and picked up the axe that had split them. It was a well-used tool, heavy and marked. He approached Niven.

Niven hadn't blinked in a long time.

'I understand the problem,' Victor said. 'You're not like the guy who thought he was watching Ben, or the others I killed tonight. You're the boss. You're in charge. You're the one who knows about your employers. You're the one who knows the price of failure. More importantly, you know the price of betrayal. So, your will is hardened right now because you think, whatever I threaten you with, whatever I do, they'll do worse. Right?'

Niven didn't answer, but his eyes answered yes.

'Which is the problem I've mentioned. But it's not my problem. It's yours. I don't have all night to explain to you, to convince you, that you're wrong. I need to prove that you're wrong. I need to prove to you that, whatever you've done, whatever they might do, I'll do worse.'

Sweat was dripping from Niven's face despite the cold.

Victor said, 'I'm going to take this axe and I'm going to hack off one of your hands. The blade is dull and I couldn't find a whetstone so it might take a couple of blows to do the job, so you'll need to be patient. The pain and the fear will be like nothing you've ever experienced, but the horror of watching the stump where your wrist used to be spray blood everywhere is going to be like nothing you can even imagine. At that point you won't be worried by what your employers might do to you. You'll bleed to death in about two minutes. Which is why I'm telling you now: don't forget the stove. When I sever your hand, you're going to be free of that post. It's only 20 feet to that stove, but it's going to feel like a mile. Focus on it now, because you're going to be in shock. When you cauterise the wound against the cast iron, you're probably going to pass out, but I'll wake you up again. If your heart stops, I'll use the epinephrine you brought to bring you back. If you don't talk to me then, if you don't give what I want to know about your employers, I'll take your other hand. After that, I'll start improvising. Are you ready?'

Niven's gaze flicked between the axe and Victor's eyes. 'You ... you can't be serious.'

Victor raised the axe.

FORTY-NINE

Ben Mayes looked a little older than Victor but Mayes spent his days working in the elements and didn't seem the kind who bothered with sunscreen and moisturiser. They had a certain similarity in appearance because they had the same buzz cut, pale skin and comparable physiques; Mayes was used to hard labour. He was used to a physical, but simple, life. In every sense, he was a civilian. An innocent by any standards. Victor couldn't help but note how their lives had played out to the most extreme conclusions.

Mayes was a reasonable man put in an unreasonable position. He had taken Victor's explanation of events in the way any reasonable man put in an unreasonable position would: with resistance. It was expected, and Victor had given the man no choice but to do as he was told. At first light, Victor unlocked the doors to a stone steading and heaved them open. Mayes was awake, and squinted as the dawn found his eyes. He looked tired, but alert. He hadn't slept. Victor removed the gag and untied him.

'You can come out now.'

'What happened last night?'

He had a curious accent, sounding more English than Scottish, but still American too. Not mid-Atlantic, though. Something else. Something different. It made Victor wonder what his own accent might be, if he ever again elected to speak in his own voice. Did that voice even exist any more?

'Some things are best left unsaid.'

He offered his hand and Mayes took it, using it as a brace to climb the short, crooked steps and out into the dawn.

Mayes attacked him.

He was strong and pretty fast, but he was an amateur. A civilian. He was on his back and winded before he understood his mistake.

Victor offered his hand a second time. Mayes hesitated and took it and Victor heaved him up. Mayes grunted as he came to his feet and swiped soil from his clothes.

This time Mayes didn't try anything. The lesson had been learned.

'I've never been in a fight before,' Mayes said. 'Does that count?'

'I'm not your enemy,' Victor said.

Mayes shrugged as he rubbed at his back where he had struck the ground. He was wary. He was unsure. He had probably spent all night in the steading trying to make sense of something that made no sense.

'Why do you smell like bleach?'

Victor didn't answer.

'I heard gunshots. Screams.'

'I expect you heard a lot of things.'

Mayes sniffed the air, smelling smoke, and turned to where Victor had made a small fire pit. 'What's that?'

'You don't have an incinerator. I had to burn things. Clothes, mostly.'

Mayes said, 'What happens now?'

Victor explained: 'We have some things to sort out here that I need your help with, and when we're finished you need to collect your wife and go on a road trip. It's a surprise, you'll tell her. You want to whisk her away and be spontaneous. Away from phone reception and distractions. Say whatever you have to say. Tell her whatever you need to, so long as it isn't the truth. Take plenty of clothes. Withdraw as much cash as you can and drive three hours before spending a penny of it. Stay moving. Don't pay for anything with a credit card. Don't show ID. Try to avoid CCTV cameras. You might be gone for a week, maybe two.'

Mayes squinted into the dawn. 'You want us to go on the run without knowing why. Who are we running from? I don't understand any of this. How am I meant to believe anything you've told me? You held me captive. I can't trust anything you say.'

Victor said, 'Come with me.'

Mayes hesitated.

'It's not an order, Ben. It's a recommendation.'

He led Mayes to a pickup truck. It was Mayes'. An old, rusted workhorse of a vehicle. Faded paint. Mud-caked tyres.

'That's my truck.'

'Do you have a heart condition? Any history of heart disease in the family? Blood pressure issues?'

Mayes shook his head.

'Then take a look under the tarpaulin.'

Mayes hesitated.

Victor said, 'I'll wait here.'

A sheet was stretched across the truck's load bed, but one corner had been left unfastened. Mayes approached, looked to Victor for reassurance he didn't receive, and lifted the flap back. He looked beneath.

The colour drained from his face and he turned fast to throw up.

Victor waited until the man had composed himself. He offered Mayes a rag to wipe his mouth with.

After he had, Mayes said, 'They're dead?'

'If they're not, they're incredible actors.'

'Who are . . . *were* they?'

Victor said, 'I don't know all of their names and you don't want to know any more than you have to. All that matters is they were sent to kill you and your wife. Your sister will find out who sent them, and make sure this can't happen again. Then you'll be able to come home.'

'You and my sister . . . you said you guys are friends.'

'I said we're acquaintances.'

'What does that mean?'

Even Victor wasn't sure. 'It means we have a complicated relationship. But at the moment we're on the same side.'

Mayes grimaced and glanced back at the truck, as if he wanted to take another look under the tarpaulin, as if he needed to see again to make sense of what he saw. He'd moved from shock to denial, but he stopped himself because he wasn't sure what he hoped to achieve.

'They're ... That's all your doing?'

Victor nodded.

'How many?'

'Why?'

Mayes was perplexed. 'I don't know why I asked that. Jesus.'

Victor frowned but said nothing.

'I don't know whether to laugh or throw up again.'

'Maybe try not thinking about them. Be glad it's those men in there and not you and your wife.'

'I am,' Mayes insisted, still pale. He looked again towards the dawn and took a few steps. He turned to face Victor. 'Man, go on the run? Is this for real? I should just wait until you've gone and call the police. I'm friends with the local PC. They'll be here within the hour.'

'That's not a good idea, Ben.'

'Why? Because you're worried they'll find out what's going on? Because you don't want them on your ass for killing all those guys?'

'There are two equally good reasons, neither of them having anything to do with me worrying. The first is that if you value your friendship with the policeman then the last thing you want is for him to catch up with me.'

Mayes understood, even if he didn't want to understand. 'What's the second thing?'

Victor said, 'In a life-threatening situation, whether terrorism or a rockslide, what kills most people is slowness to react. Regular lives are so safe, so eventless, that there is a lack of comprehension when faced with death. It's not necessarily shock. It's disbelief. It's dismissal. Civilians say to themselves: *I've got this wrong; this isn't what I think.* But it is, and by the time they've realised, it's too late. And, of course, sometimes they do in fact have it wrong. They've misread the situation, and they're left embarrassed, maybe ashamed. But . . .'

'But they're alive,' Mayes finished.

Victor nodded.

'I know what you're doing.'

'You're a smart man. So do the smart thing. When you're back from your road trip with Suzanne, if you still feel angry, call the cops. You can tell them everything. You lose nothing by waiting. But you could lose everything by acting hastily.'

'Maybe,' Mayes said.

'Does anything I've said or done make sense if I mean you harm?'

Mayes was silent for a long time. Victor said nothing further.

'When we were kids, Constance always wanted to see the world. She was never settled. Never happy. Me, I like home. I don't like travelling.'

'You don't have to like it,' Victor said.

'You never told me your name,' Mayes said. 'I'm guessing that was deliberate.'

'That's right.'

'Assuming everything you say is true, then thank you for saving my life and that of my wife.'

Victor said, 'There's no need to thank me. This is no act of altruism. I had my own reasons for coming here.'

Mayes didn't know what to say, so he stayed quiet for a moment. 'You're a hard guy to like, you know? And I'm taking it into consideration that you saved my life.'

Victor nodded. 'There are many things I aim to be, but likeable is not one of them.'

'It shows, man. It really does.' Mayes pushed his hands into the pockets of his jeans. 'You know something? I've never learned to surf. I hear they have good waves down in Newquay. Now seems like the perfect time to try, don't you think?'

'Just don't upload any selfies until you're back, okay?'

'I hear you. Will I see my truck again?'

Victor shook his head. 'I'm sure your sister will wire you money for a replacement.'

'I don't want her money.'

The sun was low. A single cloud drifted in front of it, haloed in blazing yellow against the pale sky. Mayes glanced around, then turned; looking, remembering.

'Hey, where's my dog? Where's Archie?'

'I'm sorry, Ben,' Victor said.

Mayes' face pinched. He put his hand over his mouth and turned away from Victor. He stayed turned away for a while.

Victor said, 'If I could have let you keep him with you in the steading, I would have. I like dogs.'

When he turned back, Mayes said, 'He was a good dog. The best.'

Victor continued: 'But if he had made the slightest noise,

we'd both be dead and Suzanne would have been next, along with anyone else they found at her sister's place.'

'I loved that dog,' Mayes said. 'But I understand. He would have laid down his life for us if he could have. He was that dog. In a way, I suppose he did. Where is he?'

'I buried him,' Victor said. 'Out back, under the tree.'

Mayes thought about this, and nodded. 'Thank you for that.'

Victor shrugged to say *You're welcome.*

'Would you tell Constance something for me?'

'Sure.'

'Please tell her I hate her guts. Tell her once all this – whatever it is – is over, I never want to hear from her again. She's dead to me.'

Victor nodded, then gestured to the truck. 'I'll dispose of those bodies elsewhere. I've cleaned up inside your house as much as possible, but you'll need to keep the windows open for the smell. I've also had to burn some of your clothes and some of your sheets.'

'I don't care about stuff like that. It's just stuff. Besides, Suzanne is always telling me to update my wardrobe.' Mayes spotted the wrecked Explorer. 'What's that?'

'It's their vehicle. It's a problem. You're going to have to help me hide it until a more permanent solution can be found.'

'Can't you drive it away?'

'It has four blown tyres and a lot of bullet holes.'

'Oh,' Mayes said, then: 'I have a winch for my pickup. It's not currently attached, but that won't take long. If you steer it, I can drag it pretty much anywhere.'

'Perfect,' Victor said.

'We can put it in the barn. No one will find it in there.'

'The barn's no good.'

'Why?'

'I'll come to that in a minute,' Victor said. 'What about that outbuilding?'

'It's full of stuff. Junk. All sorts. We use it as storage.'

'Can you move things into the house to make room?'

Mayes nodded. 'Sure, I guess. It'll take all morning to clear out though.'

'You don't need to clear it out, just make enough room for the truck. Do you have fuel for the farm machinery? Gasoline? Diesel?'

'Of course. Both, why?'

'You're going to need to raze the barn to the ground.'

'What does that mean?'

Victor said, 'I need you to burn it down.'

Mayes was open-mouthed. 'You want me to destroy my own barn?'

Victor nodded again, and glanced at where Mayes had vomited. 'Whatever you do, don't go inside.'

FIFTY

Victor landed in Helsinki on a flight from Oslo. He had left Scotland later than he would have liked, but disposing of six corpses took time, even for someone as practised as Victor. He arrived tired. It wasn't a long journey from Scotland, but he hadn't slept in almost two days. He knew well enough how fatigue not only drained his body but his mind. His alertness was impacted. His awareness reduced. He was used to operating on little-to-no sleep, but it was always to be avoided if possible.

The cold afternoon helped keep him alert as he performed counter surveillance.

When he was satisfied, he bought a prepaid cell phone to check if Leyland had made any progress with Phoenix. She had made significant advances in finding links in the intel from Wilders' safe. Victor didn't analyse it yet, because there was a second, more recent message. This one wasn't an update on Phoenix, but on his other problem. The message was concise.

Alvarez came to see me. He claims to know your identity.

He destroyed the phone, because he always did, and took a breath. He fought the instinct to think about his past, about himself, about who he had been before. It felt so long ago he didn't have to fight hard. He spent so much energy and thought on surviving the present that his past became ever more distant, ever hazier. But it was real. It existed. He could hide almost every aspect of himself from the world, but not all. He was a killer now, living under a myriad of false identities, but it hadn't always been that way. If Alvarez knew who he had been, he could find who Victor was now.

He located a payphone to call Raven. She would need time to sync up with him while he considered his next move. 'I need you in Helsinki.'

There was a pause before she replied, 'I'm already here.'

Victor didn't like coincidences. They were almost always bad. He said, 'Where are you?'

'Holed up at the safe house.' She gave him the address.

'I'll head straight there.'

Victor didn't like to hurry, even when he wanted answers. He didn't know the city well, but he knew it enough to get around in the same way he knew almost every major city in Europe. He spent his life moving from place to place, whether he was working or not. He hadn't been to Helsinki for a while, but not much had changed since his last visit. It was still clean, still attractive. He saw none of that beauty as he made his way to the address Raven had given him.

She was waiting for him when he arrived.

She didn't say anything. She hurried towards him as soon as he was through the door and he had to stop himself launching into a pre-emptive attack as she raised her hands. She hugged him. He managed to let her, enjoying the feel of her against him. He placed a palm on her back.

'Thank you for saving my brother.'

He nodded. 'You're welcome.'

'Is he okay?'

'Physically, he's fine.'

'Mentally?'

'He's a normal guy who has experienced his first taste of the real world. He'll develop some paranoia and mild PTSD. Maybe drink too much. He'll pick arguments with Suzanne. Usual stuff.'

'You couldn't have just pretended, could you?'

'I've told you nothing you didn't already know.'

She stepped back. 'You're right. I'm sorry. I'll be forever grateful for what you did.'

He nodded again and backed away. He didn't like praise at the best of times. He told himself he had never needed it, so it was unnecessary.

Victor said, 'What are you doing in Helsinki?'

She gestured at the apartment. 'This is where I ended up. The phone call in Prague was, as we both expected, to give me further instructions. I was told to come here to prepare and wait.'

'Alone?'

She shook her head. 'There was a babysitter.'

Victor understood. 'Where is he now?'

She showed him a corpse in the bathtub. 'You look worse than he does.'

'I am a little tired,' Victor admitted. 'Is this place safe?'

'It's safe enough for now. This guy was here for a few days, as far as I can tell. Seems he arranged it himself. He brought an arsenal with him. There's been no further contact from the old man or anyone else. I imagine they don't yet know what happened in Scotland and assume everything is going to plan. But we should go after you get some rest. You look like you could use it.'

'I do, but it can wait. I don't like us being in the same city at the same time.'

'It was bound to happen, sooner or later. Our worlds cross over, don't they?'

'This is too much of a crossover for my taste. I'd like to know why.'

'Is there a why for people like you and me? Ever think we're meant for something better? Ever think you were meant to be more than you are?'

Victor shook his head. 'I'm doing exactly what I was designed to do.'

'You've never wanted to retire?'

'Sure. Of course. In the early days, when I was beginning to understand that this was not a sustainable profession to be in long term. So I began saving more money, stockpiling resources, preparing a way out. When the job in Paris went wrong, for a moment afterwards, I was out. I was done.

I'd decided that was it. I was going to teach climbing or languages or something similarly deluded.'

'So what changed?'

'I was shot about a second later.'

'That would do it.'

'It made me realise that the world I'd built for myself had become a prison. I told an … acquaintance … of mine I couldn't retire. But I could. Maybe it would take a week or a month or maybe it would take years, but it wouldn't last. Eventually they would find me, like they did after Paris. And in retirement I would lose my edge. I wouldn't see them coming.'

'There is a certain sense in that attitude, I grant you.'

He said, 'But that's all you're getting from me. Don't think because we've been helping each other I'm going to suddenly reveal the inner me.'

'It was worth a shot. But okay, enough with the touchy-feely stuff. Let's talk about the plan. How do you want to do this? I figure keep it simple, but messy. Draw some blood. Wear a vest. I shoot you with plenty of witnesses. You stagger away. Something like that?'

He shook his head. 'There's been a change of plan. I need answers before I do anything else.'

'What answers?'

He nodded. 'I'll explain, but later. Now, I need to sleep.'

FIFTY-ONE

There had been a time when Muir had been terrified of public speaking. She hadn't been outgoing when she was young, she hadn't been confident; the thought of standing before her peers, looked at, scrutinised, judged, had been her worst nightmare. Those teenage drama days were long gone, and now she couldn't understand why her younger self had ever been afraid. She didn't stutter. She didn't mumble. She wasn't disfigured. She knew what she was talking about. She could imagine a career post-CIA, lecturing and giving speeches, seminars and classes. She fancied herself touring universities and institutes the world over, teaching what she knew about security, intelligence and terrorism. She knew some ex-Agency staff who earned a small fortune that way. Money had never been a driving factor for Muir, but a nice house in a nice part of town never hurt anyone.

This particular lecture theatre was packed. Mostly

students studying for degrees in politics, international relations and other boring subjects, but there were a few scattered adults and she tried to guess which ones were there to make notes for the SVR or PRC or whoever else had too much money and too much paranoia, hoping she might give away a few classified secrets.

Her lecturing style was conversational. She had bullet points projected on the screen behind her, but she had no lengthy notes. No one learned anything from transferring spoken words to paper or digital documents. She tried to engage as much as possible, encourage debate and even argument. She remembered her favourite professors, who had provoked more than taught, conducted more than dictated. She tried to emulate them.

The Finnish students all spoke excellent English. They enunciated better than her for the most part. She enjoyed talking with them.

She knew she had them fully engaged when they spent more time with their eyes forward than at their notebooks and computers. She would go so far as to say they were having fun, if not as much as she was having. It was all going so well until a door at the back eased open and a late arrival slipped through. There were no spare seats so he just stood at the back, arms folded across his chest, and peered down at her.

After that, she couldn't concentrate. She would lose her train of thought and forget what she was saying. Questions had to be repeated before she understood what she was being asked. Debates lost their fire. Discussion became monotonous. The applause at the end was perfunctory. She didn't bother to ask if there were any follow-up questions because the students couldn't escape fast enough.

Only the man at the back stayed behind. He approached down the steps as she collected her things and shook the hands of the university staff who had arranged the visit. She had no doubt they were sincere in their thanks, but she couldn't take their praise seriously.

After they too had left the lecture theatre, Alvarez said, 'Fascinating talk.'

'Is that a joke?'

He shook his head. 'I'm sorry I missed the start.'

'That was the best bit. You killed my rhythm.'

'And why would I do that?'

'Cut the crap, Antonio. What are you doing here? Are you my stalker now? I have nothing to say to you.'

'Your travel schedule is no secret. This lecture series has been well advertised. Thought I'd check it out while I was in town.'

'Why are you in town? Did you think he would be in the audience too? You got the university surrounded by SWAT trucks?'

'Not exactly, but I have an SAD team on campus for your protection.'

She couldn't be sure if he was serious or not.

'What's going on?'

'Well, that's what I intend to find out.'

'I don't understand you, because sometimes you act like a certified moron when I know you're actually quite smart.'

'Quite,' Alvarez echoed.

'You know full well this lecture was scheduled a long

time before you came to me. Yet you still felt the need to see it with your own eyes. You couldn't be sure it was genuine without being here personally. Did you really think it was all an elaborate charade and it would be just me and Tesseract chatting over coffee? Catching up about old times?'

'Didn't you tell me you had nothing to do with him?' Muir scoffed.

'I'm serious, Janice. This is it. This is the line. You either stay on my side of it, or you cross it and you can never come back over.'

'Is that the best you can do? Really? Grow up.'

Muir finished collecting her things into her bag, slung it over one shoulder, and headed for the exit.

'Tesseract's in town,' Alvarez said to her back.

It made her stop.

He said, 'Or he will be real soon. He's here to take care of some business.'

She turned to face him. 'I don't believe you.'

'I know. Why would you? But why else am I here? I didn't come all this way to listen to you mumble about the importance of quiet diplomacy. No offence.'

'What business?'

'Not fun, being out of the loop, is it?'

'I don't have time for this.'

'I have a feeling you're going to be missing your flight back.'

'What business?' Muir said again.

'I guess you could say it's half personal, half business. Maybe unfinished business?'

Muir waited.

Alvarez said, 'You know something, I never liked to hunt. My dad tried to get me into it, once upon a time. I have too much empathy to enjoy it. Deer have such big brown eyes. Fishing's different. Hard to care about a fish, right? Turned out to be a pretty good fisherman too. I've tried to get my kid interested in it like my dad tried with me and hunting, but sitting patiently with a rod and a line can't compete with video games, can it?'

'I wouldn't know. I don't have kids. What does any of this have to do with what you're doing here?'

'This, all this, really comes down to a single, simple question that I asked myself long ago, long before I got this job. How do you find a man without an identity? How do you find a man that doesn't exist?'

She shook her head because there was nothing else to do.

'The answer's simple,' Alvarez said. 'In fact, it's the easiest thing in the world.'

'I'm listening.'

He stepped towards her. 'The only thing anyone really knows about this guy is that they don't know anything. What does that tell you? That there's nothing to know? No way. He was born somewhere. He had parents. He grew up. He had some kind of life. He has a name. But that no one knows any of these details tells us everything. It tells us that this someone, this Tesseract, this Mr Eighty-Seven Per Cent, is a man who more than anything else wants to be anonymous. This is someone who values that anonymity first and foremost and has constructed his existence so carefully, so precisely, that he's managed to achieve it. No one knows who he is. He hasn't done that just by using an alias. He's erased each and every trace of his identity. He's killed to protect it. He *will* kill to protect it.'

Muir was beginning to understand. 'What have you done?'

'It's more a case of what *we* have done, Janice. You opened up a channel of communication with Monique Leyland, which in turn gave me a direct route to Tesseract himself.'

'You've spoken to her then,' Muir said, and he nodded. 'What did you tell her that she told him?'

Alvarez shrugged, like it didn't matter. 'Oh, nothing really. I just happened to mention I know who Tesseract really is.'

Muir stared. 'You lied.'

Alvarez nodded. 'Of course I lied. No one knows who this guy is. But I want him to think I do – or just that I might. I thought there was a chance that he might come here to talk to you in person, but I know for certain he'll come here now. He'll need to know. He'll have to find out if it's true. It'll eat him up otherwise. He can't live with that risk.'

Muir's eyes were wide. 'That's why you came to Procter, and that's why you came to me.'

'You got it. I knew you would encourage him to disappear with me putting pressure on you both, but what you were actually doing was setting things in motion so he would come to me. Kind of thing Procter would do, right? Guess we're pretty similar after all.'

'You need to tell Leyland you were bluffing.'

He looked around. 'I like it here. I like the air. It's so fresh.'

'You're gambling with your life. Don't do it,' Muir said. 'You don't know who you're dealing with.'

'He's one man.'

'You don't know what he's capable of.'

'People keep telling me that. I say in return: Let's see. Let's see. Because he's either here already or he's on the way, and if he does in fact try to kill me, then he's the one making the mistake. You see, Janice, the difference between a hunter and a fisherman is the fisherman is the smart one. The hunter has to track down his prey. He has to make all the effort. But when you fish, you use a lure and wait for the fish to come to you. You let the fish do the hard work.'

FIFTY-TWO

Alvarez had established an operations centre in the CIA annexe of the US Embassy. The station chief was a woman named Layla Jensen whom he knew from his days with the Agency. She had been happy – content – for him to commandeer her staff of analysts.

'If you had informed me of this operation, I could have made some headway before you arrived.'

'I appreciate your eagerness to be of assistance, Layla, but I've been trying to keep this as low key as possible. We're dealing with potential leaks, after all.'

'Of course,' she agreed.

It was the kind of standard operations room Alvarez had been in many times. From one wall hung numerous monitors displaying CCTV footage, video recordings, television news, documents and photographs. Two rows of desks faced the screens, with half a dozen monitors on each row, an analyst seated at each terminal.

There were three male analysts, three female. They were all Americans, all dressed in similar office attire, neat and respectable. The room wasn't quiet, even when no one was talking, because of the constant murmur of keyboards clicking and the persistent whirring of fans, interrupted at intervals by ringing landlines or cells.

The air smelled of coffee and deodorant. Air conditioning kept it at a pleasant temperature.

An Agency paramilitary team attached to the Special Activities Division had been divided between surveillance and standby duties, spread between four SUVs cruising around the city, ready to be deployed on Alvarez's command. Jensen's people were crunching data for any sign of the target. The team leader was a guy named Gaten Bradley. He was a pure badass. Alvarez knew that just from looking at him, let alone from feeling the strength of his grip or reading his extensive service record. Alvarez, who had spent four years in the Marine Corps, had never felt more like a civilian, had never felt more beta. He was the larger man, sure, but he was a German Shepherd. Bradley was a Pitbull – a pure-bred, genetically engineered Pitbull from hell. No contest.

Bradley had the respectful manners of a Southern gent and the weather-beaten face of an outdoorsman. He was a few years older, but his hair was still jet black, as was his beard.

'Afghanistan, Mogadishu and Iraq. Both invasions for the latter,' Alvarez summarised.

'I feel I should say that I saw no action in Desert Storm.'

Alvarez raised his eyebrows as he glanced through

Bradley's service record. 'You made up for it since. Rangers for eleven years; Delta for six.'

'I've tried to serve my country to the best of my ability.'

'I'll say.' He flicked over several pages with increasingly raised eyebrows. 'Two years in the Special Activities Division. You've been busy.'

'I told you: I am a warrior. I don't like to sit idle.'

'Why did you leave the army?'

Bradley stroked his beard as he mentally composed his answer. His hair reached his ears. He wore a dark denim jacket over a pale denim shirt. His trousers were black jeans. Alvarez wasn't sure he had ever seen triple denim before. Bradley's shoes were white sneakers stained by grass. He was a slight guy but the jacket was stretched across his back into a pure V.

'No future there, Mr Alvarez. I was an enlisted man. I joined as a kid at the bottom and I sweated and killed my way up, but that only gets a man so far. Truth be told, I was always happy with that. I'm not the sort of person who can send a man to do a job that he can't do himself. And by the time the next war kicks off, I'll be out of the picture. I'll be too old to be sent into battle, and I don't want the indignity of being left on the sidelines. So, barring contracting for a PSC – you'll have to excuse my language, but they're all a bunch of assholes – I figured joining the CIA would be the best chance of keeping in the action.'

'Hmm. Would it be fair to say that you're addicted to combat?'

Bradley shook his head. 'No, sir. It would not. But I am a warrior. If I don't get to fight, then what is left of me?'

'We're in Finland here, not Fallujah. This is a Western urban environment you're operating within.'

'I'm a ghost, Mr Alvarez. Put me on the streets and the first time you'll see me is my reflection on the knife I'm cutting your throat with.'

'Jesus,' Alvarez couldn't help but say.

Bradley said, 'Be glad you're on the home team. I've taken more necks than a haji on Eid.'

'I most certainly am glad to be on your side, not theirs.'

'So,' Bradley said, 'can I tell my guys to saddle up?'

'Your team as good as you?'

Bradley nodded. 'They're all former tier-one operators. All JSOC. I even have a Brit who was SAS.'

'Good,' Alvarez said. 'But this isn't a battle. I want the target captured, not tagged and bagged unless there is no other option. Do you understand?'

'Yes, I do. But you read my record before you came to speak to me.'

'And?'

'And you don't need a guy like me running the op if you expect this tango is going to cuff himself and save us the bother.'

'No, I don't expect that he will. There is every chance this won't be neat and it won't be quiet.'

'Which is why you need a man like me.'

'That's correct, Bradley. I most certainly do.'

Flights, hotel and car-hire records were being analysed; facial recognition software was combing through CCTV footage for anyone who matched the man from the Minsk tape.

A voice came through one of the audio channels: 'Muir is on the move.'

Alvarez clicked his fingers. 'Put that on screen one.'

An analyst hit some keyboard commands and on one of the large monitors a live video stream appeared of Muir leaving her hotel. The footage was being streamed from one of the SAD operators on surveillance duty.

Alvarez said, 'Stay with her.'

One of the Agency staff entered the room and approached Jensen, whispering something to her. Jensen then said to Alvarez, 'You have a visitor.'

'Excuse me, what did you say?'

'He says it's important. He says he has information you need to know. He's been put in an interview room on the second floor.'

Alvarez said, 'Did he give a name?'

FIFTY-THREE

Victor slept for a few hours. Not as long as he needed, but enough to refresh. He was used to sleeping for short periods. He had taken one of the bedrooms, sleeping on the floor so he could use the bed to barricade the door. He wasn't sure if that was simply protocol or because he didn't trust Raven. He trusted no one, but the average person required no special defence against them. Raven was another matter entirely.

A part of him expected her to be gone when he awoke, to have taken the opportunity to leave the city and the country. She wasn't going to help him do what he needed to do. He could understand that.

It was dark in the penthouse. He had slept through to the evening. A light was on in the living area.

Raven was sat at a dining table, going through a file. She didn't hear his approach.

He said, 'Hey,' and her head rose.

'You look surprised to see me.'

'I am,' he admitted. 'Why are you still here?'

'To consider my next move. I've been going through the babysitter's things, trying to gather intel.' She closed the file. 'I don't have much on the target, so I was seeing if I could learn what the Consensus hoped to achieve here. I don't want to leave with nothing.'

Victor said, 'I can't help you there. The guy who led the crew in Scotland was called Niven. He was an ex-cop. He didn't know anything about the old man or even about Phoenix. He was kept at arms' length.'

'I'm sorry you wasted your time then,' Raven said. 'But thank you again for what you did.'

Victor remained silent.

'What did you mean before, about needing answers before you do anything?'

'My SIS handler warned me that the guy after me, Alvarez, knows who I really am. Before I do anything else, I need to find out if it's true.'

She tensed. She was as surprised by this as he had been. 'How ... how is that even possible? Does anyone out there know your real name?'

'Not everyone I encountered in my youth is dead. But would any of them recognise me today? Would any of them understand who the boy they knew had become?' He shook his head. 'At one point I lived on the streets. I'd run away from the orphanage. I gave the other runaways a false name because I didn't want anyone to find me. When I enlisted, I used that alias. The recruiting officer helped me falsify what I needed to. When I left the military I invented another identity. When I went freelance I started changing identities like other people changed clothes. I've had fake names for longer than I was ever known by my real name. These days, I don't think of myself by my real name. To me, I'm someone else. I'm whoever my passport says I am. I'm nothing but the identity that is the cleanest, my name is the one alias that no one will ever break because no one will ever know it. So, Constance, what is a real name?'

She said, 'Something you'd kill to protect?'

'I told someone my name, once. Not long ago really. I won't tell you where or when, but I didn't think I was going to make it and that person showed me a kindness that was enough to keep me alive and free for another moment. They asked me my name and I told them. It felt like the right thing to do at the time. Was it reckless? Sure. Do I regret it? Yes. But it felt good in that moment. It felt like lifting a burden. Fun. Rebellious.'

He saw he had said too much from the way she looked at him. He realised his guard had started to slip in her presence. He was becoming comfortable. She knew it too.

He said, 'Why is it so dark in here?'

'None of the lights work in the whole building. Wiring, I suppose. We have gas and water, if you want coffee.'

He nodded, glad to be talking about something else, but she wasn't done.

'I have an idea,' Raven said. 'Would you like to hear it?'

'Probably not,' Victor said.

'Come away with me.'

'What are you talking about? Neither of us is done here.'

'But we could be, if we wanted. We could drop everything, disappear into the wind. Start a new life.'

'Together?'

'You watch my back and I'll watch yours.'

'You're kidding, right?'

'Why am I? We work well together. Alone, we'll always be vulnerable, but we have strength in numbers. Imagine how much better we could be with a little practice. We could get to know each other. Properly, I mean.'

'That's not a good idea.'

'You still don't trust me, do you?'

'You tried to kill me.'

'I just knew you would bring that up again. It was one time. One.'

'It's not something I forget.'

'Let's not forget that you actually did kill me.'

Victor remained silent.

'But you're just diverting the course of the conversation, I know. What you're saying is, you don't want to get to know me.'

'I'm saying you may think you want to get to know me. But you wouldn't like what you found out.'

'Talk about self-deprecating. Dude, there can't be anything worse than what I know about you already. I mean, you're not exactly the man my mother – may she rest in peace – would have approved of. Not because you're a professional contract killer, but because you're freelance. She wanted me to settle down with a man who had a steady job. What I mean is, I already know the worst of you. I'd like to find out about the best.'

'That's where you're so wrong, Constance. There is no best of me. There is nothing more than this. This is who I am. This is all I am. All I will be.'

'Even if I believed that, it doesn't have to be like that. We can be anyone,' she insisted. 'Start again. Think of the possibilities.'

'That's too much to think about. Don't feel sorry for me, Constance. I don't feel sorry for myself.'

'You should.'

'Why? Because I don't float through existence like everyone else? They may live peaceful, happy lives, but I guarantee they've never felt more alive than I have when my heart's pounding and my enemies are dead around me.'

'So, there is a reason why you do this. It's not just because you can't get out. You enjoy it.'

He shook his head. 'No, but I have enough self-awareness to understand that the closer I am to death, the more I feel alive.'

'You're the frog, slowly boiling to death without realising it.'

'No, because I know I'm boiling to death. But I'm now too weak to jump out of the pot.'

She smiled because she had trapped him. 'Which is exactly why you need someone else to switch off the stove.'

'Someone like ... you?'

She beamed. 'However did you guess?'

Victor said, 'What are you doing, Constance?'

She looked confused. 'What do you mean?'

'You've been doing a good job of keeping me talking. I'd like to know what you're hoping to achieve.'

'Nothing wrong with a little chit-chat between friends, is there?'

'It's more than simply chat. Maybe it's because I've just woken up, maybe it's because my guard isn't as high as it should be, but I've only just noticed that you've been keeping the conversation away from why you're here in Helsinki.'

'You know why,' she said. 'I was sent here.'

'To kill someone.'

Raven was silent.

Victor stood and approached the dining table.

'Don't,' Raven said.

He ignored her. He reached for the slim brown dossier.

FIFTY-FOUR

There was a Sykes, an idea of a Sykes, an *ideal* Sykes that was almost realised, that might have been realised had he only been born a little taller, a little prettier, a little richer, a little smarter. He had been destined for silver but ached for gold with such longing that silver was squandered, ignored and willingly forfeited. The end result meant less than bronze – a yearning hope for bronze.

Sykes hadn't slept well. He hadn't for years. The skin beneath his eyes was now darker than his hair had ever been. What was left of it, at least. He could see the shine of his scalp if he stood under a harsh light, and had taken to using dark bedding to avoid the sight of all those fleeing hairs on his pillowcase each morning. It was depressing, and he fought it hard with every potion and gadget money could buy. Maybe they worked. Maybe he had slowed the inevitable. Maybe his hair would be thinner without them. Which was even more depressing. He was scared of being hairless as he was scared of many things. Sykes was, and always had been, a coward. Once, he had ambition and desire. Once, he had been driven by greed for money and power. Now, he realised that this was driven by his weakness. A strong man didn't need wealth and power. Needing it meant he was weak. He was weak now and he had always been weak. That weakness had almost made him rich and almost made him dead.

He had dressed in his best suit for this. Dressing used to be such a simple thing to do as a young man. Now, a chore. A hassle. Something he hated. He had to sit down to put his socks on because he couldn't bend over far enough to reach his toes, let alone stand on one leg that long. Then he had to stand again to fasten his trousers, breathing in and pulling hard to fasten the button. Whatever pride he derived from managing to fit into the same waist size was offset by the swollen muffin-top, pale and hairy, that pride manifested.

Sykes was spent. Not physically, because he could stretch four more decades out of his listless shell. No, he was spent as Sykes. That lonely teenager had strived to be anyone else. Sykes longed to be that lonely teenager again.

He wasn't drunk enough to be under any illusions. He knew the drink was driving him, giving him a confidence and purpose that he was never meant to possess. He had followed the necessary path, the obvious path; that which was preordained. But from now on he would change that direction. He realised that there was a will buried beneath all that self-loathing, a will that was forged of something

TOM WOOD

greater than he, and which had always been there, but dormant, buried, waiting for the summons.

He summoned it now. Sykes knew what he had to do. He knew that he could not go on as this skeleton of being. Every choice he had ever made was the wrong one, so any action that contradicted those past failures had to be correct, had to be righteous.

He just hoped that he wasn't too late.

The interview room was small and nondescript aside from a table and a couple of chairs. The walls were painted taupe and the floor covered in cheap linoleum. Alvarez took a seat opposite Sykes, who stank of alcohol and body odour. Alvarez grimaced at the smell.

He said, 'What are you doing here, Kevin?'

'I need to speak to you.'

'No kidding. You flew halfway across the world. You look like you could use some coffee.'

'I don't want coffee.'

'I don't have a lot of time here. I was told you have information for me. Information that couldn't wait until I was back in the States?'

Sykes shook his head. 'You need to know now. It can't wait. Like I waited for Procter to deliver on his promises. I gave him everything I knew in return for nothing. I just became his dogsbody. Someone to bury the shit that rolls downhill. That's why I left. Even though I escaped prosecution, people had heard the rumours. I was never going to be trusted again. Which, funnily enough, is why they came knocking at my door.'

'They?'

394

'There are these people. You have to understand, they're everywhere. Sometimes you come across them and don't know it. If they don't reach out to you, you'll never know they exist. They reached out to me. I . . . I did as they asked, I've done as they ask. I have a bank account, offshore. In Rome. They pay into this account. It's laundered. It's clean. Ooo, you should see how much they pay me. It would blow your mind.'

'What are you talking about? Who are they?'

'An infestation. I don't know what they're called, but they have people like me in their pocket. I mean, I guess I'm one of them. In a way. I don't know who else is like me, but I do know there are lots of us.'

'Doing what?'

'Lying, stealing, passing on information. Sometimes it's just a phone call. I get a phone call that tells me to make a phone call. Sometimes I meet someone. Sometimes I deliver money. Sometimes I find other people they need.'

'Who do they need?'

'At first they just wanted information. They knew some of what I'd been involved with. They knew about Paris. They knew about the assassin. That's who they were mostly interested in. Him and his associates. I thought that was it. But they came back. Not for more information, though. For work.'

'What work?'

'This and that. Liaising with people. Recruiting. Hiring. Finding the right people for the right jobs.'

'What jobs, Kevin?'

'I knew they were bad because of the people they wanted

me to find. People like me. The traitors and the untrust-worthy. Criminals. Thieves and killers. Contractors. You name it.'

'What are you trying to tell me here?'

'They're everywhere. I thought of them like a shadow government, but it's much worse than that. They're more like terrorists. There are all these cells. There might be four or five guys or fifty. Each cell operates almost inde-pendently from the others. If one is compromised, it doesn't affect the greater organisation. I thought the guy who called me was in charge, but he's just a guy like me. A guy hired by another guy to hire more guys. I didn't ask questions. I went along with it, but slowly, a bit at a time, I learned more. I heard something about New York. A cover-up. I tried to find out more. I was curious, I guess, and I was scared. I didn't know what I'd got myself into. I wanted some leverage. I was careful. I thought I was. Then one morning I woke up with a snow shaker on my bedside table. It had the Statue of Liberty inside. I stopped asking questions after that. I've made a lot of bad choices in my life, but this is probably the worst. I don't see a way out because I don't even know who I'm working for. I don't have anyone to betray any more than I have anything to bargain with.'

Alvarez said, 'You're not telling me anything, Kevin. You're barely making any sense at all. I need some proof if you want me to take you seriously.'

'You'll have all the proof you need soon.'

'What does that mean?'

'It means they'll know we've talked. They'll know like

they always know. I don't care. I'm tired of being scared. I'm tired of being me.'

'You need to go back to your hotel and sleep it off. Come see me when you're sober.'

'Don't you understand? I wouldn't be here if I was sober. I can't look at myself in the mirror any more. I can't bear to see the man who looks back at me.'

'That's the booze talking.'

'The booze is allowing me to talk freely, that's all. I know what I'm saying. It's me who's saying it. I don't see myself as a bad person. I mean, not really bad. I didn't kill you that time, did I? I could have done, but I didn't. People have died because of the things I've done, yes. But if it hadn't been me, it would have been someone else. There's always someone else. I'm not evil, I'm just lazy. I've always wanted more. I've never been satisfied with what I had, but I didn't want to earn more. I just wanted more. You don't choose to be lazy. I never chose it. If I could, I would have chosen to be a doer, like you. A worker.'

'You're drunk, Kevin. And I'm tired of humouring you.'

'I'm always drunk or hungover. Neither state is really me, but they're all I am.'

'You're not making any sense.'

'You're not listening to me. I'm confessing.'

'Save it. I'm not interested. I'm not a priest. I already know what you've done. I know what you got away with. All this, whatever this is, can be someone else's problem.'

'You know what I did, not what I'm doing.'

Alvarez listened.

'There's this guy, he's an ex-cop. He's an animal. I found him. They needed him. God, the things he's done ...'

Alvarez stared. 'You're serious, aren't you? This isn't some fantasy.'

'That's what I'm trying to tell you,' Sykes growled. 'This animal. His name is Niven. Right now he's at a farmhouse. Some isolated Scottish place. He's got a crew. Bad people like him. They've got hostages. It could already be too late. They could be dead.'

Alvarez was sitting forward. 'Tell me where the farmhouse is, Kevin. Who are the hostages?'

'Ben and Suzanne Mayes.'

'What are these men going to do, Kevin?'

'It's supposed to look like a home invasion. They're going to kill them, unless the sister of the farmer completes a job for these people. She's an assassin. I don't have time to tell you all the details.'

'If this is true, then you really are a piece of shit.' Alvarez stood, tugging out his phone. 'Whatever you did before, it's nothing compared to this.'

Sykes' breathing became a series of heaves as his inebriated body tried to oxygenate itself, and it was a lot of work. He said, 'Why be merely foul when you can be vile?'

Alvarez looked down at him in disgust. He thumbed his contact and brought the phone to his ear. 'You had better hope they're still alive. You'd better pray.'

'You can't threaten me with anything. But I'm not finished. Forget them for a second. They're safe for a little while longer. They're safe because the sister, the assassin, is going to do the job they want her to do. She's here, in

Helsinki. Right now. Her name is Constance Stone, she's former Agency, now rogue. She's—'

Alvarez interrupted: 'Dammit, Sykes. I know that name, she's—'

'LISTEN TO ME.'

Alvarez did.

Sykes said, 'The sister is here in Helsinki to kill you. You're the target.'

FIFTY-FIVE

Raven got to the file first and snatched it away from Victor's grasp. But it didn't matter, because now he knew.

Victor said, 'You tensed when I said the name Alvarez before. I saw it but I didn't think why. Now, I understand. Now I get why you were talking nonsense about going away together. He's here in Helsinki, isn't he?'

'It wasn't nonsense.'

Victor said, 'I know why Alvarez is a threat to me, but what's he done to the Consensus?'

'I don't know. I don't know anything about him. But he's a problem for them, clearly. Maybe not now. Maybe soon. Maybe it's pre-emptive. But whatever it is, it's unbelievable. Just the worst cosmic luck. Of all the . . .' she growled, screwing up the file into a ball and throwing it across the room. '*Goddammit.*'

'Blasphemy, Constance.'

'Trust me, Him upstairs would be okay with it this time. I mean, He really would see the funny side. He would get just how incredibly bad this is. What. Are. The. Odds? It's some kind of sick joke. It has to be. Can you believe it?'

He didn't answer. He was already scanning the room with new eyes, picturing where she had placed her things, imagining where she had left her gun; which objects could be improvised weapons she would go for.

'I can't let you go after him,' she said.

'I know.'

'But you're going to anyway, aren't you?'

'He's left me no choice. I need to know what he knows.'

Raven said, 'There's always a choice.'

'For you, maybe. But not for me. There is no choice because the right action is always the best action.'

'I was a threat, once. Now look at us.'

'Yes,' Victor said, 'look at us.'

They were standing across the room from one another, three metres apart, out of range, but getting closer, beginning to circle, arms rising, postures changing, adopting stances; slowly, inevitably. They both saw what the other was doing. They both knew what was happening.

'We don't have to do this,' Raven said.

Victor nodded. 'We only have to if you try and stop me.'

'I can't take the risk that he corners you or you decide he's too much of a threat to live. If they want him dead, then he's a threat to them. He has to live.'

'I understand what motivates you, Constance. You need to understand what motivates me.'

401

She said, 'I know. Greed. Selfishness. Amorality. Nihilism.'

'You didn't complain about any of those things when I was saving your brother's life.'

'Which you only did to get closer to Phoenix and ensure my aid against Alvarez.'

'What matters is I did what you needed. Will you do the same for me?'

She hesitated.

'Then this discussion is over.'

'If you walk out that door, we're enemies again.'

'We've always been enemies, Constance. This has been nothing but a truce of convenience. We should have known it wouldn't last long.'

She said, 'Don't do it.'

'Don't try and stop me.'

'Will you kill me if I do?'

'You'll be a threat.'

'So that's a yes.'

He nodded. 'Keep out of my way and it doesn't have to end like that. For now, you're not a direct threat. If you want to stay alive, then stay out of my way.'

She sighed in resignation, and he headed for the door.

He stopped because he heard a hammer cocked behind him. 'That better not be what I think it is.'

'I can't take the risk.'

'Are you going to kill me, just in case? Are you going to shoot me in the back, Constance?'

'What choice are you leaving me?'

'There's always a choice. Isn't that your point? Isn't that

the reason you do what you do?' He took a step backwards. 'I've made my own choices, same as you. All this is is another decision. Shoot me, or don't shoot me.' He took another step backwards.

'Don't make me do it.'

'I've always known this is how it would end,' Victor said. 'I just never knew I would know my killer.'

'We can still work this out.'

He said nothing.

'You hear me? There's still a solution, if you'll only listen.'

Victor heard her take a step towards him. Then another, her desire to convince him to stay overriding her tactical awareness.

He moved fast, spinning on the spot, going for the gun. She was as fast as him but hesitation slowed her – she didn't want to shoot him – so when the gun went off he had already pushed the muzzle away.

The bullet shattered a window. Neither blinked.

'You almost shot me,' he said.

'But I didn't. Let's talk about this. We can work out a solution. There has to be a way.'

He nodded. 'Okay, you're right. Let's talk. But, please, lower that gun.'

As her gaze dropped, so did his closest elbow into her face. She staggered back, dazed, but not before he batted the gun from her hand. That gave her an instant to recover enough for her guard to fly up to intercept his follow-up attacks.

FIFTY-SIX

Sykes was nursing black coffee when Alvarez re-entered the interview room. He didn't bother to sit down this time because it wasn't going to take long.

Alvarez said, 'I made some calls and had a couple of local cops swing by the Mayes' place, Kevin. They spoke to Ben. He's alive and well, getting ready for a little vacation. He's pretty upset though. His dog knocked over a stove and set the barn on fire.'

Sykes' eyes were wide. 'What? That can't be true. They ...'

'You've been telling me lies, and I don't like being lied to.'

'Why would I lie? What's in it for me? Something's gone wrong, obviously. The plan didn't work. I don't know why, but everything I've told you is true. If you look into it, I swear you'll find evidence. Maybe the sister had help. I don't know. She ... Something happened and she didn't need to kill you. You have to believe me.'

'Okay,' Alvarez said. 'Despite my better instincts, I'm going to tolerate this delusion just so I can watch you wrap yourself up in this bullshit. So, tell me, why me? What have I done to them? Whoever these people are.'

'They're threatened by you, and they don't like threats. They think you know things. They think you know what happened in New York. They don't want you to find the assassin. They don't want you to know what he knows.'

'What happened in New York? Does the killer work for them?'

'No, of course not. But there was a connection. He's not a primary concern, though. They're scared that one day you'll be the Director of National Intelligence.'

'I've only just joined. If, *if*, I wanted that job, I'm ten years or more from having a chance at it. There's nothing to be gained killing me now.'

'You're not listening to anything I'm saying. They think long term. They plan ahead. There's always a narrative. They're not going to wait until you're the Director of NI before taking you out. How will they stay hidden after that? No, they're going to have you killed when no one's going to notice, not only taking you out before you can really hurt them but making room for another candidate, a better, more suitable candidate.'

'This sounds like the biggest pile of horseshit I've ever heard.'

'There'll be an easy way to know for sure if I'm telling the truth.'

'How?'

'Look at me,' Sykes said. 'I'm a mess. I'm a drunk. But I'm not suicidal. Remember that about me.'

The door opened. It was Layla Jensen.

'Sorry to interrupt, but we have reports of gunfire down-town. Might be something.'

Alvarez stood and headed to the door. 'I'm done with this crap, Kevin. When we're back in the States, expect a call from the Department of Justice. Any agreement we've had is over. The deal's off.'

Sykes swallowed the last of his cold coffee. 'It won't matter.'

Raven was fast and she knew exactly how to block his strikes, but he was far stronger. He outweighed her by at least 50 pounds. Just stopping his fists and elbows reaching her face jolted her from her stable fighting stance to an awkward, off-balance position. But that weight difference meant she was the smaller, faster target. She hit him with short punches he couldn't hope to block.

One blow caught Victor on the side of the jaw and sent him reeling, vision darkening, hearing fading. He recovered in time to block the next one meant for his temple but missed the one aimed for his ribs. The impact knocked the air from his lungs and he doubled over, grimacing and unsteady.

Hands grabbed the back of his head and pulled it down for a knee that powered upwards. He blocked it with crossed arms, but the force of the knee slammed his own arms back against his chest. He winced and shot out both hands before another knee could strike and locked his arms out, braced against Raven's hips. Kneeing from such a position was impossible and Victor powered forward, driving her back without resistance.

Raven slammed backwards into a wall. Plaster cracked, but she rebounded with the energy, twisting from his grip and going for the dropped gun.

An analyst explained: 'The call's just come in. Police won't be there for at least six minutes. Witness heard a gunshot and saw a window break from an apartment building. Penthouse.'

Jensen said, 'That's not something we have every day. There are lots of guns, but shootings are rare. Very rare. I can't see this being coincidental, can you?'

'What do we know about the penthouse?' Alvarez asked.

The analyst brought up building records, land registry, utility bills and rental agreements. 'It's owned by a private landlord but is supposed to be unoccupied while it is renovated.'

Alvarez said, 'CCTV?'

Keys clicked. 'There's a traffic camera at the intersection.'

Jensen said, 'Bring it up on screen one.'

A grainy black-and-white image appeared on the largest wall-mounted monitor showing a four-way intersection and buildings either side of the road.

'Top-right corner is the apartment block,' the analyst said. 'No sign of activity.'

'Can we adjust the camera to see more of the building?'

The analyst said, 'It's static.'

Jensen asked Alvarez, 'What do you want to do?'

He stared at the monitor, stepping forward closer to it, as if proximity to the screen would give him some more information, some answer. 'How far out are the SAD units?'

The analyst checked the map and the live GPS updates. 'Closest is Sierra One, on Muir. First vehicle is three minutes out. Second SUV is five.'

Alvarez said, 'Send them both. Tell them to hurry. If this is the killer, they're to shoot on sight.'

Victor threw himself at Raven, charging her into the side of a sheeted cabinet. The wood shuddered and flexed and splintered. Raven grunted, air-less, as Victor grabbed her arms and hauled her away, throwing her into the table.

She tumbled backwards over it, falling off the far side and knocking over chairs as she went to the floor, landing on her front.

Victor heaved the table to one side and kicked a chair out of his path as he rushed to take advantage of Raven's prone position. She rolled out of the way of a heel intended for her neck, going on to her back and kicking out a heel of her own that caught Victor in the abdomen and doubled him over.

He fell forward, on to Raven, who threw up an elbow to protect herself and catch Victor as he fell. The elbow glanced off Victor's forehead but didn't stop his size and weight pinning Raven in place, trapping her arms for a brief moment, long enough for him to shoot out both hands to squeeze Raven's neck.

Victor had tremendous grip strength, but Raven tensed her neck to flare the tendons and harden the muscles, giving her enough respite to bring up her left foot and kick it into Victor's hip while she sprawled on to one side.

The kick forced Victor to release his hold on her neck and he thumped a palm against the floor to prevent himself crashing prone as Raven scrambled out from underneath him.

Raven rolled away and flipped to her feet. She backed off and grabbed the babysitter's knife from the dining table as Victor stood and picked up a chair. He used it as a club, swinging it by two legs at Raven's head.

She ducked the first attack and sidestepped the second, the chair creating too much distance to strike back.

Victor changed tack and switched to faster jabs, thrusting the chair forward, catching Raven by surprise and hitting her in the chest and forcing her backwards, off balance. She released the knife to grab a doorframe to stop her falling over in the doorway.

She ducked the chair as he swung it at her face. Instead, it struck the doorframe and broke apart.

Muir had noticed her tail, of course, because she was CIA and even with a rotating pattern she couldn't fail to spot the three different but identical black SUVs full of tough-looking guys. She pretended not to notice, because what was the point? There was nothing to be achieved in letting on they had been made. It wasn't like it was the surveillance team's fault they were giving themselves away. That was the fault of whoever sent them to watch her, because they were not full-time shadows. This was a gun team. She figured contractors or SAD paramilitaries ready to go into action the moment Tesseract tried to make contact with her. Which wouldn't happen, because he wasn't reckless enough to show up in Helsinki.

Screeching tyres as the black SUV braked hard and pulled a fast U-turn told her something was very wrong.

FIFTY-SEVEN

Raven had no choice but to back away, to create distance, to escape his relentless, stinging attacks. She gave Victor the room to kick her in the chest, in the sternum, a solid stomp kick that catapulted her backwards over the sofa, tipping it over with her, dust sheet wrapping around her.

He went for the dropped gun while she untangled herself.

He heard her behind him, recovering faster than he expected, standing, but there were no other guns in the room to concern himself with and too much distance between them for her to make some desperate lunge. He scooped the weapon up, turning as he did, raising his arm as his gaze sought the target.

He glimpsed her back, her black hair in motion as she sprinted to the closest doorway to the hallway.

The gun came up, and the front sights came into

alignment with the back sights, muzzle aiming at the back of her skull, a moving target but running away from him in a straight line, but then disappearing as he increased pressure on the trigger; Raven dropping into a slide, anticipating a headshot and robbing him of it before he could fire, simultaneously making it to the hallway and out of his line of sight before he could adjust his aim.

He chased after her. The apartment was big, but it wasn't so large that she could lose him or hide. She was desperate, fleeing, no plan or tactics beyond trying to stay alive.

She had one advantage: she knew the layout of the interior better than he did. Fatigue and a false sense of security had overridden his innate protocol to perform thorough checks. He realised that fatigue was slowing him now, even if he didn't feel it. His reactions wouldn't be as sharp. His movements would be sluggish. So she had two advantages, because she was well rested.

But those two advantages were insignificant, because he had the gun.

Raven made it to a bedroom, the closest haven. She couldn't afford to be in the hallway a second longer. If he saw her again, she would be dead. There was a catch on the door, that she engaged. It wouldn't stop him, but it bought her a moment to drag the bed in front of the door.

Which was kicked open, but only a few inches before the bed blocked it.

A single bed was no match for his strength. He pushed it aside; it took time, it took a matter of seconds, but she made the most of each and every one of them, heaving open the window, climbing out on to the sill.

There was a balcony below her.

Victor forced his way into the room, saw it was empty, and hurried to the open window – no sign of Raven – and leaned out to see a balcony one floor below.

One of her shoes lay on the balcony, having been lost in the climb and drop.

He didn't follow. If it was him, he would be waiting on the other side of the balcony doors, ready to ambush his pursuer when they dropped down, exposed, vulnerable, gun no longer in hand.

Instead, he backed away, rushing through the apartment, making it along the hallway, through the lounge and to the front door, but stopping himself. Thinking. Realising. Remembering.

He brought an arsenal.

In the apartment's second bedroom, Raven removed one of the Estonian's weapons from the black sports bag. She was quiet but quick, knowing she didn't have much time, regardless of his actions. She could hear him moving in the hallway, racing away, assuming she had dropped to the balcony below as she hoped to convince him with the discarded shoe. Instead, she had reached across to the next window, thankfully already open, and slipped inside an instant before he would have seen her. She was fast, knowing the exterior after tricking the babysitter.

She loaded the weapon and racked the slide.

It was a noise Victor knew well, a hard, metallic crunch that was impossible to lessen, to quieten. All guns made their own unique sounds that, like fingerprints, could identify them to the right ear. Victor never forgot the sound of a racking slide. Even muffled through the door and space between them, he knew the weapon.

An MP7, a beast of an automatic gun he had last used in Russia, in a forest in Sochi. Incredible firepower.

The pistol was no match for it.

The MP7 was a short, light weapon, a perfect size and weight for Raven's build. She had used one before too. Plenty of times. This particular one had a folding stock that was pressed against her upper right chest as she charged out of the opening door. The twenty-round magazine was loaded with subsonic ammunition to make the most of the long suppressor affixed to the muzzle. It was equipped with a holographic sight, perfect for close-quarters battle – perfect for this fight.

As she exited the bedroom she only glimpsed his foot as he dashed out of the hallway. He must have heard her and recognised the noise of an automatic weapon racked. In a straight gunfight, he knew he would lose.

Now it was his turn to run.

Victor dashed out of the penthouse ahead of the storm of gunfire and descended the stairs fast, creating distance and cutting down lines of sight, but not so hurried that he didn't hear the squeal of rubber on asphalt on the street outside. A hard brake. Not the action of a driver avoiding an accident, but a fast deceleration, controlled, going from speed to stationary in the shortest possible time. He spared a second to glance out of a window.

From a black SUV he saw six men exit, quick and assured; each man knowing his job and how to act in relation to the others. They were dressed in casual clothes, from which they whipped out compact sub-machine guns or pistols while on the move towards the building, weapons snapping up and ready to fire. That wasn't all. It was night and they were ready for that. He recognised the thermal-imaging goggles they wore.

The first gunshot, he realised, had brought them here. How long ago did it happen? One minute? Two? It was hard to keep track of time in the chaos of combat. These guys weren't the police but they had responded fast. So they were one unit of a larger contingent. The odds of the only team out looking for him just happening to be in the same area weren't even worth considering. This unit had been the closest. There would be more further out, but closing fast. As more arrived, his odds of escape, of survival, exponentially diminished.

One assassin above him, but six gunmen below him.

He had to retreat back up the stairs. Raven, however capable, was the lesser threat. He pictured the building and the entrances and the hallways and rooms. They had to come for him because he wasn't going out to them. No way. They could see in the dark. He would be a glowing white target long before he had any hope of spotting them in return. Outside, he had no chance against multiple shooters. Inside, he would still be a glowing white target, but at point-blank range he could see them too. Then it was down to tactics and speed. Then, he had a chance.

They wouldn't try to keep it quiet from the way they moved. They weren't going to tranquillise him. They were a paramilitary unit of a foreign power. They would want this handled fast.

The MP7 had forced them into action. Even suppressed, it wasn't quiet. They had to act before the police arrived on scene.

The apartment building. Nine stories. Three exterior walls. Only two external doors, but with ground-floor windows that made for multiple points of entry. Impossible for him to cover them all.

That didn't matter, because unless they were planning on scaling rendered walls or had brought ladders to get up onto the scaffolding, there was only one way to reach him. The stairwell.

Choke point.

He kicked open a door to the closest apartment and went inside. Like the penthouse above, it was unoccupied for renovation, and like the penthouse it had some items of furniture protected by dust sheets. He yanked away a sheet that covered a sofa, hurried into the nearby bathroom, and turned on the shower.

Raven did not rush to follow her fleeing enemy. She might now outgun him, but she was under no illusion just how dangerous he could be. She was cut, hurt and bleeding.

Everywhere hurt. Chasing after him in the dark was no fun. Instead, she edged to the balcony door and peered outside when she too heard a vehicle braking hard, taking a mental snapshot of the exterior, seeing the gunmen exit their vehicle and approach the building.

She knew a SAD team when she saw one, because she had once been part of one. Good-humoured guys every one, but lethal.

It didn't matter if they were here for her or him, because both of them were assassins with shoot-to-kill orders on their heads.

She hurried through the penthouse, heaving open a window on the building's north side. She leaned backwards through it, took hold of the top of the frame, and hauled herself out and up on to the sill. She balanced carefully and slid the window back down. The roof above was surrounded by an overhang of stone she could just stretch her fingers to. She stretched further, inching them along until she had her fingers flat on the overhang up to the second knuckle. Not an ideal grip, given her weakened state, but it would have to do.

She exhaled and lifted, pulling herself straight up until her jaw was higher than the roof. She hooked an elbow on to it, and then swung up a leg. A moment later, she was crouched on the roof and considering her next move.

After catching her breath, she edged her way across the roof, until she was overlooking the scaffolding.

She lowered herself off the roof and dropped the remaining distance as shots of a gunfight raged from inside the building.

FIFTY-EIGHT

With weapons locked and loaded, the SAD operators entered the apartment building through both exterior doors at the same time, fast and assured, as two fire-teams of three. They were well-briefed on their target, but not on the location, so they had to take their time moving through the ground floor. They knew what they were doing, though. They knew how to clear a building. They were all former military who had seen combat, who had swept rooms for insurgents whilst looking out for booby traps and IEDs. Thermal-imaging goggles painted the interior in shades of grey: the cool floor tiles were dark, the warmer walls lighter. They saw each other's exposed skin – faces, necks, wrists – as pure white, with their clothes as pale grey. Their guns were black, except where they held them, warming the metal to pale handprints that faded back to darkness.

They converged at the bottom of the stairwell, ignoring

the elevator, which they would have done even had it been active.

They communicated with hand gestures. The action was taking place high above them, in the penthouse, which they ascended towards. They didn't like leaving floors uncleared behind them, but they had to hurry.

The six kept close as they made their way up the stairs, covering different angles, anticipating an attack. This was their most vulnerable moment, and they expected the target would exploit that, given the chance.

As a result, they moved fast, not wanting to extend that vulnerability any longer than they needed. There was no further sound of gunfire from above. They reached the eighth floor without incident. The penthouse waited. It seemed the target had wasted the best opportunity he would ever get.

Victor, lying with his front on the cool floorboards, whipped the dust sheet soaked in cold water back from where it lay on top of him, and opened fire.

Two shots at each man. Double taps to their heads. They went down, one by one; too surprised to know what was happening; too slow to react to the unknown. Four seconds. Five corpses.

He had waited until he heard no more footsteps on the stairs before throwing the sheet back. He hadn't been able to see through it any more than their thermal imaging had been able to differentiate between the cold sheet and the cool floor.

He was on his feet and approaching the stairs a moment later.

Had the sixth team member hung back?

Yes, because a sub-machine gun opened up from the floor below. Rounds puckered the banister and punched holes in the walls and ceiling.

He returned fire, shooting blind, emptying his pistol as he ran along the landing and passed the top of the stairs, tossing it aside as it clicked empty, and sliding across the floor to where the five corpses lay.

Scooping up one of the dropped weapons – a bullpup Steyr SMG – he scrambled to his feet and dashed back the way he had come as footsteps pounded the stairs.

He led with the Steyr, squeezing the trigger before he had fully rounded the wall or acquired a target.

The final guy – who was in fact a woman – caught the spray of automatic fire in the chest as she rushed up the stairwell.

The body armour saved her from the small-calibre rounds, but she tumbled over backwards down the stairs, striking the floor with the rear of her skull with all the energy of the fall and she slackened at the foot of the stairwell.

She didn't move again.

Victor waited, in case Raven was near. When he was sure she wasn't going to show up, he checked the corpses. They had just the essentials: guns, ammo, comms.

He reloaded the Steyr, stashed as many spare mags as his waistband could handle, and took an armoured vest and thermal-imaging goggles from one of the bodies. Taking the equipment burned time he didn't have, but he had an idea.

The woman stirred. A quiet moan escaped her lips. Not

dead, but not conscious either. No threat now, but she could wake at any time.

Victor pressed his left palm over the woman's lips and nostrils while he kept watch for Raven.

Victor reached the penthouse, having seen no sign of Raven, and realised that like him she had spotted the arrival of the team and fled. That reduced the immediate threat, but a second SUV had arrived outside. He should already be trying to escape, but he couldn't waste this opportunity. He might never get another one.

In the bathroom he heaved the dead Estonian from the bathtub and dressed it in the body armour and goggles he had taken from downstairs. The corpse was no longer stiff from rigor, and though awkward to manoeuvre, this didn't have to be perfect. Victor kept hold of the Steyr for now, but he wasn't going to take it with him.

In the kitchen, Victor worked the stove, twisting each of the four knobs to their maximum setting. Gas hissed. He found no clicker in the drawers, but remembered the pack of French cigarettes and lighter that had been on the dining table. They had scattered during the fight with Raven. He found them at opposite ends of the room, the pack of cigarettes by the door and a lighter beneath a window. He picked the latter up from amongst the shards of broken glass and brought it to the cigarettes.

He opened the pack and lit the cigarettes inside.

The second SAD team to arrive entered the building fast, two-by-two cover formation, clearing the hallways and stairwell and checking doors as they hurried through the building.

Bradley led, knowing they had people down, and eager to get to them and exact revenge. The enemy was still present, still dangerous, so they had to be thorough. They were fast but they didn't rush.

He was not surprised to find the corpses, and after checking for signs of life and finding none, there was only one course of action. He signalled for his men to advance upstairs.

The door to the penthouse was closed and they took up their positions, ready.

Bradley gave the countdown to breach with his fingers: three, two—

One.

They charged through the door and into the apartment, beginning to spread out to clear the rooms one at a time searching for the target, searching for vengeance, but he smelled the gas and yelled—

'ABORT.'

The gas exploded, demolishing the kitchen, the partition wall and sending a huge fireball and concussive wave through the penthouse, consuming the SAD team before they could retreat. The apartment became an inferno, lit by flames but dark with smoke.

Victor, lying in the bathtub with the Estonian's corpse shielding him, escaped the fireball and shockwave almost unscathed. The latter blasted the bathroom door off its hinges and deposited it on top of the tub, trapping him in place until he managed to work his way out, but by the time he did the bathroom was filling with black smoke.

His eyes filled with water, and he coughed and retched. He grabbed a hand towel to try and shield his mouth and nose. The hallway was aflame. He could barely see. The heat was incredible.

He held out his arm perpendicular to find the width and to brace himself as he stumbled from wall to wall, trying to avoid the flames. He manoeuvred around burning furniture, gaze sweeping for anything that might injure him or that could be used to his advantage. His eyes stung from the smoke and heat and the strain of continued staring in an effort to focus the shapeless blurs and colours. He stumbled on a corpse, losing balance, the sleeve of his suit jacket catching fire as he fell against a burning door frame, but managed to stay on his feet.

He saw there was no way out. The fire was too bad, blocking off the exit. He changed direction, shaking the sleeve as he continued, the smoke clearing enough for him to see the window at the other end of the hallway.

He grabbed a burning chair as he ran, throwing it at the window so the glass shattered as he reached it and threw himself through the rainfall of shards; landing on the scaffolding one floor below, body slamming into aluminium piping; feeling the crunch in his flank as ribs cracked, but rising despite the pain, despite the fatigue, hearing the wail of multiple sirens and knowing he had a matter of moments before the police arrived. There wasn't time to descend the scaffolding, but he saw the mouth of the rubble chute.

It was wide enough for him to fit into, but too wide to

slow his descent enough to survive the eight-storey rush to the ground. He didn't know what was in the skip at the bottom. Could be full of convenient soft wood, or maybe hard bricks or worse. Maybe he would be lucky and the skip was full of mattresses. Victor didn't believe in luck.

He drew the babysitter's knife and climbed into the chute. He stabbed the knife into the tough plastic.

He didn't hesitate and dropped.

He fell at a hellish speed, even with his limbs splayed to create friction and the knife slowing his descent. The chute was designed for waste, not a person. He saw nothing but darkness. All he could hear was a rush of icy air and the scrape of the knife slicing against plastic as he fell.

Two seconds, four. He didn't know how fast he fell, but he expected death to greet him at the bottom. This was no tactical manoeuvre. This was an act of desperation. He had no choice. Fall, else die in the fire, or get captured by the police.

The knife jammed in the chute – maybe blunted enough by the tough plastic to catch; maybe caught on something more solid – and his wrist jolted against the sudden force it was asked to support and failed.

The pain was fierce but he thrust his palms against the inside of the chute, trying to slow himself, and he smelled his own burnt flesh before he shot out of the bottom of the chute.

There was no skip, and his ankles and knees crunched with the collision of hitting the ground, but the lack of a skip with solid walls let him roll with the impact, over and over again, across an empty communal parking area until he finally stopped, face down on the cold asphalt, winded, bleeding and grimacing, his right wrist already swollen, the hand paralysed, both palms almost skinless.

He lay there for a brief moment until he knew for certain he was still alive, then stood, and stumbled into the night.

TWO WEEKS
LATER

FIFTY-NINE

Procter's front lawn was dark in the shadow of the tall trees that stood below the sun. A tiny spider spun a web between the posts supporting the porch. The web was invisible in the glare of the low sun. The spider looked suspended in mid-air. Levitating.

'The house and the land is Patricia showing me she still cares. I've always been a city boy who yearned for the country, but when you work for the Agency and your wife works for the government, you're going to spend your life in a townhouse. Maybe I turned on the old emotional blackmail with my injury, but she did what was best for my convalescence. We still have the brownstone, and she spends most of the week there, but that's another story – and you don't need to hear it, even if you came all this way just to catch up.'

'I'm in no particular rush,' Alvarez said.

'In a way. It's like a slow dance, not that you're old

enough to have ever been to a real dance hall. You slow dance with the girl you like and you try your best not to poke her with your hard-on, but all the while you're trying to do exactly that.'

'I don't understand,' Alvarez said. 'Are you the hard-on, or am I?'

'I'm saying the pleasantries are make believe. They're window dressing.'

'I know what you're saying.'

Procter looked towards the setting sun. 'Do you ever stop and think that the last honest conversation you ever had was when you were a kid? Do you ever think that as adults we never say what we really mean and every conversation is just two people doing everything they can to avoid the truth?'

'I'm more inclined to believe that every conversation is just two people fighting with words.'

'Therein lies the difference between us.'

Alvarez said, 'I'm fighting you with words while you try and avoid the truth?'

'I'd say that's exactly what we're doing.'

'That sounds surprisingly honest for someone who believes adults can't have an honest conversation.'

'Moments of honesty do not an honest conversation make.'

'Like I said: fighting with words. But we don't need to, because we're way beyond all that.'

'There's no reason for you to be here. At least, no good reason.'

Alvarez said nothing.

Procter said, 'I take it you're feeling sorry for yourself. I take it you came here with the intention of giving me a piece of your mind.'

Alvarez said, 'It started with us chatting on your porch. Maybe this can become a regular thing.'

Procter sipped lemonade. Patricia had made up a batch for him. A fat jug sat on the table next to him. Ice cubes clinked together as he set the finished glass back down. The evenings were getting chilly, but Procter didn't care.

'This stuff is delicious,' Procter said, 'but only if you like it tart. However many lemons your mother used to use when you were a kid, Patricia doubles it. I warn you, it's like paint stripper for your throat. Delicious paint stripper.'

Alvarez was undeterred. He filled a glass and took a big gulp, swallowed, and grimaced.

'Told you,' Procter said.

Alvarez cleared his throat and set the glass down again. 'It is tasty.' His voice was hoarse.

Procter smiled. 'So.'

'So,' Alvarez echoed.

'I told you last time that I'm content just sitting out here. You'll get bored first, believe me.'

'You know I'll get what I want eventually. It'll save us both a lot of time if you just lay it all out for me.'

'I've never found ignorance to be a particularly dignified tactic.'

'Then change tactic.'

'I've also found going down without a fight to be significantly less dignified.'

431

'You've mentioned dignity twice now, yet I don't detect a hint of irony in your voice.'

'If you think you can insult me into a confession, you're very much mistaken.'

'I don't intend to insult, but I'm not going to go easy on you, either with what you've done or what you say.'

'I read the report,' Procter said. 'You made something of a mess over in Finland, wouldn't you say?'

'I made mistakes, yes. But I broke no laws.'

Procter gave him a look.

'I broke none of *our* laws,' he corrected.

'Do you believe he's dead?' Procter asked.

Alvarez took his time answering. 'Unidentified male corpse of approximately the same size was found in the ruins. Just bones, basically. Incinerated in the fire.'

'You don't seem convinced.'

'I don't think I would be convinced unless I saw him dying myself,' Alvarez said. 'But it doesn't matter what I think or don't think or know or don't know. You may have no authority over my actions, but the Director of National Intelligence sure does. As far as he's concerned, Tesseract is a corpse and that's the end of it. I don't get to argue otherwise. I got good men killed over in Helsinki and another two will never work in the field again. Contractors, technically, but CIA in everything but name. My stock is rock bottom right now. For a long time I'm going to need to ask permission just to go to the bathroom.'

'So why are you here?'

'To let you know you've won for now, but I'm not going to give up the fight.'

'Then I look forward to seeing you in the ring.'

Alvarez was confused.

Procter said, 'Didn't I mention it? I'll be back at CIA soon enough.' He patted his hip. 'I'm set to make a full recovery. I'm part robot, granted. But a soon-to-be fully functioning robot. We'll be seeing a lot more of each other.'

Alvarez couldn't hide his disgust. He didn't try.

'You're nowhere near fifty, Antonio. The grey-haired men who run the intelligence world only give these jobs to other men with grey hair. It's not about experience, it's about balls. Old men don't like young men. You only get to certain places in life when your dick starts to shrivel up. It's compensation. It's the unwritten rule. Yet you jumped the queue. You didn't stop to ask why? You didn't wonder what makes you so very special?'

'I have useful friends,' he said, thinking about his golfing partner. 'But what are you trying to tell me?'

'That you're not biting the hand that feeds you, you're attempting to take the whole arm.'

'Are you saying that you got me the job?'

'I'm saying you've never had a more useful friend than I can be.'

'I might have to disagree with you on that.'

'Maybe, but I think one day you'll see why you're wrong, you'll see what you're forgetting. Because all that I have done, all the laws I have broken, have not been for me, but for this country. I'm a patriot, like you. More so, because I'll do whatever it takes to keep us all safe.'

'You can rationalise it however you want, but if you go off the reservation, you should pay for it.'

'Pay for what, exactly? For taking someone bad and making them do some good? Is that what you want to punish me for?'

'I don't make the rules.'

'No, but you're going to have to break some if you're ever going to get what you want.'

He was shaking his head before Procter had finished. 'No. That's where you're wrong. I've done things by the book up until now. That's the way it's going to stay. I'm not like you.'

Procter laughed. In part to provoke, but part of it was genuine too. 'You think you're going to get a guy like me without getting dirty yourself? Please.'

Alvarez was silent.

'We need to be careful of the lies we tell ourselves, Antonio. Sooner or later we start believing them. After that, how can we tell what the truth even looks like?'

SIXTY

The Festival Theatre in Edinburgh was a modern construction, but its metal-and-glass exterior was offset by an auditorium that was classically lavish and grand. It was beautiful enough to appreciate without any performance. Victor had seats at the back of the stalls, which had generous legroom and a perfect view. He would have preferred to be closer to the orchestra pit so he could see the musicians work their magic, but he couldn't tolerate people sitting behind him when it could be avoided. The performance was spectacular – *The Marriage of Figaro* – the production sumptuous, but, as was only right, the singing was the true joy. He had purchased two tickets so he could sit with the aisle to one side of him and an empty seat to the other. It felt wrong to deny someone else the chance to see such majesty, but protocol came before all else. At the interval, he waited a minute to let plenty of other people leave ahead of him – to the bars and toilets – and he slipped away amongst the crowd.

He hadn't seen an entire opera for years. It was too much of a risk to remain in a confined public space for so long. He hoped to be able to catch another production, but in another city, weeks or months from now, arriving for the second act, leaving before the third. Then, on another continent, maybe years from now, watching that final act, and then able to piece his memories together to form a single, uninterrupted performance. He only had to live that long. But such goals helped him to stay breathing for another day.

'How are you enjoying the show?' a woman asked him as they passed in a corridor – she had been sitting on the same row.

'Tremendous, isn't it?'

'I can't wait for the next act.'

He smiled. 'Me neither.'

Victor liked the Scots and he liked Scotland. He was fond of the accent in particular. It was one of the few he could not imitate with confidence. There were so many inflections and colloquialisms it was beyond his repertoire. He could pass as almost any European he chose to embody, but even Victor had limits.

He was only passing through, staying over for one night, having flown in from Reykjavik via Dublin, on his way to London. Not ideal after his recent trip to Scotland, but there were only so many ways to enter the UK. It was a long train journey south from Edinburgh to London and although comfortable enough, he could not relax. His last long trip on a train had been most unpleasant. He was keen to ensure this one was uneventful. He rubbed his thigh.

He sat on a leather seat in the first-class carriage, alone on a table for four people. The three other seats were all reserved with white tickets, but they were empty because Victor had booked all four. He placed his luggage on the seat opposite him to discourage anyone from asking if they were taken.

The sun was on his left and caused green leaves to shine yellow. The first-class windows had curtains, but he used the glare as an excuse to wear sunglasses. He welcomed the chance to further disguise his watchfulness.

A trolley holding drinks and snacks came his way along the aisle.

'Refreshments, sir?'

'I'll take a coffee.'

'Milk?'

He thought of the little packet of single-serving milk. He thought of what Raven might say about the plastic-leaking chemicals and the ultra-heat treatment destroying the micronutrients and the natural fat skimmed off, rendering all those fat-soluble vitamins useless, and the cattle bred to produce more milk than nature ever intended and growth hormones and anabolic steroids and antibiotics and feed that was anything but grass.

'Black, please.'

She nodded and poured from a brushed-steel flask into a paper cup.

'And some sugar.'

She raised an eyebrow in the same way he sometimes did.

He couldn't stop himself. 'You're surprised?'

She nodded. 'Yes. Well, maybe not surprised. I like to

guess what people will ask for. You know, to pass the time. I'm right more often than not. Some days seventy-thirty. I figured you for plain black.'

'I have a sweet tooth.'

She smiled and dropped three sachets of sugar on to the table next to his coffee. He watched her go. She was Eastern European. He guessed Latvian from her accent, but he also detected a hint of Estonian. He was almost intrigued enough to ask her about her background, but even if he was prepared to break protocol and make himself more memorable – and he was not – she would be asked where she was from every single day by curious passengers who didn't stop to think she might not want to have the same conversation again and again. He didn't want to make her job harder than it was already.

The coffee was awful.

In London, he booked a room for the night at three separate hotels, calling ahead from payphones, using the same name for each booking, and then found a fourth one that afternoon, stayed in the room for two hours, then left the light on and the shower running while he slipped out a tradesman's entrance to find a fifth hotel to actually sleep inside.

The next morning, the hotel was quiet save for the rustle of Sunday newspapers and the tinkling of a fountain outside. From his seat on a low couch Victor could see the statue, a cherub, spouting water. A Union flag fluttered on a tall flagpole, the breeze not strong enough to lift it proud. It seemed sad and almost dying. It was made of silk and looked thin and weak, dirtied by pollution. The sky behind it was the colour of granite.

The drawing room had a high ceiling and a once-thick carpet trodden down to almost no depth over years of use.

His coffee was brought alongside a small jug of hot milk and a little plate of shortbread biscuits. The young man assured him the orange juice had been squeezed fresh and his smoked salmon omelette used only the finest ingredients.

After breakfast, he took a cab to the closest railway station, bought a ticket to the furthest destination available, then hailed another cab outside and had the driver drive around in circles until he climbed out at random and walked on foot back to the station and caught the train. He disembarked at the first station, jumping back on at the last second, feigning confusion, before leaving at the next station and catching a train back to the city.

London had many small areas of greenery that were tucked away near busy areas, but quiet and undiscovered by the tourists. This one was busy because it was lunchtime and office workers were keen to make the most of their hour on a rain-free day, but he saw her fast in the same way she saw him fast. Both of them could be anonymous, but not from one another. Not any longer. They had spent too much time together. They knew each other too well to hide in the way they could from others.

Victor and Raven neared with a certain amount of caution, because that's how they always operated, but the crowd provided cover, it provided safety. Neither of them would choose to make a kill surrounded by so many witnesses. Which was why it had been agreed upon. A sniper would have an impossible shot to make.

There was no glint in her eyes, no glib comment, no innuendo. She had the same expression he had. All business. No emotion.

She said, 'Thank you for meeting me,' but there was no warmth in her thanks. She was being polite, but nothing more.

It had been a fortnight since Helsinki and she had healed well, but despite the time and make-up he could still see the remnants of bruises and cuts to her face, reminders of the injuries he had inflicted. One eye was still a little black. There was still a hint of swelling.

'You're walking stiffly,' she observed.

He had many minor injuries of his own from the fall down the rubble chute. His ribs ached with every breath, and his palms were still sore. 'I overdid it at the gym.'

She said, 'I hear on the grapevine people think you're dead.'

He nodded. 'For the moment, at least. Your Estonian babysitter made for a useful substitute. Whether this lasts or not is out of my hands, but it's bought me some time. You're the only one who knows for sure that I'm still alive.'

'So the original plan worked after all.'

He nodded again.

'Then we tried to kill each other for no reason.'

'Your gunshot brought them to us. Had you not tried to kill me, it wouldn't have worked itself out like that.'

'Is that a thank you?'

'I'm not going after Alvarez,' Victor said by way of

an answer. 'There's no longer any need. Whatever he knows about me is irrelevant, so long as he believes I'm a corpse.'

'Then we really did fight over nothing.'

Victor said, 'You lied to me, didn't you? The old man never mentioned me or Phoenix. You made that up so I would help your brother. I should have realised at the time that it was all too convenient, but deception is one of your many talents.'

She didn't hesitate. 'And I'd do it again in a heartbeat. Of all the things I regret, using you to help Ben is never going to be one of them. Don't even think about—'

He was offended enough to interrupt her. 'Not my style, Constance.'

He saw that she was regretful for the implication, but she said nothing.

'Why am I here?'

Raven said, 'At first, because I wanted to put things right between you and I. I wanted to call another truce, but a permanent one this time. Go back to how things were.'

'I thought you might offer me some dessert wine.'

'Funny,' she said, mirthless.

He waited.

She continued in her own time: 'But I've changed my mind. You've always told me that you're a mercenary, a killer. So now I'm going to treat you as one. I don't want a friend like that.'

'We were never friends. We had only an alliance of interests and a certain attraction.'

'Now,' she said with a smirk, 'now is the moment you

441

choose to admit it. Not that it matters. I don't want an ally like you. We're on completely different sides.'

'The only side I'm on is my own.'

She nodded. 'That's what I finally understand. If that side of yours happens to align with me, then it all works out. But as Helsinki showed, the gloves are off as soon as we want different things.'

'You didn't need to meet me just to tell me what I already know.'

'I realise that. I didn't. I wanted to meet you now, like this, one last time.'

'One last time,' he repeated.

'Because if we ever meet again it's going to be as enemies.'

Victor remained silent.

Raven said, 'I hope that never happens. I hope I don't see you again. But if I do, then I want it to be through the scope of a high-powered rifle.'

He didn't reply because he didn't have the same need to voice his thoughts she had. She waited a moment before realising that he would say nothing further. She responded to this with an exhale, a bitter smile, because she understood now:

'I never meant anything to you.'

He didn't answer. He backed away and let the crowd swallow him.

Raven stood in the centre of the square, surrounded by people, but alone.

SIXTY-ONE

People always felt the need to say *I hate funerals*. Alvarez didn't get that. Everyone hated funerals. It was universal. He was sure even undertakers weren't big fans. He was sure if he looked into it there would be a disproportionate number of incidences of depression and substance abuse among undertakers compared to other professions. This funeral was a standard Jewish affair. Alvarez had been to a few of those over the years. He had reached the age when funerals were becoming as common as weddings.

The immediate family weren't especially religious, but some of the extended relations were and had been respectfully catered for. Alvarez listened to the rabbi, not understanding when he spoke Hebrew, but the solemnity of his tone was understandable.

There were plenty of tears, as was to be expected, but there was no wife and no children and the parents were old enough to show restraint. They were so old they had to be helped to sit, to stand, and for every step between.

Alvarez went alone. He had no invite, so he stayed at the back and kept out of people's way, but he was dressed for it and no one looked at him with any suspicion, no one demanded to know who he was or what he was doing there. He knew how to keep a low profile.

It was a beautiful day: blue skies and sunshine, only a hint of white cloud. It only ever seemed to go one of two ways with funerals – perfect weather or terrible. There was no middle ground. Maybe that meant something. Maybe that meant there was more than just life and death. Alvarez didn't know. He didn't spend too much time considering spirituality and his place in the universe because deep down he didn't really want those answers. He was too scared to ask the questions in the first place.

The family hadn't wanted the cause of death to be made public, so people had been told Sykes had died of a heart attack, which was technically true, but when Alvarez heard the news the first thing he did was pick up the phone and find out from the pathologist herself exactly what had happened. Sykes had committed suicide. He had ingested enough cocaine to kill a bear, let alone a human. Swallowed, not snorted.

'No question at all it was suicide. Even someone who didn't use drugs regularly would know taking so much in one go was only going to end one way.'

'Alcohol in his system?'

'Not a drop.'

'Thank you for your time.'

Cocaine and drug paraphernalia had been found in his townhouse, the investigating officer assured him. Alvarez asked around. None of Sykes' colleagues knew of any drug use. Most knew he liked to drink and tried to hide it.

The day before the funeral, Alvarez's phone rang. It was the Director of National Intelligence himself.

'I hear you're hassling people about a friend's suicide.'

'He wasn't my friend, sir.'

The director said, 'I don't want to think you're neglecting your duties with personal enquiries.'

'Understood.'

Alvarez had heard a lot about his duties after the Helsinki debacle. He would be in trouble if word got out he had attended the funeral. Standing at the back, he was first to leave when the service was over and headed back to his car. He had parked it well out of the way. Someone else had had the same idea because a man dressed in black stood smoking on the kerb. He was alone and lost in his own moment until he saw Alvarez approach.

'How was it?' he asked. 'I couldn't bear to go inside. I hate funerals.'

Alvarez nodded his understanding and said, 'It was a moving service.'

'We enter this life not knowing we exist. We leave it wondering what that existence meant.'

Alvarez said nothing to that.

The man dropped the cigarette and stubbed it out under the toe of his shoe. At his age, he should know better than to smoke. 'Did you know him well?'

Alvarez considered how to answer. 'I thought I did.'

'Isn't it always that way?' the old man said with a sad, almost innocent, smile. 'We never really know anyone.'

SIXTY-TWO

She went by the name Phoenix. It was her handle. It meant nothing. It was just a name. It was just a word she liked that had imagery and symbolism associated with it, all of which had no relevance to her but helped throw her enemies off her scent anyway. Who was she? From what ashes did she rise? They inferred history. They misread subtext. They created a mental picture that was inaccurate. That helped her. That gave her advantages.

She needed those advantages because she was a wanted woman. She was a criminal. Her job was freelance human resourcing. She was a recruiter, a broker. Maybe the biggest. Maybe the best. In a past life she had been a lawyer and an entrepreneur and many other things, but above all she had been a networker. She knew how to make associations and keep acquaintances, and how to put the right people together when neither knew the other existed, let alone that they might be helpful to their respective goals.

She had worked for diplomats and politicians, private security firms and warlords. She had put arms dealers in touch with insurgents and supplied names and coordinates to independent intelligence outfits who in turn had passed those on to CIA officers who had authorised targeted assassinations of those same insurgents. Those contacts in the private security world were always looking for work, and some didn't care whether the targets were terrorists or civilians. She helped those transactions. She made the deals. Then she was organising the deals. Then her contacts were bringing contracts to her table for her to fulfil. She had a mental rolodex full of professional killers and those that needed their services.

Her success rate was phenomenal, but not perfect. Not all such contracts were successful. Some were open. One in particular had been in motion for a whole year, without success. This was far from common. It was almost unique. Three attempts had been made and all three had failed. She wasn't used to failure, even with a target this problematic.

She didn't know his name because no one did. If it was out there, she would know it. That she didn't was both a source of frustration and fascination. She knew so little about him it seemed impossible he could in fact be a real person. Everyone had a past. No identity could be hidden in its entirety. At least, that's what she had believed.

He had angered powerful people, and so the contract had come to her, because if anyone could fulfil it, it was Phoenix. She had sources everywhere. She put out the word for information on the target, on the assassin without a name. She offered good money for hard intel.

That request came to the attention of a man who worked for British intelligence, SIS; commonly referred to as MI6. Phoenix knew all about that man. At the time he was a spy and he was corrupt. He had a wife and daughter and a Chinese mistress. He had been a career intelligence officer who had succumbed to his base urges. Those urges had begun at lust and ended with greed.

He had a file on the assassin because that assassin had recently been hired by SIS. Threadbare, as files went, but it had enough details to make it valuable, because those details were verified. They were real. She learned more about this killer, and found herself with more than a professional interest in him, because, like her, he had managed to make himself invisible. A kindred spirit, almost. She wanted to find out more about him as much as she wanted to profit from his death.

The file supplemented what she had been given by her client and with it there was enough to pass on to contractors. One went missing in London. The second was found shot to death in Belgrade. She took no chances with the third attempt in Germany, using a traitorous subordinate as bait and a whole team, but still no joy. At least in terms of success, but she found she was enjoying this duel; the feints, the parries, the counterattacks. Her work could be so boring. Contracts came in; she distributed them to the most suitable contractor on her books; she passed on confirmation when it came in ... A few clicks of a mouse, typically, albeit clicks worth hundreds of thousands of dollars at a time.

She had not been paid for this contract because she was

paid only for success, and her potential reward for success was diminishing with each failure. Her world was a secret one, but it was small. Contractors lost meant fewer contracts could be fulfilled, and word got around. Be careful working for Phoenix, some were starting to say.

So, this particular job had to be put to one side. The nameless killer had won a reprieve. Only for now, because Phoenix knew that all it required was the simple passage of time, so that memories became foggy and new contractors emerged who would pay less attention to the failures of their predecessors than did contemporaries. Wait, she told herself. Time the next thrust just right.

She sipped champagne and soaked in her luxury Villeroy & Boch freestanding bath and lamented the unfortunate turn of events that meant this killer would remain a mystery to her a while longer. She could wait. The delay would only increase the satisfaction when it eventually came. And it would come, she thought, as one hand slipped beneath the bubbles.

In a fluffy towelling robe, and with the company of a second glass of champagne, she pondered taking her new Bentley Continental out for a quick spin along the coast as she padded to the drawing room of her chateau, where she found the nameless killer was sitting at her grand piano.

Phoenix didn't panic, because in some way she had felt this was not only inevitable, but expected. She kept her composure because she always did. As a girl she had been fast to understand the importance of appearances, of remaining dignified. She had rarely cried, even then. Children were already ugly enough.

His fingers hovered over the keys, as if poised to play, but hesitant. He would have heard her approach, but he made no immediate reaction. He didn't look at her. Instead his gaze stayed on the piano, and in his frozen silence he seemed regretful.

She set the glass of champagne down on a sideboard. She was no longer thirsty.

The killer said, 'I thought you'd be a man.'

'Men always do.'

He turned on the stool to face her. 'You're younger than I expected.'

'Ditto,' she said. 'And you're also a lot better looking in person than the pictures of you would suggest. You do look so very ordinary on a still taken from CCTV.'

'I'll take both as compliments.'

'Please do. How did you find me?'

'That would be telling.'

She smiled at him because she was somewhere between terrified and exhilarated. They had been playing this game, this duel, for a long time now. She was absorbed in its unexpected climax.

'Then allow me to guess,' Phoenix said. 'Wilders told you about his safe, his little stockpile. You got to it before me and you copied the information and had your friends at MI6 or CIA pick it to pieces. He didn't know how to put those pieces together himself, but he never had access to supercomputers, hackers, and assets all over the globe. They would have followed the money, of course.'

The killer nodded. 'It's the hardest thing to hide.'

'Indeed. If one wants to be paid for one's services, then

the money has to flow in the right direction. Oh, well. I've had a good run. Had to end sometime. But I must admit I'm a little surprised you didn't take me unawares in my sleep, or cut the brakes of my car. Or do you intend to make me suffer first?'

He shook his head. 'I try not to hurt anyone any more than necessary.'

'Try?'

'It's a grey area,' he admitted.

'Then I suppose you're here because you want to know where the contract came from. But you must understand I have no name to hand over. The client is as anonymous as I am – was.'

'I do understand that, and I don't need you to tell me who my enemies are.'

Her intrigue was growing with every passing second. 'You don't strike me as the type of man who would come here just for a pre-execution gloat. That's a bit classless, no?'

The killer stood. 'I'm not going to kill you.'

She couldn't hide her surprise. 'Well, now you have me in quite the head spin. Why ever not?'

'You're just doing your job. Same as me.'

Phoenix said, 'You mean, if you kill me there'll just be someone else who'll step into my shoes.'

'I don't take these things personally,' the killer explained. 'It's all just business, whether I'm aiming the gun or staring down the barrel of one. And you're right, the next broker might be similarly difficult to track down. I've put a lot of effort into finding you. I don't want to go through it all again if it can be avoided.'

'So you want to call a truce?'

'Truces never last,' he said with something in his voice she couldn't decipher. 'I'd prefer to start a war between us.'

'I don't understand.'

'But a cold war,' he added.

'I see,' she said. 'Mutually assured destruction.'

'I don't want you sending more killers after me.'

'Likewise, I don't want you showing up with another grievance.' She thought for a moment. 'But what's the point, if your employers know who I am? I'll be finished anyway.'

'I found you on my own,' he answered. 'They merely helped point me in the right direction.'

'Well, your proposal does make a certain amount of sense, but I'm afraid I must decline.'

'That's truly unfortunate,' the killer said, stepping closer.

'Let me finish,' she was quick to add. 'We don't need to be at war with one another. Let's call a ceasefire instead. Then disarmament. Peace ...'

He understood, as she expected him to. 'And after peace comes alliance.'

'You catch up fast.'

He said, 'You work for people who want me dead.'

'I work for myself. Contracts come in from all sorts of clients. Sometimes their goals are in opposition. I don't pick sides. I'm a Swiss girl at heart. And not all jobs can be fulfilled. It's common enough, even with the best intentions. Besides, the contract on you has been open a while now. There have been three attempts. The client understands the difficulty. I can withdraw it quietly without creating a fuss.' She paused. 'So, can I add you to my roster?'

The killer said, 'I'm going away for a while. I don't know when I'll be available.'

'I'll be around when you return. There's no deadline on talent.'

'I'm very expensive.'

'I should hope so,' she said. 'The contracts that come through me are not for amateurs.'

He thought for a moment. 'I need something first.'

'Name it.'

'I want certain people to think I'm dead. There are unidentified remains in Helsinki – an Estonian, stabbed and incinerated in a gas explosion. If there is anything you can do to help convince these people that corpse belongs to me, then I'll be open to your idea.'

She nodded. 'That's do-able. I have all sorts of friends with all manner of benefits, so I can't see why not. I can put things in motion today, if you are agreeable to my proposal. You can be dead by the end of the week, so to speak.'

'Then consider me agreeable,' he said, and sounded so. 'In fact it's been too long since I've worked on the freelance circuit. Contracting for intelligence agencies has proven more trouble than it's worth.'

Phoenix was delighted. In a closely contested duel, it was sad that someone had to lose, and yet a draw was always unsatisfying. Far better for both parties to emerge victorious.

She stepped closer to him, now there was nothing to fear. 'May I ask you a question? It's somewhat personal. Something that's been scratching at my curiosity for a while now.'

The killer said, 'You may ask.'

She understood the subtext, but asked anyway. 'How is it that, after all you've done, with all your enemies, you are still alive?'

'Simple,' he said in quick response, but then took a moment to respond fully, and when he did the answer was as ordinary as it was enlightening. 'I never pick a fight I can't win.'

She smiled at that and fetched her glass of champagne from the sideboard. 'Would you join me for one? To toast our new-found friendship?'

'Do you have a fresh bottle?'

She nodded. 'I have a cellar full. You may take your pick.'

The killer said, 'Then I'd like that very much.'